Abuse
of
Authority

Abuse
of
Authority

Edward Caputo

"Outliving your enemies is the ultimate revenge!"

Library of Congress Control Number: 2020921983
ISBN: Hardcover   978-1-6641-4096-7
               Softcover   978-1-6641-4095-0
               eBook   978-1-6641-4094-3

Print information available on the last page.

Rev. date: 11/16/2020

To order additional copies of this book, contact:
Xlibris
844-714-8691
www.Xlibris.com
Orders@Xlibris.com
821973

CONTENTS

PART 3 PRESENT DAY

In memory of my Mom, Elizabeth M. Caputo

ACKNOWLEDGEMENTS

This book is dedicated to my sister, my daughter, my daughter-in-law, my granddaughters, my women friends, and all women at risk of *Abuse of Authority* from the institution that is supposed to "Protect and Serve" them. It is intended to expose the heinous crimes hidden behind the "Police Blue Curtain Code of Silence."

All women need to be aware of the possibility of *Abuse of Authority* when complying with law enforcement officers or the possibility of deceptive uniformed men posing as police officers. The recommended procedure is to continue to a lighted facility or dial 911.

I wrote *Abuse of Authority* to raise awareness of this danger to women.

PREFACE

USA Today - Records of Police Officer misconduct published after nationwide search: [1]

At least 85,000 Law Enforcement Officers across the United States have been investigated or disciplined for misconduct over the past decade, an investigation by USA TODAY Network found.

Officers have beaten members of the public, planted evidence, and used their badges to harass women. They have lied, stolen, dealt drugs, driven drunk, and abused women.

Despite their role as public servants, the men and women who swear an oath to keep communities safe generally can avoid public scrutiny for their misdeeds.

The records of their misconduct are filed away, rarely seen by anyone outside their departments. Police unions and their political allies have worked to put special protections in place, ensuring some records are shielded from public view or even destroyed.

Protect and Serve

Law Enforcement is at the very pinnacle of humanity's trust. No other profession demands a higher *ethical* standard. The fundamental assurance is the trust we have to go to a police officer when in trouble or help is needed. Although the majority of police officers are honest and trustworthy, the ultimate betrayal is when that trust has been broken by police officers who abuse their authority and hide behind *Blue Curtain Code of Silence.*

Ironically, the police officers that commit the crimes are often assigned to investigate their very own crimes. Then, absurdly, the Judicial System decrees no punishment after it convicts the police officers. It is obvious the extent to which police impunity continues to rein as an impenetrable *Abuse of Authority.*

During a generation of police sexual abuse and murder, such as the *Golden State Killer* [2] and the *#METOO* movement, where can women go when in trouble if humanity's most trusted profession becomes the predators? Police officers sworn to *Protect and Serve* become the abusers, rapists, and murderers!

The police rape and murder incidents exposed in *Abuse of Authority* are based on actual cases. They are a select sample of the countless rape and murder incidents by police officers that have unfortunately occurred in the United States. They may seem too graphic, brutal, and unbelievable, but they are true and really happened. The adapted details of each case are woven into a dramatized story, fictionalized to take place in South Florida, with the victim's surnames changed. Some have been modified to fit the narrative of the plot. The factual legal cases portrayed in *Abuse of Authority* are documented in Footnotes and the Bibliography.

---

[2] *LAPD Police Officer Joseph D'Angelo*
Rapes and Murders in California:

After a 12-year reign of terror, the California "Golden State Killer," a serial rapist and killer identified as Police Officer Joseph D'Angelo, was finally apprehended and charged with over 52 rapes and 13 murders. Ironically, for many years he was assigned to investigate his own crimes.

PART ONE

PRESENT DAY

PROLOGUE-ONE

Blood Moon [3]

McCabe's Irish Pub
Miami, Florida

The Blood Moon cast an eerie gray, film noir shadow over the streets below as the police cruiser, driven by the "Sunshine State's Finest," slowly approached McCabe's Irish Pub at midnight in downtown Miami. It was a standard-issue black and white Ford Crown Victoria equipped with a galvanized steel cage in the backseat to imprison rowdy or uncooperative offenders. Its painted motto on the side proclaimed, *"To Protect and Serve."*

The driver was the embodiment of police law enforcement authority in his official police-issued badge, blue uniform, handcuffs, orange-tinted eyeglasses, and 9mm-Glock - locked and loaded. At six-feet-four inches, and two-hundred and thirty-five muscle-bound pounds, he was a force to be reckoned with. In his mind, he *was* the police force, and he relished the power.

The sounds of revelry got progressively louder as the police officer parked his police cruiser directly across the street to search for her. He could barely make out the words to *"Bad Moon Rising,"* blaring on the jukebox amid the laughter and shouting commotion inside the Pub.

I see a bad moon a-rising

I see trouble on the way

1

I see earthquakes and lightnin'
I see bad times today
Don't go 'round tonight
It's bound to take your life
There's a bad moon on the rise...

He chuckled to himself at the irony of the lyrics on the night of the Blood Moon, then reached over for the bottle of Johnny Walker Red scotch he had with him, took a long hard swallow, and lit a cigarette to feed his habit. He sucked a deep drag into his lungs, holding it captive for a moment, then slowly exhaled twin plumes of smoke out of his nostrils, dragon-like. The police cruiser reeked of nicotine.

He lowered the driver's side window to search through the glass front door of the Pub. His orange-tinted police eyeglasses brightened the shadowy dark cloudless night and gave a clear view of the blinking neon sign broadcasting the Pub, *"OPEN."*

He waited patiently, watching patrons come and go. Drunken men staggered down the narrow cement steps outside the Pub as they left. Some were lucky and left with a woman they had picked up or a hooker who had been working the bar, while others walked in alone and walked out alone.

It wouldn't be much longer.

She's in there somewhere, he told himself.

He could feel it. He could sense it. His instincts were combat honed. He was like an animal stalking prey, but he didn't see her... Not yet.

Inside, the Pub was rocking as Anna Swayze ordered another round of drinks. It was "Girl's Night Out Thursday," and the Margaritas were going down real easy.

2

Was this number four or five? She couldn't keep track.

Anna was a beautiful 21-year-old petite-brunette Florida college student with full breast implants and a killer body. Her hazel eyes were often mistaken for brown, and at five-feet-three-inches, she was sick of being called *"cute as a button,"* even though she was fastidious about her grooming and looks. She wore a tight Lilly Pulitzer cashmere sweater and pleated skirt tonight to display her feminine allure.

She worked hard and played hard, but this week was particularly stressful, with only one month left until the end of the semester. She wanted to shake off some college dust and have some fun tonight before focusing exclusively on her studies.

The girls flirted with the male barflies, making mindless small talk amid the cacophony of chatter at the bar. The Irish Pub atmosphere was bright and cheerful, with bartenders frenzied, grabbing rows of draft beer taps and columns of liquor bottles stacked within the multi-level shelves behind the bar for hard liquor shots with names like *Sex on the Beach*.

An imposing array of big-screen, high-definition video monitors covered the glossy painted plaster walls, displaying numerous sports channels and sporting events. A super-sized movie screen dominated the center wall in the middle of the room, tuned to the Miami Dolphins football game against their archrival, Buffalo Bills. The fans in the room cheered at each advancement by the hometown team.

Across the vast room, dart games hung on the walls, pinball machines clanged in one corner, and spirited video competitions resounded nearby. A pool table was on the other side of the partition with a group of men holding cue sticks, gathered around awaiting their turn.

Anna leered at a tall, handsome, hot, muscular blond playing pool. She watched as he slammed his cue stick into the cue ball, causing the colorful rack of pool balls to explode with a loud *bang*, knocking a couple into the pockets.

He's a strong one, she thought, *I like him.*

"Nice shot, woohoo!" She shouted across the bar in the general direction of the pool table to draw his attention to her, hoping to meet him.

The pool player looked over at her indignantly, grabbed his Guinness, and walked around to the other side of the table to take his next shot. He had an insolence she didn't expect.

She responded to his scowl with a giggle, "Sorry about that!"

She shrugged off his bad attitude, grabbed one of the Margaritas the bartender had barely finished pouring, and raised her glass high, shouting above the music and slurring the words, "Here's to the girls of Miami College."

They all laughed and clinked their glasses together to seal the final toast of the night.

Anna's best friend, Christine, watched her failed attempt at flirtation and laughed, "I guess he's really into that game." She tossed her long black curly hair back, "He doesn't know what he's missing." She was the epitome of German with vivid blue eyes, five-eleven in flats, nowhere near thirty and brilliant. Her silver sequined outfit sparkled in the harsh bright lights inside the Pub.

Anna looked over at the pool player again and smirked back at Christine, "Oh well, his loss." It was nearly closing time, so they paid their check and slipped off their barstools to leave.

They stumbled out of the Pub at almost 1:30 a.m. Christine threw her arm around Anna, "Girlfriend, you drunk!"

They burst out laughing as they surged through the door onto the cement sidewalk where they paused, taking in the Blood Moon.

Anna looked up, "Wow!"

The reddish tinted Blood Moon hovering in the cloudless black sky cast an ominous shadow over the night's otherwise jubilant festivities. Their mood became darker!

"Understated." Christine dropped her grin as she looked up at the Blood Moon in amazement. She remembered the apocalyptic prophecy of the Blood Moon forewarning the end of the world in the bible, Revelation 6:12, "It's a bad omen!"

Anna crooned the theme song from the movie, *The Legend of Princess Zelda*, "Yes. *Something Wicked This Way Comes*, hmm." She stared wide-eyed at the Blood Moon; a sense of dread filled her!

"Boohoo, 'Something Wicked This Way Comes,' hmm." Christine mocked Anna.

> *"Be on your guard, evil grows and rises to its peak under the hour of a Blood Moon."*
>
> *"By its glow, the aimless spirits of monsters that were slain, in the name of light, return to flesh."*

Anna shuddered, "Stop it! You're scaring me!"

"Home," she pointed toward Anna's car, kissed her on the lips, and hugged her, "Pity Mr. Tall, Blue-eyed, Blond, and Gorgeous wasn't interested. He could have protected you from the aimless spirits of the monsters of the night."

Anna lightened up and laughed, "I had other plans for that hunk. Too bad, Mr. Tall, Blue-eyed, Blond, and Gorgeous. Home we go. Alone!"

Anna walked south to her car while Christine went north. They weren't worried; this was their "hood," an upscale downtown where all the graduate students partied. It was a *what-happens-at-McCabe's-stays-at-McCabe's* mentality.

Anna pitched her purse onto the passenger seat and glanced up at the Blood Moon once again as she got into her little red Mazda Miata, two-door, two-seat convertible. It took a couple of tries, but her key finally found the ignition switch.

She giggled thinking of the night, turned the rearview mirror toward her eyes, and put some lipstick on, "Need a few less Margaritas next time, Anna." She talked to the mirror as she spread the lipstick onto her lips. They stayed too late, had too much fun, and drank too much.

She slowly pulled away from the curb, dreading the long drive home, but careful to look for any signs of authority, fearful of a *DUI* arrest. She knew she was driving under the influence of alcohol, so she proceeded slowly and cautiously out of downtown. She left the top open but closed the side windows. The wind blowing through her hair felt good.

I'll be okay, she thought.

PROLOGUE-TWO

Rhapsody in Blue [3]

Dark, Back Road
Outside of Miami

As Anna traveled home from the Pub, the road quickly changed from bright streetlights and neon store signs in downtown Miami to a dark desolation outside of the city. She looked up again at the Blood Moon gloom from her open convertible, apprehensive about the total absence of other cars on the road. But, then again, she thought, *it's probably typical for this late at night.*

She took a deep breath and did her best to drive carefully, obeying traffic laws, staying under the speed limit, and within the traffic guidelines. She knew she had too much to drink and was careful to appear as law-abiding as possible, to avoid any potential trouble with the police.

Suddenly, a few miles outside of the city, red and blue rolling lights exploded. It looked like the scene from *Close Encounters of the Third Kind*, with bright lights shining and rolling red and blue police cruiser lights flashing from the rooftop lightbar behind her, reflecting in her rearview mirror, onto her face.

"Fuck, fuck, fuck!" She murmured, wondering what she had done wrong. She had been so careful.

Instinctively, her right hand sought and fished her purse for breath mints. She took her time easing over to the curb as she popped one, chewing fast, trying to think of some excuse for why she was being pulled over.

He sat still in his police cruiser, watching her squirm, knowing she was drunk and in trouble. *DUI - Driving Under the Influence, a "Rape Cop's" best friend,* he told himself. *The perfect excuse to pull over a beautiful woman in the middle of the night on a dark, deserted road.* He chuckled sarcastically, "You take care of me, *baby*, and I'll take care of you."

He knew the longer he waited, the more worried and scared she would get. So, he grabbed the bottle of scotch next to him and gulped down another mouthful, savoring the moment.

He'd played this scene many times before and wanted to let the drama play out. He enjoyed the chase. She was under his control, and he knew she couldn't escape him. Police authority trumped all.

He especially liked her size. She would fit well in the back cage of his police cruiser. It would be a good night. He fantasized about the moment he would rip her blouse open. She'd struggle, her breasts would jiggle, her nipples would rise to the chill of the night, and then he would have her. His manhood throbbed and thumped in tune with his heartbeat, as he slowly got out of the police cruiser.

She jumped as he rapped on her window! Her eyes came level with his crotch. She stared at a large silver belt buckle with a very stiff zipper bulging back at her. She swallowed hard.

He watched her eyes widen, "Out of the car," he ordered. His official police badge, blue uniform, handcuffs, orange-coated police eyeglasses, and especially his gun, made it official: *The Law Must Be Obeyed.*

She unbuckled her seat belt, staring up at his police badge, "What did I...?" She couldn't finish the sentence as he reached over the top of the convertible's window, grabbed her by the hair, and opened the door.

He hauled her painfully out of the car.

Her hands flailed defensively as her nails scratched his arm, "STOP!" She shouted.

His fist suddenly crashed into her jaw.

Dazed and hurt, she felt tears leak down her face.

"What are you doing?" She rubbed her jaw to ease the pain.

He jerked her head back, "Shut up, bitch! I'm the law!"

"You won't get away with this, I'll report..." She never finished the threat as he slugged her in the stomach, but she couldn't lurch forward because he held her head back. She wanted to vomit, but salvation made her swallow rather than suffocate.

He pulled his 9mm-Glock out of its holster, shoved it between her eyes, and laughed, "Really? I could shoot you right now. Who do you think they'd believe? I'm a cop, and you're a drunk who just offered me a blowjob to avoid arrest. Hahaha."

His laugh sounded like something from a horror movie.

"Unless you want a DUI *and* prostitution arrest, well," he holstered his gun, "that's your choice."

"No. I'm not..." She tried to look up, but he spun her away, wrenched her right arm up behind her back, as pain shot through her shoulder.

His grip on her hair snapped her head back, and he steered her toward the police cruiser.

Terror shrieked through her, but she couldn't cry out because he held her head so far back that it was all she could do to breathe. Then, he opened the back door and slammed her face-first into the cage of his police cruiser. Her nose stung, her eyes watered, and she tasted blood as he shoved her inside the galvanized steel-wire cage.

He let go of her hair long enough to slap a handcuff on her left wrist, then another on her right, and rolled her over onto her back.

Anna was terrified, "Please!" She cried out. "I'm not a prostitute!"

He pushed her legs apart, "Hmm, legs spread apart, in the back of my police cruiser... Looks like prostitution to me." He attached her right wrist handcuff to the front of the cage and her left to the rear, and then he cuffed her ankles spread-eagle.

Anna was frightened about what was happening to her, handcuffed in a cage, in the back of his police cruiser like an animal, in pain from the beating she'd taken. She struggled with her arms and legs, but she could not move. He had her trapped!

As he went around to the front dashboard to switch-off the police lights, she screamed, "HELP ME! SOMEBODY! PLEASE HELP ME!"

She didn't see his fist coming down, but stars suddenly exploded. Her head throbbed, her jaw fell slack... she blacked-out. When she woke, she heard his zipper, felt his hand under her skirt, and her panties torn away. And then he was there, inside of her. Too large, too hard, and she screamed in pain again, "HELP ME! SOMEBODY! PLEASE HELP ME!"

"Scream, baby. Scream all you want," he dared her, "I'm a cop; it's two o'clock in the morning, and no one will even hear you." His big, strong hand snaked around her throat. She thought she would die on the night of the Blood Moon.

In her torment, as he ravaged her, she thought she heard the muffled sound of a car crushing stones on the shoulder of the road behind her. She faintly heard music... strange music playing in the distance... She hoped it was a savior coming to rescue her from her nightmare, and she prayed to live, a prayer she had little hope of being granted. She listened to the music, trying to block out her agony – it was some kind of symphony, *maybe*... Then she recognized it.

Rhapsody in Blue.

He was vicious! He hurt her, but there was nothing she could do to stop him! He had her chained to the cage, imprisoned. She cried from the pain, but he didn't care. It went on and on. She focused on the music coming from behind the police cruiser to help her get through her torture.

Rhapsody in Blue, she thought. *It should be Rapist in Blue.*

Finally, he exploded inside of her, and it was over. She let her head fall backward. Tears swelled in her eyes and rolled down the sides of her face, making it difficult to see. Blood seeped from her nose and mixed with her tears, filling her ears.

He slowly backed out of the cage but left the cruiser backdoor open.

It was dark all around her, and then the music just stopped. It was eerily quiet for a moment, except for some distant voices mumbling and laughing. He had beaten and raped her. Now she wanted to be set free, but then she heard footsteps crushing stones on the shoulder of the road coming back toward the cruiser.

Suddenly he was back inside the cage; the strange music started again – *Rhapsody in Blue*. She remembered *'Blue' was a cop thing. Blue Uniform… Blue Blood… Blue Curtain.* She struggled with the handcuffs, but she was powerless.

He positioned himself between her spread legs again, looked down at her, and grunted as he unbuckled his pants. Then his hands were on her again!

She gulped in fear and cried, "NO!" She screamed, "NO! NO MORE! PLEASE NO!"

But he pushed inside her again, bigger this time, throbbing harder than before. He thrust deep, too deep inside of her.

She felt her cervix crush. She cried out in pain, "NO! PLEASE STOP!"

"That's right, scream baby, scream all you want. You've had this coming for a long time." He growled; his voice was different, lower this time.

The orange-tinted police eyeglasses, the outline of his face, and the blond hair were the same, but without the police badge and uniform, and his scent had changed. His breath smelled of beer, instead of scotch and tobacco, and his touch was crueler this time.

Her tears leaked out of control, drenching her face. She was in the hands of a madman, Dr. Jekyll, and Mr. Hyde, both as evil as the worst. She felt him push inside her, more searing pain as *Rhapsody in Blue* played in the background.

The car heaved as his weight shifted. One more crushing thrust, and he gasped in climax. He panted for several seconds on top of her and then moved away, "Remember this next time you get out of control. Rude to interrupt a good shot!" He snarled and slapped her face.

At that moment, she remembered him - *the pool player.*

The car shifted again as he backed out of the cage. He looked over at the cherry-red glow of a cigarette on the other side of the patrol car, "Gus, quit knocking all the fight out of them, will you?"

A chuckle followed the arch of the cigarette butt being flicked away, sitting on the hood of the car behind. Gershwin blaring on the radio, "Stop complaining, Angelo. You know she was great."

They both laughed. They were brothers and *always* shared everything.

They were still laughing when suddenly they were drenched in headlights. A black and white car with high-beams blinded their eyes. It looked like a police patrol car.

Gus exchanged looks with his brother, "Are you expecting company?"

"No!" Angelo responded with surprise.

Then, a blue-uniformed figure stepped from the patrol car and walked toward them, "Was it good?"

Gus laughed. Just another cop looking for some action, "Very good," he said, "Take a turn. Have at it."

"But don't expect any fight," Angelo added, chuckling.

Anna Swayze started screaming in the police cruiser again, "HELP ME! PLEASE HELP ME!"

The blue-uniformed intruder glanced over at the woman screaming, chained inside the cage of the police cruiser, then responded to Angelo, "Oh, don't worry. I won't."

Gus and Angelo looked at each other. The voice sounded familiar, like they'd heard it before.

Suddenly, *BAM!* Gus saw the gun flash in the dark, as a bullet slammed into Angelo's chest and it splattered him red with blood. His brother crumbled to the ground.

Gus was shocked! *Why would another cop shoot them?* He screamed, "WHAT THE HELL ARE YOU DOING?"

Then he saw the shooter turn the gun toward him. He instinctively reached for his own gun and dove to the ground just as the shooter's gun flashed again, *BAM!* It hit him in his left shoulder, bleeding, as he fired back at the shooter in rapid succession, *BAM! BAM! BAM!* Gus hit the shooter in the leg, firing up from ground level.

The shooter staggered back into the patrol car, bleeding badly, and shoved the transmission into reverse, squealing the tires backward onto the roadway, leaving a trail of blood on the gravel shoulder. Then the car lurched forward and sped off.

Gus continued firing his gun at the fleeing rear-end of the patrol car, *BAM! BAM! BAM!*

Anna Swayze was crying, bleeding, chained inside the cage, and struggling to be free as she witnessed the gunfight, and continued screaming for help! She shouted at the car as it raced away, "NO! NO! DON'T GO! HELP ME!"

Gus was down on the ground in pain, bleeding from his shoulder wound. He crawled over to Angelo to feel for a pulse, "Angelo, Angelo." There was no pulse, and there was no response. His dead eyes stared wide at the Blood Moon. *Rhapsody in Blue,* still playing on the radio.

Angelo Slayton was dead! Gus Slayton was wounded and bleeding!

---

[3] *NYPD Police Officers Eddie Martins and Richard Hall, New York City Rape:*

Police Officers Eddie Martins and Richard Hall arrested Anna Chambers on drug charges in Coney Island, NY. They handcuffed the 18-year-old woman and took turns raping her in the back of their police van while on duty. They admitted their crime and were sentenced to probation - they received no punishment!

PART TWO

ONE YEAR EARLIER

CHAPTER ONE

The Governor's Daughter [4]

Florida State Capitol

Tallahassee, Florida

Tallahassee became the Florida State Capitol in 1824 because it was equidistant from the two largest cities at the time, St. Augustine and Pensacola. It eventually grew larger than both cities in the state and became home to the Florida Supreme Court, the Florida Governor's Mansion, and the Florida Department of Law Enforcement - FDLE.

Casey Collins was a smart, ambitious and relentless Senior Agent at FDLE, competing in a world dominated by aggressive, uncompromising men, that often made it difficult for a woman to succeed in what was still very much a *man's* police force. She was a true type-A personality and excelled at her job, but her attractive looks were more of a hindrance than an advantage to her in "The Department."

She couldn't help that she was a natural blonde with baby-blue eyes and burst a D-cup bra, or that she had to shop in the JR's department for a pant size that fit her narrow hips and small bottom. She was often compared to the beautiful model, Kathy Ireland. Given the nature of her job, she maintained her fitness and took pride in her physical endurance.

Casey climbed the long set of concrete steps and entered the front doors of the Florida State Capitol building deep in thought, contemplating her impending meeting with Brendan Scott, the Governor of the State of Florida. She was apprehensive and anguished because she knew it would be a difficult and emotional meeting.

She flashed her FDLE badge at the guards, bypassing the metal detector, and rushed into the elevator for the Governor's office. She watched the doors close and was alone with her thoughts as the elevator ascended. Tears formed in her eyes as she reminisced about the Governor's daughter, but she tried her best to be strong.

In the vestibule outside the Governor's office, the Governor's long-time friend and trusted Security Guard, L.B. Rouselle, stood watch to check the identification of visitors and protect the Governor from any harm. He was a former Marine, tall and strong, and served alongside the Governor in the Vietnam War.

They had been in deadly wartime battles together, and L.B. saved the Governor's life during a brutal Viet Cong attack. He was awarded the Medal of Honor and gained the Governor's loyalty for the rest of his life. He was also a retired police officer and worked side-by-side with Casey on many arrests and trials when the Governor was the District Attorney.

The three of them had grown to become trusted work colleges and good friends. They were like the "Three Musketeers."

L.B. stood up and hugged Casey as she walked into the vestibule, "Great to see you, Casey. How are you doing?"

Lawrence Bourbon Rouselle was native born in New Orleans and still maintained the old "N'orleans" southern accent as he spoke. With strong Creole roots, the "Bourbon" in L.B.'s name came from his French royal-family lineage, dating back centuries to the days when the Rouselles first set foot in Louisiana, then a French colony on the North American continent.

Casey hugged him back, "I'm doing okay, L.B. How is Brendan holding up?"

"It's been hard, Casey. Brendan is struggling every hour of every day. He'll be glad to see you."

It was all very sad. The Governor's daughter was raped and murdered, and his wife had been so distraught by her daughter's murder, that she had a massive heart attack. She's been on life-support ever since her daughter's death, hopelessly sealed in her mind and incommunicado with the outside world. The Governor refused to give up on her, even though the doctors at Tallahassee Memorial Hospital diagnosed her condition as terminal. He hoped that capturing their daughter's killer could revive her. It was the Governor's top priority to find her killer.

Their daughter, Susan, was found in a drainage ditch alongside Alligator Alley near the Seminole Indian Reservation at Big Cypress in Southwest Florida. Her cause of death was strangulation. She was only twenty-five-years old.

L.B. opened the door into the reception area, as the Governor's secretary looked up from her desk and bristled.

"Hello, Agent Collins." Her voice was polite beneath suspicious eyes. She was in her early 50s, petite, five-feet-two-inches with short, stylish reddish hair, and always perfectly groomed. She had been with the Governor from the start of his political career and fully intended to stay until her retirement.

Just then, a group of Florida Senators walked past them and out the door through the vestibule, following their meeting with the Governor.

Casey and L.B. waited until all the politicians marched by, talking and patting each other on the back, and then proceeded toward the Governor's office.

The secretary bared her faux smile, "He's waiting, go on in." She had strict orders not to disturb the Governor while Casey was in his office.

Casey smiled at the woman, then quickly dismissed her as she slipped through the half-open door. She knew the Governor's secretary had invested several of the best years of her life trying to seduce her boss away from his wife of thirty-plus years. Now that his wife was barely alive, she anticipated replacing her when the time came. Casey also knew she was a threat to her, because of the closeness and fondness between her and the Governor, and now she was working on the most important thing in the Governor's life… his daughter's rape and murder.

Casey wrestled with her emotions as she entered his well-appointed, stately office. She knew it would be a disheartening reunion. She closed the door firmly behind her and leaned her back against it.

A few soft green potted plants added life to the wood, brass, and glass surroundings. At one end of the room, there were three Second Empire couches, a marble wood-burning fireplace that always radiated a cozy charred oak scent, and exquisite gilt-framed original artist oil paintings on the walls of hunting scenes that could easily have held their own at the Metropolitan Museum of Art – The horses and lead rider dressed in riding pinks, brass fox hunting horn in hand, jumping fences and chasing packs of beagles looking for a fox to corner, trap, and rip to pieces. Considering Susan's killer, Casey sympathized with the fox.

"Hello Casey," the Governor said as he approached her with outstretched arms. He wrapped his arms around her and hugged her tightly, holding her for several moments longer than his usual friendly greeting.

Casey answered in her softest voice, "Hi, Brendan."

The Governor finally released her, and they walked over toward his favorite antique leather couch and coffee table, beneath an oversized picture window that framed the Capitol City of Tallahassee. As he considered what to say, he stared blankly at the landscape of the city below, which shimmered through the three-dimensional windowpane in his corner office.

"Please sit down, Casey."

Casey sat down, and the Governor sat close next to her, "How are you holding up, Brendan?" She could see the sadness in his eyes.

"It's been hard. First, my daughter was murdered, and then my wife had a heart attack, and now she's in a coma. I've lost both of them." He wondered how this double tragedy could have ever happened to him. He had been so diligent.

Casey put her arm around his shoulder, "I know. I am truly sorry. On both counts."

At first, he was at a loss for words. Then, he let down his defenses and just honestly described what he was going through, "Casey, I'm sorry I've been so self-absorbed. It's just that I was finally on top of the world after all those years of hard work, and then *bang*, it's all over because this senseless killer raped and murdered my baby."

Casey empathized and could totally relate to what he was going through because she also had an unsolved family murder tragedy in her life. She looked up with sad eyes, "Please, don't blame yourself. There was nothing you could have done to save her."

"She was so good and so talented. She was just gathering facts from the Seminole Indian Reservation for the book she was writing for her graduate studies. Now she's gone. It's just not fair." The Governor's eyes welled up with tears, "Casey, you have to find her killer. I will not rest until we punish him for what he did to Susan."

Casey's voice dropped even lower as she spoke what was in her heart, "Brendan, I will help you and support you, however I can, and whenever you need me. I want you to know I'm here to help you in any way I can. All I ask is that you let me help you. Let me know what you're going through. Please don't shut me out. Let me into your life."

For a split-second, Brendan thought he was going to cry. It was the most beautiful thing she could have said to him. He leaned over and kissed her tenderly on her cheek.

Casey hugged him tightly as they both sobbed into each other's shoulders. It was a tragedy of immeasurable proportions.

He reluctantly left her shoulder and cuddled her next to him. He swallowed hard and peered at her through watery eyes, "Thank you, Casey. With your help, we'll get through this. How are you holding up?"

"It's been quite a week." She sighed as she gently nestled into his body. She loved the way he molded into her, sheltering her with his warm body, protecting her vulnerable position.

At fifty-seven-years-old, Governor Brendan Scott was a strong, tough man. Formerly a Marine, he fought in the Vietnam War and returned a hero, which helped him get elected Governor. His spare six-foot-three-inch frame and aristocratic features were aging nicely thanks to good genes and fine living, accentuated by chemical and surgical science. He had a rugged face, one that might fit with a romance novel hero. His chiseled features were feathered with what others called laugh lines, but in his case, they were due to the degree with which he studied plans, legislative reports, and financial records for the State of Florida. He kept his dark brown hair trimmed short enough to expose his lightly graying temples. Not handsome per se, but still the heartthrob of the state, as fit of mind as anyone she knew. It was his manner, his calm presence, and his quiet ability to get things done that made him a great Governor.

Brendan hugged her tighter and spoke softly, "You're upset."

"Yes, I am. I wish things were different." She allowed him to draw her into his shoulder. She nestled in and fought the melancholy. If things had been different for them, she knew they would have been together. But there were too many things on his side and her side, making the idea hopeless. She thought they both knew it, but occasionally he broke ranks. He truly loved her, and she loved that. And she loved him back, but she didn't want to think about that at this point because of his anguish about his daughter and wife.

He tried to compose himself, "How is the investigation going?"

The Governor was her boss, so she had to give him her honest assessment, "It's frustrating. There were two other rapes in Southeast Florida in the past month, and the semen sample rape kits matched the DNA from Susan's killer, so we are tracking that down, but the victims were so badly beaten and so frightened they couldn't recall important details we need."

"I understand the DNA shows a single rapist, same as Susan, but the victims claim they were raped by *two* men posing as police officers. How does that affect your investigation?"

Casey reached over and sorted through her bag to pull out a notepad, "DNA indicates the rapist is Caucasian. According to the victims who survived, he's likely tall and muscular. It matches the victim's descriptions, except for the possible second rapist, but honestly, it could fit the description of millions of men."

The Governor scanned Casey's notes, "All three rapes matched the DNA? Are the accounts similar?"

"Yes. They are all very similar." She looked up at him, "Except for Susan's murder. Serial rapists disguised as cops. Or maybe they actually are cops?"

He stared off into the distance for a moment, then picked up an official-looking document from the coffee table and handed it to Casey, "I agree that a serial rapist and murderer might be attacking women in our state. I want you to lead the 'Rape Task Force' I'm forming to investigate the crimes and find my daughter's killer."

He chose Casey based on her crime-solving reputation from past cases they had worked together, at FDLE, when he was the District Attorney. Their history together made Casey especially important to him.

"Thank you, Brendan. I'll do my best."

The Governor pointed to the document again, "As you can see, I budgeted a $125,000 reward fund for informants to come forward. I'll request more if you need it."

She studied it, "Good. That will help. I'll start with $25,000 for Susan's killer."

"I know I can trust you to do the right thing. You always do. This is personal for me, so keep me informed." He smiled and hugged her, touching her tenderly, lovingly, feeling everything he wanted to say, but couldn't. So, he said it with his touch.

She felt his sadness. A tear dripped down her cheek as she held him close. Life had been so unfair to him. There was nothing she could do about the losses he'd suffered - first his daughter, now his wife - but she could find the answers he needed and give him closure, which she vowed to do!

---

[4] *NJ Governor Brendan Byrne Daughter's Rape in New York City, New York:*

New Jersey Governor Brendan Byrne's 25-year-old daughter, Susan, was dragged into an alley, and gang-raped by two men on the Upper East Side of Manhattan, while she was returning to her car on East 78th Street between Second and Third Avenue at 12:40 a.m.

CHAPTER TWO

Cold Case

Florida State Capitol
Tallahassee, Florida

Casey had her own tragedies to deal with. At eighteen, she ran away from a toxic, abusive family and home environment, and received a scholarship at Florida State University, while working part time at the local Police Station. Her family had deep roots in the Police Department.

She competed in the Miss America Beauty Pageant and had been named Miss Florida, but unfortunately, placed runner-up to the beautiful black contestant from New York, the judges favored. She cringed when the Master of Ceremony made the announcement, *"And the winner is... Miss New York."* She was disappointed but went on with her life.

After graduation from college, she met the man of her dreams in Tallahassee. He proposed to her on bended knee beneath the full moon on Apalachicola Beach following three weeks of dating. Casey married Jeremy Collins a month later on the beach overlooking the Gulf of Mexico sunset at the Buccaneer Inn on Saint George Island, south of Tallahassee.

A small group of friends attended the wedding. Casey did not invite her family!

They had chosen Saint George Island because it was close to Tallahassee, but far from the hustle and bustle of the big city. It was a beautiful and tranquil barrier island in the Gulf of Mexico, situated four and one-half miles off the coast of Florida's Panhandle, connected by the Bryant Patton Bridge, a long and narrow two-lane bridge that spans Apalachicola Bay. Their wedding was in-season, so Saint George Island Beach was crowded, as were the quaint little boutique shops in town, and the Blue Parrot Ocean Front Café they frequented, night after night.

Casey Collins was deeply in love and planned to spend the rest of her life with Jeremy Collins until, unfortunately, one evening on the way home from work, he was shot in the head while driving on Monroe Street in Tallahassee. He died at Tallahassee Memorial Hospital the next day. Witnesses said the killer pulled up next to his car and shot him at point-blank range. They thought there could have been two men in the car. It seemed like it might have been an assassination.

It was just one of those strange, bewildering things that happened because of a series of bizarre events that shifted what she thought would be the course of her life. In the months that followed, Casey grew fanatical about finding her husband's murderer. She spent weeks researching crime reports of similar incidents in surrounding areas and tracking down the whereabouts of criminals living close to the crime scene.

She drove the police crazy with her constant phone calls and theories. Unfortunately, they never found the killer or killers, after months of arduous searching for the criminals. They relegated the murder to the cold case files at the Tallahassee Police Department. That troubled her and she wanted to do more.

This life-altering event drove her ambition in the field of criminal justice. Law Enforcement was in her DNA. It was the "Family Business." She attended law school in the evenings and worked her way up from street cop to FDLE Detective First Class in record time – where she dedicated herself to solving murders, like the one that had killed her husband.

The pain of losing her husband and failing to find his killer haunted her since the day he died. She could understand the pain of not getting answers to the death of a loved one, and especially the Governor's loss of his daughter, Susan. Casey vowed to work tirelessly to find the answers the Governor so badly needed, and she so badly longed for herself.

CHAPTER THREE

Rape Task Force [5] [6] [7]

FDLE Headquarters
Tallahassee, Florida

The Florida Department of Law Enforcement - FDLE headquarters in Tallahassee was a massive, gleaming structure in the heart of the Capital City. It's the epicenter of law enforcement for the state, controlled by the Governor and the Florida State Cabinet. They divided the building into different sections, each devoted to major areas of focus: Computer Crimes, Domestic Security, Forensics, and Investigations. A staff of agents handle specific crimes, categorized by the type of crime and location.

The top floor consists of a broad array of offices for the department heads and facilities with the latest technology to help fight crimes. The video conference center provides access from Tallahassee to the six Regional Operations Centers in Pensacola, Jacksonville, Orlando, Tampa Bay, Fort Myers, and Miami.

The smell of roasting coffee permeated the conference room from the coffeemaker on the small countertop below the oversized whiteboard on the wall. Senior Agent Casey Collins sipped her coffee at the conference room table, dressed in a modest dark blue skirt suit, a white blouse, and low heels. She had her blonde hair pulled back into a neat ponytail.

Casey was meeting with her partner, Agent Darren Turner and FDLE Profiler, Jack Higgins, for a brainstorming session. They had been working nonstop, collecting information, and conducting interviews, so they covered the conference table with newspapers, photographs, and reports. They reviewed everything to build a "Profile" of the rapist and killer to help them track him down as members of the "Rape Task Force," which the Governor had established.

Darren leaned forward in his chair and admired his attractive FDLE partner and boss. He subtly inhaled her lightly scented perfume and silently congratulated himself. Having given up his patrol job in Miami Beach a month ago, beach bunnies and Ocean Drive party girls, as good as they looked and performed, failed to stimulate the rest of him. Casey, on the other hand, was always cheerful. Her baby-blue eyes were as bright as her mind, and she dressed for success. She was in her mid-thirties and wore little makeup; she was naturally beautiful.

He found his gaze grazing her cleavage while they spoke. Everything from her marvelous bust and body screamed sex, but everything above her bust was pure law and order. Sadly, FDLE policy stated that there was no fraternizing allowed, though he constantly fantasied, telling himself it could happen… someday.

Jack reviewed the reports and photographs. His wire-rimmed glasses were cockeyed, and his pockmarked complexion was paler than usual. He tilted his head sideways to look into Casey's face, "The killer has a deep contempt for women." Jack observed, "He probably grew up in a home with a dominant father figure and women subordinated to the father. Overall, the killer has a total disdain and lack of respect for women. He sees them as objects for his selfish pleasures and then discards them like garbage."

Casey agreed, "Judging by the way he raped and murdered Susan, I think that's very accurate."

Darren concurred, "What a shame."

"We have to find her killer." Casey picked up the Tallahassee Democrat newspaper on the table and displayed it to Jack, "And now we have another rape to investigate." The headline read: *Victim Accuses Police of Rape.*

Jack repositioned his eyeglasses and peered at the newspaper, and then at Casey, "Last night," he said, shaking his head. A few unruly wisps of hair dangled across his balding forehead, defying the hair-sprayed comb-over. He shoved them back into place with his fingers.

Casey responded, "Accusing the Police."

Darren walked over to the coffeepot to refill his cup and corrected, "Accusing two cops. She's claiming she was pulled over and forced into a police cruiser and raped twice. Not a mark left at the scene."

She opened up the paper to read the article for herself.

Newsflash: Victim Accuses Police of Rape
Fort Pierce, Florida
By The Tallahassee Democrat

Police responded to a 911-cell phone call made by 21-year-old Lindsay Baily, claiming she was gang-raped by two policemen, who took turns on her inside their police cruiser. Ms. Baily said they pulled her over for a minor traffic violation. However, instead of writing a ticket and moving on, they used their authority to rape her. They kidnapped her, handcuffed her, threw her in the back of their cruiser, drove to a vacant car lot, and raped her.

FDLE questioned Ms. Baily, in hopes she could offer some clues as to the identity of the perpetrator or perpetrators since she claimed two men raped her, but the DNA indicated only one rapist, "They were dressed as cops and pulled me over for speeding. Then, they handcuffed me behind my back, beat, and raped me. They had this music turned up loud as they took turns on me. It sounded like... Rhapsody in Blue." She said, "They told me they had multiple warrants out for my arrest, and I could avoid jail time by having sex with them."

A semen sample confirmed that she had been raped, but the DNA results remained unidentified after a search of criminal databases. They also tied the DNA to three other unsolved rapes in Florida, including the rape and murder of the Governor's daughter. The similarities in all the crimes prompted the Governor to form a Special Task Force to investigate the serial rapes and murders in our state.

FDLE Senior Agent Casey Collins would lead the Governor's Rape Task Force. They established a special phone line to collect any relevant information: (850) 555-1212.

The press dubbed them, "The Rhapsody Rapists."

Casey snapped the paper closed, "Lindsay Baily said two men raped her, but semen indicated a single rapist." An expression of regret crossed her compressed lips, shaking her head, "Where do we go from there? If it was a cop or cops, sworn to uphold the law, they're breaking it in the worst way."

Jack added some background. He was always on, commanding every step in a radio announcer's voice. His demeanor exuded professorial confidence, and he always appeared to be sanctimonious, making a big show of clearing his throat before speaking, to convey the image of the expert he was, "If the perpetrator is a cop, he is an evil thrill seeker and has no remorse."

He cleared his throat to continue his dissertation, "How many law enforcement officers are accused of sexual misconduct? There is no definitive answer. The Federal Bureau of Justice Statistics, which collects police data from around the country, doesn't track actual arrests of police officers, and states aren't required to collect or share that information. Plus, they do not require police to provide DNA samples."

"The 'Blue Curtain Code of Silence' protects all cops. It's just not right." Casey slapped the newspaper back down on the conference table in frustration.

Jack picked it up and stared at the article, "Was there one rapist or two? That is a definite complication when trying to build a Profile. Are they cops or just posing as police officers? It's easy nowadays to get a uniform and badge and put a blue rotating light on your car."

Casey added, "You can easily buy a uniform at any costume store for Halloween or a party. If he's a cop, he already had the uniform, handcuffs, and police car. But the Blue Curtain makes it difficult to investigate these crimes because the police departments all protect each other."

"Right," Jack went on, "and to measure the problem, the *Associated Press* [5] obtained records from 41 states on police decertification, which is an administrative process that revokes a police officer's law enforcement license. They reviewed cases from 2009 through 2014 to determine whether they stemmed from sexual misconduct meeting the Department of Justice standard for sexual assault: *'sexual contact that happens without consent, including intercourse, sodomy, child molestation, incest, fondling, and attempted rape.'* Nine states and the District of Columbia said they either did not decertify officers for misconduct or declined to provide information."

Darren sounded surprised, "Why?"

Jack shared his knowledge of the subject and his psychological expertise, "The Blue Curtain again. Of those states that released records, the AP determined that over 550 police officers were decertified for sexual assault, including rape and sodomy, sexual shakedowns in which they extorted citizens into performing sex to avoid arrest or gratuitous pat-downs. Some 440 police officers lost their badges for other sex offenses, such as possessing child pornography or sexual misconduct that included being a *'Peeping Tom,'* sexting juveniles, or having on-duty sexual intercourse. About one-third of the officers decertified were accused of incidents involving juveniles."

"Because of gaps in the information provided by the states, it was impossible to discern any other distinct patterns, other than a propensity for police officers to use the power and authority of their badge to prey upon vulnerable victims. Some decertified police officers, faced criminal charges; some offenders were able to avoid prosecution by agreeing to surrender their certifications."

Darren interjected, "Why aren't more of these crimes reported?"

Jack responded with an expert's conviction, "The Blue Curtain again. Police have all the authority. Police officers avoid charges or beat a conviction because they are so steeped in the system. They know the district attorneys. They know the judges. They know the safe houses. They know how to testify in court. They know how to make the accuser's accusations look questionable. How are you going to get anything to happen when the police are part of the system, and when they threaten you, and when you know they have a gun, and you know they can find you wherever you go?"

Jack continued, "Victims include unsuspecting motorists, schoolgirls forced to raise their skirts in a supposed search for drugs, police interns taken advantage of, women with legal troubles who succumb to performing sex acts for promised help, and prison inmates forced to have sex with guards. The AP's findings, coupled with other research and interviews with experts, suggest sexual misconduct is among the most prevalent types of complaints against law enforcement officers. Phil Stinson, [6] a researcher at Bowling Green State University, analyzed news articles between 2005 and 2011 and found over six-thousand-seven-hundred arrests involving over ten-thousand police officers.

Probably more than double that number have never been caught or prosecuted."

"Unfortunately, giving us good cops, a bad name," Casey added.

Darren looked at Casey, "Bad cops doing bad things. It's a much more prevalent problem than I originally thought."

Casey turned to Darren, "They are cops... and cops investigating other cops won't be easy—both because they too serve, and because of the Blue Curtain. It's a double-edged sword because the Blue Curtain does some good too—protecting officers who are truly innocent. The system designed to protect good cops has been hijacked and is now used to commit crimes."

Darren agreed, "How true."

Casey looked saddened, "Cops sworn to 'protect and serve' are the abusers, rapists, and murderers."

The ultimate betrayal!

[7] **_Deputy Evan Cramer Police Rape in St. Lucie, Florida:_**

Sheriff's Deputy Evan Cramer pulled over a young Florida woman named Kelly for a minor traffic violation. However, instead of writing a ticket and moving on, he used his police authority to kidnap her, throw her in the back of his cruiser, drive her to a vacant car lot, and rape her.

CHAPTER FOUR

The Rhapsody Rapists [8] [9]

FDLE Headquarters
Tallahassee, Florida

"Do you think the rapist and killer is a cop?" Darren asked directly to Casey.

Casey squinted her eyes, curiously, "Or cops." She corrected him, "I'm not sure, but that's what Ms. Baily is claiming."

"Sounds nasty." There was a time when having a female boss would have bothered Darren, but now it didn't, especially since his boss was drop-dead gorgeous. He knew he could take his weekends back down to Miami Beach and find any manner of female comfort with little effort and little expense. Yes, he was a male chauvinist, with no intent to change. For the moment, though, he would enjoy both of his worlds.

"It does," she agreed.

As usual, Casey was all business. A workaholic. She was, in fact, his boss, and that thought always made her smile. *She Who Must Be Obeyed.* She tried not to let it go to her head. Getting to the top of the Florida Department of Law Enforcement was an achievement her family had always aspired to. She, being the only female member of the family, was the only sibling family member to achieve it.

She enjoyed working with Darren but kept her guard up. He was too confident, impeccably groomed, and exceedingly handsome. She'd heard through Betsy, her secretary, that the office staff referred to them as *Mr. and Mrs. Smith,* from the Brad Pitt and Angelina Jolie movie, although Darren reminded her more of James Bond than Brad Pitt. His athletic five-foot-eleven-inch frame was built to carry a heavy briefcase in one hand and a two-suiter in the other while dashing for the last flight out of the Tallahassee International Airport. She took his wisecracks in that context and reined back her suspicions.

Darren pulled a report from the stack of papers and reviewed it, "I've questioned the first responders at the scene, and they said they don't have any solid leads. Lindsay Baily was so frightened she didn't notice any police identification or the squad car's numbers. The rape scene was in a deserted car parking lot, so there were no surveillance cameras or eyewitnesses. They found nothing that looked suspicious to them."

Casey scratched her head, "I haven't gotten much from forensics either. Besides the vaginal swab, there were no fingerprints or tire tracks."

"Same as the others. The plot thickens." Darren sounded frustrated, "So, where does that leave us, Jack?"

Jack scratched his bald spot, thoughtfully listening to the discussion between Casey and Darren, "The DNA should have told us whether there were one or two rapists," he said, "but it indicated only one. Based on that, we have to assume one rapist as the key to building our Profile. Of course, handcuffs are also easily acquired, but from what I can derive from the interviews, forensics, and photographs, the rapist must have had some law enforcement or military background. Based on the victim's testimony, he is probably white, in his early 30s, over six-feet tall and physically fit. I believe he is personating a strong dominant male role model from his past, who was guilty of analogous behavior and actions."

Darren was curious, "How did you reach those conclusions, Jack?"

"Well, he needs to appear as an authoritative figure so women will obey him, and tall men portray that image better than shorter men.

36

Ms. Baily indicated the rapist or rapists were young-looking Caucasians. Usually, rape is a learned behavior, not naturally acquired at birth. Since his mentor raped without punishment, so can he. Plus, he's unafraid of taking risks, such as raping a woman in the middle of a parking lot. The police badge, the uniform, and the gun all bolster his sense of power and authority, which enhances his masculinity and control. That's probably why he became a cop, in the first place."

Jack stood up and explained it further to Darren as if he were lecturing in a classroom, "Remember the case against Oklahoma City Police Officer Holtzclaw. [8] According to pretrial testimony, Internal Affairs detectives reviewed the names of the women Holtzclaw had come into contact with during his 4:00 p.m. to 2:00 a.m. shift and interviewed each one of them. The GPS device on his patrol car put him at the scene of the alleged incidents, and department records showed that he had called in to check all the women for warrants. By the time the investigation concluded, they had assembled a six-month narrative of alleged sex crimes they said started December 20th, 2013, with a woman taken into custody and hospitalized while high on angel dust."

"Dressed in a hospital gown, her right wrist handcuffed to the bed rail, the woman said Holtzclaw coerced her into performing oral sex, suggesting that her cooperation would lead to dropped charges. The woman said, *'I didn't think no one would believe me,'* while testifying at a pretrial hearing, *'I feel like all police work together.'"*

Jack continued his diatribe incessantly, "Holtzclaw faced 36 counts, including rape, sexual battery, and forcible oral sodomy. Many of the women had struggled with drugs. Some had been prostitutes or had criminal records. Most lived in the same rundown swath of the city in sight of the state Capitol dome, and they were all women of color. Many of their allegations were similar, with the women saying they were accused of hiding drugs, then told to lift their skirts or pull down their pants. Some claim they had been groped, and others said they were forced to have sexual intercourse or oral sex."

"The youngest accuser said Holtzclaw first approached her when she was with two friends who were arguing, and he learned that she had an outstanding warrant for trespassing. He let her go but found her again later that day, walking to her mother's house. She said she offered her a ride and then followed her to the front porch, reminding her of her arrest warrant, accusing her of hiding drugs and warning her not to make things more difficult than they needed to be. She claimed he touched her breasts and slid his hand under her panties before pulling off her shorts and raping her. When it was over, the teen said he told her, *'He might be back to see me again.'"*

"She said, *'I didn't know what to do,'* she testified at the pretrial hearing, *'Like, what am I going to do? Call the cops? He was a cop!'"*

Casey interjected, "Thankfully, he's in prison for the rest of his life. Sentenced to 263 years."

Darren shook his head, "Horrible. It's hard to believe police would do that to the people they are supposed to *protect and serve.*"

Casey was shuffling through the papers and photos, then placed them in stacks, face-up on the table. She handed Darren one of the stacks of photos, "These are photos of the previous rapes and Susan's murder, which I printed out from the computer."

Darren sorted through the stack of photographs and stared at one of the Governor's daughter at the time of her murder, "She's lying in a drainage ditch alongside Alligator Alley. Judging by the scars on her wrists, they had handcuffed her. Same as the others."

Casey glanced at the photo in Darren's hand, "Exactly. There's a pattern here that might help us correlate the crimes. The same MO as the others." She placed some of the other photos on the conference table in a lineup.

"The killer or killers have gotten more brazen with every victim." Jack observed, "He or they are feeling infallible, sort of god-like, continuing to take more risks and will continue to do so until stopped."

He shuffled through the photographs, "They had handcuffed them all. Susan had the deepest wounds. She must have fought hard to survive."

"But sadly, she didn't survive." Casey had a special fondness for the Governor and his daughter. She had been involved in law enforcement ever since her husband's murder and had worked with the Governor on several previous assignments in the past when he was the District Attorney. She was also very close to his daughter. The two of them were like sisters... now she was dead.

"Her car was discovered a couple of miles from her body with the keys still in the ignition, following her meeting at the Seminole Indian Reservation." Darren added, "The only things missing were her license and registration."

Casey concurred, "She must have been stopped for a fictitious traffic violation and asked for her license and registration."

"That makes sense. Why else would they be missing?"

"She had been a graduate student at Florida State University, studying Seminole Indian History for her forthcoming book about the forced relocation of Native American Indians from Southwest Florida in the mid-1800s. Her manuscript, *Tamiami Trail of Tears,* was found lying on the front seat."

Casey picked up Susan's manuscript from the table and thumbed through it, "She had hand-written notes all over the neatly typed manuscript that she must have added during her discussions with the Seminole Indian elders. The notes scribbled in the margins of the document, alluded to buried pirate treasure on Seminole Indian land. Could there be any connection between her investigation into Seminole Indian history and her death?"

Jack scratched his chin as he thought, "That's a feasible theory. However, the book was going to be about history that happened two-hundred years ago. It's all very interesting about the *Dade Massacre* in Big Cypress Swamp and Indian War Chief, *Osceola.* It probably would have been a great book, but I don't see a motive for murder. In fact, the Seminole Indians beat the Army so badly, that the US government would probably be the ones to want to quash the book from publication."

Casey grinned, "I know. It was never a fair fight. The Army used their arsenal of guns and rifles against an Indian defense of mostly bows and arrows. The Seminoles were vastly outnumbered but fought courageously and never surrendered. I was cheering for the Indians as I read her manuscript."

Jack grinned, "I especially liked the quote from the Army soldier fighting the Seminoles along the Tamiami Trail in the Everglades in 1836, 'If the Devil owned both Hell and Florida, he would rent out Florida and live in Hell.'"

They all laughed for a moment at that quote from the past.

Darren said, "You've got to give them credit, they fought hard utilizing guerrilla tactics in a treacherous swampy wilderness with devastating effects to defend their homeland."

Casey replied, "Yes. They knew how to move within the Everglades swamp and used it to their advantage against an enemy invading their land. The government eventually gave up. At that time, it was the most expensive military campaign in our country's history."

Jack flashed a sarcastic look to Casey, "Well, at least they named Dade County, Florida, after poor Major Dade. He commanded the worst US military defeat in history."

Darren added, "I didn't realize that until I read Susan's manuscript, but I still don't see a connection to her murder."

Casey questioned, "I wonder if her notations about pirates and buried treasure could have been a motive. Maybe she inadvertently discovered something, like a buried treasure map or something?"

Darren agreed, "Could be. Pirate Gasparilla and his buccaneers had quite a run for a long period of time and must have amassed a small fortune."

Jack intervened, "Or a large fortune. Gasparilla plundered merchant ships for almost 40 years, according to history and Susan's notations."

Casey questioned, "Do you think the killer knew that she was the Governor's daughter?"

Jack shook his head, "It looks like it was just an unfortunate coincidence to me. But I can't be sure of that or anything else at this point. We need to get this Profile typed up and distributed."

Darren was puzzled, "What about the music, Jack? That's something we've never encountered before. Music to rape by?"

"The Rhapsody Rapists." Jack nodded, "That is unusual. I believe it was probably to drown out the victim's screaming while he or they raped her. It might be something from a childhood memory that brought pleasure and replaying the music reinforced that pleasure. If there are two men, they are working like a team sport. Almost as a tag team while the music was playing."

Darren looked disgusted, "Tag team? That's awful."

Jack concurred, "Yes, it is! They target a woman and track her down, like a pack of wolves chasing and cornering prey. Then they take turns raping her."

Casey listened to Jack and Darren and remembered her painful experiences as a child. She had been repressing those painful memories for many years, but the references to the music forced her recollection. She wanted to change the subject.

"Jack, thank you for all your help. We have to catch this guy." She flashed her brows then scooped up her notes on the killer's profile, photos, and Susan's manuscript into her voluminous bag, draped the bag over her shoulder, and stood up, pushing her chair back.

Jack shook hands with both of them, "Or guys, I know. Good luck to you."

"Yes, thank you, Jack." Darren slid out of his seat and followed Casey out the door.

---

[9] *LAPD Police Officers Luis Valenzuela and James Nichols, California Rapes:*

Los Angeles Police Department Officers Luis Valenzuela and James Nichols repeatedly raped and sexually assaulted women while on duty. They took turns like a tag team; one partner served as the lookout, while the other carried out an attack in the backseat of the police car they drove together while on duty.

CHAPTER FIVE

Red Stilettos [10]

Diva's Topless Gentlemen's Club
Fort Lauderdale, Florida

The Slayton brothers smoked a cannabis joint as they drove to *Diva's Topless Gentlemen's Club* on 24th Southeast Avenue in Fort Lauderdale, a topless dancing club with sexy dancers and beautiful waitresses. One waitress, in particular, had caught their attention, and they always sat in her section of the club.

Gus turned into the parking lot, past glowing neon signs with sexy dancer animations kicking-up long lean legs in slow motion, as the blow slowly seeped out of his nostrils. He flicked what was left of the roach out the open window, parked, and they strolled into the building's entrance. They were regulars, so the bouncer just nodded as they walked in and took a table in front of the main stage.

The DJ played a modern, souped-up version of *Stayin' Alive*, although it wasn't the Bee Gee's singing it. The words were appropriate, but the song sounded like it was playing at high speed with a steady beat. *Bubble-gum music.* It blasted loudly in the smoke-filled room, providing a rhythm for the topless dancers shaking and jiggling their bodies to the constant drumbeat.

A scantily clad cocktail waitress walked over to take their order. Since they were sitting down, she bent over, displaying her bountiful breasts and smiled seductively as she greeted them, "Hello gentlemen, my name is Rosie. What would you like?" She leaned a little lower to accentuate the *"what would you like"* part.

They both leered at the tattoo of a long-stemmed red rose on her left breast as they contemplated her offer. It was obvious Rosie really knew how to sell drinks. Although, they already knew her real name was Kimberly.

The smell of her cheap perfume momentarily overpowered the stench of smoke and stale body odor that permeated the room. Her blonde wig was sprinkled with sparkling sequins that matched her glistening outfit, which rode high on her thighs, exposing her fishnet stockings and six-inch Red Stiletto's. It was a sexy bar waitress uniform, the club management required her to wear, to generate more business from the male patrons. And it worked!

They both grinned devilishly as Gus ordered a double Johnny Walker Red on the rocks, and his brother, Angelo, ordered a Budweiser beer. They helped themselves to premium cigars from the small cash-box tray Kimberly balanced on one hand.

Their eyes followed her wiggle back toward the bar. Her lower back revealed a "tramp stamp" tattoo of two long-stemmed red roses intertwined together at the stems just above the dimples on her behind, a perfect match in color with her outfit and her Red Stiletto high-heels.

Gus reached into his jacket pocket to retrieve his guillotine cigar-cutter to clip the end of the cigar, as he watched her strut away. He ceremoniously lit the head of the cigar with his Zippo torch lighter, embossed with a rippling American flag and a police badge silhouetted among the folds, "To Protect and Serve" in bold block letters at the base. He turned it over a few times toward the flame and inhaled his first few puffs. Then he passed the cigar-cutter over to his brother.

The black walls of the massive club, the revolving mirrored globes hanging from the ceilings, and the heavy cloud of smoke all evoked a dark and seductive mood. Small tables and scattered grungy metal chairs surrounded several stages, strategically located in corners, and the large main stage in the middle of the room. Colored spotlights penetrated the murky darkness, and bright white spotlights targeted the stages, illuminating the scanty, sparkling, sequin-decorated outfits worn by the dancers until they stripped them off.

They were like the proverbial little kids in a candy shop. They didn't know where to look first. Gorgeous topless dancers strutted their stuff all around them. Gus feared he might get whiplash from jerking his head to look at all the women's breasts moving in time to the music. Their nipples gleamed from baby oil. Each stripper was more well-endowed than the last.

Where to look next?

Customers screamed and hollered excitedly as they watched the dancers strip off their tops. Some patrons stood by the center stage and waved beer-soaked dollar bills while the dancers seductively pulled down their panties to allow them to place the money into their garter belts. As a thank you, they would lie down on their backs and spread their legs, rotating their hips salaciously in time to the drumbeats.

Kimberly returned with the drinks and set them down on the tiny table. Flirtation was also part of her job description, plus it got her bigger tips.

She smiled seductively as she looked from brother to brother and asked curiously, "Are you two, twins?"

Angelo answered, "Yes, we are Darlin', and you are so beautiful."

She placed the bar tab on the table, "Well, thank you, gentlemen. That will be $35, please."

Gus took out a wad of bills, peeled off a fifty, and shoved it into her bra. His finger caressed her nipple, "Keep the change, honey."

She took the bill out of her bra and looked at it, "Thank you."

As she walked away, they turned their attention to the center stage, which resembled the "after" models at a breast implant convention. The music continued with *Dancing Queen* by Abba. The song had a strong beat, and the girls were doing it justice.

Gus turned to his brother, "Kimberly would be a great addition to our collection."

"She's got to be done, Bro. She's a hot one! She drives a red Jeep Wrangler and takes the same route home every night after the bar closes."

Gus grinned, "I'll bet she's in a real hurry to get home after a long night working here."

"Yeah Bro, she's probably speeding on her way home and, you know… that's against the law."

Gus chuckled, "Just doing our job, Bro. Just doing our job. *To Protect and Serve.*"

The brothers' fist-bumped each other, "It's a tough job, but somebody's got to do it."

They both laughed.

Gus added, "The funny thing is, the Chief issued a police bulletin to be on the lookout for her red Jeep as she drives home late at night. It seems some stalker has been harassing her on Route One, and she needs protection. The stalker was tailgating her and flashing bright lights behind her. Almost forced her off the road one night."

"Hey, that's horrible. What a terrible man." Angelo laughed, "We must follow orders, Bro. *Protect and Serve,* you know what I mean, Bro?"

CHAPTER SIX

The Badge of Betrayal [10]

U.S. Route One

Fort Lauderdale, Florida

After her shift ended, Kimberly walked out to her red Jeep Wrangler parked underneath the bright, flashing animated neon bar sign at a little before 2:00 a.m. A rainstorm had passed while she was inside the club working, and the parking lot glistened with wet pavement and scattered puddles. The lights from the neon sign shimmered on the wet pavement, creating a colorful dancing light show.

As she opened the driver's side door to get into the Jeep, water dripped down from the rain-soaked tan canvas top onto her hair from the weight of the water displaced by the open door, "Oh no. That was smart, Kim." She ridiculed herself as she wiped the dampness from her hair with her hand.

She had changed out of her sexy, sequined bar waitress uniform and Red Stilettos, into a more conservative white sweatshirt, shorts, and sneakers for the long drive home to Coral Gables, twenty-two miles south of Diva's. She had called her husband to tell him she was on her way home.

The red Jeep Wrangler pulled out of the parking lot and turned south onto Route One. She crossed over 17th Street, the main causeway to the beach, and continued on her regular route home. The bright lights of the club, stores, restaurants, and streetlights on the thoroughfare eventually became dark, empty, and desolate, which was usual for her ride home this late at night.

Kimberly became especially vigilant and apprehensive as she approached the area where a stalker had previously harassed her and tried to force her off the road. She noticed a police cruiser pulled over on the shoulder up ahead of her and felt a little safer. She looked inside the front driver's side as she passed the parked police car and observed a police officer smoking a cigarette. Thinking nothing of it, she continued on her way, but when she glanced in her rearview mirror, she saw the cruiser's headlights had suddenly switched on, and the police car turned from the shoulder onto the main roadway. Since she had requested police protection, she assumed the cruiser would safeguard her on her way home. She felt safer as she drove, knowing she was being protected by the police.

Gus took a long, deep drag on his cigarette, then flicked the butt out the open window onto the gravel shoulder below after he watched the red Jeep Wrangler pass him by. *There she is,* he thought as he switched on the ignition and pulled onto the road.

He followed behind the Jeep, heading toward an area where he and Angelo intended to rendezvous. The scheme was for Gus to pull her over and put her in his police cruiser to drive to the designated, isolated area off the main road where they would both "party" with her.

Gus noticed another car following behind him and worried momentarily about being identified, but he knew he would have to act soon to maintain the schedule with his brother. Besides, he was the *law* and had *absolute authority*. He switched on the siren and the rolling red and blue police lights and tailgated close behind the red Jeep. The Jeep's brake lights flashed momentarily as it slowed to pull over to the side of the road.

Gus chuckled to himself as he watched the Jeep's predictable reaction to the police cruiser's lights and siren, "That's right, Kimberly. *The law must be obeyed.*"

Just as the Jeep and the police cruiser pulled onto the shoulder of the road, the driver in the car following slowed down and watched the scene curiously. He scrutinized the police officer in the cruiser with lights and siren going, and then he noticed the pretty young blonde in the Jeep Wrangler obeying the police car's authority. He couldn't imagine why the Jeep was being pulled over because he didn't think she had done anything wrong. He wondered if the police officer pulled her over just because of her good looks, but since he had an expired driver's license and didn't want to get into any trouble himself, he continued on his way.

Kim stopped her Jeep, grimaced at the bright red and blue lights swirling in her rearview mirror, and wondered why she was being pulled over. She started fishing through her purse, searching for her license, car registration, and insurance card, as the police officer approached the driver's side door. She rolled down her window.

Gus ordered, "License and registration ma'am," looking down at her with his orange-tinted glasses.

She looked up at his official police badge and assumed it was a legitimate traffic violation stop, "Why did you pull me over, officer? What did I do wrong?" She reached for her wallet and pulled out her license and registration to hand over to the police officer. She left her wallet on the passenger seat.

Gus took her documents and put them in his shirt pocket without even looking at them, "Out of the car," he ordered.

It startled her as he grabbed the door handle and opened her door, "What? Why?"

"Out of the car," he repeated without explanation. He reached behind his back to take the handcuffs from his belt.

"What did I do?" Kim pleaded, compliantly releasing her seatbelt.

Gus grabbed her left wrist, slapped the handcuff on, and forcefully dragged her out of the car by her arm, "You're resisting arrest."

"What? Why are you arresting me?" He then slapped the handcuff onto her right wrist so both hands were handcuffed in front of her. She was frightened and wanted to run away, but he gripped her arm tightly and pushed her toward the patrol car as she struggled.

"You're under arrest. I'm going to take you to police headquarters." He continued pushing her toward the passenger side of his police cruiser.

Kim tried to twist free of his grip, but he was too strong, "Under arrest for what? I did nothing wrong!"

Gus opened the passenger side door of the cruiser and pushed her into the seat, "Resisting arrest," he repeated and slammed the door.

Kim was confused and terrified. She watched Gus walk around the front of the police car and then turned her head around, hoping for another car on the road behind, but it was dark and empty. She panicked as she tried to figure out how to escape him. There was a two-way radio on the dashboard crammed between the electronics in the police cruiser. Just as she reached for the handset, Gus ripped it from her and punched her in the face from the opened driver's side door. Her mouth was bleeding, and she screamed for help, "HELP ME! SOMEBODY! PLEASE HELP ME!"

Gus reached for the dashboard to switch off the police lights.

"Scream baby, scream all you want. I'm a cop, it's two o'clock in the morning, and no one will hear you." He put the police cruiser into drive to pull back onto the main road.

She was handcuffed, and her face was all bloody and swollen. Kim realized she was in trouble, big trouble. She shouted at him, "WHAT ARE YOU DOING? WHO ARE YOU?"

"Just a secret admirer of yours, that's all."

Suddenly, she recognized him from Diva's last night, "Oh, my God. I know who you are. What do you want from me?"

CHAPTER SEVEN

Stomped to Death [10]

Old Charlotte Highway
Davie, Florida

A cloud of dust encircled the police cruiser as Gus drove onto Old Charlotte Highway, a deserted dirt road west of U.S. Route One, toward his brother's predetermined destination.

Kimberly feared for her life and knew she had to escape somehow. Her eyes darted around the inside of the car, looking for a way to get away from her captor. She was handcuffed in the front seat as the cruiser was speeding down the dirt road. She had to get away. She spotted the "door unlock switch" on the side of the door. In desperation, she forced it to unlock, then opened the passenger door and dove out of the police cruiser, head first.

She crashed onto the dirt road from the speeding vehicle, bruised and bleeding. She rolled and rolled painfully until she used her legs to curl around to stop the momentum. Still handcuffed, she staggered to her feet and started running down the dirt road away from the police cruiser, screaming, "HELP ME! SOMEBODY! PLEASE HELP ME!"

It stunned Gus that she dove out of the speeding car and immediately slammed on the police cruiser's brakes as it skidded to a stop in the dirt. He quickly got out of the car and sprinted after Kim. He was a big man, with long legs, and raced down the dirt road after her. He heard her screams for help in the distance ahead of him and eventually saw her awkward, handcuffed run. He could not let her get away from him.

Kim was running for her life, screaming. As she ran into the darkness, she didn't see the tree root on the ground in front of her that caught her foot, and she tripped painfully onto her face. She hit her head on some rocks on the ground and was knocked out cold, lying face-down in the dirt.

Gus was rapidly racing along the dirt road after her, in his official police-issued boots, when he suddenly stomped on something unexpectedly in the middle of the road. It felt like it might have been a dead animal or bird. He stopped in the darkness to see what he had stepped on and then gazed into the distance to see if Kim was still running ahead of him. He didn't see or hear her, so he took out his flashlight and started probing around to determine what he had stepped on.

The light from his flashlight illuminated what appeared to be blonde hair in the dirt. He moved the light farther down and saw the white sweatshirt Kim was wearing and realized Kim must have fallen, and he must have stepped on her with his boot while he was running after her. His boot print was visible on the back of her sweatshirt and the middle of her neck.

He shook her shoulder and yelled, "Kim, Kim, are you all right?" She didn't answer, and she didn't move. He felt her neck for a pulse, but there wasn't one. She was dead.

He realized he must have crushed her neck when he stomped on her with his boot, after all, he was two-hundred-and-thirty-five-pounds, and all of his weight landed down on her back and neck with one foot. He stood up to figure out what to do next. He knew he had to tell his brother what had happened, but he didn't want to use his cell phone because he knew from police training, the cell-tower location could incriminate him.

He removed the handcuffs from her dead wrists and pushed her body off the dirt road underneath some bushes. Then he shoveled dirt with his hands and shoved tree branches and brush on top of her body to hide it.

When he was done, he dusted off his police uniform and hiked back to the police cruiser. He lit up a joint and inhaled hard, trying to calm his nerves while he figured out how to tell his brother what had happened.

"What do you mean, she's dead?" Angelo's voice boomed loudly.

"I accidentally stepped on her while I was chasing her. I think I broke her neck." Gus explained sheepishly.

"What? You stepped on her neck and killed her?" The brother was incredulous, "How the hell did you do that?"

Gus sucked the joint into the bowels of his lungs from the sodden evaporating stub of marijuana and flicked what was left of the roach onto the ground, "She jumped out of the car while I was driving over here to meet you, and then she ran down the road, screaming. I ran after her, but it was dark, and I didn't see she had fallen down. I stomped on her back accidentally while running after her."

Angelo was infuriated, "We planned this for weeks, and now you killed her? Why didn't you put her in the cage?"

"I know. You're right. I should have. I figured I handcuffed her, and she wouldn't jump out of a fast-moving car. I guess I was wrong."

"I guess you were! It wasn't the jump out of a moving car that killed her. You stomped her to death in the dirt with your boot."

---

[10] _Police Officer Griffin Murder in Charlotte, North Carolina:_

Police Officer Josh Griffin, serving a life sentence for the murder of 26-year-old Kimberly Medlin, finally confessed to killing her, after years of vehement denials. He admitted he stalked and murdered her after he used the red and blue lights on his police cruiser to pull her over. He handcuffed her and drove her to a deserted road to rape her. When she tried to flee, he hit her, stomped on her back, and strangled her to death.

CHAPTER EIGHT

Tamiami Trail of Tears [11]

Casey Collin's Apartment
Tallahassee, Florida

The Spaniards were the first Europeans to arrive in Tallahassee in 1528 when their merchant ship with four-hundred men survived a hurricane off the coast of Cuba and landed on the Florida panhandle. Their original destination was Mexico City, but the hurricane stranded them in Tallahassee for over eight years. Most of them died, fighting off more hurricanes, tornadoes, and the Apalachee Indians.

Casey Collins still lived in the Apalachee Ridge neighborhood of Tallahassee, named after the Apalachee Indian tribe centuries ago. She and her husband, Jeremy Collins, first moved to Apalachee Ridge after they got married. It was a happy home before his murder, but now it had become a constant reminder of what could've, should've and would've been, had he not been murdered. Monroe Street, where he had been shot and killed, was one block away.

It was a sparsely furnished, cozy two-bedroom apartment on the third floor with a den. Her police background guided her desire to be on a higher floor because most robbery break-ins occurred on the ground floor of buildings. Her den had all the comforts of a home office: a large flat-screened video monitor attached to the wall with an oversized, scratched, wooden file cabinet below supporting a video player, a metal desk with a computer station, a small credenza with a lamp, and of course, her glass-doored gun case, stocked with well-oiled and ready weaponry. Not exactly feminine, but she was a cop after all.

Casey poured herself a glass of Pinot Noir and pulled Susan's manuscript out of her bag. She sat down next to her coffee table in the den to read it thoroughly. The cover displayed a full-color artist's rendition of Seminole Indian War Chief, Osceola, dressed in his complete ceremonial ensemble, including feathered headdress and regalia from 1838. The painting, by renowned artist George Catlin, captured a proud, angry, and determined Indian Chief Osceola. She stared at it for a moment, thinking of Susan.

She flipped to the first page, and as she read, paid particular attention to the handwritten notes Susan had scribbled in the margins of the document which alluded to the Florida Pirate Gasparilla, and also a Seminole Indian treasure. That bolstered Casey's nagging suspicion that the research Susan was doing may have somehow been connected to her murder.

Tamiami Trail of Tears [11]

"If the Devil owned both Hell and Florida, he would rent out Florida and live in Hell."

Quote from a white U.S. Army soldier's letter home, while fighting the Seminole Indians along the Tamiami Trail in the Everglades in 1836.

At the U.S. Army encampment, deep within the Big Cypress Swamp in the Southwest Florida Everglades, Major Francis L. Dade, swatted the huge mosquitoes assaulting him as he walked cautiously along the drizzle-soaked, slick, rocky and muddy trail through rows of pitched Army tents. He maneuvered past smoldering campfires and battalions of sleeping soldiers, to check on his spooked horse, pulling nervously on the tie line. He could smell the rot of the swamp and feel the bone aching dampness deep into his joints; the sounds of bullfrogs, snakes, crickets, alligators, and countless wild animals surrounded him. Glowing eyes seemed to blink at him from every shadow.

It was December 28, 1835, a dark, moonless, rainy, and sweltering night alongside what would eventually be named the "Tamiami Trail" that would ultimately connect Tampa and Miami in the "River of Grass," as the locals called the Everglades. The trail was cold and wet in the winter and hot and wet in the summer, where only the native Indians, alligators, snakes, and mosquitoes knew how to exist. Dysentery and malaria would be the primary rewards for Major Dade's military troops if they survived the miserable, ill-fated Seminole Indian Wars.

The Seminole Indian War Chief Osceola, watched the white man quietly from behind a tree at a distance, careful to be as invisible as possible. The Seminole Indian leader was dressed in red war paint in his full ceremonial warrior outfit of buckskin shirt, leggings, silver coin earrings, a feathered gray turban, ostrich plumes, silver spurs, a tomahawk, knife, and bow and quiver with arrows. A decorated powder horn, bullet pouch, and rifle completed his arsenal. He was ready for war, and so were his warriors.

Chief Osceola had planned his war tactics for killing in total darkness. They encircled the encampment in the dead of night and attacked when their adversaries were least prepared and most vulnerable. The Indians would totally annihilate their enemy, then torch whatever was left, leaving nothing but smoldering piles of rubble when they were done. They wanted to teach the white man a lesson and set an example of devastation to drive them out.

Earlier, Chief Osceola had addressed the Seminole Indian War Council assembled in a semi-circle beneath a majestic oak tree in the River of Grass. The "Council Oak," would become symbolic, as the place where important Seminole Indian decisions were made, "We hate the white man. We must drive them out. The spirits of our ancestors' demand that we hold the lands of mother earth, which our forefathers owned. I will not sign any treaty to give away Indian lands, and I will kill any Chief who does sign it."

The gathering of Seminole Indian leaders signaled their defiance, and stood with fists in the air, shouting praise and support for Chief Osceola. The pack of Indian warriors listening nearby rallied and started war dances and chanting, to embolden the tribal elder's decisions. The Seminole Indians declared war against the white man.

Although Chief Osceola was half-white himself, he was dedicated to halting the onslaught of the white man in Florida. He was born Billy Powell, to an Indian mother and a white father in Alabama, and he learned to hate the white man after watching his white father continuously brutally bully, beat, and bruise his Indian mother while he was growing up. Eventually, his Indian mother escaped his father's viciousness, and they relocated to the Everglades to join the Seminole Indians. Although he was a half-breed, he became Indian Chief Osceola in the Seminole tribe because of his leadership in the war against the white man.

Francis Dade, a Major in the U.S. Army, was just following orders. The United States was at war with the Seminole Indians, and he was just doing his duty. The fledgling U.S. Government triggered the Seminole Indian Wars after Andrew Jackson, the "Indian Fighter," became Andrew Jackson, President of the United States, and pushed the "Indian Removal Act of 1830" through Congress. This Act became the official policy of the U.S. Government, a policy of displacement and extermination of all native American Indians, including the Seminole Indians in Florida, to systematically remove them from the path of "civilized" European-American settlement.

The clash that inevitably resulted from the Indian Removal Act frames the last, the worst, and arguably the most tragic years in the history of the United States against native American Indians. The conflict took place mostly along a rough, uninhabitable, and wild terrain in the Everglades: The Tamiami Trail.

It was never a fair fight! The U.S. Army used its arsenal of guns and rifles against an Indian defense of mostly bows and arrows, with a predictable outcome. But the Seminoles fought courageously and never surrendered. They proved to be fierce adversaries for the United States Government.

Major Dade approached his horse and tried to soothe the animal by gently stroking her mane, but the mare, sensing the Indian war party in the nearby trees, continued to fuss and whine. Dade was unaware of the ambush that surrounded him and his troops, as he continued to comfort the animal, but soon the entire string of military horses also began to snort and fuss.

Concerned about the horse's commotion ruining his surprise attack, Chief Osceola removed one of the arrows from his quiver and nocked it onto his bow and then signaled his two Seminole under-chiefs, Chief Jumper and Chief Alligator, to do the same thing. They were as fierce as Chief Osceola, hated the white man as much as he did, and wanted to kill them and drive them out of their tribal homeland. Chief Jumper and Chief Alligator followed Chief Osceola's lead and nocked an arrow onto their bows, ready for action. They motioned their Seminole warriors to get ready.

Silently, Chief Osceola released his arrow, impaling Major Dade's back. Dade screamed out in agony and arched his back to reach for the bloody arrow but could not remove it. Another arrow came from Chief Jumper and another from Chief Alligator. The Major fell onto the muddy trail next to his horse, dead.

It startled the encampment awake by the commotion, and the troops grabbed their weapons. They spilled from their tents, disoriented and stumbling into the darkness of the swamp against an unknown threat. The Seminole Indian warriors swarmed the unprepared troops.

With their campfires reduced to smolders and their kerosene lamps providing minimal light, they couldn't see the brutal rush of death descending upon them. The soldiers shot toward the Indian warriors surrounding them, but many friendly fire bullets hit their fellow officers. The onslaught was bloody and ferocious.

The Seminole Indian warriors had the advantage of surprise in the blackness of night and familiarity with the onerous swamp. Bloody skirmishes ensued from the hand-to-hand combat more accustomed to the Indian warriors with knives, tomahawks, bows and arrows, and the few *rifles they had stolen from the white man. The soldier's scalps were cut off from their heads as trophies to prove their success to Seminole Indian elders and further inflame the tribe to promote broader warfare to recruit additional warriors to their vengeful campaign.*

History would call it the "Dade Massacre" because only three U.S. Army troops survived. Chief Osceola and his Seminole warriors killed 110 soldiers in that battle, but also suffered huge losses of their own tribesmen.

They fought many other skirmishes with similar results, but the white man kept on coming with more armies and more weapons. The end of the Second Indian Seminole War eventually decimated the Seminole Indian population of about 5,000, to only 500 Seminole Indians left in the territory.

They arrested Seminole Indian Chief Osceola, in a breach of honor, when he came under a white flag of truce to negotiations with the U.S. Government in 1837. He was callously arrested and decapitated in jail. They buried his body without his head.

After more than a decade of fighting, on May 10, 1842, a frustrated President John Tyler ordered the end of military actions against the Seminole Indians. Scholars estimate the U.S. government spent nearly $50 million on the war, a huge sum at that time, and over 2,000 American soldiers had died. It marked the costliest military campaign in the young country's history.

A few hundred Seminole Native Indian Floridians retreated into the Everglades. In the end, the U.S. government gave up trying to subjugate the Seminole

Indians and left the survivors in peace. The Seminole Indians never relinquished sovereignty or signed a peace treaty with the United States.

Casey sipped some more Pinot Noir and lowered the manuscript to her coffee table, deep in thought, questioning any connection to Susan's murder in her mind. *It would have been a good book,* she thought.

The manuscript was well-written and easy to read, but what Seminole Indian research might have caused her murder? Was it her handwritten notes scribbled along the margins of the manuscript, during her meeting with the Seminole Indian Chief, referring to a buried Pirate Gasparilla treasure, or was it just a random coincidence? The manuscript remained in the car when Susan was kidnapped, so logically, it might not have been the motive. It might just be a blind alley.

Still skeptical, she called Darren on her telephone, "I just finished reading Susan's draft manuscript again," she told her partner, "I'm suspicious it might somehow be connected to her murder, especially since her handwritten notes refer to a Seminole Indian pirate treasure of some kind. Money can be a powerful motive for murder. That may provide some clues."

Darren responded, "I read it too Casey, and I've interviewed the Seminole Indian Chief Susan met with before her murder. I tried to delve into the significance of the handwritten notes, but I haven't found any connection."

Casey looked at the title of the manuscript on the coffee table again. "Tamiami Trail of Tears," she thought the title was appropriate, since it was a *Trail of Tears,* because of Susan's rape and murder, "Meet me for breakfast at Rosa's Café tomorrow morning and bring the transcript of your interview with the Seminole Indian Chief. I want to investigate this further."

"Okay, Boss."

After hanging up the phone, Casey took her Pinot Noir and moved to her home office computer on the desk in her den. She sipped on her wine and started researching anything she could find regarding Pirate Gasparilla and the Seminole Indian tribe.

CHAPTER NINE

Pirate Gasparilla [12]

Rosa's Cafe

Tallahassee, Florida

The next morning, Darren Turner peered over the top of his newspaper as the entrance door chime to Rosa's Cafe in downtown Tallahassee jingled. The aroma of sizzling bacon drifted through the air.

Casey rushed in a little too late for breakfast, and a little too early for lunch. An expression of regret crossed her compressed lips. He chuckled, it was not the first time in the past few weeks he'd been forced to wait for her.

Casey was exhausted and slightly hung-over. She had researched the Seminole Indian tribal land records thoroughly all night long with several glasses of Pinot Noir, going back over 200 years, but could not find that little window, that long-forgotten footnote, that saving amendment or annotation someone had thoughtfully inserted so many years ago to provide credibility to the Pirate Gasparilla buried treasure theory. She found nothing.

Darren nodded as Rosa emerged from the kitchen and dropped the two plates she'd kept warm for the past hour and two coffees in front of them. She gave Casey a disapproving frown with her squinty, dark-brown shadowed eyes. Her bright red lips puckered before she sauntered her substantial figure back to the cash register and her crossword puzzle.

Darren laughed and snapped his paper closed.

Casey looked up from the plate Rosa had set in front of her and smiled at Darren, "My favorite." He was getting to know her a little too well. He'd ordered her favorite food, kept it warm, and was not surprised or annoyed at her tardiness. And, although she caught his side glances and thinly veiled innuendos, he'd been a model agent so far.

She forked up a mouth full of scrambled egg, as her gaze strayed to the newspaper on the table. She flinched, set her fork down, and reached for the headline. *"Woman Found Stomped to Death in the Dirt."*

Darren's gaze met hers, and he sighed, "Last night," he said while shaking his head as he sawed into his steak. He didn't appear to enjoy it.

She could understand why, "I know. That's why I'm running late this morning. I have Dennis Hollis and his crack team from FDLE out of Miami working on it. Could it be a second serial murder?"

Darren nodded, "Not sure. This one looks like it was an accidental murder. She was stomped to death while running away on a dirt road."

Casey scanned the article. The more she read, the more her appetite faded, "Accidental murder is still murder. The question is, did he rape her?"

Darren shrugged, "I am sure that will be determined."

Of course, it will, she thought, before picking up the paper to read the article for herself.

Newsflash: Woman Found Stomped to Death in the Dirt.

Davie, Florida

By The Tallahassee Democrat

Authorities discovered a young woman, 26-years-of-age, lying face down on a dirt road off U.S. Route One early this morning in Fort Lauderdale. The young woman, identified by her husband as Kimberly Merrick of Coral

Gables, was declared dead at the scene. She was badly bruised and appeared to have been stomped on, which resulted in her broken neck. Boot prints discovered on her back will be examined for possible identification of the perpetrator.

Tire tracks and footprints indicate she jumped or was pushed out of a moving car at a high rate of speed and then got up and ran before tripping on a tree root. They estimated time of death between 2:30 and 3:00 a.m. She had called her husband a little before 2:00 a.m. to inform him she was on her way home. When she didn't arrive, he alerted the police.

An autopsy is being performed to determine the exact cause of death. The state awaits the result of DNA and Toxicology screens.

Casey stared pensively into her coffee cup as she sipped, looking for answers, and shaking her head, "Someone very large stomped on her back with big boots, while running, and broke her neck. It was a dirt road, so we have tracks all over the crime scene, including on her back."

Darren agreed, "Sounds like we have to rely on forensics to solve this one."

"Right. It looks like she was being chased and tripped and fell while running. My guess is the killer didn't see her fall and just stomped on her back accidentally while running at full speed, chasing her in the dark, based on the boot print on her back and the middle of her neck."

Darren looked shocked, "Do you think it was one of *our* boots?"

"I don't know. Forensics is looking at the boot prints and the tire tracks. It could take a while. Her wrists were scarred too, like from handcuffs." Casey set the paper aside, shaking her head, "If this murder is related to Susan's murder, the killer just didn't happen upon them. These women were cherry-picked and hunted." She wasn't crazy about vigilante justice, but as a woman, she wanted revenge.

Darren shrugged, "No pun intended." He chugged his coffee and avoided looking at her, "That far apart? That's some complex homework. 'The Rhapsody Rapists' are really 'The Rhapsody Rapists and Killers?'"

"It gets uglier and uglier," She sipped her coffee and went back to her meal. Eggs scrambled, bacon crispy, one slice of toast, white, butter.

"Speaking of which, here's the Seminole Indian Chief interview transcript you requested." Darren set his plate aside and pushed the document over to Casey. He glanced at Rosa for more coffee, but she ignored them.

Casey swapped him the *Tamiami Trail of Tears* manuscript from her massive shoulder bag and slid it across the table to him. She moved her plate, then placed the transcript in front of her.

Darren held the manuscript, "I read it. I just don't see any connection."

She flipped the Seminole Indian Chief transcript open and started to study it, "I know... So far."

Rosa finally came over to their table with a coffeepot and filled their cups.

Darren added two packs of sugar and stirred, "I like coffee with my sugar," he joked.

Casey gave him a disapproving expression and looked back at the transcript, "In my research last night, I discovered that in December 1821, the United States Navy Warship, USS Enterprise, attacked Pirate Gasparilla and his pirate crew, after almost 40-years of plundering merchant ships for their treasures. In the battle that ensued, cannonballs riddled Gasparilla's ship, and it sank in the Gulf of Mexico."

"Rather than surrender, in a gesture of final defiance, Gasparilla wrapped an anchor chain around his waist and dramatically jumped from the bow of his sinking ship, shouting, 'Gasparilla dies by his own hand, not the enemy's!' Gasparilla committed suicide, and all his crew died in that battle."

Darren placed his coffee cup back down on the saucer, "And... Their vast treasure remains buried somewhere in unknown locations in South Florida. Perhaps on Seminole Indian tribal land, no one knows for sure, and the only people who would have known, are all dead."

"Unless there's a buried treasure map." Casey could not prove or disprove whether Gasparilla's pirate treasure had anything to do with Susan's murder. She thought, after over a decade in law enforcement, her skills could help her find a clue to help solve the Governor's daughter's murder. She was, for the first time, alone and forced to venture across new, unexplored territory based on history and legend. And, in a legal system built for nearly a millennium on the concept of indisputable facts, there was little tolerance for improvisers.

Darren shrugged his shoulders, "Right. Unless there's a buried treasure map."

"Let me review your questioning of the Seminole Indian Chief to see if that sheds any light on the murder." She started reading the transcript.

Seminole Indian Chief Interview by FDLE Agent Darren Turner

Turner: "Susan met with you just hours before she was raped and killed. What was she looking for?"

Seminole Indian Chief: "She said her research revealed that there may have been buried pirate treasure discovered by the Seminole Indians near the edge of the Tamiami Trail in the Everglades."

Turner: "Is that true?"

Seminole Indian Chief: "I don't know. It was over 200 years ago, but history indicates that legendary Spanish Pirate Gasparilla and his band of murderous buccaneers secretly buried the treasure they had pilfered from the English, French, and Spanish, on Seminole Indian tribal land."

Turner: "Pirate Gasparilla?"

Seminole Indian Chief: "Yes. I'm a bit of an antiquity aficionado, and swashbuckling Pirate Gasparilla terrorized the coastal waters of Southwest Florida during the late 18ᵗʰ and early 19ᵗʰ centuries. His greed and avarice were legendary because of the large number of ships that fell prey to Gasparilla and his buccaneers during the 38 years he ravaged Southwest Florida waters."

Turner: "Wow. How much pirate treasure was there?"

Seminole Indian Chief: "Again, we don't know for sure, but the legend is that it was a wealth of gold and silver bullion worth over 30 million dollars at the time, confiscated through years of bloody battles with more than 400 merchant ships on the high seas. Gasparilla was determined to keep it hidden for himself and his men. That was a lot of money in those days."

Turner: "Did the Seminole Indians discover it?"

Seminole Indian Chief: "The legend is that a young Indian boy tracking deer to feed his family with his bow and arrow happened upon Pirate Gasparilla and his dastardly band of pirate crew digging into the sandy soil. Gasparilla chugged a bottle of rum while he marched around the perimeter of the dig site, guarding the treasure chests."

Turner: "Did the Indian boy eventually return to dig up the treasure chests?"

Seminole Indian Chief: "We don't know, but that was what Susan was probing."

Turner: "It wasn't in the main body of her manuscript, but I saw notes that she scribbled around the edges alluding to this."

Seminole Indian Chief: "She was writing non-fiction, and these legends are not confirmed history. They were just handed down verbally from generation to generation. That's what she was trying to authenticate."

Turner: "Anything else?"

Seminole Indian Chief: "Well, Susan was a bit of a romantic. She was also interested in any love story component she could weave into her book."

Turner: "Was there one?"

Seminole Indian Chief: "Yes. Even though Pirate Gasparilla routinely plundered and kidnapped the women on the ships he seized for his pleasure and held them captive on nearby Captiva Island where there was no chance of escape; he fell in love with one of his captives. The most famous encounter involved a Spanish Princess. Gasparilla had captured and fell in love with a princess named Useppa. She steadfastly rejected the Pirate's advances until he threatened to behead her if she would not submit to his lust. Still, she refused, and he killed her in a rage. He then took her body to a nearby island, which he named Useppa Island in her honor, and buried her himself."

Casey stopped reading the transcript and looked up at Darren, "Well, the romance part is interesting, but the buried treasure chests might be more of a motive for murder."

Darren agreed, "Yes. If the Indian boy recovered the treasure and if it then became Seminole Indian treasure. That's what we don't know."

Casey finished her last bit of coffee, "To be continued... Let's meet back at the office later to dig into this latest murder in Fort Lauderdale."

"And dig into the buried treasure on the Seminole Indian Reservation... Pun intended." Darren smiled, signaling Rosa. He flipped the green check over and laid some bills on top.

Casey added to the pile. Their deal was Dutch, with no exceptions.

Rosa smiled when she saw Casey's tip. Apparently, she was forgiven for being late after all.

---

[12] *Pirate José Gaspar, also known by his nickname Gasparilla (lived 1756 – 1821), is claimed to have roamed and plundered across the Gulf of Mexico and the Spanish Main from his base in Southwest Florida. He amassed a huge fortune by stealing many fortunes and ransoming many hostages. He died by leaping from his ship rather than face capture by the U.S. Navy, leaving behind an enormous and as-yet undiscovered treasure somewhere in South Florida.*

CHAPTER TEN

The Rhapsody Killers [13]

FDLE Headquarters
Tallahassee, Florida

Casey walked through the front doors into the frigid air of the FDLE Headquarters in Tallahassee and cringed. As usual, Lieutenant Mike Weller and Sergeant Jon Benjamin, or the "B-team," as Darren sarcastically called them, hovered near her office door at the water cooler.

Darren caught up to her as he arrived, and joked to Casey, "There's our B-team. They look like a chubby version of Joe Friday and Frank Gannon from *Dragnet*. Don't they? *Just the facts. I want just the facts.'*" Darren chuckled.

Darren's pompous attitude always cranked up the tension between them. The three of them bickered constantly. It was a miracle they had survived working together in the same office through the grueling, never-ending stream of investigations. They argued over every detail of the criminal evidence they pursued, and Weller and Benjamin often upstaged Darren in ways that nearly subverted his carefully orchestrated analysis of perpetrator motives.

Casey choked back a laugh and sent Darren a glare. She'd have to explain harassment to him again. He seemed to fail to understand that she, as their superior, was open to all manner of perceived harassment simply by the virtue of her sex.

71

It didn't help that Weller and Benjamin had partnered at the FDLE for seven years, and to say that neither of them was pissed at her advancement would be an understatement. Worse, she ended up with a new partner - who again was neither of them – compounded by, of all things, her physical appearance.

Of course, Casey was not oblivious to her appearance. She was neither proud nor ashamed nor embarrassed by it. She accepted it as an accident of birth that *Mother Nature* had bestowed on her, just as she had her entire life. The overall package she presented was one that most women would kill for, and most men would die for. Given all of this, she was under the gun to outperform. Her private motto was, *pick up the slack or suffer the flack*. And flack there would be.

And, if all of that were not enough, her new partner showed up looking like the accumulation of Cary Grant, Clark Gable, and worst of all, George Clooney. It was her one and only prime directive that sheltered her from the storm of sexual harassment - *no fraternizing between the ranks*. No exceptions.

Darren passed her without a word and went into his office, but he gave a nod to the boys at the water cooler as he passed. Casey walked into her own office, then turned back to the pair whose eyes were all over her, "Reports?" Her brows rose with the question.

Weller answered, "On your desk, Boss." The pair fidgeted before retreating to their squad room cubicles.

Casey chuckled, shoved her door closed with her high-heels, crossed over her office, and dumped her voluminous bag on the chair next to her desk. She tackled the mountain of paperwork, divided notes, newspapers, and shuffled papers between folders.

She took one of the newspapers and walked out to the squad room.

Weller was leaned back in his chair with his feet up on his desk as he thumbed a file folder, his black-rimmed reading glasses wedged onto his forehead. Benjamin was hunched over a leftover fast-food burger that she wouldn't have cared to guess from when. His outsized belly fat rippled over his desk as he chewed.

As expected, they both came to attention when they heard her heels click across the floor.

She handed *The Tallahassee Democrat* newspaper to Weller, "You and Benjamin follow up on this murder in Davie. It's possibly the second murder and fifth rape by the same killer. This is getting bigger and bigger. I don't like it. Run the investigation for hits statewide and see if we get any matches."

"Okay." Benjamin held up his file, "We're on it. We started the investigation already this morning, and we'll follow it through."

"Darren and I will be video conferencing the Lindsay Baily Fort Pierce rape interrogation with Dennis Hollis from FDLE in Miami. We are running short-manned, so if this operation doesn't go as planned, I may need you on the Baily rape as well."

The pair scowled at her; they were already working two shifts.

Casey added, "Come to think of it, you two have considerable experience in rape cases; maybe I should just hand it over to you now." She turned as if to make the arraignments.

"No, no." Benjamin held up his file, "We're swamped with three rape cases already, and now this new one in Davie makes it four. Our plate is full."

Casey turned back, "Well, if you're sure." Innocence spread across her face with a small practiced smile.

"Oh, yeah, we've got them covered." Weller was on his feet, nodding in complete agreement with his partner.

"Okay, then." She turned and walked back toward her office with a grin.

Darren slipped out of his office beside her as she passed, "You can be truly evil."

"Eavesdropping?"

"No, boss, the air vent just happens to exit over Weller's desk."

Casey pictured him on a chair with his ear pressed to the vent. She made a mental note to look next time, "We have to share and play nice, Darren." Casey tried to sound like a schoolteacher, "Weller has a history of making complaints."

"That's why they're the B-team."

He followed her into her office and handed her a sheaf of papers.

Casey looked curious, "What's this?"

"Background on Lindsay Baily for our video conference call with Hollis. It begins in fifteen minutes."

Casey's head came up and looked him square in the face, with a "WTF" look, "She has a record?"

Darren shrugged, "Drug possession a few years ago. She was on probation. cops prefer to hit on drug users and prostitutes for sexual favors… If it was a cop or cops?"

Casey shook her head, opened the file, and read a few lines, "Wow." She looked back at Darren, "This should keep us busy for a while." She slipped the folder into her middle drawer, the one she would lock when they left, "Okay. Let's get to the video monitor in the conference room."

Dennis Hollis led Lindsay Baily into a small, windowless interrogation room at the FDLE Regional Operations Center in Miami. The room might have been painted white at one time, but now the walls were dingy and yellowish-brown from years of smoke-filled interrogations and neglect. A tarnished coffeemaker sat on a scratched steel table with broken drawers in one corner of the room.

Hollis had a coffee in his hand, sitting across from Ms. Baily at a square table with a video camera on a tripod trained on her. She tried to adjust her demeanor, so she squinted at the camera as if trying to recognize someone she thought she had once known. A bright light mounted on the side glared into her face. She still looked black and blue from the beatings, and scars were visible on her wrists.

Hollis began the interrogation, "Ms. Baily, as you probably are aware, this interview is being recorded."

She turned her gaze to Dennis Hollis, glanced at the file in his hands, and again looked up at him, "Yes, I understand."

Hollis: "I know that you recently got out of the hospital. How are you feeling?"

Baily: "Still sore, but feeling a little better."

Hollis: "Senior Agent Casey Collins, the head of the Governor's Rape Task Force and Agent Darren Turner, are joining our interview through video conference from Tallahassee." He pointed to the video monitor attached to the wall.

Collins: "Hello, Ms. Baily."

Turner: "Good morning, Ms. Baily."

Baily: "Hi."

Hollis: "We're going to be asking some questions today in the hopes you can remember vital information that could help us identify and arrest the men who abducted and accosted you."

Lindsay Baily looked up with black and blue eyes, "Yes, I'll try to remember as best I can, but it all happened so quickly."

Hollis: "My first question is, you said your assailants were two white men dressed as cops. Did they have badges and did you see any badge numbers?"

Baily: "They were dressed in police uniforms, and they had badges on, but they hit me and handcuffed me so quickly, that I don't remember the badge numbers. I was in a state of shock, just trying to survive."

Hollis: "I understand. Have you ever seen these men before?"

Baily: "No."

Hollis: "Can you describe what they looked like?"

Baily: "They had these orange-tinted glasses on so I couldn't see their eyes." She said, thinking back to that night. "They looked over six feet tall with fair skin and light-colored hair."

Collins: "Ms. Baily, this is Casey Collins. You're describing two different men, but your description of them sounds the same." Casey thought about how this description sounded familiar to her. Bells started going off in her head.

Baily: "It was all such a blur. They beat me, handcuffed me, and raped me. They terrified me. That's all I can remember."

Hollis: "The DNA analysis from your rape test kit evidenced semen from a single male, but you said there were two rapists. Is there anything you can tell us to shed some light on that?"

Baily: "I don't know. There definitely were two men. They took turns raping me. Maybe one of them didn't ejaculate? I don't know?"

Hollis: "They left you in a vacant car lot. Did you see the license plate number or police car identification number?"

Baily: "They dumped me out of the car when they were done with me, like a bag of trash. I was lying on the ground in pain, without my pants, and they sped off. By the time I was able to get up and get oriented, they were gone."

Turner: "Ms. Baily, this is Darren Turner. Is there anything else that stands out in your mind to help us identify them?"

She took a moment to think and then said, "Well, I remember they cursed a lot and kept saying how they were the law, and nobody would believe me. Oh, and one of them smelled like cigarettes, and the other smelled like beer."

Collins: "Ms. Baily, were you sober at the time, or did you have any alcohol or drugs in your system?"

They could see on the video screen that she was fidgeting and upset by this line of questioning. She knew they were aware of her background and arrest record, and it put her on the defensive, "Agent Collins, I am clean and have been for over a year. I know that you have access to my arrest record, but that was a long time ago. I have been totally sober."

Hollis: "Were there any other distinguishing features about them you can remember? Were they wearing rings or watches? Did they have facial hair, scars, or tattoos?"

Baily: "I'm sorry. I really don't remember."

Hollis: "Agents Collins and Turner, any other questions?"

Turner: "What about this music? Did they play it during the rape?"

Baily: "Yes. It was really strange. They had this music on loud while each one of them took turns raping me, *Rhapsody in Blue*. The other one was on guard for any intruders. I know the newspapers have named them 'The Rhapsody Rapists.'"

Turner: "Yes, that is strange," *or The Rhapsody Killers*, he thought to himself.

Casey cringed. It brought back horrible memories from her childhood that she had repressed for many years.

Hollis: "Anything else?"

Collins: "No. I think we're all set for now. Thank you, Ms. Baily."

Baily: "Thank you."

Hollis: "Ms. Baily, we would like to have a police sketch artist draw a likeness of each assailant. Can you remember enough to help us build a portrait of their faces?"

Baily: "Yes, I'll try."

Hollis: "OK. Let's go next door to begin that process."

Casey switched off the video screen, picked up her bag, and set it on the conference table. She let out a long sigh, "Well, that didn't give us anything new."

They both stood and started walking out the door. Darren commented, "Maybe the sketch artist will help us with identification."

Casey pondered Lindsay Baily's description of the rapists: *They wore police uniforms and had these orange-tinted glasses on, so I couldn't see their eyes. They looked over six feet tall with fair skin and light-colored hair. One smelled like cigarettes and the other smelled like beer.*

She was putting the pieces of the puzzle together in her mind and began to realize; maybe they were real cops and not imposters.

---

[13] **_Police Officer Stephen Maiorino Rape in Boynton Beach, Florida:_**

Police Officer Stephen Maiorino kidnapped and raped, a 20-year-old woman at gunpoint on the hood of his police cruiser in an abandoned field in Boynton Beach, Florida. During the assault, the officer held her face down on the hood of his police cruiser with his right hand, and pointed a gun at her with his left.

CHAPTER ELEVEN

Topless Dancers [10] [14]

FDLE Headquarters
Tallahassee, Florida

Casey walked out of the video conference center and almost ran into Weller and Benjamin, waiting to ambush her.

"We have updates on the Davie murder to tell you about."

She noticed the notebook Lieutenant Weller was carrying, "Great. Fill me in. Let's go into my office."

Weller and Benjamin sat down in the two chairs in front of Casey's desk, eager to boast about their detective skills. Casey walked around to her chair and plopped her bag onto the floor, "What've you got?"

Weller started flipping through his notes.

"Well, her name was Kimberly Merrick. She was a waitress at Diva's Topless Gentlemen's Club in Fort Lauderdale, working the late shift. She clocked out of the Club at 1:38 a.m. and was driving home. She suspiciously pulled her car over onto the shoulder of U.S. Route One and was abducted. The killer apparently took her to this dirt road where she tried to escape. It looks like she tripped on a tree root while she was running away from him, and he stomped on her neck and broke her back in pursuit. She died instantly. We have a boot print on her back and boot tracks all over the dirt in surrounding areas."

Benjamin piped in, "The Police Chief said someone had been stalking her and tried to force her off the road a couple of nights before her murder. He put out a bulletin to his station to be on the lookout for this stalker as she drove home."

Weller flipped another page, "It seems she had a red Jeep Wrangler and always took the same route home every night, at about the same time. This stalker must have been waiting for her and abducted her based on her travel routine every night."

Casey was thinking, "Tell me more about how she died."

Weller continued, "It was between 2:00 a.m. and 3:00 a.m. on a dark, deserted dirt road off of U.S. Route One. She had called her husband earlier to tell him she was on her way home and was driving to Coral Gables when she pulled over onto the side of the road."

Casey was listening intently, "On Route One?"

Weller looked at Benjamin, "Yes. On Route One, and then the stalker apparently put her in his car and drove her onto this dirt road where she died trying to escape."

"Why did she stop to begin with? Did she have car trouble?"

Benjamin responded, "No. We don't think so. The keys were still in the ignition, and it started right up when the Fort Lauderdale police found the car. Her wallet was on the passenger seat with her money still intact. The only thing missing was her driver's license."

"So, it wasn't a robbery." Casey took a notepad out of her drawer and started writing, "The only reason I would think the driver's license would be missing is if she took it out of her wallet to show it to a cop or someone posing as a cop."

Weller smiled, "That's what we're thinking too. And maybe the killer wanted to keep it as a trophy. The stalker might have had a blue revolving police light on his car and pulled her over, then kidnapped her."

Benjamin continued, "There's more. Her wrists have scars like she was in handcuffs, and her legs have cuts all over them. We think she jumped out of a moving car to escape the stalker and was running away when she tripped on a tree root and fell facedown. It was dark that night. Her killer probably didn't see she had fallen, and he just stomped on top of her with his boot."

Weller chimed in, "Her husband went searching for her when she didn't arrive home on time. He backtracked her usual route and found her car. That's when he called the police at about 4:00 a.m. They searched the area near her Jeep and discovered her dead in the dirt."

Casey summed it up, "So, do you think this stalker is the killer? Was there any sign of rape?"

"We don't think so. She was fully clothed when she died, but they did a rape test kit anyway, and an autopsy. We have to wait for the toxicology results."

"They are analyzing the boot size, treads, and tire tracks forensically."

Casey gave them both orders, "You need to find any regulars at this Diva's Topless Gentlemen's Club who might be her stalker. These men fall in *lust* with the women working at strip clubs, so we need to track them down. You need to interview the servers, bouncers, and dancers."

Weller and Benjamin looked at each other with big grins, "Interview the dancers?"

Casey smiled, "That is, unless you're too busy? I can assign the interrogations to Hollis if you're too busy."

Weller stretched his hands out, "No, no, we can do the interviews. It's an important part of the investigation, and we're dedicated to solving this murder."

Casey was sarcastic, "I'm sure you are. We need to know who the regulars are that might have had aggressive behavior toward the women working at the club."

Just then, Darren poked his head into Casey's office, "How's it going?"

Weller looked at Darren with a shit-eating grin, "Well, it seems we need to go to a topless bar in Fort Lauderdale to do some fact-finding interviews with the staff. Tough duty, but somebody has to do it."

All the men laughed.

Darren added, "If you need any help to interview the topless dancers, let me know. That's my specialty. I have plenty of dollar bills."

Casey interrupted, "Very funny guys, but this is a murder we're investigating. Show a little respect."

They all chimed in, smiling, "Yes, Boss."

"And Darren, put out a $25,000 reward post for information leading to the capture of Susan's killer. Weller and Benjamin, we'll probably do the same for Kimberly." Casey always referred to the victims on a first name basis.

Weller and Benjamin stood up and headed out the door, smiling. They were eager to begin their surveillance.

---

[14] _Police Officer Tim Harris Police Rape and Murder in Indian River, Florida:_

Police Officer Tim Harris confessed to the rape and strangulation of 43-year-old, Lorraine Hendricks, after falsely stopping her car for a fictitious traffic violation. Searchers found her badly decomposed body four-weeks after her rape and murder under a pile of brush in a heavily wooded median of I-95. He said that the woman reminded him of his wife, who had just divorced him, so he killed her!

CHAPTER TWELVE

Full Code

Tallahassee Memorial Hospital
Tallahassee, Florida

The Governor looked out his window on the top floor of the sleek, twenty-story office building in midtown Tallahassee and watched the world go by on the streets below. He could hear the sounds of the city, like a distant rumble, through the plate-glass window. He thought back to the night the police told him and his wife, their daughter, had been raped and murdered on Alligator Alley. His wife collapsed immediately, and the police called for an ambulance.

The ambulance brought his wife to the Emergency Room at Tallahassee Memorial Hospital at one-o'clock in the morning. Her blood pressure was under 59 over 18; her heart rate was over 200, her blood sugar was over 700, her potassium level was over 10, she was breathing erratically and unconscious. She was comatose and near death.

She was wheeled into the Emergency Room and surrounded by a flurry of doctors, nurses, and technicians frantically trying to keep her alive. Then, suddenly, the heart monitor sound changed to a steady buzz, and a straight line formed in place of the wavy line that indicated her heartbeat. She suffered cardiac arrest, and her heart stopped beating.

A nurse shouted, "CODE BLUE! CODE BLUE! STAT!"

The doctors immediately began CPR, and they quickly shuffled the Governor out of the room.

Five-minutes later, a young woman resident doctor, apparently from India with a strong accent, rushed out of the room, "Your wife's heart is unresponsive, Governor. Do you want us to continue?"

"Yes, of course. Continue!" It shocked the Governor they would even ask that question.

Five more minutes passed, and once again, the door burst open, "We've been working on reviving your wife for ten-minutes now, and we've broken some of her ribs in the process. She's not responding. Do you want us to continue?"

"Yes. She's Full Code. Continue!" Although the Governor didn't like to hear they broke her ribs, her heart was much more critical. *Did they want to let her die because of a broken rib?* He had refused to sign the document designating her as "DNR - Do Not Resuscitate." Instead, she was "Full Code," meaning to do anything and everything necessary to keep her alive.

"Very well." She hurried back into the ER.

Another five more minutes passed, and the same doctor burst out of the emergency room flustered, "We've been working on your wife for twenty-minutes now, and she is still not responding. Normally, at this point, we have no hope of revival. Do you want us to continue? She's suffered more broken ribs."

"Yes. She is Full Code. Continue!"

She returned to the ER once again, and the door slammed behind her.

The Governor was left to imagine what was going on in there and what his wife was going through after finding out her daughter was dead. She had a heart attack and now broken ribs. He was heartbroken too, over his daughter's death, but for the moment, he had to focus on saving his wife.

Ten more minutes passed slowly, and two nurses calmly came out of the ER to talk to the Governor, "Governor, could you please follow us to the Quiet Room?" There was a change in the hospital atmosphere, and the nurse's demeanor went from the feverish pitch of an Emergency Room to the quiet calm of a funeral home.

The Governor responded anxiously, "What happened? How is my wife?" Fully expecting the worst.

The nurse signaled him down the hallway, "The doctor will meet you in the Quiet Room to explain."

It reminded the Governor of a movie or television show. *Grey's Anatomy, ER,* or *Ben Casey.* They always brought you into the Quiet Room to deliver the bad news.

The Governor sat down in the Quiet Room, knowing it had been over thirty-minutes since they started CPR, and the human brain can't survive without oxygen for more than five minutes. His wife must be dead.

Two doctors entered the Quiet Room with somber expressions on their faces.

The Governor stood up beseechingly, "What happened to my wife?"

The same female resident Indian doctor spoke first, in a very calm and deliberate tone, "Governor, we worked on saving your wife for almost thirty minutes, which is a record at this hospital. We normally don't continue past twenty minutes except, since you are the Governor, we continued based on your orders."

The Governor stared at her and then looked over at the doctor sitting next to her, waiting for the words that she had passed away or whatever they say about someone who had just died, but those words were not said, "Doctor, please tell me what happened."

She had tears in her eyes, "At the twenty-ninth minute, her heart started again." She looked over at the male doctor sitting next to her,

"We were all amazed because we were just about to give up. It was a miracle."

The Governor stared dumbfounded at the Indian doctor, a feeling of relief washing over his entire body, "Oh, thank God." Then he hugged her, "You saved her life. Thank you."

The other doctor in the Quiet Room chimed in, "Governor, she is alive, but there's been a lot of damage. She has many broken ribs, and even though we did tracheal intubate her, there may be brain damage from lack of oxygen."

At this point, all he could focus on was that she was alive, "Can I see her?"

"Yes, but be prepared. She is not coherent, and there may be brain damage." He repeated that point again to prepare him for the worst.

The Governor followed the doctors back into the emergency room. When he got there, it was a cacophony of beeping lights, groaning monitors, and the repetitive sounds of a breathing machine keeping his wife alive. He looked down at his wife in the tiny bed in this large, white room, and she looked horrible. Tubes shoved down her throat, and intravenous lines jabbed into her arms with blood and black and blue marks everywhere.

Her eyes kept circling the room.

"Mary. Thank GOD you're alive."

No response. Her eyes continued circling the room.

He thought for sure there must have been brain damage, "Mary, it's me, your husband. Do you recognize me?"

Still no response. Her eyes still circled the room. He looked over at the doctors who were watching him, "Is she brain-dead?"

"We don't know. She's been through a lot. Thirty minutes without a heartbeat is a long time."

The other doctor agreed, "It will take a while to know if she can come back."

Eventually, the doctors were able to stabilize the Governor's wife, and admitted her to the Intensive Care Unit of the hospital. But the nightmare continued. It was a painful roller coaster ride with many highs and lows. She had kidney and congestive heart failure; her heart ejection fraction was only ten percent, she had pneumonia, infections, blood in her digestive tract, a bedsore on her back that doctors said would never heal and, to top it off, she was probably brain-dead.

Later, they thought she had tuberculosis and put her in an isolation room where the Governor couldn't visit her without wearing a mask, gloves, and gown. She had more drugs pumped into her than he ever knew existed. They needed to operate because of her internal bleeding, but they said they couldn't because she was too weak, and the doctors thought the operation would kill her.

Three-times by three different doctors, he was told she was going to die. They asked him if he wanted them to make her "comfortable," which is code for "give her morphine and let her die comfortably."

His daughter was already dead. He refused to give up on his wife.

CHAPTER THIRTEEN

Heartbroken

Tallahassee Memorial Hospital
Tallahassee, Florida

The next morning, the Governor visited his wife at Tallahassee Memorial Hospital. He went to the Intensive Care Unit of the hospital and walked into her room alone. He surveyed the blinking lights and whirring sounds of the breathing machine and medical equipment connected to her body that poked, monitored, and kept her alive. She was lying on her back in a white gown with a tube shoved down her throat, and intravenous lines jabbed into her arms, which were tied down so she couldn't unconsciously pull them out.

The nurses were busy tending to other patients in other rooms, so he just stood over her and gazed down at her beautiful sleeping face and reflected on all they had been through together. While he watched her peacefully resting, he considered what the future might hold in store for the two of them. *Would Mary ever recover from her heart-attack? Would they ever recover from their daughter's rape and murder? Could he and Mary live happily after the tragedy that had befallen them?* He was hopeful. It was always better to move forward than to go backward. He loved her so much.

She was in a vegetative state, with her eyes closed, but he hoped she could hear him. He held her hand as he whispered to her, "Mary, it's me, Brendan. I love you."

Mary didn't move, but he thought he noticed a slight flutter of her eyelids.

He continued to try to connect with her subconscious, "Mary, Mary, can you hear me? I will find Susan's killer. I will make sure there is justice for our daughter."

Again, there was a slight flutter of her eyelids. He hoped she heard him.

Just at that moment, the nurse entered Mary's hospital room, and she saw the Governor holding his wife's hand and talking to her. She knew from experience that the chances of her recuperation were doubtful at this point. She wanted to tell him it was too late, and she was already gone. But she didn't.

He was heartbroken.

CHAPTER FOURTEEN

Ratings Game

NBC6 Television Station

Miami, Florida

The worldwide news media descended on Florida. The serial rapes and murders were big news, and the fact it involved the Governor's daughter made it even bigger news.

FDLE knew they had to be careful with the press. The press always accentuated the titillating downside of every story and FDLE had enough problems already without the press magnifying them. This painful situation was something for the FDLE Communications Office and public relations experts to handle.

Television and cable news media were stirred to a frenzy. *Neilson Media Research* utilized rating systems to determine audience size and composition of television programming. The higher the ratings, the more money a network could make. Consequently, news reporters were like vultures ripping dead flesh. *Where are the good bits? What secrets can we find?* They hunted for some tidbits of sensational information that would outmaneuver the other networks in the ratings game.

Even the venerated news anchors from the four major television stations and cable news networks, broadcast their nightly news shows from FDLE Headquarters in Tallahassee or the scenes of the crimes in Florida. CBS, NBC, ABC, and FOX, as well as CNN, *Bloomberg,*

The Wall Street Journal, Forbes, Newsweek, Time Magazine, and all the others, set up temporary offices in Tallahassee to cover the story.

International correspondents also wanted in on the action. BBC and The Guardian from London, Le Monde from France, Spiegel from Germany, and other European media, as well as coverage from practically every other country in the world. The national and international news media all wanted the latest updates.

FDLE was getting a continuous barrage of phone calls, emails, letters, and even some surprise visits from reporters, wire services, radio stations, magazines, and other assorted news services. The reporters called anybody and everybody they could to get information.

The statewide coverage of the Rape Task Force drew big ratings for the local networks, too. Every Florida station from Tallahassee, to Jacksonville, to Tampa, to Miami, and beyond, also wanted every scintilla of the story. NBC6 "Investigators" was a team of news reporters in Miami designated by NBC6 to dig into the details of news covered by the station, and this one was getting the most attention, especially the rape and murder of the Governor's daughter.

The six and eleven o'clock news anchor was a beautiful, voluptuous bleached blonde named Tina Evanston, who looked like a Barbie doll. Her aggressive ambition moved her up fast at the station, and now she was trying to make it big nationally. She thought this story might be her opportunity to promote herself from a local news station to a national or cable news network like CNN or FOX.

Darren Turner had been dating Tina off and on for the past year, but suddenly, not surprisingly, he had become the epicenter of her world. She figured he could be her ticket to get insider information about the Rape Task Force investigation, which could propel her into the big-time news media limelight. So, she called him constantly for a cocktail, date, or small talk to pry any incriminating evidence out of him. She used her feminine charms to extract confidential info. She wanted to be the first on the air with any news scoop he could give her that could increase her *Neilson* ratings.

Being the playboy, he was, Darren was never one to pass up an opportunity for a sexual quid pro quo. He was using his position and knowledge to gain an advantage with Tina that could help him gain her affection. He loved the sudden attention from this beautiful television news star and, in a way, it was a symbiotic relationship because FDLE wanted the public to know as much information as they could divulge, but not too much that could give the perpetrator an advantage or promote copycat criminals. And, since Darren wanted sex with Tina, it was a mutually beneficial, win-win situation for both of them.

Technically, press releases were supposed to be released exclusively via the FDLE Communications Office. Still, Darren didn't see any harm in giving Tina an exclusive, early news tip every now and then, especially if it would help him with her romantically.

Tina called Darren in his office, "Hello, Darren, how are you doing?"

Darren summoned his sexiest voice, "Great Tina, how are you?"

"I'm fantastic. Do you plan to come to Miami anytime soon? There's a great new restaurant on the beach I want you to take me to." She started slowly and built to a crescendo.

Darren thought about the investigation progressing in South Florida and the B-team getting the plum assignment interviewing topless dancers at the bar in Fort Lauderdale, "As a matter of fact, I probably will be down there soon. If not for business, then for pleasure. Maybe we can go over this weekend. What kind of food do they serve?"

"Well, being Miami Beach, their specialty is Cuban cuisine. It's the new hot spot in town, and they have a great Salsa band so we can do some dancing after dinner."

Darren was not a big fan of dancing, but he did whatever the ladies wanted to advance his agenda with them, "Sounds good. Let's plan this weekend."

"It will be great to see you." With the small talk concluded, Tina went for the jugular, "So how goes the investigation? You know the press has labeled them, '*The Rhapsody Killers*.'"

"Yes, I heard they've been upgraded to 'Killers.'" Darren liked to drag it out a little, rather than give her the important morsels right away. He knew what she really wanted. So, they played a little "cat and mouse" game, "It's going well. We have teams working around the clock."

"How about the investigation into the Governor's daughter's case? Anything new?"

Darren took a deep breath, "As a matter of fact, there *are* some recent developments."

Suddenly, Tina got very excited, "Really? What can you tell me?"

"Well, it hasn't been released yet by the FDLE Communications Office, but I guess I can tell you."

Tina let out a frustrated, "Daaarrreeen, what is it?"

Darren figured he had teased her long enough, "We're posting a $25,000 reward for information leading to the arrest of Susan Scott's killer."

"Oh, good. It hasn't been released yet?"

"No, you got the scoop."

"Great. Thank you. Anything else?"

Darren hesitated for a moment, "Well... There may be one other potential lead we're investigating, but we have found no correlation to the murder yet."

Tina was getting impatient, "What is it, Darren? What is it?"

He was backing off telling her for a moment, "I really don't think I should tell you... yet. It's really kind of premature. We haven't fully investigated it."

"C'mon Darren, tell me." Tina resorted to her sexy, seductress voice, "I'll make this weekend *extra especially* nice for you." She knew how to push Darren's buttons, and she was pushing them - hard.

"Tina, it's just a very preliminary hunch and not yet ready for release."

Tina knew she could convince him to divulge the information with the proposition of sex, "Saturday night dinner and dancing. Then, you can stay overnight at my condo on the beach with me. How does that sound?"

Her bribery was working, and Darren was starting to give in, "Oh my God, that sounds wonderful."

She smelled a big scoop, "Then tell me. What is it?"

Darren's testosterone was now pumping at high speed, and he couldn't resist her sexual innuendos, "Well, it's very preliminary, but Susan was writing a book for her graduate studies, and she might have stumbled across something important while doing her research. It could have been the motive for her murder."

Tina's investigative news reporter antennae went up instantly. Her instincts told her that this was much more than a preliminary hunch, "What did she stumble across?"

He hesitated for a moment, "Umm, well, it seems that... Her research uncovered the possibility of pirate treasure buried on Seminole Indian tribal land."

"What?" Tina practically jumped out of her skin.

Darren tried to backpedal, based on her reaction, "Tina, remember I said it's just a preliminary hunch."

She wanted more, "How much pirate treasure?"

"We're not really sure... but it might be as much as thirty million dollars."

"Yikes." This was explosive news. She was already scripting her monologue in her mind, "How did she discover this buried pirate treasure?"

Darren already knew it was a mistake telling her, but the proverbial cat was already out of the bag, "Well, she didn't really *discover* the pirate treasure. She interviewed the Seminole Indian Chief, and he mentioned a legend that had been handed down from generation to generation about a young Indian boy who was hunting in the Everglades and happened onto Pirate Gasparilla and his buccaneers burying their treasure chests."

"Wow. Wow. Pirate Gasparilla." This was getting juicier and juicer. Tina thought she was going to have an orgasm, "So, where is this pirate treasure?"

Darren started to backtrack the entire episode, "There is no pirate treasure that we know of... Just the legend of a pirate treasure. The legend is that it's on Seminole Indian tribal land."

She started developing theories in her mind, "Do you think she discovered a pirate's treasure map of some kind, and it led to her murder? Or maybe she was strangled to get her to disclose where the pirate treasure was buried? What do you think, Darren?"

At this point, Darren was getting exasperated, "Look, we really don't know. It's just that the book she was writing for graduate studies at the University of Florida about Seminole Indian history over 200 years ago coincided with the time frame that Pirate Gasparilla was pillaging merchant ships in South Florida waters. It might just be an insignificant coincidence."

Tina continued to develop her monologue in her mind, "And Pirate Gasparilla stole treasure worth thirty million dollars and buried it on the Seminole Indian reservation? What would that be worth in today's money? A billion dollars?"

Darren knew she was getting a little carried away, "That might be an exaggeration, Tina."

"It may or may not be an exaggeration. Nobody really knows how much treasure may be buried, and what it might be worth, right?"

"I guess technically, that's right. But, Tina, this is all just a preliminary hunch. We have no solid evidence."

Tina was now in a hurry to get off the phone, "OK, Darren got to run. I'll see you this weekend." *Click.*

Darren just sat there, listening to the dial tone. He hung up the telephone and stared at it for a moment. He started regretting what he had told her. He thought to himself, *Oh GOD, that was a mistake,*

Tina hung up the phone and ran to her producer and the NBC6 Investigators office to announce her big scoops. They would quickly produce a "Breaking News" segment to air immediately to beat their competitor stations and gain viewer loyalty as the news station to watch for the latest developments in this important story. Then, they would develop a bigger and more titillating news segment for the six and eleven o'clock news, which would be the real *Neilson Ratings* bonanzas.

CHAPTER FIFTEEN

Breaking News!

FDLE Headquarters
Tallahassee, Florida

Riddled with many critical questions from the victim's families and friends about the murders of their loved ones, Casey regrettably had very few answers. All the ongoing investigations had yet to turn up anything concrete. She hoped the $25,000 reward post would generate some valuable leads which could help them solve the cases, but usually, most of the leads were absurd claims whipsawed to a dead-end after countless hours of investigation. It was a painful, protracted, inexorable process that crashed and burned all the participants, from the victims to investigators, with extreme highs and lows like the Coney Island Roller Coaster Ride, "Cyclone."

Casey's secretary, Betsy, kept buzzing her office. Reporters stalked Casey and anyone else at FDLE they could pin down, looking for information. This journalist or that reporter wanted to get through the line with questions regarding the investigations, but all she answered was, "No Comment."

In an attempt to maintain the integrity of her office, her team, and her investigation, Casey had to level the playing field by keeping tight control over the information divulged to the press. Therefore, it was mandatory that all communications emanate from the FDLE Communications Office, and nothing gets leaked to the press from internal FDLE sources. It was an essential component of FDLE that the exact same truth about the progress of the investigations was available to the public through professionals, licensed, trained, and required to put the needs of the victims and their families first.

Her heart broke every time she talked to the victims and the victims' families. It was depressing and demoralizing to continually answer their questions with, *"we're working on it,"* or *"it's under investigation, and we can't divulge any information."*

They wanted answers, and she knew they were counting on her to find the rapist and killer who had destroyed their lives. But she had no answers... Not yet.

After completing her last phone call with a victim's family member, Casey glanced over at one of the flat-screen television monitors on the wall in her office. Her heart sank. Tina Evanston's face filled the screen, apparently delivering a monologue about the latest breaking news regarding the Governor's daughter's rape and murder investigation. The volume was muted, but she saw the caption at the bottom of the screen:

BREAKING NEWS!

The Rhapsody Killers

Seminole Indian Pirate Treasure Clue to Murder of Governor's Daughter.

Casey sat immobilized by the immensity of what she had just seen. Her eyes moved from Tina's face to the captions below on the monitor, but her body remained immobile as if it glued her to her seat. Tina Evanston appeared to move her lips in slow motion, saying something important. The caption at the bottom of the screen changed to:

"$25,000 REWARD"

In capital letters, as she continued moving her lips.

What is she saying?

Casey shot up from her chair to the television and turned the volume higher. *Unbelievable,* she thought, *how bad can this get?* At that moment, everything froze in time and space as she listened to Tina Evanston's oration:

> *"... Based on a trusted source inside FDLE, close to the investigation, we have confirmation that the Governor's daughter was researching a project for the University of Florida prior to her murder and inadvertently discovered that Pirate Gasparilla had buried treasure chests on Seminole Indian tribal land over 200 years ago. The pirate treasure had an estimated value of thirty-million-dollars at the time, but in today's dollars, it could be worth almost one-billion-dollars. FDLE is investigating whether it had anything to do with the Governor's daughter's murder, and they have posted a $25,000 reward for information leading to the arrest of her killer. They have established a special phone line to collect any relevant information: (850) 555-1212."*
>
> *"This is Tina Evanston Reporting for NBC6 Investigators."*

Casey's face turned an alarming shade of red as she shouted at the television, "OH MY GOD! HOW COULD HE DO THIS?"

Casey knew this information had not been released by the FDLE Communications Office and immediately suspected Darren. *Tina Evanston's in Miami and Darren parties in Miami. It had to be him.*

She wanted to strangle him.

She rushed toward Darren's office, stopping outside to question Darren's secretary, Darlene, "Has Darren been talking to any reporters?"

Darlene was protective of Darren but couldn't lie to Casey, "Well, I know Tina Evanston called him this morning. I don't know what they talked about."

Casey exploded, "Darren should not be talking to the press. Everything should go through the FDLE Communications Office... Period."

Darlene shrugged her shoulders with an expression that implied she knew that, but there was nothing she could do about it, "He's my boss. What can I do?"

Casey barged through Darren's door with an energy that made it feel like a tornado had just touched down. Her forehead was visibly wrinkled, and her face was flushed with anger, foreshadowing a temper ready to explode. She grabbed the telephone receiver out of his hand and abruptly hung it up, "WHAT DO YOU THINK YOU'RE DOING?" Her voice was full of rage.

Darren lifted his head to face his expected whipping, and his eyes opened wide in shock, "Well, I thought I was talking to a friend on the phone until you just hung up on him."

Casey leaned over his desk and looked into his eyes, "Have you been talking to Tina Evanston?"

Darren looked up sheepishly, knowing he was guilty, "Yes, I did, but I told her it was all preliminary hunches. I didn't think she'd run with it."

"I can't believe it." Casey threw her arms up, "Are you aware of the damage you're causing? We have FDLE Communications Office and public relations experts to help us deal with communications during an investigation like this, and you're circumventing the entire process. How can you take it upon yourself to talk to these vultures? You have no right to provide that kind of information to anybody without my authorization. Do you understand me?"

Darren dropped back into his chair and apologized, "Look, I'm sorry. I told her it was just a hunch we were pursuing. I didn't think she would broadcast it."

"You're either naïve, Darren, or you're playing me. I know you're hot for her and trying to use your position at FDLE to improve your romantic opportunities with her, but you need to stop it! NOW! If you grant one more interview to her or anybody else without my prior approval, I will fire you. Is that clear?"

"Yes. I'm sorry," Darren declared with a pout.

Casey controlled her urge to jump across the desk and smack him. Shaking her head in disgust, she stormed out of Darren's office.

Back in her office, Casey's voice mailbox was bombarded with phone messages from the irate press corps. Most of the messages were derogatory attacks about the fact that FDLE had given this scoop to Tina Evanston, while *they* were all playing by the rules, working with the FDLE Communications Office. These abrasive messages continued all day. Reporters were justifiably upset because they were outdone by Tina Evanston and NBC6 news in Miami, because of her intimate relationship with Darren Turner.

CHAPTER SIXTEEN

Family Traditions [15]

Gus Slayton Home

Miami, Florida

Five-year-old, blond-hair, blue-eyed Gustavo A. Slayton, Junior, ran gleefully into his father's arms with a toy gun in his hand as the six-feet-four-inch rookie policeman knelt down to greet his son, a smoking cigarette stuck to his lip, "Daddy, daddy, daddy."

"Hi, Buddy." Gus Slayton slammed the apartment door closed with his boot and hugged his son with a smile upon returning home to his perfect little family after a long hard day in a hot Miami squad car. It was late August in Southeast Florida. His uniform was drenched with perspiration from the day, and he reeked of tobacco and scotch, although little Gus Junior didn't seem to notice. Gus picked up his son in one arm and walked through the toy-cluttered living room toward the aroma of dinner cooking in the kitchen.

Little Gus Junior took his Dad's police cap off and put it on his head sideways to play policeman, the toy gun still in his hand, "Bang, bang, bang." The prodigy aimed his toy gun at the cops and robbers cartoon blaring on the television.

Police Officer Gus Slayton looked the part: tall, blond hair, blue-eyed, muscular, and handsome with his official police-issued orange-tinted glasses still covering his eyes. He could have been an actor in

Law and Order, at least the "Law" part. Growing up, he really had no choice but to join the police force. It was a family tradition. His Father, Grandfather, twin brother, and even his sister were cops. And he, like his grandfather and father before him, and his twin brother and his sister, started playing cops long before kindergarten.

Gus's father set the traditions as the siblings were growing up. Police Chief Gustavo Slayton Senior, was strong and tough, and always in-charge. His father was the boss and got whatever he wanted, one way or another. Gus grew up in a home where his father was Chief of Police, Chief of the city, and Chief of the household. There was no backtalk, or he, or his twin brother, or his sister, or his mother got whacked with the back of the Chief's hand... *Hard.*

He verbally and physically abused his wife and his children with impunity. He was always in control and not to be denied.

The Law Must Be Obeyed.

His daughter was a convenient sex-toy for the Chief from the early age of eight-years-old. He would sneak into her bedroom after his wife fell asleep and have his way with her. He turned on the music of Gershwin's *Rhapsody in Blue* to mask any suspicious noises emanating from her bedroom so his wife couldn't hear him screwing her daughter. Of course, his daughter didn't know any different at the time and thought this was normal because it was all she had ever known. The brothers also got to share her after their father was done. They took turns on her, with *Gershwin* still playing in the background.

The brothers *always* shared everything.

As Chief of Police, their father could even put through an exception to the sacrosanct police department rule that says siblings can't work together in the same precinct, which was further "grandfathered" in by future Police Chiefs.

This exemption allowed Gus and his twin brother, Angelo, to partner together in the same squad car. His father figured that way they could take care of each other while on duty and, for the brothers, that also made their extracurricular activities of sharing women together even more exciting.

His wife, Rachel, was stirring pot-roast on the stove, the aroma filled the kitchen, when Gus slapped her tight ass with his free hand, "Hey, good-lookin', what-cha got cookin'?"

Little Gus Junior chuckled at that, as his Daddy roughly twirled his mother around to embrace her. He crushed the stub of his cigarette in an ashtray and kissed her hard on the lips as he slid his hand down to clutch her behind, pushing her into his bulging groin, "Put the stove on simmer," he commanded.

Rachel, a young, petite black-haired beauty of Cuban descent, married Gustavo Slayton upon the diagnosis of her unexpected pregnancy. She had dated both Gus and his identical twin brother Angelo for a while and wasn't really sure which was her baby's father, but she chose to marry Gus because she wanted her child to have a father and a stable home. A decision she now regretted as an abused police wife. Especially since it turned out to be a package deal that included both Gus *and* Angelo, anyway. The brothers *always* shared everything.

She turned the stove dial lower, as ordered.

"Daddy, daddy, can we play cops and robbers?"

"Later, Champ, Daddy and Mommy have something to do right now." Gus slowly slid his son down to the floor.

Little Gus Junior watched adoringly as his father clutched his mother's arm and directed her toward the bedroom. The bedroom door closed behind them, and the music started to play from behind the closed door. Gus Junior stared at the closed door and listened for a moment thinking, *I want to grow up to be just like my Daddy.* Then, he returned to his cartoon and toy guns in the living room.

Inside the bedroom, Gus shoved his wife onto the bed and switched the CD player on the night table to play *Rhapsody in Blue.* The strong beat of the music with rough sex further aroused him. Rachel lay face down on the bed sobbing, dreading his inevitable assault. He whacked her behind hard, flipped her over onto her back and ripped her blouse off. Then, he pulled her bra down and unzipped her skirt as he straddled her.

He leaned sideways to unzip his dark-blue police-issued pants and pushed them off. Then he slid down her body and pulled her skirt and panties off. He held her neck tight to hold her steady while he spread her legs and entered her. His grip on her throat strengthened, and she almost passed out as he pumped rhythmically to *Gershwin's* music.

She was gagging uncontrollably and started coughing. She groaned in pain as he pushed hard into her with his powerful leg muscles, giving her no reprieve. She was small compared to his large size, but he was on a mission, and he didn't really care how she felt. She held back her tears as he hammered away, slapping flesh on flesh. His grip on her throat tightened more, and she felt like she would pass out again, but she held on until he finally exploded inside of her. She collapsed on the bed, trying to catch her breath. Her face and neck were red and sore.

Suddenly, Angelo entered the bedroom and started undressing.

Rachel dreaded what was going to happen next because it had happened so many times before. She tried to get up out of the bed to escape, but Angelo pushed her back down as his brother grabbed her and pulled her back.

"No, stop!"

The brothers ignored her pleas. Angelo got on top of her, spread her legs apart, and brazenly had sexual intercourse with her while her husband watched.

The brothers *always* shared everything.

---

[15] ## [15] *Police Officer Sergio Alvarez Rapes in West Sacramento, California:*

Police Officer Sergio Alvarez prowled the streets in his police cruiser during his graveyard shift and used his police authority to abduct and rape women in his patrol car or in dark alleys. His wife, Rachel Alvarez, was also raped and abused by her husband and testified against him at trial. She was relocated to Naples, Florida, as part of the "Witness Protection and Relocation Program."

CHAPTER SEVENTEEN

Sitting on Gold [16] [17]

Medley Police Range
North Miami Beach, Florida

"BAM! BAM! BAM!" Gus Slayton fired in rapid succession at the mugshot image of an arrested black man they used for target practice. The North Miami Beach Police Department routinely used a photo lineup of arrested African-American human image mugshot targets at the shooting range to help its sniper team practice marksmanship. [17]

Angelo watched his brother's shooting, "Right between the eyes, Bro. Nice shooting."

Gus retracted the target, removed the mugshot, and replaced it with another mugshot image of an arrested black man. His bullets had gone right between the eyes of the African-American man's mugshot.

"BAM! BAM! BAM! BAM! BAM!" Angelo took his turn firing in rapid succession. The mugshot was so riddled by bullets that the human face was unrecognizable.

Gus laughed, "We should put a photo of the head of the Governor's Rape Task Force as a target, Bro. We need to teach her a lesson."

"Hey, that's our flesh and blood, Bro, and we love her," Angelo laughed.

"You're right. We love her. Maybe we should target the Governor instead. Hahaha."

They both removed their eye goggles and ear shooting protection and walked over to the metal-doored massive gun cabinet that stored a vast array of firepower. It was stocked with ready weaponry: Remington 12-gauge shotguns, .44 Magnums, some reworked Glocks, an Uzi, AK47s and a Vietnam-era sniper rifle, the Springfield M21.

Gus picked out the Springfield M21 sniper rifle. He ran his fingers up and down the well-oiled gun barrel and raised the weapon up to his shoulder, feeling the weight. He cocked the bolt of the rifle with his right hand. Peering through the high-powered scope, he aimed at an imaginary figure of the Governor in his mind and slowly squeezed the trigger. The unloaded rifle clicked harmlessly, "Bam, Bam. You're dead. Rot in hell, Governor."

His heart was filled with hatred, his soul restless to exact vengeance - but he had no heart, and he had no soul. He turned to Angelo, laughing, "Hahaha. You know, maybe we should have some fun with Little Sister again, just like the good old days, Bro."

Anglo smiled back, "We certainly had some good times with her, back in the day."

Gus laughed, "She belongs to us, Bro. She's ours, as her dead husband soon found out. Hahaha. Poor Jeremy Collins. Wrong place, wrong time. He didn't know what hit him."

Angelo laughed back, "Ha. It *was* a beautiful wedding. Too bad poor Jeremy picked the wrong woman to marry. He shouldn't have interfered with *our* family and *our* woman."

They placed their guns into the gun case and moved to a quieter spot in the shooting-range to talk.

Gus looked from side to side to make sure no one was listening, "Sis put out a $25,000 reward for information leading to the arrest of the Governor's daughter's killer."

Angelo laughed again, "Ha-ha. Maybe I should turn you in? I need the money."

Gus laughed also, "Maybe I'll turn you in. I need the money too."

They both had a chuckle over that.

Gus continued, "Tina Evanston's broadcast on NBC6 news publicized there's some buried pirate treasure on the Seminole Indian Reservation that the Governor's daughter had been researching and that could be the motive for her murder."

Angelo chuckled at that, "Well, we both know she was sitting on gold."

Gus burst out laughing, "Sitting on gold. That's a good one, Bro. Ha."

"She was pretty good. Too bad she was the Governor's daughter. Who knew?"

They continued laughing until some other police officers walked nearby. One of them commented, "Hey, what's so funny?"

Thinking quickly, Gus picked up the mugshot from his target practice and showed the police officer, "I got him right between the eyes."

The officer looked at the mugshot and smiled, "You sure did. Nice shooting." He walked away toward the showers.

Angelo turned to Gus, "Seriously, do you think there might be some buried pirate treasure out there."

Gus snickered, "I don't know. You should've asked her before you killed her."

Angelo didn't laugh at that, "Gus, that was an accident. You know I didn't mean to strangle her. I was just having rough sex with her."

"Rough is an understatement. Now we have the Governor up our ass. Plus, his wife is dying, and he blames that on us too."

Angelo got defensive, "Hey, you should talk. You killed beautiful Kim Merrick before we even got a chance to party with her."

"You know that was a total accident, Angelo. I didn't touch her."

"Ha-ha, you just stomped her to death."

Gus apologized, "My mistake. It was dark, and I didn't see her fall."

"Whatever... Too late now."

"Right. It is."

"Back to this pirate treasure hunt... If Tina Evanston's report is right, maybe we need to return to the Seminole Indian Reservation to check it out."

"I'd rather check beautiful Tina Evanston out."

"I know, Bro, and I hope we get that opportunity sometime soon."

Gus agreed, "Let's head over to Everglades City to pick up the trail."

---

[16] **_Police Officer Jimmy Fennell Murder in Austin, Texas:_**

Police Officer Fennel is suspected of killing his fiancée, Stacey Stites, because he was angry she had sex with a black man, Rodney Reed. Fennel allegedly strangled Stacey to death with a belt and framed Reed for her murder. Dr. Michael Baden, a highly respected forensic pathologist, concluded that Stacey had been killed before midnight, a time that pointed to Fennell as the killer, not Reed.

CHAPTER EIGHTEEN

Treasure Hunt [18]

Seminole Indian Reservation

Big Cypress, Florida

The First Seminole Indian War took place between 1814 and 1818, when the military and political opportunist, General Andrew Jackson, was named Military Governor of Florida and brazenly marched across Florida's international boundaries to settle the "Indian Problem." Over a period of several tumultuous years, he burned Seminole Indian villages, hanged and shot the native Seminole Indians to death, as well as foreigners he suspected of inciting the Seminole Indians. He provoked an international furor.

During the Second Seminole Indian War, 1835-1842, the U.S. Government subjected the Seminole Indians to the fiercest of all the wars ever waged against native peoples. Seminole Indian Chief Osceola was the brave and determined leader of the resistance, and his Seminole Indian warriors fought back valiantly. Unfortunately, he led a vastly outnumbered and poorly armed force, pitting roughly 900 Seminole Indian warriors, against a combined U.S. Army and militia force of 9,000 troops.

The Third Seminole Indian War ended with another 250 Seminole Indians slaughtered by the U.S. government. This was the only Indian war in U.S. history, in which not only the U.S. Army but also the U.S. Navy and Marine Corps participated. The Seminole Indians were outnumbered, outmaneuvered, and overwhelmed in the Seminole Indian Wars.

Finally, after the U.S. government spent nearly $50 million on the war, a huge sum at that time, and more than 2,000 American soldiers and many more Seminole Indians dead, the US government gave up, and the Big Cypress Seminole Indian Reservation was officially established.

The Slayton brothers used their police authority to pose as investigators for the Governor's Rape Task Force investigating the Gasparilla pirate buried treasure correlation to the Governor's daughter's murder. Of course, they were only interested in the buried treasure since they already knew who killed the Governor's daughter.

Although the Seminole Indian Reservation had its own internal law enforcement organization, they fully cooperated with state and local authorities. When the Slayton brothers arrived, the Seminole Indians rolled out the red carpet to be as helpful as possible, especially since the Governor's daughter was murdered on their tribal land.

The Slayton brothers made it look official. They drove their official Miami police cruiser to the Seminole Indian Reservation headquarters in Big Cypress dressed in their official blue police uniforms and were greeted by members of the Seminole Police Department. Gus Slayton flashed his official gold-plated Police Badge to the Captain, and they all shook hands.

"Hello, I'm Officer Gus Slayton, and this is Officer Angelo Slayton. We are here to investigate the Governor's daughter's murder."

The Police Captain was very cordial, "Hello. Welcome to the Seminole Indian Reservation. We are very sorry about the tragic murder of the Governor's daughter, and we will be eager to assist in any way we can."

They walked into the Police Captain's office and sat down to talk. It was all very modern and high tech. Not exactly what you would expect to see from watching *John Wayne Cowboys and Indians movies.* On the back wall, there were rows of video screens that monitored the Seminole Indian Casinos and their other business enterprises. On another wall, there was a large map of Florida, highlighting the six Florida Seminole Indian Reservations in Tampa, Brighton, Immokalee, Fort Pierce, Hollywood, and Big Cypress.

Gus initiated the questioning, "Captain, we are here to get to the bottom of the buried pirate treasure mystery that may have been the motive to the Governor's daughter's murder." He looked over at Angelo before continuing, "Did Susan Scott uncover any facts about the authentication or location of this buried treasure?"

The Police Captain answered, "As I'm sure you are aware, Agent Darren Turner from FDLE has previously interviewed our Seminole Indian Chief extensively, and many of those questions have already been covered."

Gus looked back at Angelo with a dumbfounded expression but faked his response, "Yes, Captain, we have read the transcript of that interview, but still many questions remain."

The Police Captain stood and walked over to the map on the wall as he started answering Gus's question, "We really don't know if there was or wasn't any buried pirate treasure. It was over 200 years ago, and we have no record of what might have actually occurred." He pointed to a spot on the map in the Everglades within the reservation, "The legend is that a young Seminole Indian boy was hunting deer in this approximate area when he heard the pirates digging in the sand. At first, he didn't know what the sound was and thought maybe it was an animal, so he quietly approached the sound and hid behind some trees, watching the pirates dig a hole in the ground. He most likely didn't understand the concept of burying treasure, anyway."

Gus walked over to the map as well, to pinpoint the exact location the Captain was indicating, "Did the Indian boy ever go back to retrieve the buried treasure?"

The Captain shook his head, "Again, that was over 200 years ago. I doubt he would have understood the significance of buried treasure to want to go back to retrieve it. Remember, it was a very simple existence for Seminole Indians in those days. We didn't know what we know now, and we didn't think the way we do today."

Gus shook his head, "Has any excavation of that area been done to search for the treasure?"

"We have done some preliminary searches of the swamp area, but it's very large, and with all the hurricanes, fires, lightning, rain, animals, alligators, and who knows whatever else over the past 200 plus years, any trace of the dig site has been lost... If there ever was one."

Angelo questioned the existence of a treasure map, "Did the Governor's daughter discover a map of the location of the treasure the Indian boy or anybody else might have drawn?"

"To the best of my knowledge, there is not a treasure map in existence for Susan Scott to have found. So, I would have to say my answer is, no."

Gus continued his fake line of questioning, "It's just suspicious that on the night, Ms. Scott was murdered, she was here at the reservation discussing buried pirate treasure."

The Police Captain scratched his chin, "I understand that. You may want to go to the AH-TAH-THI-KI Museum here in Big Cypress. I know Susan spent the afternoon there, prior to meeting with the Seminole Indian Chief."

The brothers looked at each other quizzically, "What is that?"

"In our language, Ah-Tah-Thi-Ki means 'a place to learn,' sort of a Museum. We invite tourists to come to the Big Cypress Seminole Indian Reservation and learn about our history and culture. The Seminole Tribe of Florida is one of the most successful native Indian business tribes in America. We run casinos, hotels, cattle, citrus, and other business enterprises and employ thousands of people. The Museum's exhibits and artifacts show how our Seminole ancestors lived in the Florida swamps and the Everglades, and how they survived and eventually prospered."

Gus was hopeful, "Ancient artifacts may be a clue to what happened 200 years ago. Maybe that's where she discovered something to do with the pirate's buried treasure."

The Police Chief just shrugged his shoulders, "Maybe."

------

[18] *Police Officer Arthur Lee Sewall Rape and Murder in Las Vegas, Nevada:*

Construction workers found 20-year-old Nadia Iverson's body in an apartment they were renovating in Las Vegas, with a gunshot wound to her head. Las Vegas Police Officer Arthur Lee Sewall's DNA matched the DNA tested in Iverson's rape test kit. They charged Sewall with raping and killing her.

CHAPTER NINETEEN

The Tombs [19]

FDLE Headquarters
Tallahassee, Florida

Casey smelled the coffee brewing in the FDLE kitchen and decided to get some to clear her head. She hoped it was strong. She was still upset with Darren for leaking classified information to Tina Evanston. Plus, her feelings were mixed with a little jealousy because she had a special fondness for Darren, which she kept secret.

When she arrived, Lieutenant Weller and Sergeant Benjamin were there, chatting at a small table while Casey poured herself a cup of coffee, "Good morning. How are you guys doing?"

They both replied in unison, "Good morning, Casey." In an attempt to make their coffee break appear productive to their boss, they brown-nosed her about the investigation.

Weller took the lead, "Casey, we were just discussing the geographic location of all the rapes and murders. The killer or killers must live in south Florida since they have covered their tracks so well."

Casey took a sip of her coffee, standing by the counter, and processed their supposition, realizing that her theories were similar, "Yes. At this point, we shouldn't rule out anything or anybody."

"Except for the Governor's daughter," Benjamin added, "all the rapes and murders have occurred on the east coast of South Florida."

The Profile they had developed implied that the rapist and killer – or both, if there were two of them - probably lived and worked in that vicinity nearby the crime scenes, so she knew the center of the investigation had to focus on that region, mostly between Miami and Fort Lauderdale and the surrounding areas.

She responded as she started walking back to her office with her cup of coffee, "Yes. Keep working on those assumptions. I'll catch up with you later."

Casey returned to her desk and opened the emails on her computer. Her emotions were whirling around because of Tina Evanston's breaking news scoop thanks to Darren, but she knew she needed to calm down and focus on the investigation. The first email she read changed everything:

CONFIDENTIAL

FDLE Interoffice Communication

To: Casey Collins, Senior Agent, Governor's Rape Task Force

From: FDLE Regional Operations Center - Miami

Subject: Everglades City - Cara Jones Murder

Authorities responded to a missing person's call from the parents of a 20-year-old female, Cara Jones, last seen leaving her boyfriend's house the night before. They followed the route she would have presumably taken and eventually discovered her white Volkswagen Beetle early this morning below an abandoned bridge off Mercy Road, an eerily dark and desolate area commonly called "The Tombs."

Her body was discovered below a nearby bridge in a creek bed. She appeared to have been strangled with a rope, badly beaten with a blunt object, and thrown off the bridge. Vaginal samples have been sent to the lab to determine if there was a sexual assault involved and to identify the DNA of the perpetrator.

She had been a Junior at the State University studying to become a teacher. They declared the young woman dead at the scene.

The state awaits the result of DNA and Toxicology screens.

"Oh, my God. Another one!" This murder just blew her theory about the killer's location out of the water. Now, it was Southwest Florida, in addition to Southeast Florida. Or was this a copycat killing? She printed the email and headed over to Darren's office.

"Another murder." She handed Darren the printout, and he glanced at it.

"I know. Last night in Everglades City. Sheriff Alan Robertson is working on it down there."

Casey pointed to the email, "This murder broadens our search area. So now we have Everglades City to Fort Lauderdale to connect with the Profile. Southwest to Southeast Florida."

"Everglades City is a stretch. Why would he or they venture outside of their comfort zone in the Profile? It doesn't fit."

She stood by his desk, thinking, "I don't know. Except for Susan, the other crimes have occurred in the same east coast region of South Florida, until now. You're right. It doesn't fit. Unless there is some reason to venture outside of the Profile zone or it's a copycat killer."

Darren connected the dots, "Everglades City is near where Susan was murdered. Could there be a connection between these two murders?"

"It's also near to the Seminole Indian Reservation in Big Cypress and the legend of the buried pirate treasure chests." Casey knew they had to get more involved in this one, "We need to dig into this," she said, "Pun intended. We need to go to Everglades City to investigate whether this is the same serial rapist and murderer we're already chasing, or if there is another one."

Darren's expression faded to horror, and he looked at her with a face that almost made her laugh out loud, "No, no, no. It's Friday. I don't want to spend Friday night in Everglades City." He sagged back in his chair, looking deflated.

She smiled curiously, "That is the scene of the crime, and we are cops."

"Everglades City?" He cringed more.

Casey fixed him with a look that said, *really?* "In your interview, you said you liked to travel."

"Of course, to warm, lush mosquito-free Islands. Paris in season..." He dropped the charade, "But this is so far into the Everglades that even the alligators worry about the mosquitoes eating them."

Casey turned and walked back to her office. She returned a few seconds later with a can of deep woods mosquito repellent that she had stored in her desk and set it down in front of him, "Here, spray this on, crybaby." A satisfied smile curved her lips.

He picked up the spray bottle and studied it, "Thanks a lot," he said sarcastically, "When do we leave?"

Casey thought for a minute, "In about an hour. I want us to get down there while the body is still at the crime scene. There's no convenient airport near Everglades City, so we'll get there quicker if we just leave immediately and drive down. It will give us some time to talk and consider the evidence."

"Yuck. This is not good, Boss."

She flashed him a cynical look, "We'll have to be there for a couple of days. I'll get some things from home and pick you up back here."

"Wonderful."

She added sarcastically, "Why? Do you have big plans for the weekend? Maybe in Miami Beach?"

"I was thinking about it."

"Well, it's on the way to Miami Beach, you can head over there when we're done." She gave a combination laugh and sigh, "You can go see Tina if you can keep your big mouth shut."

"That's a thought," Darren said.

Casey gave him a dirty look, "Okay, I'm heading home. Be ready to go in an hour. We have to catch this guy."

Darren stood-up and started collecting some folders, "Or guys," he reminded her.

Casey turned and walked out the door. She needed to call the Governor and make him aware of this latest murder and her plan to go to the scene of the crime.

---

[19] *__CHP Police Officer Craig Peyer Murder in San Diego, California:__*

California Highway Patrol Police Officer Craig Peyer stalked and murdered 20-year-old Cara Knott. He used his police red and blue lights to pull her car over to a darkened exit-ramp after spotting her at a gas station. When she refused to have sex with him, he strangled her, beat her with a blunt object, and threw her body off a 70-foot high bridge to eliminate any potential forensic evidence.

CHAPTER TWENTY

Road Trip [19]

Casey Collin's Car
Everglades City, Florida

Everglades City had never been fortunate enough to prosper and grow like its sister cities on the east coast, or the "other" coast, as most inhabitants of the Tamiami Trail called it. The "illegal industries" had been the primary occupation for most of the locals and had progressed from Plume feather poaching for ladies New York fashion hats in the 1920s; to Rum running during Prohibition in the 1930s; to skinning alligator hides in the swamps for manufacturers of boots and pocketbooks up North in the 1940s; to prosperous marijuana and drug smuggling using the drug route from Cartagena, Columbia, to the Tamiami Trail in the 1950s.

They did anything and everything to survive in those days, legal or not. It was an outlaw's refuge where criminals and wanted men would go because there was little or no law enforcement in Everglades City. Guns were the law.

Casey made it home, took a quick shower, changed, and sprayed on some perfume. Her "Go Bag" was always packed and ready, and she grabbed it on her way back out the door. She pulled up to the Government Center less than an hour later.

Darren was leaning against the stainless-steel handrail, waiting with his Go Bag at his feet, looking more handsome than she recalled in his Stanley Blacker periwinkle checkered sports jacket, beige Polo Ralph Lauren slacks, and a glorious mane of thick black hair. She watched as he nonchalantly pushed his athletic five-foot-eleven-inch frame from the rail, grabbed his bag, and made for the passenger door. She wondered how she would get through this assignment; *He was probably hung like Johnny Wad and exerted pheromones like a gorilla in heat.*

He jumped into the passenger seat, "Wow. You smell good." He dumped his Go Bag at his feet, and seemed to pull a CD from thin air, "Music, Boss?"

"Thank you. Sure, anything but Gershwin." Casey fell back slightly, pushing the transmission into reverse as soon as his door slammed shut. She pulled the sun visor down and slid her Eagle Eyes Apollo Gold shooting glasses over her nose, aware that Darren watched her every move, even as he popped the CD case open and launched the player.

The first song from Led Zeppelin filled the car with perfect harmony accompaniment.

> *There's a lady who's sure*
>
> *All that glitters is gold*
>
> *And she's buying a stairway to heaven*
>
> *When she gets there, she knows*
>
> *If the stores are all closed*
>
> *With a word, she can get what she came for*
>
> *Ooh ooh and she's buying a stairway to heaven...*

He was ready when she turned to look at him, "'Stairway to Heaven,' very appropriate, since we're on our way to Everglades City. Don't you think?" He chuckled.

"Perfect." She responded.

"Like 'em?"

Casey shook her head, "Of course."

"Yeah," he grinned, leaned back in his seat, and closed his eyes, "How is everything going with the Governor?"

"Good," she replied automatically, weary of his new line of questioning. The Governor crossed her mind... His hands... His face... His smell. Darren fell silent for a moment, except for the sound of the CD. And she was grateful for that.

It was short-lived. He interrupted her thoughts, not opening his eyes, "So, first road trip?"

"First road trip," she confirmed, not looking over at him as she veered the SUV off the main road onto the Interstate 10 ramp.

"How long?"

"Must be five or six-hours." She responded.

"Five to Naples, so probably six to Everglades City."

She glanced at the in-dash GPS map. The green dot flashed their current position on the back-lit map, adding, "And forty-minutes." Six-hours and forty-minutes echoed in her mind, and she resisted the urge to close her eyes. His pheromones were in overdrive, and hers wanted to respond in kind.

"Been there before?"

"Everglades City? No. Not much experience with Southwest Florida."

Darren shivered, "Rough country."

Casey laughed. Given the reports she had read about the terrain, climate, and conditions, she thought that too. Especially after reading Susan's manuscript, *Tamiami Trail of Tears*.

Darren laughed too as he shook his head, "Talk about gator bait."

She smiled, "Well, we have the Forensic teams and the FDLE ranger rescue teams on call." Pretty much guessing what was going through his mind, "I am surprised. You have a little more field savvy for this than I thought you would."

Darren shrugged and looked as though it embarrassed him.

Then she remembered his résumé; he had search and rescue in the Ozarks, firefighting in Northern California, and nine-eleven rescue and recovery in New York City experience. He was accustomed to hostile conditions — the very reason she hired him.

Darren relaxed back in his seat, and closed his eyes again, "Must be the Florida air."

"Must be." Casey glanced at her watch as the sun drifted lower and lower in the sky, then slipped behind the western clouds, its dying rays streaking the darkening blue horizon. It looked like a giant knife had cut vibrantly colored iridescent scars across the electric red-and-orange clouds in the sky. The green foliage rolled past outside, marking the miles left behind.

He opened his eyes and spotted a Waffle House sign, "I'm starving. There's a Waffle House at the next exit."

She smiled at him, "Sounds like a plan."

He looked across at her, "So, where are you from?"

God, here it comes, she thought, "Actually, I'm from Miami."

"Oh, really? Florida girl. What brought you to the police force?"

She laughed, "It's a long story. My father was Chief of Police back in the day." It was a truth she wasn't ashamed of. Her mind flashed through her history of family personalities and problems like an old-time silent movie.

"Wow. No kidding. Is he retired?"

"Dead. Accident at home," She lied.

"Tragic..."

Not really, she thought, and briefly recalled her horrible childhood. She was the victim of domestic violence, rape, incest, and beatings. All made possible thanks to the "Blue Curtain" of protection the police live behind, "It was a long time ago."

She glanced at the golden streaks of clouds hovering over the western sky and reflected on the freedom her father's death had brought her. She thought she should feel guilty about her thoughts, but she didn't.

"This exit?" She brought herself back to reality with ease. Things were changing. Memories were fading. For once, she was in charge, and it would only get better.

CHAPTER TWENTY-ONE

Old Florida [19]

Rod and Gun Club
Everglades City, Florida

The Rod and Gun Club had seen it all since its opening in 1864 as a 10-room hotel and restaurant in Everglades City. It was about as "Old Florida" as it gets, and it hasn't changed much since the 19th century. Back then, tarpon fishing was the major tourist attraction and source of business following the demise of the Seminole Indian population. President Andrew Jackson's Indian Removal Act of 1830, caused the annihilation of most of the native Southwest Florida Seminole Indians, through a genocidal machination that became known as the "Trail of Tears."

Casey jabbed at the ENTER button on the ATM as though it would change the red flashing "OUT OF ORDER" message on the black screen. She was hot, tired, and irritated for many reasons, most of which at the moment was lack of coffee and the damn cash machine.

Her racing mind kept her awake all night, trying to connect the dots to the serial rapists and killers, for fear she may already know who they are. She paced around the hotel room, occasionally looking out the window at glowing eyes outside that seemed to blink at her from every shadow. *Probably alligator eyes,* she thought - the wild, wild Southwest.

It was 7:00 a.m. on a steamy Everglades City morning. Perspiration had already soaked her black Tee Shirt. The plastic embossed State Police Senior Agent emblem on her front and back suffocated her flesh, making the heat feel worse as she stood inside the un-air-conditioned Rod and Gun Club. Her bra was saturated, and her knees were sweating inside her pants. *Why do they make these uniforms black,* she thought? *Don't they know it's Florida?*

Darren's black shirt matched hers, minus the enlarged "Senior" on her bosom. They both wore cargo pants secured with a thick black leather police utility belt, their guns strapped at the hip.

Darren noticed her frustration, "Give it up, Boss."

"What kind of city is cash only?" She looked through the windows at the storefronts across the single-lane street, "Not a *Dunkin' Donuts* or *Mickey D's* in sight. Who lives here, anyway?"

"Hey, it's not New York City."

"You knew this, didn't you?" She accused.

He smiled, and half shrugged, "If I did, I forgot - lots of history here. The anarchic civilization carved out of the swampy wilderness in the Everglades remains implacable."

They heard a cavalcade of cars crushing stones pulling into the parking lot in front of the Rod and Gun Club and watched a trailing cloud of dust follow them. Two marked Collier County Sheriff cars and two unmarked, black SUV's with the Forensic teams pulled up to the front door.

Casey took the ATM card and tucked it back into her bag, "Let's go," she ordered, not looking back at Darren.

The heat of the morning stole her breath as she pushed through the doors, Darren close behind. The agents marched in tandem over to the lead car. Casey's fragrance preceded her as one of the uniforms approached them.

"Sheriff Alan Robertson," said the first officer to reach them, thrusting his hand out at Darren.

Darren took the hand, "Agent Darren Turner, and our boss, Senior Agent, Casey Collins," he said loud enough for everyone to hear.

Robertson was caught off guard. He had never seen Casey Collins before, and her beauty was quite disarming. He didn't expect that.

Casey tried not to scowl, frown or otherwise look peeved, which wasn't easy knowing that the word Senior Agent was splattered on her sizable chest, and Robertson managed to miss it, "Officer Robertson, what have we got?"

Robertson had the grace to redden as he shook her hand, "Cara Jones. Young, dead woman with unfortunately very little evidence, Senior Agent." Robertson's eyes were glued on Casey, "Her parents found her first."

Casey responded, "I know. How devastating for them."

They both shook their heads sadly in agreement.

Darren asked, "How far from here?"

Robertson reluctantly refocused his eyes on Darren. He gave a "go" nod to his partner, and then two officers surrounded the front of the SUV as they spread out maps on the steaming hood, "We're here." Robertson jabbed at a red spot on the map, then followed a pre-drawn blue line to an isolated area near a bridge marked with a red X, "A couple of miles. Five minutes away."

"Is that where the body is," Darren asked before Casey could speak.

Casey shot him a look, "Cara" she corrected. Casey always used their first names to treat the victims as people, not just dead bodies, as a way not to become desensitized. She thinks *everyone matters, or nobody matters.*

Detective Piper, the next officer, pointed to the red X, "Yes. The killer threw her body. . . excuse me, Cara, off the bridge into a creek bed which unfortunately filled with water from all the rain. We built a dam around her body to divert the flow of water and a tent because of the animals, but a lot of damage had already been done before we discovered her. The killer obviously hoped the fall from the bridge would dislodge a lot of evidence, and it did." He slid his finger from the X to the C on the map. A drop of sweat smeared the X, and Casey was grateful it wasn't hers, "We found her car over here."

Casey questioned, "Animals?"

"We had to protect the body from Gators," Piper said, as a matter of fact.

"Gators?" Darren prodded.

Piper answered, "These waters are infested with Alligators."

Casey looked at Piper apprehensively, "Besides the Alligators, are there any witnesses? Any neighbors? Anything else?"

"No. Unfortunately, it's a very deserted area under the bridge. Nothing there except Alligators and mosquitos."

Casey turned and started walking toward the car, "Let's get going."

Robertson watched Casey Collins's exquisite figure from behind as she strolled over to the front passenger door to get into the lead Sheriff's car. He didn't know FDLE agents could be so good-looking... She closed the door behind her, ending his momentary infatuation. He went around to the driver's side and got in.

Turner and Piper got in the back seats.

Piper began, "The other problem..."

"Rain," Darren said, looking skyward, "I'd say one-ish if we're lucky."

Robertson nodded, "Predicted for after two at the moment." He also looked skyward.

Casey wanted to scream. The forecast made the heat and humidity even more oppressive.

Robertson added, "When the day starts this hot, the rain forms early."

CHAPTER TWENTY-TWO

Forensic Evidence [19]

The Tombs

Everglades City, Florida

Underneath the bridge for the main roadway off of Mercy Road, in an eerily dark and desolate area commonly called, "The Tombs," Cara's abandoned white Volkswagen Beetle was hidden from view. In the creek bed below the bridge, investigators had erected a small tent covering the murdered body of twenty-year-old Cara Jones. Cara had been thrown 70-feet from the top of the bridge to the ground below.

Casey stood at the railing of the bridge and looked down at the tent. She turned to Officer Robertson, "Why do you think the killer drove her body all the way up here just to throw her off the bridge?"

He had just measured a set of skid marks on the bridge roadway, assuming it might have been caused by the killer's car, "Well, I agree with Detective Piper. I suppose the killer wanted to eliminate any evidence from Cara's body. A fall from this height could probably dislodge a lot of incriminating trace evidence when the body hit the ground."

Darren was looking down also and concurred, "Plus, the water in the creek could also wash her body away, or alligators could devour it."

Casey grimaced, "What a horrible way to die."

Officer Robertson showed them his tape measure, "The skid marks are 53 inches apart, so they were most likely caused by the tires of a full-size car."

"I assume that would rule out a Volkswagen Beetle," Casey questioned.

Robertson answered, "Yes, it definitely would have to be something larger to have tires that far apart."

Darren asked, "Like maybe a Police Squad Car?"

Robertson looked at Darren suspiciously as he responded, "I don't know, but I suppose it could be from a squad car. Why do you think it might be a police car?"

Casey interjected, "At this point in the investigation, we want to pursue all angles."

They all got into Robertson's SUV and drove down to Cara's white Volkswagen Beetle on a small abandoned paved road that led from the roadway above to The Tombs below to examine the car.

The driver's side window was halfway open, the keys were still in the ignition, and Cara's purse was still on the seat inside the car. They noticed a receipt for gas from a Chevron gas station located a few miles from the crime scene on the Tamiami Trail.

Darren put on a pair of sterile gloves and picked up the receipt, "It's dated at 10:13 p.m." He put it in a clear plastic envelope and handed it to Casey.

Casey studied it, "We'll have to go there later to find any additional clues to her murder. Maybe she met the killer there?"

"Yes, I agree. That was her last stop... alive."

They talked as they made their way toward the tent, "Since her purse was left untouched, it obviously wasn't robbery. Money and credit cards were intact."

At the entrance to the tent, Casey also put on a pair of sterile gloves. They bowed their heads down low and went inside. Casey felt saddened as she looked down at the lifeless body of Cara Jones lying in the dirt of a soggy creek bed. She was sprawled out on the ground after being thrown from the bridge above, her arms and legs stuck out in all directions, propped up by dirt and grit from lying in the mud and soaked from the rain. There were ligature wounds around her neck and a mysterious bruise on her forehead and cheekbone. The smell of human decomposition permeated the tent.

Casey meticulously examined the body and the crime scene, careful not to disturb any evidence. She surmised the cause of death appeared to be strangulation. A tear formed in her eye, and she silently said a prayer.

The Forensic Criminalist Hair and Fiber Expert had discovered a gold fiber on Cara's sweatshirt that could not be explained. It looked like a foreign fiber that did not belong to Cara and could have been a cross transference from contact with the killer. There was also a drop of blood discovered on Cara's shoe.

John Steele, the hair and fiber expert, placed the gold fiber into a sterile plastic envelope with his sterile tweezers and showed Casey, "This is the microscopic piece of gold fiber I discovered on Cara's sweatshirt."

They walked outside the tent to discuss the forensic findings further, "Do you think it's from the killer?"

"I'm not sure, but I could find no indication it belonged to the victim or anything she was wearing. We will need to scientifically analyze this evidence to determine its composition and source."

Darren asked, "Based on your expertise, do you have any idea of the origin of this kind of fiber?"

"Well, at first sight, it is an unusual piece of fiber because of its unique gold element, and I have a hunch it's probably from a uniform of some kind. Maybe military or something?"

Casey interjected, "Or a police uniform?"

He looked back curiously, "Yes, perhaps. We'll need a Forensic Research Microscopist to examine it under a microscope at the lab, to be certain."

"What about the bruises on her head and the blood on her shoe?"

"We will need an autopsy to discover what caused her bruises and a blood test to determine whether it's Cara's blood or her killer's. That will take some time."

Officer Robertson walked over to Casey and Darren as it started to drizzle, "What have you got?"

Darren answered, "The Forensics team discovered a suspicious gold fiber on Cara's sweatshirt and a spot of blood on her shoe. They will need further analysis at the lab to determine whether these are clues to who the killer was."

Casey finished the reply, "She looks like she was beaten in the face and strangled to death with a rope or something. The marks will have to be analyzed to determine what the murder weapon was and where it might be."

Robertson responded, "That fits our initial findings. We will need to go check on the Chevron Gas Station based on the receipt we found in her car. Maybe their surveillance cameras captured something or someone on video."

Casey agreed, "Let's go. I think we've gotten everything we can get from the crime scene."

CHAPTER TWENTY-THREE

Video Tape [19] [20]

Chevron Gas Station
Tamiami Trail, Everglades City, Florida

The Tamiami Trail was gradually and painfully hacked out of the Everglades swamps over countless centuries by animals, alligators, Indians, and eventually the white man. The white man believed they were civilizing Florida through the Everglades, but opened a deadly corridor to a much larger tragedy in a treacherous wilderness. From the time the "Trail" was first unearthed, it has been the scene of innumerable violent, murderous, and tragically historical events over the past 500 years, from Pirates, to Indian Wars, to Serial Killers, to Drug Smugglers, to Human Trafficking, to Gangland Murders, and beyond.

Cara Jones was just one more murdered victim to add to the frightening, bloody history of the Tamiami Trail and the "River of Grass or The Endless Glades," as the locals called the Everglades. It has been alleged to be the largest "Drop Dead Dump Zone" in America, to dispose of murdered bodies because they were often eaten by alligators or rapidly decomposed by the swamp.

It was still drizzling when Casey Collins and Darren Turner entered the Chevron gas station on the Tamiami Trail not far from the scene of the murder, based on the receipt discovered on the seat of Cara's white Volkswagen Beetle. They had observed several cameras mounted outside and hoped they might discover video surveillance tapes showing the final moments of Cara's life, and maybe her killer prior to her murder. They were hopeful something useful to the investigation might have been recorded by the cameras.

The gas station was attached to a convenience store, and Darren revealed his gold-plated FDLE shield as he asked the dark-skinned man at the counter to speak to the manager.

"I am the manager," he was of Pakistani descent and spoke with broken English. He shook his head in a combination "Yes," "No," "Maybe" swirl characteristic of his heritage, "How may I be of service to you?" The "V" in "service" sounded more like a "W," as his white teeth glinted against his dark complexion.

"I'm FDLE Agent Darren Turner, and this is Senior Agent Casey Collins." Darren held out his hand to the manager.

Casey extended hers next, also shaking the man's hand, "Hello. We need to review your video surveillance tapes from around ten o'clock two nights ago, based on the time shown on this receipt." She showed the manager the receipt in the plastic envelope recovered from Cara's car.

"Certainly, follow me." He signaled the clerk stocking shelves in the corner of the store to take over the cash register.

The manager led them toward a small door in the back of the store that opened into a tiny office with a cluttered desk and messy shelves containing bound receipt books, water bottles, extra supplies, a video monitor, and a recording machine with stacks of VCR tapes nearby. The monitor displayed six equally divided screens recording the real-time activities from the six cameras located throughout the store and the outside fuel station, "You want to see the recording from two nights ago, right?"

Casey answered anxiously, "Yes, please, a little prior to 10:00 p.m." She mentally noted that the store was using an older VCR system and not a newer CD system.

The manager scanned the hand-written dates on the white labels attached to stacked VCR tapes and removed one of them. He slid it into the video player. It showed the time in the left-hand corner of the monitor and six divided screens with various activities. He fast-forwarded the video to 9:30 p.m.

The tape started playing video that was streaked, grainy, and poor quality, making it difficult to follow. Darren asked, "Why is this video so grainy and hard to view?"

The manager responded, "I'm sorry, but our surveillance system is old, and we reuse the tapes over and over to save money. This is probably one of the older tapes."

Darren thought to himself, *Well, it is Everglades City. Everything here is old and outdated.*

After a few minutes, Casey noticed a police car in one of the divided screens. She pointed to the image, then said, "Hold on. Can you enlarge this area of the monitor?"

The manager pushed a few buttons on the player, and the six divided screens instantly became one, with the image of the police car in the center.

As Casey watched, the camera located in the parking lot showed one of the police officers getting out of the car and walking into the convenience store. She gasped because although she couldn't make out the face of the police officer in the grainy video; she thought his mannerisms and movements looked familiar.

Darren also watched as the officer in the video walked up to the counter and bought a pack of cigarettes. He wondered if the forensics team had recovered any discarded cigarette butts at the murder scene or if they were washed away in the rain. In the video, the officer then walked outside and lit up a cigarette near the police cruiser. There was another officer sitting in the car, waiting. After the first officer was finished smoking, he flicked the cigarette butt into the parking lot and got back inside the police cruiser.

Darren pointed to the screen, "We need to go outside to find that cigarette butt if we can."

"Yes, I agree." She turned back to the manager, "Can you go back to the full video of all six cameras, please?" Casey was unnerved on the inside by what she had witnessed but held it together on the outside, so Darren wouldn't notice.

They watched as the two police officers just sat in the cruiser. After about fifteen minutes, they noticed a white Volkswagen Beetle pull up to the gas station pumps and turn off the engine. A pretty young blonde girl emerged from the driver's side and started pumping gasoline into her car.

Casey exclaimed, "Oh my God, I think that's Cara."

Darren agreed, "Yes, that's her white Volkswagen Beetle."

They watched as Cara finished pumping gas and walked past the front of the police car into the convenience store.

Casey could imagine what the reaction was in the police car as they watched this beautiful young woman pass by.

On another screen, Cara walked up to the counter and paid for the gas. The clerk printed a receipt and handed it to her.

Casey turned to the manager, "We need this tape for evidence."

"Of course, whatever you need." The manager asked, "Is she the woman who was murdered at the bridge?"

"Yes. Unfortunately, she is."

As they continued to watch the video, they saw Cara walk back to her car and drive off in the direction of the bridge. A moment later, the police cruiser eased away from the curb and followed her car.

---

[20] *Sheriff Deputy Jose Sanchez Police Rapes in Los Angeles, California:*

LA Sheriff Deputy Jose Rigoberto Sanchez spotted a 24-year-old woman at a gas station in Palmdale, California. He ran her license plate and discovered she had an outstanding arrest warrant. Deputy Sanchez then arrested her, drove her to a secluded area, and raped her in the backseat of his patrol car.

CHAPTER TWENTY-FOUR

Collateral Damage [21]

Rod and Gun Club

Everglades City, Florida

Rain started falling first as an intermittent drizzle, then as a steady downpour, as Casey and Darren drove back to the Rod and Gun Club in Everglades City. Thunder rumbled loudly throughout the blackened sky. Occasional bolts of lightning shot to the ground behind the grungy hotel buildings, radiating the undersides of the dark, foreboding clouds overhead.

The windshield wipers slapped rhythmically back and forth across the windshield of the black Collier County Sheriff's SUV, as it splashed through bone-jarring potholes, leftover from the never-ending rainfall. Casey gazed out the rain-streaked window. Her view of the world outside seemed to crawl along in slow motion, as if it transformed her into an alternate, parallel dimension. It had been a brutal day and a whirlwind kaleidoscope of facts, theories, and hunches that had just come to an abrupt ending, as though someone had suddenly stepped on the brakes while she was still hurtling through space at full speed.

The investigation and her suspicions of the identity of the rapists and killers exhausted and bewildered her. Her first impulse was to share her theory with Darren, but she knew that revealing her suspicion was potentially subject to laborious scrutiny and fraught with authoritarian complications. So, for now, she decided to keep it to herself.

When they arrived back at the hotel, they said their goodbyes, and Casey and Darren went to their respective hotel rooms to rest and contemplate the investigation. They agreed to meet later for dinner.

Casey owed the Governor a status call, since she reported directly to him. She picked up the telephone receiver when she arrived in her hotel room and dialed.

The Governor's secretary answered the phone bright and cheery, "Governor Scott's office."

Casey had her most polite, authoritative, all-business voice on, expecting the usual attitude from his secretary, "May I speak to the Governor please, this is Senior Agent Collins." Of course, it was his secretary's job to screen calls for the Governor, but Casey knew there was much more to it than that. She clenched her fist, imagining the reaction on the other end of the telephone.

His secretary had a steely edge to her voice and a no-nonsense attitude, "He's in a meeting with his chief of staff and will be with you as soon as he finishes. Please hold." She was a ball-buster. Once she realized it was Casey Collins on the phone, there was no respect or friendliness.

Casey waited on hold and visualized his secretary pouting with those full red lips of hers. Her finely manicured, polished fingernails tapping fiercely on the desktop, stalling, hesitating to put her call through to the Governor.

Finally, she came back on the phone, "I'll transfer you to his office now."

He answered the phone with his gentle, caring voice, "Hello, Casey."

She answered him back in a soothing tone, simply saying, "Hi." Relieved to hear his voice on the other end of the phone.

She could almost hear a smile in his voice, "How are you? How is the wild, wild Southwest?"

She smiled back into the telephone receiver, "Well, it feels a little like I'm on Mars. They have no *Starbucks,* no *McDonald's* and no *Dunkin' Donuts.* Plus, they only take cash in this place. No credit cards. You're the Governor, how can you allow this?"

"Ha, I guess it's not New York City."

She thought about how Darren had said the same thing, "No, it's definitely not."

"How is the investigation going?"

"I'm piecing together some clues, and it's not a pretty picture."

The Governor's attitude transformed into serious concern. His tone changed to all-business. This was personal to him; this killer raped and murdered his daughter, Susan, "What have you uncovered?"

"We found a gold fiber on Cara Jones's sweatshirt."

"A gold fiber? What's the significance of that?"

"It's a foreign fiber that apparently did not belong to Cara and could have been a cross transference from contact with her killer. We have a Forensic Criminalist Hair and Fiber Expert examining whether it could be a clue to who the killer was. It will need further analysis at the lab."

"When you say gold, is it just the color gold, or does it have metallic qualities?"

"It appears metallic, as if it came from a uniform."

"Hmm, do you mean like a military uniform?"

"Yes. Or a police uniform."

"That fits the Lindsay Baily case since she claims two policemen or impostors attacked her."

"Yes. Although, the DNA evidence showed it was only one rapist."

"That seems like a difficult conundrum."

"Yes, but we have more. We also found a spot of blood on Cara's shoe. Hopefully, the DNA will provide another clue to who the killer was."

"That could be strong forensic evidence. What if the DNA is not in the Criminal DNA Database? Lindsay Baily claimed two police officers attacked her. Also, Kimberly Merrick had what appears to be a police boot print on her back. The Criminal DNA Database will not have police officer DNA."

Casey thought about that for a moment before answering. She wondered about her DNA, "That will complicate things, but eventually, we'll find a match. We'll just have to utilize different techniques."

Brendan probed further, "Do you have any hunches or educated guesses?"

Casey caught her breath, "We discovered surveillance video of Cara Jones at a Chevron gas station on the Tamiami Trail the night she was murdered."

It encouraged the Governor, "Really? Was there anything helpful to the investigation on the video?"

Casey hesitated for a moment.

"What is it, Casey?"

"Yes. Unfortunately, the gas station has an old, out-of-date VCR recording system, and the video is very poor quality and difficult to follow. We need to get it enhanced at the lab, but it shows Cara at the gas station in her white Volkswagen Beetle. She filled up her car and then walked to the counter to pay the bill. We discovered the receipt in her car at the crime scene."

"Wow. That's helpful. Anything else?"

"Yes." She took another deep breath, "There was a police car parked by the curb. When Cara drove away, the police car followed her."

"Oh, my God. Could you see the police car identification?"

"It was a poor-quality recording. Very grainy, so we can't identify the police car until we send it to the lab for further diagnostics."

"Could you identify the police officers?"

She played the scene over again in her mind, remembering the familiar mannerisms and movements, "We couldn't make out faces or badge numbers. We need to wait until the lab can enhance the video."

"What about GPS tracking? Can you find out what police car was at that gas station that night?"

"We're checking that, but unfortunately, GPS tracking can be disabled if the police car computer is turned off."

"My God, that doesn't sound right."

"I know. I guess it was assumed there would be no reason to turn a police computer off in a police cruiser."

"That needs to be changed." He measured her response and thought about whether they could also be his daughter's killers, "Do you think they could be responsible for killing Susan?"

She could hear the desperation in his voice. His daughter was everything to him. She was his only child. Any father would feel pain and guilt for not being able to protect his children. But Susan was twenty-five-years old and had a life of her own. Obviously, a father can't always be there to protect his children. Still, a father and daughter relationship, is different, at least if the father is normal, which was something she couldn't relate to because her father was not normal, "We can't be sure yet, but I'll continue to push hard to find her killer or killers. I can promise you that."

"I know, Casey. Thank you."

Her last question was about his wife's condition, "Brendan, how is Mary doing?"

"Not good. The doctors tell me she's fading fast. This monster murdered Susan, and now he or they are killing Mary as well."

"We'll catch whoever is responsible. I promise."

She hated keeping secrets from him, but before she could tell him her theory, she needed to be sure.

---

[21] _Police Officer George Gwaltney Rape and Murder in Los Angeles, California:_

California Highway Patrol Police Officer George Gwaltney, raped and murdered 23-year-old, aspiring actress, Robin Bishop, after a routine traffic stop, off of a deserted stretch of Interstate 15 in the Mojave Desert. He handcuffed and raped her in the backseat of his patrol car, then shot her to death in the head with his service revolver.

CHAPTER TWENTY-FIVE

Broken Man

Governor's Mansion
Tallahassee, Florida

Governor Brendan Scott stared out his office window contemplating his conversation with Casey Collins as rain continued falling throughout overcast skies in Tallahassee. He was shaken and distraught by her latest revelations regarding the Rape Task Force investigation. He knew he could never recover from his daughter's murder unless he found her killer. He obsessed about finding her killer. Susan deserved justice.

He wanted some time to think, to be alone for the evening, and decided to drive himself to the Governor's Mansion in Tallahassee instead of having his Security Guard drive him. He approached L.B. to give him the night off.

"L.B., I just got off the phone with Casey, and she gave me the latest update regarding the investigation. It left me feeling a little downhearted. I'm going to take a drive home by myself tonight, to contemplate everything. You can have the night off."

L.B. completely understood. He'd been the Governor's friend long enough to appreciate his mind and his moods. He knew that driving his car occasionally helped the Governor think more clearly, "Okay, Brendan. If you're sure."

"I am L.B. I'll see you tomorrow."

"Okay, boss. Drive carefully."

He drove out of the parking garage with the windows wide open in his new, blue BMW 740i. Although it seemed ill-timed now, he had treated himself to the Beemer following his election victory. He figured he had earned a reward after countless years of backbreaking effort. But now he felt guilty driving the plush, polished vehicle since his daughter was murdered and his wife was comatose, and his life was crumbling all around him.

He thought to himself, *whenever you celebrate success, it will always be a bit too early and then, look what happens... the world comes up and bites you in the ass.*

He turned onto the entrance ramp of the highway and moved to the outside lane. He downshifted from fourth to third gear and eased the accelerator pedal down. The engine roared as the valve timing tweaked and burned the high-octane fuel as he charged down the highway. The velocity felt as if it were giving him additional power passing all the other vehicles on the road.

The Florida Governor's Mansion was magnificent, even on this morbidly gloomy evening. Perfectly groomed lush green rolling hills, with expertly pruned trees and meticulously manicured shrubbery, lined the freshly mowed grass surrounding the circular driveway leading up to the mansion's main entrance. The sounds of rippling water rapidly churning over cobblestones echoed from a meandering brook as it flowed inevitably to the vast Gulf of Mexico. A trace of rock maple smoke wafted in the air from a wood-burning fireplace in a nearby neighbor's home.

He maneuvered his BMW around the circular driveway and sat with both hands on the car's steering wheel, staring into the distance. He listened to the powerful engine idling and imagined his daughter running outside to greet him with a big happy smile and a big hug.

"Daddy's home, Daddy's home," as she used to long-ago before he was Governor. He wished he could go back to that happy place and space in time. He felt overwhelmed with grief, knowing that could never happen again. He switched the engine off and slowly lumbered out the car door.

He walked despondently toward the stone and granite steps, dragging his feet one step in front of the other, in a gloomy daze. Usually, he would dash home from the State Capitol, spend an hour or so with his wife Mary, grab some dinner, and then rush to his home office as quickly as possible, tending to the business of the State. Now, he was standing in the driveway, frozen in time, feeling emptiness and pain, not knowing what to do next.

Walking inside the oversized double mahogany doors, even the beauty of his home, which once was his haven, no longer comforted him. The wood paneling, marble floors, and mural walls provided a nineteenth-century ambiance. The leaded glass windows sparkled, and the bronze trim glowed. He walked through the grand two-story living room dominated by an ancient stone wood-burning fireplace. Over the mantle hung a huge oil portrait of the Governor standing with his wife and daughter sitting in front of the same fireplace. It stopped him in his tracks as he pondered it. He truly loved his wife and had continued to hope she would snap out of her coma, but he knew down deep inside, it would probably never happen. The center of their world, their only child, was dead. They had no hope. Susan could never come back.

In his den, he opened the liquor cabinet, poured a double brandy, and sat at his handmade Maitland-Smith oak executive desk in his well-appointed home office. The matching oak credenza displayed photographs of his wife and daughter smiling broadly in sterling silver frames. The largest photo captured them in front of the family beach house down by the Apalachicola coast on the Gulf of Mexico. He reminisced about happier times as he gazed out over the shadowy trees at dusk overlooking the grounds of the Governor's Mansion.

The Governor was at the pinnacle of his political career, but that didn't matter to him anymore. He was a broken man, and the only thing that mattered was finding his daughter's rapist and killer. He would get vengeance for Susan, one way or another.

CHAPTER TWENTY-SIX

Dinner Date

Rod and Gun Club

Everglades City, Florida

Darren spotted Casey walking into the restaurant from a distance. She looked stunning as she stepped through the doorway and searched the room for him. She moved like a goddess - slim and silky, her hair and dress floating as if a breeze were blowing even in the quietest air. She reminded him of *The Girl from Ipanema*. As he watched, he played the song in his mind.

He saw heads snap as male patrons turned to look at her as she passed. He hoped they didn't recognize her and searched around the room for familiar faces. She sashayed over to the bar to meet him, "Well, hello. You look beautiful tonight."

Besides being smart and successful, Casey was so attractive; she could have chosen to be a model. She was ten years younger than Darren, and the dimples that flashed in her cheeks whenever she smiled made her look even younger. She parted her long blonde hair on the side, and had it brushed across her forehead, just above her baby-blue eyes.

She smiled back at him, "Thank you, Darren. You clean up pretty well yourself."

Just looking at Casey aroused him. He gazed at her every feature: her creamy complexion, her luscious lips. He leaned forward discreetly and strained to sniff the perfume fragrance she was wearing.

The bartender stared openly at Casey as he walked over to take their drink order, then stood there, wiping off the bar in front of her several times over.

Darren spoke up sharply, "Excuse me." Pointedly interrupting the bartender's gawking, "We'd like two Bombay Gin Martinis straight up, very cold. And some spares on the olives."

The bartender grinned at Casey, "Why don't I just bring over the entire bottle of olives for you?"

Darren laughed, "Why didn't I think of that? Then we could skip dinner altogether and just have Martinis and olives all night."

The bartender reluctantly turned away to get the drinks, and Darren poured his attention on Casey.

Casey was all business as usual, "Dennis Hollis got back to me today. The boot print on Kimberly Merrick's neck and back are positively from police issued boots. Someone very large stomped on her back with a big police boot, running at full speed, and broke her neck. The tracks on the dirt road also match the boot print on her back."

"What size boot was it?"

"Size twelve."

Darren considered her answer, "I assume they are tracking down anyone that wears a size twelve in the department."

"Yes, they are."

"So, all we have are boot prints, and I assume tire tracks."

"There's more. The tire tracks measured 53 inches apart. The same measurement as the tire tracks on the bridge above Cara Jones."

Darren smiled, "So it's all beginning to point in the same direction."

The bartender returned with their drinks and two dinner menus.

Darren sipped his Martini thoughtfully as he looked at the dinner menu.

Casey raised her glass as if to propose a toast, "And we have some better news with the Cara Jones forensics also." She took a drink before continuing.

Darren perked up, "What'd they find?"

She turned to look directly at him, "Gary Harmon, with the Serological Research Institute in Fort Lauderdale, analyzed the blood spot found on Cara's shoe, and it did not match Cara's blood type. Harmon said he used a complex and sophisticated scientific test to match the so-called genetic markers derived from the blood spot on the shoe to genetic qualities found in a sample of Cara's blood."

Darren mulled that over, "That means it has to be the killer's blood. Maybe Cara scratched him as she fought off his attack?"

"Yes, she did. They discovered skin cells under Cara's fingernails, in addition to the blood on her shoe. So, we have DNA but just need to find who it belongs to."

"Gary said the blood spot on the shoe definitely did not come from Cara and only about one percent of the world's population has similar genetic markers in their blood. This percentage amounts to one in every seventy-five Caucasians and not at all in non-Caucasians."

"So that means our killer is definitely white."

"Right. Or killers."

Just then, the bartender returned to take their orders. He looked at Casey first, "What would you like to order?"

Casey joked with him over the menu, "What's good tonight? Any specials? Anything we should avoid?"

He grinned, "Actually, everything's good, now that I just served the last order of dishwater soup." He laughed, adding, "Really, the Grouper is super-fresh; just came off the boat today."

Darren and Casey replied in unison, "That sounds good."

The bartender smiled and turned away, "All-righty then."

Casey returned to business, "More good news. The microscopic piece of gold fiber found on Cara's sweatshirt was further studied, and a police hair-fiber expert determined that the fiber possibly matched thread samples found on Florida Police Patrol patches."

Darren's eyes widened, "So, the killer could be a cop."

"Maybe, or someone with access to a uniform."

"Any DNA from the rape kit?"

"Unfortunately, it's inconclusive. I think she fought so hard that the rape never occurred. I'm surmising she scratched him, and that caused the blood we found on her shoe and the skin cells under her fingernails, which will match his DNA."

After dinner, Darren walked Casey back to her hotel room. They were both loosened up by multiple Martinis. He kissed her tenderly on her lips, "Can we go inside your room for a nightcap?"

Casey had her back against the hotel room door as he planted his kiss. She had trouble resisting him. What was between them was too powerful. They were edging closer toward the cliff, treading on dangerous ground. She looked at him pensively for a moment, then turned and unlocked the door.

Once inside, Darren tried to get closer and kiss her again, but she turned her head sideways.

He whispered, "C'mon Casey, you know I love you." He continued hugging her tightly and ran his hand up her dress to unbutton it. He kissed her again, and this time, she kissed him back.

She struggled with her feelings for him, and the alcohol only intensified her emotions. Their relationship had been limping along, frozen in place by the need to sustain business contact, but without intimacy. So, all Casey and Darren could do was talk shop and try to keep their hands off each other.

Darren walked Casey backward toward the bed as he kissed her and started to undress her.

Casey's thoughts turned to Brendan. She loved him and missed him. She couldn't do this and firmly pushed Darren back, "Darren, I don't think we should do this. Not now."

He acted like he didn't hear her and continued to caress and kiss her.

She said it more forcefully, "No, Darren, I can't do this. Please leave."

Darren reluctantly stopped and looked at Casey, persuasively, "Casey, you can't stop our feelings for each other."

She shook her head and said, "I can't, Darren. I'm sorry."

Darren released his embrace and slowly walked toward the hotel room door. He turned to Casey, "Goodnight, Casey."

"Goodnight, Darren." After Darren walked out, she closed the door firmly behind him and locked it.

She thought about Brendan and wondered if he was thinking about her too.

Little did she know, Brendan was seven hours away kissing another woman!

CHAPTER TWENTY-SEVEN

The Last Kiss

Tallahassee Memorial Hospital

Tallahassee, Florida

The Governor kissed Mary tenderly on her lips as she took her last breath in life, "I love you, Darling," were the last words she heard, if she could hear at all.

He was distraught and held her hand as he watched his wife finally succumb to her fatality and pass away at the hospital. He leaned over, put his head on her shoulder, and started to cry. She was gone... Forever.

Whoever raped and murdered his daughter had now also killed his wife.

The funeral was five-days later on an overcast, rainy day. The line of black limousines, police cruisers, and motorcycles, with lights flashing, for the official State Funeral Procession, seemed to go on forever. All the top dignitaries in the State, the Vice President of the United States, and several US Senators and Congressmen attended the funeral service. There were almost as many Secret Service and police officers, dressed in black and blue uniforms, protecting all the dignitaries, as there were guests attending the funeral.

L.B., Casey, and Darren sat in the front row leading the FDLE contingent, as the Governor solemnly delivered his wife's eulogy over her casket at the cemetery:

"Today is the day I have dreaded for the past year. Because Mary has been in-and-out of life-threatening complications caused by her heart attack for the past year. Today is the day we bury a very special and classy lady, who I am proud to say was my wife."

He paused to clear his throat, "For the past year, I have watched Mary slowly, but steadily fade away, in the Intensive Care Unit of Tallahassee Memorial Hospital. I thought we were going to lose her many times, but she kept fighting back. I began to believe she was a cat, with nine-lives, and became conditioned to her surviving even the most difficult medical symptoms... Until now. Mary fought hard to live and almost made it, but ultimately the doctors ran out of options, and Mary ran out of time."

Brendan paused to wipe a tear from his eye, "Everyone who knew Mary loved Mary, and it's difficult to find words adequate to honor her memory. So, the best thing we can do today is share some of the fond memories we have of her. We will all miss Mary very much, and after this service this morning, we will bury her next to her beloved daughter, Susan, to rest for all eternity. We can only pray she is now reunited with Susan and at peace. And also hope Susan and God have a glass of champagne ready for her when Mary arrives in heaven."

"In reality, Mary died the day our daughter, Susan, died. In reality, the same man that raped and murdered our daughter killed Mary. We all want justice... Justice for two senseless and needless deaths caused by this murderer, who didn't even know how truly wonderful Mary and Susan were. As the Governor of the State of Florida, I vow to catch this killer and make sure he gets the punishment he deserves. I will not rest until justice is served for the murders of Mary and Susan."

The Governor bent over and kissed the mahogany casket containing the body of his beloved wife and placed a single rose on top, "God Bless Mary. The world will be a sadder place without her." He stopped at the gravesite of Susan, next to the gravesite of Mary, and briefly said a prayer while reading her granite gravestone.

Casey led the procession of mourners following the Governor and his security guard, L.B. Rouselle. Each placed a single rose on her casket before Mary was lowered into the ground, forever. Casey expressed her condolences to the Governor, "Brendan, I am truly sorry for you. Mary was a wonderful woman and Susan was a wonderful daughter and also a wonderful friend of mine. They did not deserve to die like this."

Tears filled his eyes. He hugged Casey tightly and whispered in her ear, "Casey, who killed them? You've got to find him. He killed my daughter and my wife, and he destroyed my life. You've got to find him."

CHAPTER TWENTY-EIGHT

Badge of Deceit [22]

---

22 Tyler Street
Miami, Florida

Police Officers Gustavo and Angelo Slayton were patrolling their regular route around the city when an emergency 911 call came across the scanner in their police cruiser. It was three o'clock in the afternoon.

"Woman reports attempted break-in at 22 Tyler
Street. Units in the vicinity respond."

Gus looked over at Angelo, "That's the next street over. Should we take it?"

Angelo agreed, "Sure, why not. Let's see what this bitch looks like." They both had a chuckle over that.

Gus responded, "This is car 54, heading over to the Tyler Street break-in." He switched on the siren and the rolling red and blue police cruiser lights from the cruiser's rooftop lightbar and raced to the house on Tyler Street.

The twin police brothers stood at the front door of 22 Tyler Street and rang the doorbell. It was a single-story ranch home with a brick front and a paved walkway, a typical style house for the neighborhood. Everything appeared normal and undisturbed from the outside.

Suddenly, a frantic 19-year-old female answered the door in a panic, "Oh my God, thank God you're here. I'm really scared."

Angelo and Gus grinned at each other deviously, as they admired this beautiful young damsel in distress and walked into the house. She was sexy, well-endowed, and vulnerable in her tight blue jeans and sweatshirt.

Gus tried to quiet her down, "Calm down, ma'am. Tell us what happened."

A young boy came running over to the three of them standing in the foyer. He looked about 15-years old, "Officer, they shattered the window. There's glass everywhere."

Gus took the lead, "Who broke what window? Where?"

The young girl blurted, "In the bathroom. Someone threw a brick through the window. Come on, and I'll show you."

First, Angelo wanted to know if there were any men in the house, "Wait a minute, wait a minute. Who else is in the house besides you two - and what are your names?" He took out a pad and pen to make it look official.

"My name is Brenda Romney, and this is my brother Luke. There are also two young children asleep in bed upstairs. Thankfully, they weren't awakened by the break-in."

Angelo flipped the pad over to a new page and posed as if he were ready to write down every word, "Did somebody break into the house? Was anything stolen? Anybody hurt?"

Brenda answered, "I don't think so. We heard a loud crash coming from the bathroom, and when we opened the door, we noticed someone had smashed the window in by a brick. That's when we called 911 for help."

The twin brothers looked at each other again. A plan was coming together in their minds instinctively without even talking about it. This was too good an opportunity to pass up.

159

Gus took charge, "Okay, Brenda, take me to the bathroom so I can investigate what happened. We'll have to write up a report, which you'll probably need for your insurance company as well. Angelo, you stay here with the boy and be on the lookout to make sure everyone is safe."

"Okay. Will do." Angelo gave his brother a wink and then turned to the boy, "Luke, do you have any purified water? I'm thirsty."

"Yes, officer. I'll get you a glass." The boy started walking toward the faucet in the kitchen.

"No, Luke. I only drink bottled water." He made up a story to get the boy out of the house.

"I'm sorry, officer, but we don't have any bottled water."

Angelo opened the front door and walked outside with the boy following him, "Well, son, there's a convenience store up the street. Could you get me a couple of bottles?" Angelo took a 10-dollar bill out of his pocket and handed it to Luke, "And get something for yourself with the change."

The boy looked at the money and then at the police officer. He smiled excitedly, "Sure. Thanks. I'll be right back."

Angelo watched him walk up the street and then closed the front door and locked it, before heading to the bathroom to join Gus.

Gus followed Brenda through the hallway leading to the bathroom. He admired her tight ass in tight blue jeans ahead of him as they walked. She was a beautiful redhead, about five-feet-six-inches, with a voluptuous figure and big breasts under her baggy sweatshirt. He could feel his groin tighten as he followed her. He knew this was going to be good.

They reached the bathroom doorway, and Brenda walked over to the window above the bathtub with Gus behind her, "See, somebody threw a brick through the window and smashed it."

Gus pretended he was investigating the damage. A brick was lying in the bathtub surrounded by glass and broken framing from the window. He was thankful there wasn't any glass on the bathroom floor. As Brenda turned around to speak to Gus, he punched her hard in the face and forced her on her back onto the floor. He jumped on top of her to hold her down while her legs were thrashing around his back.

Her face exploded in pain. She felt her nose break and blood splatter all over the floor. She struggled to escape his grip. She cried out in fear, "STOP! WHY ARE YOU DOING THIS? STOP!"

He hit her again with such force that it loosened a few teeth in her mouth.

Gus was strong; he held both her hands up over her head with his large left hand and reached for a small washcloth from the towel rack above him with his right hand. He crammed the washcloth into her mouth to shut her up and ripped open her sweatshirt.

Angelo entered the bathroom from behind and helped hold her down on the floor while Gus unzipped her blue jeans and slid them off one leg. Gus unfastened his belt buckle and unzipped his pants.

Angelo stripped her blue jeans off and held her legs spread apart.

Brenda fought back, but she was no match for these two large, powerful police officers holding her down. She felt her panties torn away, and then they pushed her legs up toward her chin.

Gus had a mean, sadistic, crazy look on his face, and overpowered her.

She tried to cry out as he raped her, but the washcloth choked-off her screams. It went on and on. It hurt her so much, but there was nothing she could do to stop him until he finally exploded inside of her.

When Gus finished, he backed away and got off her. Then Gus and Angelo traded places, and Angelo got on top of her.

She mumbled through the washcloth and tried to cry out in pain, "NO! STOP!"

Angelo hit her in the face so hard it knocked her out. She stopped moving. His eyes rolled back behind his eyelids, and he groaned as he raped her.

When he finished, Angelo stood up next to Gus and pulled his pants on. They both looked down at Brenda spread out on the bloody bathroom floor.

They heard the doorbell ringing in the foyer.

Angelo looked worried and said, "Uh-oh, we didn't report back to dispatch. That might be them at the door."

Gus replied, "Shit."

CHAPTER TWENTY-NINE

The Blue Curtain [22]

22 Tyler Street

Miami, Florida

Little Luke was outside frantically ringing the doorbell while holding two bottles of spring water and a half-finished bottle of soda. He started banging on the door, "Let me in, Brenda. Let me in."

Angelo answered the door disheveled, tucking in his shirt and pulling up his zipper. Gus was close behind. It relieved him to see Luke and not police officers, "Oh, Luke, right... Thank you for getting the water." He grabbed the water bottles from the kid and handed one off to Gus behind him.

Seeing how tousled they both were, Luke was concerned that there really might have been an intruder who had attacked the police officers. He watched Angelo straightening his uniform, "What happened? Where's Brenda?" He was looking past them, searching inside the house for his sister with his eyes.

"Oh, she's in the bathroom. She had a little, umm... Accident, slipped on the broken glass and fell down." Angelo glanced back at Gus and grinned.

Suddenly, Brenda came screaming out of the bathroom, naked from the waist down with only a torn sweatshirt on and bleeding, "THEY RAPED ME! THEY RAPED ME!" She started hitting Gus in the chest with her fists.

Luke watched the scene unfold with his bloody sister punching the police officer in the chest, "Brenda, what are you doing?"

"THEY RAPED ME!" She screamed in anger, tears rolling down her eyes.

Angelo reached behind his back to get the handcuffs from his belt and seized Brenda's arms to subdue her, "Brenda, you're under arrest for hitting an officer of the law." He handcuffed her behind her back and started leading her out to the patrol car.

Luke was dazed and confused, "What are you doing? You can't arrest her. She's hurt and needs medical attention."

Angelo pushed Luke away, "Step aside, little man. Your sister is going to jail for attacking a police officer."

"What?"

A crowd of neighbors had gathered on the street, as Luke watched the two police officers take Brenda to their squad car and place her in the galvanized cage in the back seat. All the while, Brenda was squirming to get free of Angelo's overpowering grip. She was in shock, and all she could scream was, "THEY RAPED ME! THEY RAPED ME!"

The twins knew that no one would believe her at the police station. The Blue Curtain protected all police officers. They figured she was young and naïve and probably wouldn't know enough to ask for an attorney. They would book her, fingerprint her, and put her in jail until she agreed not to press charges against them for rape.

Later, the District Attorney, citing a lack of evidence, declined to prosecute the police officers.

---

[22] **_Police Officer Ladmarald Cates Rape in Milwaukee, Wisconsin:_**

When a brick crashed through her bathroom window, the 19-year-old single mother of two in Milwaukee, Wisconsin, dialed what are supposed to be the most trustworthy three numbers: "911." Police Officer Ladmarald Cates responded and asked to see the broken window. She led him down a narrow hallway to the bathroom, and at that moment, the police officer she had summoned to protect her, instead punched her in the face and raped her. Her revulsion was so visceral that she ran outside, screaming the police raped her. Police Officer Cates immediately handcuffed and arrested her. She was charged with the assault of a police officer and jailed.

CHAPTER THIRTY

Law & Out of Order [22]

NBC6 Television Station

Miami, Florida

The next day, Tina Evanston and the NBC6 Investigators reported breaking news:

BREAKING NEWS!

The Rhapsody Killers

"She tried to commit suicide while in jail. This is a case of Law & Order... Out of Order."

Tina was on the attack:

"The District Attorney cites lack of evidence, even though the rape test kit tested positive for semen and Brenda Romney had a black eye and a broken nose. If this was consensual sex, then I'm an Orangutan."

Her outrage over the police cover-up by the District Attorney was broadcast loud and clear:

"The 19-year-old mother of two is in jail, while The Rhapsody Rapists and Killers that raped her are somehow

out on the streets and remain employed as cops. This is all wrong. Where is the justice for Brenda Romney?"

"This is Tina Evanston Reporting for NBC6 Investigators."

Brenda felt like they had brainwashed her. She began to doubt her own sanity and her own self-worth. The Slayton brothers called her a liar, the Chief of Police called her a liar, Internal Affairs called her a liar, the District Attorney called her a liar, and she was even beginning to doubt her own story. Maybe, she thought, *she really was a liar.* She was so distraught and depressed that she decided to take her own life, thinking her children would be better off growing up without her.

The Slayton brothers would have been happy if Brenda Romney had been successful in her attempt to commit suicide, but unfortunately, a prison guard heard the commotion in her prison cell and rescued her before the noose which she had fashioned out of bedsheets, tightened around her neck.

Gus and Angelo realized they had made a strategic mistake letting her live in the first place. They could have claimed that whoever threw the brick through the window, came back and killed her. Now, they had to defend themselves against the charges of rape, and they could not deny that they were at the scene of the crime, since they took the police 911 call. And, on top of everything else, they had the television "Goddess of Miami News" on their case. Luckily for them, the Blue Curtain continued to shield them... so far.

The Slayton brothers watched Tina Evanston's Breaking News report, from the large video screen, usually reserved for broadcasting sporting events, in the bar at McCabe's Irish Pub where they had stopped to eat on their late-shift. There were no major games at six o'clock, so the news was on. Tina looked like a beautiful movie star as she moved her lips in slow motion, apparently saying something important, but all the noisy clatter and chatter in the bar drowned the words out. The headline at the bottom of the screen shouted in capital letters as she continued moving her lips:

BREAKING NEWS!

The Rhapsody Killers

"SHE CALLED 911, AND WAS RAPED BY THE POLICE."

Then Gus saw the photo of his face, and then Angelo's face flash across the screen. He poked his brother in the side to get his attention, "Bro, did you see that?"

Angelo was chewing on a burger and looked up, "Yes, I see her. She's hot, Bro." He said, laughing, "Maybe we should arrest her and put her in the back of our cruiser."

Gus was getting frustrated, "Angelo, I know she's hot, but did you see the headlines? We're on the news."

"Shit. No, I was just looking at her."

Gus looked around the bar at the other patrons in the Pub to see if anyone had noticed that his face had just appeared on NBC6 television, but no one looked back at him... No one had noticed. It was Happy Hour, and they were all drinking beer, eating chips, laughing, and talking. Unless there was a game on, nobody paid much attention to the video screens. *What happens at McCabe's, Stays at McCabe's.*

Rachel Slayton saw Gus Slayton's face on the television in Miami, as she watched the news at six o'clock from her kitchen while feeding Gus Junior his dinner. She put her hand over her mouth in shock, "Oh, my God."

BREAKING NEWS!

The Rhapsody Killers

"SHE CALLED 911, AND WAS RAPED BY THE POLICE."

Little Gus Junior also saw his father's face on television, "Mommy, Mommy, Daddy's on television." He giggled and was excited to see his father on the news.

Even though he was only five-years-old, Gus Junior was beginning to understand the world around him, so Rachel quickly picked up the remote control and turned the television off before he could hear any of the details of the report.

Gus Junior looked up at his mother, confused, "Mommy, why did you do that? Daddy was just on the television."

"Because, little boy, I want you to eat your dinner. You'll see Daddy when he gets home from work."

The Governor was watching the news from his office in Tallahassee. He had several video screens arranged to monitor events in multiple cities across the State. He was particularly interested in the coverage from Miami and Fort Lauderdale, since that had been the scene of most of the crimes. When he saw Tina Evanston, he turned up the volume on that television and focused on NBC6 news from Miami.

Tina Evanston posed in front of McCabe's Irish Pub, waiting to confront the Slayton Brothers as they exited the Pub. Bright lights glared at her and the Irish Pub behind her from lightbars held by her camera crew. There were crowds of curious onlookers eager to watch the live television coverage or perhaps get a chance to be part of the surreal scene if the camera panned over toward them.

BREAKING NEWS!

The Rhapsody Killers

"This is Tina Evanston, NBC6 Investigators, reporting live from McCabe's Irish Pub in downtown Miami."

"The police officers accused of raping Brenda Romney are inside their favorite hangout right now, and we are waiting for them to come outside."

Just then, the brothers walked out of the pub, and into Tina's waiting ensnarement. The television camera panned over to Gus Slayton's face. She couldn't tell them apart, so she just asked a general question:

"Officer Slayton, what is your reaction to the accusations of rape against both of you?"

Gus looked Tina up and down lustfully and brusquely pushed the camera aside.

"We have no comment."

Angelo leered at Tina and followed close behind Gus out of the pub. The camera crew followed them to their police cruiser until they both got in and drove away.

The Governor watched and noted the brothers and their location. He questioned the television screen, "Did you rape and kill my daughter?"

Casey Collins watched Tina Evanston on the 6 o'clock news from her apartment in Tallahassee. They replayed a video clip from earlier in the day.

BREAKING NEWS!

The Rhapsody Killers

"I called 911 for help." Brenda Romney said into the microphone held by Tina Evanston in front of the Police Station. "I didn't call 911 to be the victim."

She was standing on the steps leading to the entrance to the building near the sign that proclaimed, "To Protect and Serve."

Casey thought it was either ironic or well-planned to have Brenda interviewed next to that sign.

The District Attorney walked out, and Tina ran over to him with her camera crew and shoved the microphone into his face.

"Sir, will your office be charging the accused Slayton brothers with rape?"

The District Attorney was a little roughened by the intrusion, but answered Tina directly. He looked into the television camera for his 15 seconds of fame:

"No. While I found the victim's version of events credible, I do not believe her testimony would be strong enough to successfully prosecute the police officers."

He turned and got into his waiting limousine to leave.

Tina turned to the television camera to sum things up:

"So, there you have it. The Blue Curtain once again protecting the Police and the Police Department. The justice system is so stacked against the victims that most of the time, they just give up and drop the charges. That is what they want to happen to Brenda Romney. But not this

time. The NBC6 Investigators want justice for Brenda, and we will stay on this story until justice prevails. The Rhapsody Rapists and Killers will not get away with this violation of Brenda Romney!"

"This is Tina Evanston, NBC6 news."

Casey had no doubt her brothers had done it again. They were trying to tap-dance their way out of it, but she was sure, eventually, they would get caught. Even if they were found guilty of raping Brenda Romney, it was not the conviction she wanted. Rape is bad enough, but Casey wanted them both for murder. *Especially* the murder of the Governor's daughter. She just had to find a way to prove it.

CHAPTER THIRTY-ONE

Salsa [22]

CUBACU Restaurant

Miami Beach, Art Deco Historic District, Florida

In 1870, father and son Henry and Charles Lum purchased the land comprising Miami Beach for 75 cents an acre. The first structure built on this desolate oceanfront was the Biscayne House of Refuge, constructed in 1876 by the United States Life Saving Service through an executive order issued by President Ulysses S. Grant. Its purpose was to save the lives of people shipwrecked in the Atlantic Ocean. Eventually, the United States Life Saving Service became the United States Coast Guard in 1915.

The new Cuban restaurant and dance club named "CUBACU," an acronym for Cuban Cuisine, was in the Miami Beach Art Deco Historic District on Ocean Drive. It had a hip Miami Beach upbeat, contemporary design, and the aroma of the charcoal-fired grill permeated the restaurant, enticing the patron's appetites.

Tina Evanston loved to Salsa dance, and Darren Turner was a pragmatist: *he did whatever was necessary to get Tina into bed.* So, there he was, Salsa dancing at the newest Miami Beach hotspot, trying his best not to step on Tina's eight-hundred-dollar "Jimmy Choo" alligator leather six-inch high-heel shoes. It was Saturday night, and the dance floor was packed, so he was thankful when the band took a break.

They were seated at a "front-row table" overlooking the expansive beach and the vast Atlantic Ocean, thanks to Tina's celebrity status. It was spectacular. In between interruptions from fans asking for Tina's autograph, they were having a beautiful dinner, and a fantastic bottle of 1998 Cabernet Sauvignon Reserve.

Tina interrogated Darren about the latest details of The Rhapsody Killers investigation. "So, Brenda Romney identified the Slayton brothers as her attackers. Why are they still cops, and why are they still walking around free?"

Darren swirled his Cabernet in his glass and enjoyed the aroma before answering her questions, "We have visual identification, but we don't have evidentiary proof that a rape actually occurred or who did it."

She looked at him like, *Duh.* Then, cut into her filet mignon steak, "You have a semen sample from the rape test kit, don't you?"

He placed his glass down on the table. It felt like he was getting cross-examined on trial, "Yes, but it could've been consensual, and it doesn't match any DNA we've searched in our Databases."

The server came over to their table and poured more Cabernet for them, "Consensual! What are you drinking? She is all bruised and beat-up. Definitely not consensual."

He looked back at her, "I agree with you, but the DA doesn't want to prosecute."

Tina continued her questioning, "Do you have a DNA Database for cops?"

Darren needed another drink. He knew she wouldn't like this answer either, "No. We do not require Police to provide DNA samples."

She stared at him incredulously, "Well, that's pretty stupid. Why is that?"

Darren agreed cops should provide DNA, although they do not require it according to police policy, "I don't know. Although I agree we should."

She slammed down her fork on the table, "This is crazy. We have a victim identifying cops as her attackers, you know who the cops are, and you don't have the DNA to prove it?"

Other patrons in the restaurant looked over at their table as the discussion got more and more heated. Darren chewed on his lobster tail before answering, "No. I'm afraid not."

Tina was working up a temper tantrum, "Well, how about this? Get the Slayton brothers to submit their DNA. Why don't you do that?"

He was getting frustrated trying to enjoy dinner out with Tina, but constantly getting interrogated, "We would need a judge to order that, and since the District Attorney is unwilling to prosecute, the judge will not order it on the grounds of insufficient evidence."

That got her even more annoyed, "Oh, my God! Oh, my God! The Blue Curtain again. This is crazy. Really insane."

Darren was getting defensive, "Hold on Tina. It isn't all that cut-and-dried. There are also inconsistencies in Romney's story. She claims two men raped her, but the DNA only indicates one man. Her story has some holes in it too."

The break was over, and the band started playing again. Tina just blankly stared at him in frustration, "I can't believe this." She gulped down more of her Cabernet.

Darren was frustrated too, "I'm sorry Tina. We're working as hard as we can on this case, believe me."

She turned her attention back to the music and grabbed his hand to drag him back onto the dance floor.

He was both happy her questioning was interrupted for a while, but unhappy he had to dance again.

The dance floor was filled with Cubans since Miami is the home of "Little Havana" just a short distance across Biscayne Bay from Miami Beach, and it was a Cuban Club. Cubans were natural Salsa dancers, and everyone looked like they were competitors on, "Dancing with the

Stars." Darren tried his best to keep up with them, but it was a lot of effort and an impossible ambition.

Both Tina and Darren were working up a sweat as the tempo of the music kept mounting with every song. After several energetic dances, they returned to the table to rest and have another glass of Cabernet. Darren dreaded the long night of dancing, that in typical Miami Beach fashion did not stop until 4:00 a.m. He really just wanted to leave and go to bed with Tina. Now!

Tina was ecstatic about the music, "Wow. They are one of the top Salsa bands in Miami Beach."

"Yes. Great band," Darren feigned agreement while wiping the sweat off his brow with a napkin. He was relieved to take a break and sit down for a while. Then suddenly, the band started playing "Carlos Santana, Evil Ways."

> *You've got to change your evil ways... Baby*
> *Before I stop loving you*
> *You've got to change... Baby*
> *And every word that I say, it's true*
> *You've got me running and hiding*
> *All over town*
> *You've got me sneaking and peeping*
> *And running you down*
> *This can't go on...*
> *Lord knows you got to change... Baby*

Tina grabbed his hand again, "C'mon. I love this song." She dragged him back onto the dance floor.

No rest for the weary, he thought, but wholeheartedly followed Tina's lead. He was a good soldier with a battle plan.

CHAPTER THIRTY-TWO

Miami Herald

Slayton Home

Miami, Florida

Rachel Slayton read the Miami Herald newspaper at her kitchen table while sipping a glass of Merlot. Her husband, Gus, had gone on second shift duty, and it was nap time for little Gustavo Slayton, Junior, making it Happy Hour for her.

She was reading about the serial rapes and murders in South Florida. The sexy sizzle was perfect fodder for the tabloid news, and the media had exploited the story unremittingly. The newspaper sprinkled the article with scintillating photographs of the beautiful women who had been abused and murdered, along with a sexy portrait of the Governor's daughter they had dug up from her days as a swimsuit model.

Vivid red dots on a map of South Florida highlighted the locations of the rapes and murders, showing the victim's name next to each dot corresponding to the story.

Newsflash:

Rhapsody Rapists and Killers Running Rampant in South Florida

By Miami Herald

A serial rapist and murderer terrorizing the Sunshine State. Is there one, or are there two rapists / killers, and are they disguised as police officers, or are they really police officers? Authorities are investigating all angles in several recent serial rapes and murders in South Florida. So far, they reported five rapes and three murders. It is a shocking murder mystery that needs to be solved as quickly as possible.

The Governor has formed a special task force to investigate the serial rapes and murders. We urge anyone with information to call the Governor's Rape Task Force at (850) 555-1212. There is a $25,000 reward.

Here's some of what we know:

The Governor's only daughter, Susan, was raped and murdered. Her body was discovered in a drainage ditch alongside Alligator Alley near the Seminole Indian Reservation at Big Cypress Swamp. The cause of death was strangulation. The killer or killers are still at large.

Susan was a 25-year-old graduate student at Florida State University researching the ethnic cleansing and forced relocation of Seminole Indians from Florida following the Indian Removal Act of 1830, for her college thesis entitled the "Tamiami Trail of Tears." She may have inadvertently discovered that pirate treasure chests were buried on Seminole Indian tribal land 200 years ago, but that has not been confirmed.

Unfortunately, she was murdered before she could publish her writings, which documented the thousands of Florida Seminole Native American Indians that suffered from exposure, disease, and starvation while on route to their forced destinations and died; thus, it has also been called the "Trail of Tears and Deaths." The Governor dedicated a State Park near the Big Cypress Seminole Indian Reservation to honor Susan's work and her memory.

Lindsay Baily, 21-years-old, is a rape survivor who asserts she was assaulted by two men posing as police officers in Fort Pierce, Florida. She claims she was pulled over by a Police Squad Car, and then gang-raped by the two policemen, who took turns on her inside the cage in the backseat of their police cruiser. Ms. Baily said they pulled her over for a minor traffic violation. However, instead of writing her a ticket and moving on, they proceeded to use their authority to rape her. They kidnapped her, handcuffed her, threw her in the back of their cruiser, drove to a vacant car lot and took turns raping her.

FDLE questioned MS. Baily in hopes she could offer some clues as to the identity of the perpetrator or perpetrators since she claimed two men raped her, but the DNA indicated only one rapist. "They were dressed as cops and pulled me over for speeding. Then, they handcuffed me behind my back, beat, and raped me. They had this music turned up loud as they took turns on me. It sounded like… Rhapsody in Blue." She went on to say, "They told me they had multiple warrants out for my arrest, and I could avoid jail time by having sex with them."

A semen sample from her rape test kit confirmed she had been raped, but the DNA results remain unidentified after a search of criminal databases. The DNA was then tied to three other unsolved rapes in Florida, including the rape and murder of the Governor's only daughter, Susan.

Kimberly Merrick was 26-years-old when her dead body was discovered in Davie, Florida, lying face down on a dirt road off U.S. Route One. The young woman had been badly beaten and stomped on, which broke her neck and killed her. They forensically analyzed boot prints discovered on her back to identify her killer.

Tire tracks and footprints indicate she jumped or was pushed out of a car at a high rate of speed, and then got up and ran before apparently tripping on a tree root, falling face down, and then stomped on and killed.

She was working as a waitress at Diva's Topless Gentlemen's Club in Fort Lauderdale, driving home to Coral Gables at the end of her shift at 2:00 a.m. when she pulled her red jeep over to the side of the road and was kidnapped. Her car was found later with her wallet inside after her husband alerted police she hadn't returned home that night.

Cara Jones was discovered, murdered in Everglades City, Florida, following a missing person call from the parents of the 20-year-old female. She was last seen leaving her boyfriend's house the night before. Her parents followed the route she would have taken and eventually discovered her white Volkswagen Beetle below an abandoned bridge off Mercy Road, an eerily dark and desolate area commonly called "The Tombs." Her body had been thrown off the 70-foot high bridge into a creek bed where it was discovered by her family.

She had been strangled with a rope and badly beaten with a blunt object. Vaginal samples were sent to the lab to determine if there had been a sexual assault involved, and to identify the DNA of the perpetrator, but proved inconclusive. She was a Junior at the State University studying to become a teacher. The young woman was declared dead at the scene.

The FDLE and Police authorities have developed a Profile of the killer to help track him down.

Brenda Romney, a 19-year-old single mother of two young children, was allegedly brutally raped and beaten by two police officers. Ironically, she was studying criminal justice at the University of Florida, with the thought of becoming a police officer or a lawyer.

When a brick crashed through her bathroom window, she dialed what are supposed to be the most trustworthy three numbers, "I called 911 for help," she later told detectives. "I didn't call 911 to be the victim."

Within minutes, two police officers responded, "One took me into the bathroom to review the damage and the other cop, took my 15-year-old brother outside to speak to him." The police officer gave her brother $10 and told him to go to the store to get some bottled water. "I only drink bottled water," he told my brother. "Obviously, a way to get him out of the house."

"The other cop asked to see the broken window, and I led him to the bathroom in the back of the house."

She showed the police officer the bathtub littered with broken glass and pointed to the brick. The cop she had summoned to protect her, instead chose that moment to punch her and rape her. Then, the other cop also raped her. Her revulsion in the aftermath was so visceral that she ran out to confront the police officers and shouted, "They raped me! They raped me!" as she punched one of them in the chest. Other police officers and neighbors began arriving and saw a woman screaming incoherently about being raped. She was arrested, handcuffed, and told at the station house that she was being charged with assaulting a police officer.

She became more coherent, but no less outraged and vocal, as she continued to cry out from a holding cell that they had raped her. The other police officers dismissed her as a liar.

After 12 hours, they took her to the county jail and held for four days before being released without actually being charged. She took her story to the District Attorney's office. The prosecutor subsequently wrote, "While I found the victim's version of events credible, I did not believe her testimony would be strong enough to successfully prosecute the officers."

Rachel folded the newspaper on the table and started sobbing. She wondered whether her husband and his brother had anything to do with these serial rapes and murders? She knew how it felt to be beaten and raped by two men because it happened to her practically every night. The brothers *always* shared everything, including her. And the music... there had to be a connection.

The fact that she didn't really know which brother was little Gus Junior's father haunted her. Their DNA was identical because they were identical twins. She knew her son loved her husband, but she wished Gus would have been a better role model for him to admire and emulate. She worried about what her son was learning from her husband and his brother.

She was aware of the lineage of *Blue Blood* in the Slayton family and her son's fascination with cops and robbers' cartoons, but she wanted a new life for her and her son. She wanted a better environment for him to grow up in.

She knew where Gus kept his police uniforms and guns, and she knew how to shoot them. She thought she might have to use them someday to defend herself against Gus and Angelo, but she didn't want to go to jail and leave her son without his mother. She was trapped and had no way out. She had to do something.

Then she suddenly realized what needed to do!

CHAPTER THIRTY-THREE

Evidence [23]

FDLE Headquarters
Tallahassee, Florida

Senior Agent Collins and Agent Turner met with FDLE Profiler Jack Higgins and Forensic Investigators at FDLE Headquarters in Tallahassee to identify the killer forensically. They sat around the conference table, brain-storming the evidence they had.

Darren addressed the videotape evidence from the Chevron gas station on the Tamiami Trail, "We asked NASA in Cape Canaveral to help us enhance the quality of the images on the videotape from the night Cara Jones was murdered. They have the sophisticated technology we need to recover the film's details. They plan to have it completed by next week."

Casey added, "We know a police cruiser was at the Chevron station at the same time Cara was there fueling her white Volkswagen Beetle. When Cara drove off, it appears the police cruiser followed her. Until we get the enhanced videotape, we can't identify the cruiser or the police officer."

Darren reminded her, "You mean police officers, don't you?"

Casey corrected herself, "Yes, that is correct. Police officers, plural. It appears there were two officers in the police cruiser."

Darren continued, "The videotape also showed one officer flicking a spent cigarette butt into the parking lot. We tried to recover it for DNA evidence, but it apparently was washed away in the rain down a sewer grate."

Jack Higgins reviewed his Profile analysis, "Brenda Romney accused the Slayton brothers of raping her when she called the police for help. I've reviewed their profiles, and they fit the killer's Profile we created."

Casey cringed as Jack read his Profile analysis to the team. It sounded all too familiar to her.

Weller and Benjamin added to the identification, "The staff at Diva's Topless Gentlemen's Club also identified the Slayton brothers as regular customers, and they always sat in Kimberly Merrick's section of the club."

Darren smiled, "Well, guys, I'm glad to hear your tireless dedication to interviewing topless dancers provided a positive identification. How many lap dances before you could ID the Slayton brothers?"

Weller laughed, "It was a tough assignment. Hours of visual surveillance in a sweaty topless dance club, but somebody had to do it."

All the men in the room laughed.

Casey didn't think it was so funny, "Okay boys, let's stick to business. Sheriff Robertson, what did you find out?"

"The skid marks we photographed on the bridge above Cara Jones's body were from a set of Goodyear R14X100 radial tires, fifty-three inches apart. The same tires used by the Miami Police Department and the width checked out with the squad car driven by the Slayton brothers on the night of the murder."

Based on seniority, Casey turned to Dennis Hollis from FDLE in Miami, "Dennis, what have you determined?"

Dennis responded, "Well, as my report states, the tire tracks were also from a set of Goodyear R14X100 radial tires, fifty-three inches apart. It was a dirt road, so we have tire tracks and boot tracks all over the place, including on Kimberly Merrick's back. Someone very large stomped on her back with a big boot and broke her neck. We determined the boot was police issued size twelve, and we checked all the police records in Broward and Miami-Dade counties. We found a lot of size twelve matches in the police departments. Unfortunately, it's a common size for police officers."

Darren considered his answer, "So, have you reached a conclusion?"

Dennis turned to Darren and shrugged his shoulders, "We can't reach any definitive conclusions, but we can't rule out anybody that wears a size twelve boot either, including the Slayton brothers. They both wear a size twelve boot too."

Casey reflected on that piece of evidence for a moment, then moved on to the next expert, "John, what can you report?"

John Steele, the Forensic Criminalist hair and fiber expert, described his theory about the gold fiber, "The microscopic piece of gold fiber found on Cara's sweatshirt appears to be a foreign fiber that does not belong to Cara Jones. It is potentially a cross transference from contact with the killer."

Jack Higgins questioned further, "I read in your report the gold fiber could match thread samples found on Florida Police Patrol patches."

John responded, "Yes, that is correct. All the Patrol patches in the State are manufactured by one company, and they only produce this patch with this gold thread for Florida Police patches."

Darren observed, "So, it points toward a dirty cop as the killer?"

John was not so sure, "Not necessarily. The forensic evidence cannot determine that beyond a reasonable doubt. It could be a cop, or it could be someone with access to a cop uniform. We just don't know."

Casey turned to Gary Harmon, a serologist with the Serological Research Institute in Fort Lauderdale, "The best forensic evidence we have to identify the killer is DNA. What are your conclusions, Gary?"

Gary reported, "The DNA from Cara's shoe is definitely not from Cara Jones. It can most likely be classified as Caucasian, but only about one percent of the world's population has similar genetic markers in their blood. This percentage amounts to one in every seventy-five Caucasians and not at all in non-Caucasians."

Jack Higgins added that to his notes on the profile list, "That drop of blood can nail our killer. Can you match the DNA to CODIS – the Combined DNA Index System?"

Gary shook his head, "We checked CODIS and several other DNA Databases, but didn't get a match."

Darren asserted, "If the killer is a cop, there will not be DNA on file... anywhere."

Casey thought about her DNA. If her brothers are the rapists and killers, her DNA would match. But she kept quiet.

Jack Higgins carefully looked over his Profile Sheet, "The Slayton brothers fit the Profile, but how do we get their DNA?"

Darren turned to Gary, "Can we check with hospitals or blood tests?"

Gary looked doubtful, "We checked police records, hospitals, blood banks, blood testing facilities, and found nothing."

Darren looked over at Casey, "So, where does that leave us?"

Jack answered for her, "I suggest we ask the Slayton brothers to volunteer their DNA samples or find a way to get it. Then, we can match it to all the DNA we have on file from the Rape Test Kits from the Governor's daughter, Lindsay Baily, Brenda Romney, and all the others."

Darren interjected, "If they are the rapists and killers, I doubt they'll volunteer their DNA. Also, asking them will heighten their resistance and make it even more difficult. I suggest we set up surveillance on them while they are still unsuspecting. Maybe we can get their DNA that way?"

Casey joked, "So you're eager to return to Everglades City?"

Darren laughed, "Yes, boss. That's how dedicated I am to law enforcement. Besides, they are in Miami, and that's just fine with me."

Casey smiled, "Okay, pack your bag. We'll leave tomorrow."

Darren smiled back, "It's already packed, Boss."

---

[23] **_Sheriff Deputy Randy Comeaux Rapes in Lafayette, Louisiana:_**

Sheriff Deputy Randy Comeaux was a serial rapist who preyed on the women of Lafayette, Louisiana. He took advantage of his position of power in Law Enforcement. DNA evidence taken from his covertly obtained cigarette butt matched evidence from six rape cases.

CHAPTER THIRTY-FOUR

Rachel

FDLE Headquarters

Tallahassee, Florida

After the meeting concluded, Casey barricaded herself in her office to contemplate the results of the meeting and her own suspicions regarding the rapists and killers. As she was reviewing some of the documentation, her office telephone rang.

Casey's secretary, Betsy, was on the line, "Casey, there's a woman who wants to speak to the head of the Governor's Rape Task Force. She says she's Rachel Slayton."

Sirens went off in Casey's head, *Rachel Slayton?* Casey knew she was Gus Slayton's wife, although they'd never met, and Rachel probably didn't know Casey Collins was her sister-in-law. Nobody knew her maiden name was Slayton, "OK, make sure the recorder is on, then transfer the call."

The call came through, and Casey made it sound official, "Hello, this is Senior FDLE Agent Casey Collins of the Governor's Rape Task Force, who am I speaking with, please?"

Rachel answered nervously, "Hello, I'm Rachel Slayton, Police Officer Gus Slayton's wife from Miami."

Casey pretended unfamiliarity, "Hello Mrs. Slayton, how can I help you?"

She was hesitant, "Umm... Well, I might have some information about the rapes and murders reported in the Miami Herald newspaper."

Casey sat up in her chair, "OK. What information do you have?"

She started sobbing on the phone, "Agent Collins, I'm scared about what could happen to me if I tell you what I know."

Casey realized she would need to calm her down to get any information, "It's all right. We can provide police protection for you, Mrs. Slayton."

She was trying to catch her breath, "I have a son, and I need to be sure we will both be safe."

Casey sounded sympathetic, "Well, depending on what you tell me, we can offer every protection possible for you and your son, including relocation to another city, plus you'll be eligible for the $25,000 reward."

Rachel started to calm down, "That is what we need. Relocation to another city for my son and me and some money to get a fresh start. I'm afraid they will kill me if I tell you what I know."

Casey tried to reassure her, "Well again, based on the quality of the information you provide, I can assure you we can move you and your son anywhere in the United States, provide a nice place to live, a job and give you enough money to get settled in your new home. How does that sound?"

She felt encouraged, "That sounds like what we need."

Casey added, "You will have to testify publicly in court, but we will grant you immunity from prosecution."

That got her upset again, "Publicly in court? No, I can't do that, they will kill me."

Casey's antenna went up, "They? Who are *they*?"

"My... My husband and his brother. They will kill me if I do that."

Bells started ringing in Casey's head. *Brothers? My brothers?* It was all fitting together, "Rachel, you'll be fine. We'll protect you and your son. We'll move you to a safe house during the trial and then relocate both of you when it's over."

Rachel panicked, "Trial? I don't know about that? Let me think about it."

Casey knew she was losing her, "Rachel, I'll be in Miami tomorrow. Can we meet to discuss this further?"

She started sobbing again, "I don't know? Maybe I shouldn't have called." Rachel hung up the telephone, and the dial tone sounded.

Casey tried to get her back, "Rachel? Rachel, hello?" The line went dead. She called her secretary, "Betsy, the call dropped, can you reconnect it?"

Betsy responded, "I'll try, but it looks like she hung up the phone?"

Casey thought better of it. She didn't want to spook Rachel any further, "OK, never mind, Betsy."

She looked at the receiver in her hand, thinking, *I've got to get to Miami... and Rachel.*

CHAPTER THIRTY-FIVE

Happy Hour [24]

McCabe's Irish Pub
Miami, Florida

The Slayton brothers had gone on second shift duty at two o'clock, and so, by six o'clock, it was lunchtime for them and Happy Hour for everybody else at McCabe's Irish Pub.

Gus sat solemnly at a table among the early evening Happy Hour crowd, thinking about the mounting pressure from the Governor's Rape Task Force, as he swallowed a mouthful of Scotch. He appeared uncharacteristically wrinkled and disheveled, as if he had spent the night in his uniform, "Did you read the Miami Herald story?"

Angelo gulped down an icy cold Budweiser as he stared across the rim at Gus on the other side of the table, surrounded by Happy Hour chatter. This would not be the kind of conversation either of them wanted to have at the police station, "Yeah… 'Serial Rapist and Murderer in South Florida.' I read it. I'm getting worried. Now we have television *and* newspaper pressure. What should we do?"

Gus smiled and responded glibly, "I don't know, but I'd like that babe Tina Evanston, from NBC6 news, to interview us in person. We can show her some breaking news in the back of our cruiser."

Although it was against police department policy to be drinking on duty, both brothers needed serious alcohol to get through this conversation. The patrons and staff at the Pub looked at them curiously in their police uniforms drinking cocktails, but they knew that no one would report them because, *What happens at McCabe's, Stays at McCabe's.*

The cocktail waitress interrupted their exchange, "Would you like anything else, gentlemen?" She was an attractive, large-breasted woman who wore cheap perfume and a sweater at least one size too small. Not that anyone complained.

They stopped all conversation and looked up to marvel at the sight. Gus cleared his throat and grinned, "Well, hello, Darlin'. What are you offering?"

She giggled girlishly, "All I can offer you right now are drinks, baby."

Angelo smiled, then continued flirting, "What time do you get off work, Darlin'?"

She smiled back suggestively, "Depends on how busy it is, but usually around 1:00 a.m., baby."

Angelo winked his eye, "Hey, you're worth waiting for."

She feigned modesty, "Well, thank you. Would you like some more drinks?"

"Yes, please. Another round Darlin'."

"Coming right up, baby."

They both watched as she turned and walked toward the bar, and then they looked at each other in unison with that all-knowing man smirk. Angelo remarked, "Beautiful legs and butt too! I really want to get to know her better."

Gus smiled at her timing and turned back to Angelo, "Get her name, and we'll check with the station, later."

Angelo knew the routine all too well, "Definitely."

Gus got back to business, "Angelo, there is nothing that can connect us to any of this."

Angelo wasn't so sure, "What about Brenda Romney? She is still pushing the District Attorney, accusing us of rape."

Gus smirked, "They should have let her commit suicide in that jail cell."

Angelo looked from side-to-side to make sure nobody was listening, "We should have taken care of her ourselves, while the kid was out getting water. We could have blamed it on the brick thrower."

Gus agreed, "You're right about that. We also probably shouldn't have done the Governor's daughter. That was another big mistake."

Angelo burst out laughing, "You think? Who knew she was the Governor's daughter?"

Gus laughed back, "Shit. The Governor's daughter. Now he's out for revenge."

Angelo grinned, "But we have connections, Bro. Sis is heading the Governor's Rape Task Force. Do you believe that? How lucky can we get?"

Gus was more cautious, "Hopefully, she still loves us the way we love her, and remembers that we are her family."

Angelo added, "And her lovers."

Gus held his glass up, and they clinked glasses, "And her soulmates."

The waitress returned with their order, and they promptly turned deadly silent as she juggled a tray with a Budweiser beer and scotch-on-the-rocks just below her cleavage. She smiled at them with this "I-know-what-you're-looking-at" smile and delivered the drinks, "Here you go, gentlemen."

They both looked up simultaneously. Angelo replied, "Thank you, Darlin'. You're beautiful. What's your name?"

She winked at him, "Well, thank you, baby. My name is Rita."

Angelo Grinned, "Well, hello, Rita. Where are you from?"

She smiled, "I'm from Puerto Rico."

"Puerto Rico. Really? Do you have a last name?"

She giggled, "You ask a lot of questions. Am I under arrest?"

"Just trying to get to know you a little better, Rita, that's all. My name is Angelo, and this is my brother, Gus. Angelo and Gus Slayton. Pleased to meet you."

She curtsied, "Nice to meet you both too. My name is Lopez. Rita Lopez."

"Nice to meet you, Rita Lopez."

"Thank you, Angelo and Gus Slayton." She arched her back as if to accentuate her breasts. Then she turned to slowly saunter away.

They both leered at her as she left the table.

---

[24]-Sheriff Deputy David Rogers Rapes and Murders in Bakersfield, California.

The bullet-riddled body of Jeanine Benintende, a 21-year-old Los Angeles prostitute, was fished out of a canal near Lamont, in Kern County. The fatal bullets were fired from Sheriff Deputy David Keith Rogers's gun, and the same weapon was identified a year later, when Tracy Clark, a pregnant 15-year-old hooker, was found dead in the same canal. Convicted on one count each of second-degree murder (Benintende) and first-degree murder (Clark), Rogers was sentenced to die on the latter charge.

CHAPTER THIRTY-SIX

Priors [25]

McCabe's Irish Pub

Miami, Florida

After patrolling their assigned route around the city for several hours, Gus and Angelo parked their police cruiser outside McCabe's Irish Pub after midnight. Angelo talked into the police radio, "This is Car 54 checking priors for Rita Lopez, Miami. Over."

The police operator responded, "Checking priors for Rita Lopez. Any other information on her? Over."

Angelo answered, "She's from Puerto Rico working at McCabe's Irish Pub in Miami. Over."

"I have a Rita Lopez living at Grove Street Apartments, Miami, registered working at McCabe's Irish Pub, on probation for prostitution. Over."

Angelo switched off the microphone and grinned at Gus, "Bingo." Then he switched the microphone back on, "Thank you. Over and out."

Rita Lopez clocked out of work at McCabe's at 1:18 a.m. and said her goodbyes to coworkers as the lights in the Pub were methodically clicked off by the Pub manager. She closed and relocked the front door behind her and started walking home to her apartment on Grove Street.

The police cruiser followed close behind as Rita crossed the intersection of Flagler Avenue and Mizner Street. She didn't know she was being followed, but had an uncomfortable feeling she wasn't alone.

The streets were getting squalid, as the Slayton brothers slowly turned their police cruiser onto Grove Street near Rita's apartment building. Grove Street had once been a proud, upscale middle-class neighborhood, populated with a mix of strong, hard-working Cuban and Puerto Rican immigrants. It had been a bustling community filled with pastry shops, fresh fish markets, and outdoor vegetable stands. The limestone buildings had been meticulously maintained, brightened with colorful flowers in the gardens, and freshly painted railings.

Now, unfortunately, the neighborhood looked like a dismal, bombed-out ghetto. Many of the buildings had long since been abandoned and converted into dirt and rat-infested hideaways for drug users, prostitutes, and vagrants. Rusted piles of scrap metal and old burned-out cars lined the dark and grimy streets. Large piles of rubble and debris filled the cluttered lots where stately buildings had once stood. The boarded-up shops were decaying.

The Grove Street Apartment building had a rundown brick facade covered with different colors of graffiti, artfully done, as if the city of Miami had sponsored a competition for the biggest, boldest, and most colorful rendition.

Most people would agree "The Wanderers" had the lead for the most distinctive logo and brightest colors. They plastered their name all over almost every building on Grove Street, and the graffiti style appeared to have been drawn by the same person. They were obviously vying for street-gang immortality.

Rita passed by a man pushing a shopping cart alongside the shoddy street. The cart overflowed with dark green and brown plastic bags, probably containing all the man's worldly possessions.

He shuffled along, dressed in tattered trousers and several layers of worn-out sweaters and coats. Occasionally he picked up the wreckage from a long-forgotten collision: a hubcap here, a spear of chrome there. Above his grimy, unshaven face, hair stuck out in all directions, propped up by dirt and grease accumulated from too many nights sleeping on the ground or on a park bench.

The vagabond looked at Rita as she passed him and then, twisting his cart away, returned to his task, his attention shifting to the smashed headlight of what must have been a fine Mercedes Benz at one time.

Gus drove the police cruiser passed the vagrant and alongside Rita as she walked. Then he pulled over to the side of the road to stop next to her.

Angelo greeted Rita from the front passenger seat window, "Good evening, Rita. How are you doing?"

Rita appeared surprised as she turned to greet the police cruiser, "Well, hello, officers. What are you doing in my neighborhood tonight?"

Angelo jumped out of the police cruiser with his handcuffs ready, "Well, actually, we're here to arrest you for a probation violation." He grabbed her wrists and slapped the handcuffs on her behind her back.

Rita was shocked, "What? I don't have a probation violation. What are you doing?"

Angelo took her arm and directed her toward the police cruiser. He opened the back door and shoved her into the back seat, "You're under arrest. Anything you say can and will be used against you." He pushed her over and sat in the backseat next to her.

Gus turned the police cruiser's headlights off and lit a cigarette. The street was empty except for the vagabond walking by with his shopping cart. He briefly watched the commotion by the police cruiser and then turned and shuffled down the street.

Rita struggled with the handcuffs and tried to reason with Angelo, "I've done nothing wrong. Why are you doing this?"

Angelo moved closer to her and started feeling her, "Honey, you are looking damn good tonight." He kissed her neck and put his hands on her breasts.

Rita screamed and shoved him back, "STOP! LEAVE ME ALONE!"

Angelo sneered, "Do you want to go to jail tonight, Darlin'?" He continued to fondle her breasts, "Oh, you feel so good."

She tried to push back, still handcuffed, "No! I did nothing wrong!"

Angelo grinned, "Prostitution is illegal Darlin', but if you take care of me, I'll take care of you." He reached down, unbuckled and unzipped his pants.

She resisted, "No! Stop it! I'll report you!"

He knew she could never squeal on him. He laughed, "Who are you going to tell? You're a prostitute."

Rita realized sadly she had no choice but to cooperate with him. Her hands were still handcuffed behind her back, "Can you at least take these handcuffs off?"

"You don't need the handcuffs off for what I want, baby." Angelo grabbed the back of her neck and pushed her head down into his lap, "Like I said, you take care of me, and I'll take care of you."

She knew she had to give in.

"Easy, big guy, you're going to hurt me."

He suddenly pulled her head up and slapped her hard in the face, "Hell, I'm just starting to have fun with you, bitch."

With a burning red cheek and bleeding nose, she screamed, "PLEASE STOP!" But he hit her again with such force that it loosened a few teeth in her mouth. She cried out in fear, "You're hurting me!"

"You shut up, bitch. Just be damn good tonight, and I promise I won't hurt you... *too* much." He hiked up her skirt and ripped off her panties.

He was on top of her with her wrists handcuffed behind her back, "NO! STOP!" She cried out in pain.

He hit her in the face again, so hard it knocked her out. She stopped moving. He pushed her legs apart and raped her.

Gus was watching, smoking a cigarette in the front seat.

When Angelo finished, he sat up. Rita was passed out on the backseat.

He looked over at Gus in the front driver's seat exhale a cloud of cigarette smoke as he watched, "Your turn." He laughed callously.

---

[25] *Maryland Police Officer Macklin Charges:*
Raping a Woman at Traffic Stop:

Authorities say it may not be Officer Ryan Macklin's first crime, and they are looking for other victims to come forward. Macklin has been suspended and stripped of his gun and badge after being accused of raping a woman.

CHAPTER THIRTY-SEVEN

Love Again

Governor's Office
Tallahassee, Florida

The next day, Casey arrived for her regularly scheduled weekly status meeting with the Governor, weary after another long, sleepless night.

She was eager to resolve the most important thing in the Governor's life - finding his daughter's rapist and killer. It totally consumed her. She hoped maybe that conclusion would help them find a way to be together, following his wife's untimely death. She had four rapes and two murders, all potentially tied to a serial rapist and murderer posing as a police officer. Or were there two? And were they actually police officers and could they be her twin brothers? And now, a pirate's treasure on Seminole Indian tribal land confounded the investigation. To top it off, she had an out-of-control news media, thanks to Darren's big mouth or big something else.

Casey opened the door to the Governor's vestibule, and L.B. was standing guard as usual. Marine Corps paraphernalia decorated the perimeters of the small vestibule. L.B. was proud of his medals, ribbons, and insignias from past battles. His tour of duty included eighteen months in Vietnam. He prominently displayed the ceremonially encased awards for military honors and marksmanship.

L.B. greeted her with a warm hug, "Hello, Casey. Good to see you."

"L.B., how are you doing?" She hugged him back.

"I'm doing fine, Casey. Brendan is expecting you."

The Governor's secretary looked Casey up and down as she rushed into the reception area, "Hello, Agent Collins. He's waiting, go on in."

Casey smiled at her as she slipped through the half-open door into the darkened office. She closed the door firmly behind her and leaned her back against it. She wondered why the lighting was turned down so low and struggled emotionally with the impropriety of being alone with the Governor in his office.

Casey's whole world had turned upside down since she first met Brendan. She found herself mesmerized. His quiet confidence and broad smile aroused a feeling in her that she had thought was gone forever. For her, it was love at first sight. She had not been that love-struck since she met her late-husband ten years earlier. She yearned for a partner, a friend, and a lover. She wanted to be like the other couples she saw laughing, connected, and in love. She desperately hungered for romance with the man of her dreams, who could satisfy her both emotionally and physically. But there was one problem... he was married. But not anymore!

Suddenly, he approached her from the side, his body pressed into hers, and he kissed her. She was startled by his advance and hesitated for a fleeting moment. She wasn't sure how to react. She knew she loved him, and she knew he cared deeply for her. Their lips met. He gently slid his hand toward the back of her neck. She leaned forward into his kiss.

As soon as he held her, her best intentions were quickly abandoned, and they flung into each other. Their mouths fused, kissing more urgently and embracing each other more tightly. Months of her trying to resist her true feelings exploded into pure passion.

Casey tore at his jacket, and he tugged at her blouse. They continued to kiss more and more deeply and began peeling off each other's clothes. The kiss deepened as Brendan steered her toward his couch. His hands slid down her back, pressing her into his growing virility. She moaned and grasped for the buttons on his shirt, her hands on his chest.

She yanked at his tie while his hands explored her body. He slid his hand under her blouse, shoving her bra aside and cupped his hand around her breast, her nipple hard against his palm. Unwilling to break, they caressed each other as they stumbled onto the couch. Brendan rolled on top, pulled her blouse over her head, and pushed her skirt fabric down out of his way. He felt her bare skin. Her flesh glowed.

Casey was filled with passion. She released his belt buckle and unfastened his zipper.

He moved and helped her push his pants to the floor. At last, they were naked against each other's bodies. Animal instincts had taken over. The Governor pushed into Casey, and she clutched him as though she were drowning. They drove forward blindly in a burning, savage manner that required no excuses and no apologies. Tenderness would have to wait for another time.

A moment of panic swept over her, "No!"

"Yes!" His free hand slid down her body.

She gasped and moaned. Her desire filled her. Her hips moved over his. She leaned into him, and he clutched her breast, releasing more of her inner passion.

He groaned and grabbed her from behind, grinding deeper as she flung her head back, breathing hard. His mouth captured her cry of release that threatened to rock the entire government building. She clutched him hard as she climaxed, which sent him over the edge, and he erupted inside her.

She held him, and he held her back, her breasts coddled between them, locked with him, his mouth still on hers as their breathing came to check. His heart pounded hard into hers, nearly changing her rhythm. His sweat trickled over her, dripped into her hair, trickled between their still locked mouths. She loved the taste of him.

He reluctantly left her lips and sighed hard. He swallowed and peered at her through the dim light of the shuttered office, "I couldn't resist you today, Casey."

It took several minutes to regain their composure, and they both felt awkward. They stared into each other's eyes, "We'll find a way," she whispered.

He smiled back, "Of course, if you marry me..."

If things had been different for them, she was all for marrying him. She smiled and tightened her hug on him. She feared the inner-most secret she held inside her about his daughter's rapist and killer. She knew if it were true, he would be devastated, and it would change their relationship forever.

CHAPTER THIRTY-EIGHT

Surveillance

Miami Police Station

Miami, Florida

The next morning, Casey was still reeling from her intimate encounter with the Governor, and she was careful not to show her emotions visibly to Darren as they flew down to Miami from Tallahassee. She was feeling both guilty and enraptured, since making love to Brendan yesterday afternoon. It was quite startling. She knew she loved him, and she thought he had strong feelings for her too, but now their unbridled passion had brought their relationship to a whole new level.

She was confused about where it could go from this point. It was complicated. He was the Governor of the State of Florida, and she reported directly to him. Plus, as a police officer, she was a state employee, and in charge of investigating the rape and murder of his daughter. The biggest complication was that she suspected her brothers might be the rapists and killers who murdered his daughter and now his wife too. If her brothers were responsible for the death of Susan and Mary, he would never forgive her.

Casey and Darren checked into the Miami Marriott Hotel on Brickell Street the day before their surveillance assignment was due to begin. Casey stopped at a Pharmacy to purchase hair dye and cosmetics to change her appearance so her brothers would not recognize her.

In the morning, she went into the bathroom in front of the mirror and dyed her blonde hair black, then she took tanning cream and rubbed it onto her arms, hands, and face to make her complexion darker. When she was finished, she admired her extreme makeover in the mirror. She looked Cuban, which fit perfectly into the Miami environment.

Now… She would have to explain to Darren why she was incognito. He needed to know the Slayton brothers were her brothers.

The next morning, Darren was waiting in the Lobby to meet Casey for breakfast when this beautiful, tan, black-haired woman approached him, "Good morning, Darren."

At first, he thought maybe it was his lucky day to meet this beautiful Cuban lady at the Hotel. But, as he looked closer at her face and her features, he recognized her, "Casey, is that you? What are you doing?"

Casey smiled and admitted, "Yes, Darren, it's me. It's a long story. Let's go have coffee, and I'll explain it to you."

Darren was shocked by the revelation that the Slayton brothers were Casey's brothers, and even more shocked when she told him about her childhood, growing up with them. He felt very sorry for her, but he knew she was a strong, resilient woman, and it would not stop her from doing her job. He would fully support her and help her through this difficult and very personal investigation.

Casey and Darren arrived at the Miami Police Station at one o'clock in the afternoon in a nondescript Chevrolet four-door sedan that fit seamlessly into the environment. They sat in the car listening to the air conditioner blow cool air around the hot interior during the sweltering peak heat of the day in Miami. They were sipping coffee from Styrofoam cups and could smell the aroma of sizzling hamburgers at lunchtime drifting through the air from a local Greek Diner across the street.

Casey noticed the large sign posted in clear view at the entrance door to the police department, "To Protect and Serve." She thought about the irony of that motto, given their assignment to capture cops, who were both rapists and murderers - the ultimate betrayal.

It was in-between shifts, so the parking lot was lined with police cruisers, as the cops went off and then back on duty. The Slayton brothers' police cruiser was within their sight.

Darren was in the driver's seat and turned to Casey, jokingly, "Okay, Maria, we are ready and waiting."

Casey laughed, "Maria. Very funny. But maybe you should call me that Cuban name while we are working undercover?"

Darren thought about it for a moment and agreed, "You know, I was just teasing, but I think you're right. Maria, it is." He started crooning the song from West Side Story:

Maria

I just met a girl named Maria

And suddenly that name will never be the same

To me...

Casey joked back, "Okay, Frank Sinatra. Enough."

They watched for another half-hour before the afternoon's activities got underway. Then, throngs of police officers began leaving the police station, heading to their police cruisers to begin their shifts.

Darren took out his binoculars and surveyed the stairway leaving the police station searching for her twin brothers. He spotted them walking together down the stairs, apparently joking with each other, "There they are."

Casey recognized them immediately based on their mannerisms and movements, which brought back painful memories.

The Slayton twins got into their cruiser and drove off.

Darren tailed the police cruiser from a distance until the brothers parked it outside of McCabe's Irish Pub. As they vanished into the Pub, Darren turned to Casey, "Okay, Maria. It's showtime."

He parked the Chevy nearby, got out of the car, grabbed the black suitcase containing their surveillance equipment from the trunk, and headed into McCabe's Pub. They planned to confiscate a glass or fork or anything that might provide saliva for DNA evidence and hopefully catch them in a conversation about their rapes and murders.

Legally, they could use any discarded item at their table but needed to videotape and audiotape the entire surveillance assignment so they could use it as evidence in court.

They casually walked into the Pub and surveyed the layout. They spotted Gus sitting at a table, drinking a cocktail. Directly across the table from Gus, they saw Angelo, who was drinking a beer. They appeared to be having a very intense conversation.

Darren and Casey found a good middle-distance table with a clear view of a mirror that would let them spy on her brothers without them feeling the gaze. Darren opened his briefcase, creating a shield for the camera mounted inside, switched on the video and audio recorder, and inserted an earpiece into his ear facing away from their table. He maneuvered a tiny parabolic microphone hidden inside a black cube on the table and tried to hone in on their conversation. To anyone watching, it would appear he was working on some business papers inside his briefcase while he was waiting for lunch.

The ambient restaurant noises interfered with the audio, but he continued to video record the brothers while they drank from their glasses and ate lunch with their forks and spoons.

A waitress approached Darren and Casey to take their order, "Hi, my name is Jennifer. Can I get you something to drink?"

Darren saw her eyes taking inventory of the paraphernalia on the table. She was staring at the black cube sitting on the edge of the table and the wire coming out of Darren's ear into the opened briefcase.

Casey shuffled some papers around as a decoy and looked up at her, "Yes, please. Two iced teas would be great."

"Let me guess, you're Spanish, right?" Her eyes were still searching for a clue as to what was going on in the briefcase.

Casey noticed her focus on the black cube, "Close, umm... Jennifer. I'm from Cuba, and my friend here is from New York City."

Darren looked up for a minute, "Hello."

"Oh, darn, I like to guess the accents of travelers visiting Miami. Anyway, I'll be right back with your drinks."

Casey watched her walk away, noting she glanced sideways at Darren's briefcase, still curious.

Darren worked the video camera hidden inside his briefcase as Angelo drove his fork into a dish of nachos and beans. Across the table, Gus was licking a spoonful of soup. *That is going to be a great source of DNA evidence,* he thought to himself.

Darren noticed their body language shifting as they got deeper and deeper into their conversation, but unfortunately, he could not record the audio because of the Pub's noisy commotion.

Gus had a somber expression on his face, as Angelo hung on each and every word he said. They were engaged in a deeply emotional conversation, melted into their own little world, blocking everything else out.

Darren assumed they were talking about the risks of getting arrested. He barely noticed Jennifer deliver his drink, as he looked up distractedly and fumbled around his briefcase to camouflage the camera.

"Here you are, sir, iced tea. And, madam for you, iced tea, as well." Jennifer struggled to place each glass on the table between his briefcase and the black cube without disturbing anything.

It was the most inopportune moment. Darren kept looking from his briefcase over to the Slayton's table and back again. Jennifer finally turned away, just as he noticed the brothers getting up to pay their check. Darren nodded to Casey that it was time to collect the evidence, and they grabbed envelopes out of the briefcase, just as Gus and Angelo walked out the door.

Casey and Darren sprinted toward their table before anybody else could touch it. They left the camera rolling so it would record them collecting the DNA evidence. They took sterile gloves out of one of the envelopes and two sets of sterile tweezers out of another envelope. They started collecting forks, spoons, and glasses into previously labeled "Gus" and "Angelo" envelopes for forensic DNA analysis.

The servers stood around staring at them, wondering what they were doing, until Darren flashed his badge and said, "FDLE."

CHAPTER THIRTY-NINE

DNA

Marriott Hotel

Miami, Florida

Darren dropped Casey off at the Marriott Hotel so she could undo her disguise before meeting with the Rape Task Force at FDLE Headquarters in Miami. She wanted to avoid questions or controversy regarding why she was incognito. She and Darren decided that until they were absolutely positive her brothers were the rapists and killers, she should remain active on the case and consider recusing herself only after their suspicions were definitely confirmed based on the DNA evidence.

Darren drove to FDLE Headquarters alone to deliver the DNA evidence they had confiscated at McCabe's to Gary Harmon, the serologist with the Serological Research Institute in Fort Lauderdale, for analysis.

About an hour later, Casey received a phone call in her hotel room from her secretary, Betsy, "Casey, Rachel Slayton is on the phone. She wants to talk to you."

Casey had just stepped out of the shower and still had a towel wrapped around her head. She hesitated for a moment, thinking of an approach to gain Rachel's trust and confidence, "OK, Betsy, put her through, but make sure you record the conversation."

"I will, Casey. Here she is."

Casey was excited Rachel called, but calmed her voice down as much as possible, "Hello, Mrs. Slayton. How are you today?"

The other end of the phone line was quiet for a moment, but then Rachel answered, "Hello, Agent Collins, I'm OK."

Casey was careful not to scare her off again, "That's good, Mrs. Slayton. I'm in Miami, and I would like to meet with you."

Rachel was hesitant again but then responded, "I've been thinking... About your offer. You know, relocation, the reward and everything. I think that's what we need."

Casey was silently cheering inside her mind. She decided to address her more personally, "Good, Rachel, we can relocate you and your son to a safe area. Think of where you would like to live. We can relocate you anywhere in the United States."

Rachel sounded hopeful, "Well, actually, I was thinking about the West Coast. My son likes sunsets."

Now, we're finally dancing, Casey thought, "California? No problem. We can make that happen right after the trial."

"No, no, I mean the West Coast of Florida. Maybe Naples or something. You know, with a sunset."

Casey grinned to herself. Rachel just wanted something simple. To be happy, "Naples is beautiful. We can definitely arrange that. Can we meet today?"

Silence once again for a moment, "Yes, I like Naples."

"We can move you immediately after the trial."

Rachel was still concerned about testifying at a trial, "I'm still scared about what will happen to me if I do that."

Casey needed to get her testimony, "Let's discuss it when we get together. When can we meet?"

"I can meet you today. My son is at my Mom's house for the afternoon, and my husband is working."

"Great. Do you know where FDLE Headquarters is in Miami?"

Rachel was cautious again. She didn't like the idea of meeting at a police facility. She was scared her husband might find out, "I'd rather not meet there. Is there somewhere else?"

Casey understood. She wanted a less threatening environment, "Do you know where the Marriott Hotel is on Brickell Street? That's where I'm staying."

"Yes."

"Can you meet me here? I'm in Room 307."

"Yes. I'll be there in an hour."

"Okay. See you then."

Casey immediately called Darren, "Darren, you need to come back to the Marriott. Rachel Slayton is coming over to talk to us."

Darren was surprised, "Rachel Slayton, wow. How did you pull that off?"

"It's a long story, but bring an audio recorder with you."

"Sure, boss. On my way."

Casey hung up the phone and surveyed the room. There was a little table in the corner that would work, but she'd need two more chairs. She called the Front desk.

CHAPTER FORTY

Wife Testimony

Marriott Hotel

Miami, Florida

About an hour later, Rachel knocked gently on the door of Room 307 at the Marriott Hotel in Miami. She was in a conservative dress with low heels, her black-hair styled up in a bun on her head, and a purse hung over her shoulder. She was Cuban and looked a little like Casey did when she was incognito.

Casey opened the door and greeted her, "Hello Rachel, I'm Casey Collins, pleased to meet you." They shook hands, and Casey introduced her to Darren, "This is Darren Turner." She wanted to keep the "agent" term out of the introductions, hoping to make Rachel feel more at ease.

Darren walked over to introduce himself, "Hello, Rachel." They both shook hands, "Please come in and sit down."

The room was spacious and viewed the Intercostal Waterway. It was painted in calming pastel colors with several water-color paintings hanging on the walls. The queen-sized bed dominated the middle of the room. In the corner, they sat at three chairs around a small table in front of the sliding glass door leading out to a balcony, with several water bottles, pads of paper with pens, a tape recorder in the center, and a box of tissues near where Rachel was sitting.

Rachel was nervous, "I'm very scared. They will kill me if they find out I'm talking to you."

Casey tried to calm her down, "Rachel, I can assure you, nobody knows you're here. We will protect you and your son." She tried to change the subject to something more positive, "We can relocate you and your son to Naples, and nobody will know where you are. So, you can't tell your friends or family for a while."

That seemed to divert her attention, "Yes, I know. As I said, I like Naples. My son loves sunsets, and it seems like a nice place to start a new life."

"I agree. It's a beautiful city." Casey was anxious to get down to business, and the audio recorder was running, "Tell me who do you mean, when you say 'they?'"

Rachel looked from Casey to Darren. She understood that she had to tell them what she knew in order to go into the Witness Protection and Relocation Program with her son, "My husband Gus Slayton and his brother, Angelo. They are both police officers with the Miami Police Department."

Rachel began to let down her defenses, and her true feelings poured out. She was crying and started to empty the tissue box. She likened Gus Slayton to a firestorm that destroyed everything in its path. His family... His home... His marriage... His law enforcement career... The lives of the women he kidnapped and raped, "Gus's corruption has destroyed my community and my sense of security. The women Gus and Angelo hurt will never forget and will never trust law enforcement again."

Rachel Slayton dabbed the tears in her eyes with another tissue. She described Gus Slayton as a violent man out of control who, "Lost the moral compass and direction in his life. His moods became darker, his increasingly suspicious behavior alarming. He beats me. He lets his brother, Angelo, rape me. I can't live like this any longer." She broke down in tears.

Rachel grabbed another tissue and sobbed harder, "Gus and Angelo will never *choose* to stop raping women. They must *be* stopped."

Casey got emotional listening to her. She had experienced everything Rachel had been through and double that with her father.

Rachel continued crying, "I have to escape this man; he became my abuser, not my husband or friend."

Casey put her arm around Rachel to console her, "We know. We believe they are both sexual predators and murderers. We have been investigating them for almost a year now, including reviewing all vehicle stops and record checks they made, and we have also contacted the women to determine if they were subjected to improper conduct."

Darren added, "FDLE has a lot of evidence against the Slayton brothers. They were prowling the streets during their graveyard shift and using their position as police officers to abduct and rape at least half-a-dozen women that we know about. Plus, murders related to these incidents. They have been preying upon prostitutes, drug addicts, and other women, described as 'down-and-outers,' they believed would not report their assaults."

Rachel wiped the tears from her eyes with a tissue, "I know. They are monsters. They have to be stopped."

Casey hugged her and was on the verge of crying herself, "They used phony DUI stops and computer warrant searches to single out their victims, some of whom they attacked in their patrol car or in dark alleys. As sexual assault victims, the women have not been publicly identified, but the murders have been."

Rachel hugged Casey back, "His crimes also destroyed our marriage, and his son will grow up without a father because we need to escape him."

"We will protect you," said Darren, "Your testimony will be important to get the jury to convict them and put them away, so they can't harm any other women."

CHAPTER FORTY-ONE

Desperados

FDLE Regional Operations Center
Miami, Florida

With little fanfare, Casey brusquely entered the conference room, closed the door, and sat down at the head of the conference table. Her Rape Task Force investigative team sat on either side of the long rectangular table in a glass conference room with a large whiteboard behind Casey at the front of the room. Directly across the room on the opposite wall was a large flat-screen video monitor with a built-in camera for video conferencing. The B-Team attended the meeting from Tallahassee. Weller and Benjamin looked like two bauble heads on a car's dashboard.

Weller tapped the microphone with his wedding ring, "Can you hear us?"

Darren looked over at the screen, "Yes, Lieutenant Weller, we hear you loud and clear."

Casey wore a blue-striped skirt, with a white blouse and an open navy-blue jacket with gold metal buttons on which were etched elaborate flowers. She looked tired from lack of sleep and stressed from the rigors of the investigation. She felt like they were closing in on the perpetrators and wanted to summarize the evidence with her team.

Casey briefly surveyed the attendees, making sure everyone from her team was in attendance. Besides Weller and Benjamin, her sidekick Darren sat to her right. Profiler Jack Higgins was on her left. Dennis Hollis from Fort Lauderdale sat next to Darren, and Sheriff Alan Robertson sat next to Jack with Detective Piper next in line to Robertson.

Casey called the meeting to order, "All right then, let us begin. After almost a year of investigations, we are finally close to solving this hideous case."

Darren reinforced her comments, "Thank God."

Casey stood up and drew a few of circles on a large whiteboard in the conference room with a black marker, representing each of the rapes and murders and all the known evidence. On the top, in a rectangular box, she wrote, "The Slayton Brothers" and underlined it. She connected the circles from one to the other with her marker. Then, she wrote the name, "Rachel Slayton" in one of the circles and underlined it.

She turned to face the team sitting around the conference table, "Agent Turner and I have just interviewed Rachel Slayton, the wife of Gus Slayton. She's turning state's evidence and will go into the Witness Protection and Relocation Program after she testifies at the Slayton's trial. She is an abused and battered wife and will provide powerful testimony regarding the character of both Gus and Angelo Slayton."

The team all looked at each other and shook their heads in approval at this new turn of events. They responded their approval in unison, "Nice job, Casey."

"Thank you. Rachel told us that her husband and his brother beat and rape her constantly. They treat her like a sex slave and share her sexually. Both brothers take turns with her." Casey was reliving painful memories of her own childhood, as she described the testimony of Rachel to the team.

Darren interjected, "Yes. She knows their modus operandi and is willing to testify in court. They are evil twins, two halves of a sinister whole!" He turned to face Casey, "Nice job, Boss."

This was not yet the time to celebrate... Not yet, "Let's sum up the evidence we have. First of all, we now have the Slayton brother's DNA and await a positive confirmation from the lab that it matches the semen samples collected from the rape kits."

Weller interrupted in an effort to gain some brownie points, "Boss, as you also know, we got confirmation at Diva's Topless Gentlemen's Club that the Slayton brothers were regulars there."

Darren responded sarcastically, "Nice job, Lieutenant."

All the men in the room laughed.

Casey didn't think it was funny, "Ok. Settle down. We'll get to that. Secondly, we have the drop of blood from Cara's shoe. She wrote it on the whiteboard with a question mark and circled it. This could be the 'Big Kahuna.' We get a match here, and we know for sure we have the right assailants."

"Thirdly, the tracks in the dirt from the Kimberly Merrick murder and the tire skid marks on the bridge from the Cara Jones murder both match the squad car driven by the Slayton brothers. I believe the enhanced videotape from NASA will confirm they followed her from the Chevron Station." She wrote 'Chevron' and circled number three with another question mark."

"Number four is the eyewitness testimony that two cops are the rapists and murderers, and they work as a tag team. The Slayton brothers are identical twins with identical DNA." She looked over at Jack Higgins, "So that explains why we thought it was a single rapist, Jack."

Jack smiled back at Casey, "Bingo. Now I understand."

Darren added, "Their biggest mistake was Brenda Romney because she can positively identify them even though the so-called Blue Curtain tried to protect them. Plus, the semen in her rape test kit will be compared to the Slayton DNA."

She picked up photos of the brothers and displayed them to the team, "The rape victims have identified these photos as their attackers." She drew an arrow from point number four up to, The Slayton Brothers, "And of course, the hard work and many hours of investigative interviews by Weller and Benjamin, at Diva's Topless Gentlemen's Club to confirm they were regulars there."

The room laughed again at the sarcasm by Casey.

Darren Turner enjoyed watching her slight wiggling movements and legs stretching from behind as she wrote on the whiteboard. It was a great view from where he sat, "Slayton brothers," Darren repeated, "They've got to be the killers."

"Right." She handed the Slayton brother's photos to Turner.

Turner studied the photos provided by the Police Department, "They look really mean." He grabbed the grainy surveillance photos from the Chevron Station and compared them, "There are many similarities here with this Slayton brother. If, indeed, it is him."

Casey turned back to the whiteboard and started writing again, beginning with number five, "Lastly, they fit the Profile to a T. Jack Higgins supplied us with a psychological Profile of the killers, and the Slayton brothers definitely fit that Profile."

Sheriff Robertson turned to Jack Higgins, "What about the music? They played Gershwin's Rhapsody in Blue while they were raping women. What was that all about?"

"The Rhapsody Killers." Jack stood up to address the entire team, "I believe the Gershwin symphony is a predisposition conditioning from events in their lifetime. The music both excites them sexually, elicits memories of past sexual conquests, and provides a familiar, safe psychological compartmentalization for them. They probably grew up with this music in their household as children."

Casey just stood there, listening to Jack's theory. He was right on. That symphony was drummed into her head, night after night, to mask sounds emanating from her bedroom. To her, it was horrible music and elicited painful memories.

She briefly faded into those memories as Jack postulated, *First, her father would quietly enter her bedroom after her mother had fallen asleep. He turned on the symphony and tenderly held her in his arms and gently kissed her. Initially, the music actually soothed and relaxed her, and she thought she enjoyed it. At eight years old, she was innocent and assumed this affection from a father was normal behavior. He was a violent man, but at that moment, she felt safe and comforted in his arms. She thought she was in love with him. She didn't realize he was a pedophile.*

When her father finished, he would leave the music on and go back into the bedroom with her mother. Then her brothers would enter her room. They were not as gentle and loving as her father. First, the older brother, Gus, would rape her, and then Angelo took his turn with her. They always shared everything. They were both mean and abusive. She screamed and fought them off, but they overpowered her, and the music drowned out her agony. Her brothers acted as if she was their property, and, as she grew older, they would not let her go out or date anyone. They always controlled her and disrupted any potential romantic interest from other boys. They had a perverted, controlling relationship with her until she ran away from home.

Darren observed Casey as Jack Higgins was going through his explanation. Although he didn't know the entire story, he could sense the pain Casey was experiencing and wanted to hold her and comfort her. But, in a roomful of cops, he had to maintain his distance.

When Jack finished, she wrote, "Rhapsody in Blue" and circled that as well. She drew another arrow to The Slayton Brothers, "That's their signature. The symphony playing in the background. That's another nail in their coffin." She again drew more arrows from the names of the murder victims up to The Slayton Brothers on the whiteboard.

Collins had enough circumstantial evidence to bring the Slayton brothers in for questioning. She had methodically reconstructed all the incidents and all the major players in the rapes and murders and had come to the same conclusion - the Slayton brothers are the rapists and killers.

Turner stood up and grabbed a red marker from the tray. He circled The Slayton Brothers on the whiteboard twice, "Let's bring them in."

Casey picked up the black marker again and went back to the whiteboard, pointing at the question marks with the marker, "We just need to get the lab confirmation, and then we can go arrest them."

CHAPTER FORTY-TWO

Catwalk

The Breakers

Palm Beach, Florida

The Breakers Hotel in Palm Beach, Florida, originally opened on January 16, 1896, by oil, real estate, and railroad tycoon Henry Flagler, a founder of Standard Oil and, at the time, one of the wealthiest men in America. He was responsible for building the Florida East Coast Railway from Daytona to Key West, and he needed hotels for tourism, so he built them. The Breakers was one of many hotels he built in Florida.

The Palm Beach Charity Fashion Show luncheon took place at The Breakers, on prime beachfront property, within full view of the Atlantic Ocean. The charity was to benefit the Veterans America Organization for wounded and deceased soldiers and their families. They lined wheelchairs on either side of the Catwalk for disabled veterans to have ringside seats to enjoy the attractive models parading the latest fashions.

It was a beautiful sunny day, and the powerful waves were breaking on rocks below the huge outdoor patio, which is how the hotel got its name: "The Breakers." Governor Brendan Scott was scheduled to give the keynote address at the historic hotel during the height of Florida Fashion Week when the world's top designers invaded Palm Beach with their latest fashion designs.

They arranged the luncheon tables and chairs around the Catwalk behind rows of wheelchairs overlooking the Olympic-sized swimming pool. Champagne and caviar were the order of the day for the five-hundred-dollar a plate charity event, and they were flowing generously to the delight of the wealthy donors. The waiters were decked out in their finest formal regalia with black bow ties, bright white shirts, tuxedo jackets, pants, and suspenders, and poured the Champagne with white-glove service.

The Governor took the stage, and L.B. stood behind him, surveying the crowd, protecting the Governor. He unfolded his notes on the podium deck and tapped twice on the microphone with his wedding ring to get audience attention before reading his speech.

"Good Afternoon. Welcome to the Palm Beach Charity Fashion Show at the beautiful Breakers Hotel. It is indeed a privilege to be here, with all the talent assembled for today's fashion design luncheon for our veteran's charity. I particularly want to thank the management of The Breakers Hotel for hosting this momentous event."

The crowd applauded perfunctorily.

The Governor continued, "We are all gathered here today for a very important reason. To honor our veterans who have given so much for our country, so we can be here today enjoying our freedom in America."

The crowd stood up from their tables this time and gave a standing ovation to the veterans in wheelchairs and those seated around the Catwalk with their families.

"I want to thank Veterans America Incorporated for organizing this event today, and remind you to please continue to support our veterans generously by contributing to," he paused to put on his reading glasses and read from a note on the podium, "VeteransAmerica.org. Thank you."

The crowd applauded once again.

The Governor and L.B. walked off the stage and sat down.

The emcee took over the podium and made a big show of opening his notes and clearing his throat as if he were preparing to give the "Gettysburg Address." He loved being on stage, the center of attention, and he loved being in control. It was his sweet spot, and he was relishing every second. He began his long-winded speech by telling the Governor how sorry everyone was for the loss of his daughter and his wife.

The Governor stood up from his seat on stage to say thank you to the emcee. The audience applauded their agreement with his sentiment.

The emcee then switched to extolling the remarkable talent and enormous success of the Governor of the State of Florida, and how lucky they all were to have him at the charity event today. The audience listened politely but looked like they wanted to hang themselves, reminiscent of the scene from the movie *Airplane.*

At the end of the dissertation, there was polite applause directed at the Governor, and then the emcee kicked his voice up a notch, "And now, I am pleased to announce the Demetrius Collection created by the ingenious designer, Jose Demetrius."

Almost right on cue, the music started pounding, and several anorexic women in scanty outfits wiggled their way down the Catwalk one jerk step in front of another in time to the beat. A billow of pastel fog simmered around the stage. It smelled like bad hairspray. The crowd stood up and applauded with great vigor.

As the Governor watched, one garish model after another came marching through the mist with strange multicolored hair, sometimes protruding in many different directions looking like a poodle bouffant, with thick layers of makeup intended to accentuate the designs they were flaunting. The carnival-like procession continued for almost an hour as the emcee went into excruciatingly detailed descriptions of each outfit with melodramatic enthusiasm.

When they got to the beachwear fashions, the audience oohed and aahed, applauding the cavalcade of models wearing skimpy bikinis. The veterans in the audience were grinning from ear to ear.

Finally, the rock music died down, and the emcee announced the guest of honor, "Ladies and gentlemen... Jose Demetrius."

Standing uproarious applause followed in pandemonium as the spotlight turned to Jose Demetrius emerging from the crowd. His bright white tuxedo with Mylar vest and rainbow shirt accentuated his dark Mediterranean complexion. The music bellowed once again, and more colorful vapor blasted into the air, imbuing the designer slinking down the catwalk as if he were one of the models. He threw kisses to his fans from the left side to the right side of the runway, "Thank you, thank you, thank you."

The music stopped, and the emcee announced, "Jose Demetrius, we love your new fashion collection. Thank you for the honor of participating in this important event today for charity."

Contagious applause again exploded as another standing ovation greeted the designer.

He shook hands with the emcee and walked over to the Governor to shake his hand as well, "Thank you, thank you very much." He took a little bow.

CHAPTER FORTY-THREE

Recusal

Marriott Hotel

Miami, Florida

It had been a long day, a long week, a long month, and a long year for Casey Collins. She crashed onto the queen-size bed in her hotel room at the Marriott Hotel in Miami, and laid on her back, staring at the ceiling fan slowly revolving around the room, feeling the cool breeze on her face. The brightness from the Intercostal Waterway outside and the television screen in the room intermittently blasting various colors across the ceiling were the only lights she could see.

Her feelings had gone through many levels of sadness and depression, regarding her brothers' potential criminality, to elation and exhilaration at the prospect of finally nailing the rapists and killers of the Governor's daughter - if they got positive DNA confirmation. Her mind flashed through the history of personalities and problems she'd experienced, like an old-time silent movie. The hundred-hour workweeks, lost weekends, little triumphs, late nights. Potential evidence that turned out to be a false positive, like the pirate treasure hunt, and good investigative efforts that turned the tide on finding the killers and saved the day.

Despite the fact she had been through hell and back because of her abusive family history, and despite the fact the killers could be her own flesh and blood, Casey felt relieved in a strange emotional sense because the evidence to convict them might be conclusively established.

Whether her feelings were right, wrong, or indifferent, and even though in a way, it would be a vindication of her own terrible childhood, she was thankful it could soon be over. It had been a long, painful, and tedious journey.

She thought about how she was going to tell the Brendan she needed to recuse herself from the case, if the DNA evidence confirmed her brothers are, in fact, the killers. *Oh, by the way, I am sorry to tell you my brothers raped and killed your daughter and raped me for years, so I have to recuse myself.* It was not going to go over well.

As she pondered her problematic explanation to Brendan, the telephone rang. She anxiously picked up the receiver, hoping it might be Brendan calling her, "Hello," she answered brightly.

"Casey, it's Darren. We have some good news."

She felt like a pin had just deflated her balloon, "Oh, hello, Darren. What's the good news?"

"Well, given your family relationship with the Slayton brothers, maybe it's not such good news, but the lab just finished their analysis. We have a positive DNA match."

Casey's stomach wrenched as she grasped the finality of the implications of what the DNA match proved, even though she had suspected it all along. Her brothers were the definite serial rapists and killers of South Florida. Her brothers had, in fact, raped and murdered the Governor's daughter.

It hit her like a ton of bricks. She placed the telephone receiver down on the bed and reached for the remote control to turn off the television. Feeling queasy, she watched as the tiny green and yellow lights flickered off, and the television screen went blank. She forced down the bile in her throat and looked out the sliding glass doors at the lights from the boats on the Intercostal Waterway outside of her hotel room.

Darren thought they had gotten disconnected. He said, "Hello? Casey, are you still there?"

Casey picked the telephone receiver back up, "Yes, Darren, I'm still here." She had an overwhelming feeling of shame. Her brothers were guilty of all those rapes and murders, "Oh, my God," Casey mumbled, losing control of her emotions. She thought about how outraged Brendan would be to learn the truth. Her brothers had raped and killed his daughter.

Listening on the other end of the telephone receiver, Darren was concerned, "Casey, are you, all right?"

She put her head down, ashamed of what her brothers had done, "Yes, Darren. Give me a moment." Tears formed and rolled down her cheeks.

"Of course." Darren waited on hold.

She managed to regain her self-control, "Darren, I need to inform the Governor, and I need to recuse myself from any further involvement in this case."

Darren understood, "Yes, I know."

"Let's meet tomorrow at FDLE in Miami, so we can inform the team and explain the situation. I'll call the District Attorney tonight to get arrest warrants after I tell the Governor."

"Okay. I'll organize the meeting for tomorrow." Then he said, "Do you want me to come over?"

"No... Thanks. I've got some serious thinking to do. I'll see you tomorrow, Darren."

He hesitated a moment, "Goodnight, Casey."

"Goodnight." She said softly as she held onto the telephone receiver for a moment. Then, she listened to the dial tone and slowly placed it back in the cradle.

She lamented what she would have to do next. She stood up and straightened her back, trying to find some measure of strength and dignity. She opened the sliding glass door to feel the night air outside and listen to the sounds of the harbor below her room. She started to cry.

The Governor had finished his dinner meeting, and just returned to his hotel room at The Breakers Hotel, when the telephone rang, "Hello."

"Brendan, it's Casey." She was still trembling.

The Governor could tell she was upset, "Casey, are you all right?"

"No, not really, Brendan. I have something to tell you."

The Governor was anxious, "What is it, Casey?"

"We have a positive DNA match on the serial rapists and killers."

"Oh, my God, Casey. Is it the Slayton brothers?"

Casey was sobbing on the other end of the phone, "Yes."

Enraged, he slammed his fist down on the desk in the hotel room, "Those bastards. They killed my daughter... and my wife."

Casey was still sobbing, "Yes, they did. The DNA matched without any doubt. The reason we discovered only one DNA sample was because the Slayton brothers are identical twins."

The Governor's anger was intensifying; he screamed wildly into the telephone receiver, "WHAT DOES THAT MEAN?" He shouted, "THOSE BASTARDS SHOULD NEVER HAVE BEEN BORN!"

As their abused sister, she couldn't have agreed more, "I know. Brendan... identical twins have the exact same DNA."

He was like a bull in a china shop, thrashing around, transfixed in furious rage, still screaming, "WHEN ARE THEY GETTING ARRESTED?"

"I will call the District Attorney as soon as we hang up to get the arrest warrants issued."

The Governor was quiet for a minute, thinking. He calmed down, rubbed his forehead, and thought about vengeance, "Do they have any clue they are going to be arrested?"

"No. Darren and me, and now you are the only ones that know the DNA is a match. I plan to meet with my team tomorrow morning to announce it."

"Casey, I want you to wait until tomorrow morning to inform the District Attorney. There are some loose ends I want to tie up." He quickly added, "Do you understand me?"

It sounded to Casey like a direct order, "Yes, I do, Brendan. I will comply with your order."

As the Governor was thinking, he started to come up with a plan, "Good – Tomorrow," he said absent mindedly.

"Brendan, there's one more thing I need to tell you."

He was still deep in thought, "What is it, Casey?"

She was struggling to get the words out, "Well, uh, this is difficult..."

Brendan was confused, "What is it, Casey?"

"My... umm." She just blurted it out, "My maiden name was... Slayton."

"What?" It didn't register at first, "What are you saying?"

She started crying again, "I'm so sorry, Brendan. The Slayton brothers are... *my* brothers. My horrible psychopath brothers. I hate them. I've always hated them."

"What?" The Governor started to put the pieces together in his mind, "*Your* brothers?"

She was crying uncontrollably at this point, "Yes. I'm sorry."

His anger flared up again, and he shouted, "THOSE MONSTERS ARE YOUR BROTHERS? WHY DIDN'T YOU TELL ME?"

"Because I wasn't sure they were guilty until tonight."

His face turned a bright red. The veins in his neck bulged as he shouted, "YOU... YOU BETRAYED ME, CASEY! I TRUSTED YOU AND YOU LIED TO ME!"

"Brendan, I'm so sorry. I didn't lie to you. I was planning to tell you and recuse myself once I knew for sure they were guilty."

The Governor was furious, "Recuse yourself? Recuse yourself! Do you think you can just *recuse* yourself? CASEY, YOU'RE FIRED!" He slammed down the phone.

CHAPTER FORTY-FOUR

Revenge

The Breakers Hotel

Palm Beach, Florida

The Governor's entire world had fallen apart because of the Slayton brothers. The Slayton brothers raped and murdered his daughter. His wife was dead because of the Slayton brothers. And now Casey misled and lied to him, because of the Slayton brothers. His life was a dismal disaster because of the Slayton brothers.

As a man, a father to a murdered daughter, a husband to a murdered wife, and as a former Marine - honed in combat in the field of battle - he had to retaliate, to avenge the murder of his daughter and his wife. He needed to act now!

After he calmed down from his confrontation with Casey, the Governor continued to formulate a plan in his mind. He had given his Security Guard, L.B., the night off after dinner because he had planned to retreat into his hotel room for the evening, but that was before Casey's revelations.

L.B. was a retired police officer and still wore a police uniform and drove an unmarked patrol car when on duty protecting the Governor. As such, they had adjoining rooms at the hotel. Since he knew L.B. would not be in his hotel room, he opened the door to his security guard's adjoining room and took his police uniform out of the closet. L.B. and he were about the same size.

Back in his own hotel room, the Governor took the police uniform off of its hanger and rolled it up, military style, so it would fit into a hotel laundry bag. He had retained his Black Sig Sauer 9mm pistol from the Marine Corps, as most soldiers did, and placed it into the bag as well. He took the laundry bag, walked out of his hotel room, and down to the front entrance of the hotel.

A huge parking area surrounded the entrance to The Breakers Hotel with a central island in the middle surrounding a massive granite water fountain, about one-quarter mile from the main roadway. It was beautifully landscaped with varieties of palm trees, exotic plants and flowers, meticulously groomed and maintained. The sounds emanating from the pervasive splash of the water fountain continuously filled the outdoor ambiance.

Parked in front of the main portico of the building, were rows of the most glamorous and expensive automobiles owned by the wealthiest, and sometimes famous, guests, staying at the hotel. Nestled among the lines of Ferraris, Rolls-Royces, Lamborghinis, and Bentleys was a black and white 4-door Ford Crown Victoria unmarked patrol car that looked entirely out of place.

The valet thought it was a little peculiar when the Governor himself asked him to retrieve the unmarked patrol car from its parking space and drove out of The Breakers Hotel parking area onto the roadway. He had expected the Governor's security guard to chauffeur the car, not the Governor himself, but he just did his job and delivered it to the Governor, as instructed.

The Blood Moon ignited the night sky, as the Governor turned the patrol car south onto Route A1A toward Miami. He placed the hotel laundry bag containing his Marine Corps Black Sig Sauer 9mm pistol and the L.B.'s police uniform onto the passenger seat. He drove a few miles and turned right onto the Lake Worth bridge across the Intercostal Waterway and toward US Route 95 South.

After a few miles, he pulled into a McDonald's restaurant on the way to change his clothing. Fortunately, he wasn't recognized as he walked into the bathroom in a suit and tie with a laundry bag and walked out of it in a police uniform, like Clark Kent transformed to Superman. He carried his suit and tie and his Black Sig Sauer 9mm pistol in the laundry bag back out to the patrol car.

Tina Evanston's reporting had indicated that the Slayton brother's favorite hangout was McCabe's Irish Pub in Miami. About an hour away. He headed over there to find them.

He was a man with a dead family to avenge.

PART THREE

PRESENT DAY

CHAPTER FORTY-FIVE

Locked and Loaded [3]

McCabe's Irish Pub

Miami, Florida

It was after midnight by the time the Governor arrived at McCabe's Irish Pub in downtown Miami. He drove slowly and checked each car on the street until he eventually spotted a standard-issue black and white Ford Crown Victoria Miami police cruiser parked directly across the street from the Pub. Its painted motto on the side proclaimed, *To Protect and Serve.*

The Blood Moon cast an eerie gray, film noir shadow over the streets below as the Governor passed by the Miami police cruiser, and saw the police officer inside, light-up a cigarette. He assumed it was one of the Slayton brothers. He questioned to himself, *what is he doing at midnight sitting alone in the police cruiser in front of McCabe's? And where is the other brother?* He wanted them both.

The sounds of revelry got progressively louder as the Governor parked his unmarked patrol car to observe the police officer in the Miami police cruiser. He could barely make out the words to *"Bad Moon Rising,"* blaring on the jukebox amid the laughter and shouting commotion inside the Pub.

I see a bad moon a-rising

I see trouble on the way

I see earthquakes and lightnin'

I see bad times today

Don't go round tonight

It's bound to take your life

There's a bad moon on the rise...

He thought about the irony of the lyrics on the night of the Blood Moon and lowered the driver's side window to search through the glass front door of the Pub. It was a shadowy dark cloudless night, but he had a clear view of the blinking neon sign broadcasting the Pub, *"OPEN."*

He waited patiently, watching patrons come and go. Drunken men staggered down the narrow cement steps outside the Pub as they left. Some were lucky and left with a woman they had picked up or a hooker who had been working the bar, while others walked in alone and walked out alone.

He reached over to the passenger seat and took his Marine Corps Black Sig Sauer 9mm pistol out of the laundry bag. He held the weapon in his hand, feeling the weight, and released the bullet clip to make sure it was loaded and ready. It was! He slid the clip back into the gun, locked and loaded. *Semper Fi. Just like Nam,* he thought, recalling his vivid memories of his time as a Marine in the Vietnam War.

The conquests of combat echoed in his mind. Tracking the enemy in the hot as hell jungle, sweating into the site, wiping it away, seeing the mark - then the gentle, ever so gentle, squeeze and *thwack* - the sound of lead tearing through flesh. The dry-throated thrill of the hunt pounding in his ears, drowning out the jungle noise. The ecstasy of the conquest and the slow, slow easing of his heart.

Suddenly, he saw two women stumble out of the Pub at almost 1:30 a.m. The taller woman in a silver sequined outfit with long black curly hair threw her arm around the shorter petite-brunette and burst out laughing as they surged through the door onto the cement sidewalk. They both paused and looked up at the reddish tinted Blood Moon hovering in the cloudless black sky and started teasing each other. He couldn't make out what they were saying, but it seemed like it had something to do with the Blood Moon.

The taller woman, with long black curly hair, appeared to start singing. Then she pointed down the street.

The two women kissed each other on the lips and hugged. They continued razzing each other before they eventually parted in opposite directions. They both appeared to be very drunk.

A few minutes later, the Governor watched the Miami police cruiser, driven by one of the Slayton brothers, ease away from the curb and drive away. Likewise, he also eased away from the curb and tracked the cruiser from a distance, careful not to be discovered as it drove out of the downtown business district. He could see another car in front of the police cruiser in the distance.

As the Governor followed the Miami police cruiser from the Pub, the road quickly changed from bright streetlights and neon store signs in downtown Miami to dark desolation outside of the city. He looked up again at the Blood Moon gloom, apprehensive about the total absence of other cars on the road. But, then again, he thought, *it's probably typical for this late at night.*

Suddenly, a few miles outside of the city, he saw red and blue rolling lights explode up ahead as the police cruiser appeared to pull over the car he was following. The Governor switched off his headlights on the patrol car and pulled over onto the side of the road into a wooded area, close enough to observe the Miami police cruiser up ahead, but hiding the car so it wouldn't be exposed.

It was eerily quiet for a moment as the bright red and blue rolling lights of the police cruiser lit up the Blood Moon night sky. Eventually, he watched the police officer get out of the cruiser and walk up to the car in front that he had pulled over. He wondered, *where is the other brother?*

The police officer grabbed the woman driver by her hair and forced her out of her car. The Governor watched as the police officer pulled out his gun, pointed it at her head and shoved her into the back door of his police cruiser. He couldn't see clearly what was happening because of the distance and the bright rotating police lights glaring in his eyes, but he could tell the woman was struggling and heard her screaming for help. His plan required both brothers to be present, so he had to wait and couldn't help her. He questioned again, *where is the other brother?*

Suddenly, the bright rolling red and blue lights were switched off. The woman continued screaming in the back of the police cruiser, but he couldn't help her... not yet. The Governor watched and waited patiently inside his unmarked patrol car because he wanted both the Slayton brothers together in the same place, at the same time.

After a while, he saw another Miami police cruiser pull up behind the first Slayton brother's Miami police cruiser and switch off its headlights. He heard music playing from that police cruiser. He recognized the music as Gershwin's, *Rhapsody in Blue*, so he figured it must be the other Slayton brother.

Fueled by his thirst for blood, the Governor could almost taste the revenge he so badly needed. It was time for the Slayton brothers to die.

CHAPTER FORTY-SIX

To Protect and Serve [3]

Dark, Backroad
Outside of Miami

The Governor watched the twin brothers move back and forth between the two Miami police cruisers and heard *Rhapsody in Blue* playing on the radio. He felt sorry he couldn't help the woman screaming in the forward police cruiser, but the timing to execute his plan had to be just right.

He saw the cherry red glow arch of a cigarette butt being flicked to the other side of the police cruiser and heard the two brothers laughing after they had both probably raped the screaming woman. He became uncontrollably enraged, and his rage surged.

Did they laugh when they raped and murdered my daughter?

Furious, he started the patrol car and switched on the high-beam headlights.

The brothers were still laughing, sitting on the hood of the police cruiser with *Rhapsody in Blue* blaring on the radio when suddenly, they were drenched in high-beam headlights. They squinted into the bright lights blinding their eyes and thought they recognized the car as one of their own. A black and white police patrol car.

243

Gus exchanged looks with his brother, "Are you expecting company?"

"No!" Angelo responded with surprise.

Then, a blue-uniformed figure stepped from the patrol car and walked toward them, "Was it good?"

Gus laughed. Just another cop looking for some action, "Very good," he said, "Take a turn. Have at it."

"But don't expect any fight," Angelo added, chuckling.

The woman in the forward Slayton police cruiser started screaming again, "HELP ME! PLEASE HELP ME!"

The Governor cringed when he glanced over at the woman chained inside the cage and the motto on the side of the police cruiser, *To Protect and Serve*. He listened to them laughing, then responded to Angelo, "Oh, don't worry, I won't."

Gus and Angelo looked at each other. The voice sounded familiar, like they'd heard it before.

Suddenly, *BAM!* Gus saw the gun flash in the dark, as a bullet slammed into Angelo's chest and it splattered him red with blood. His brother crumbled to the ground.

Gus was shocked! *Why would another cop shoot them?* He screamed, "WHAT THE HELL ARE YOU DOING?"

Then he saw the shooter turn the gun toward him. He instinctively reached for his own gun and dove to the ground just as the shooter's gun flashed again, *BAM!* It hit him in his left shoulder, bleeding, as he fired back at the shooter in rapid succession, *BAM! BAM! BAM!*

The Governor was hit in the leg by Gus firing up from ground level. He staggered back into the patrol car, bleeding badly, and shoved the transmission into reverse, squealing the tires backward onto the roadway, leaving a trail of blood on the gravel shoulder. Then the car lurched forward and sped off.

Gus continued firing his gun at the fleeing rear-end of the patrol car, *BAM! BAM! BAM!*

Anna Swayze was crying, bleeding, chained inside the cage and struggling to be free, as she witnessed the gunfight, and continued screaming for help. She shouted at the car as it raced away, "NO! NO! DON'T GO! HELP ME!"

Gus was down on the ground in pain, bleeding from his shoulder wound. He crawled over to Angelo to feel for a pulse, "Angelo, Angelo." There was no pulse, and there was no response. His dead eyes stared wide at the Blood Moon. *Rhapsody in Blue,* still playing on the radio.

Angelo Slayton was dead. Gus Slayton was wounded and bleeding.

CHAPTER FORTY-SEVEN

Postmortem

Backroad

Outside of Miami

Agent Darren Turner looked down at the bloody, dead body and the dried blood and tire tracks on the shoulder of the road. He immediately recognized the dead man as one of the Slayton brothers, even though he was not in his police officer uniform. His mind was racing as he pondered who might have killed him.

Was it the victims themselves, or victim's family members, or his wife, Rachel Slayton, or... his sister, Casey Collins?

Casey had been unavailable since last night. *Where was she?* She wasn't answering her phone. *What was going on? And where was the other Slayton brother?"*

Darren called her office from his cell phone and spoke to Betsy, "Have you heard from Casey? I need to talk to her. It's very important." He didn't tell Betsy the reason, because he assumed she didn't know that the Slayton brothers were Casey's brothers, "I left messages at her hotel, on her cell phone and her house, but she hasn't answered."

"I haven't heard from her either," Betsy was concerned as well, "I've been trying to reach her all morning."

Darren couldn't figure out what was going on, "Call me immediately when you locate her. It's very important."

Most murders are committed by family members or close relatives, and it was incriminating that Casey was missing at the same point in time that her brother had been killed. He surveyed the crime scene while he spoke to Betsy and wondered if the remaining Slayton brother might have hurt or kidnapped *Casey*?

The forensics teams were busy making plaster molds of the tire tracks from the killer's car, although the gravel made it difficult to get an accurate pattern. They had taken detailed photographs of the entire crime scene, awaiting the arrival of the Miami Medical Examiner to inspect the body before they could remove it.

There was an ambulance nearby, and the brunette woman inside was wrapped in a blanket, shivering in the early morning chill. Anna Swayze had a bandaged head, and her wrists and ankles were bleeding from struggling to be free of the handcuffs all night.

Just as he hung up from Betsy, a television news crew pulled up, and Tina Evanston descended from the NBC6 Investigators News van with a microphone in her hand and a cameraman following close behind her. She quickly surveyed the area, the black and white Miami police cruiser, and the dead man on the ground. She knew she had struck gold. She looked into the live television camera feeding the breaking news back to the studio and then, in turn, out to her worldwide audience.

BREAKING NEWS!

The Rhapsody Killers

"This is Tina Evanston from the NBC6 Investigators, streaming live breaking news from the crime scene of a murdered police officer outside of Miami."

Darren was working with the Forensics Team to gather and document evidence at the crime scene when suddenly Tina walked up to him and shoved the microphone into his face.

"We heard on the police scanner that there was a police officer down."

The cameraman panned from Tina to the dead body and the black and white police cruiser, then over to the ambulance with the bloody woman inside.

"Can you tell us what happened?"

Other police officers came over and started cordoning off the area, pushing the cameraman back. They preserved the area with yellow police tape railing off the entire crime scene. The cameraman continued to take video while adjusting his positions.

Darren spoke into the microphone while looking at his girlfriend.

"Tina, we don't know what happened. We are still investigating the crime scene."

She looked back at the dead body, sprawled out on the ground next to the police car, and directed the cameraman to take a video of the body.

"Is it a cop? It looks like he was driving a police car. Can you reveal the identity of the dead body?"

Darren looked into the camera for a second, trying to think of the politically correct response before answering Tina's question.

"No, we can't. We haven't verified the identity, and we haven't notified the next of kin."

She was suspicious and looked Darren straight in the eyes. She had been face-to-face with the Slayton brothers before, and the dead body looked like one of the identical twins. But which one?

"Is it a dead Slayton brother?"

Darren was getting frustrated. He wanted to answer her question directly and honestly, but there were other considerations and department policy procedures he had to adhere to.

"I told you, we haven't verified the identity, and we haven't notified the next of kin."

Tina then changed the direction of her questioning and focused on the disheveled brunette woman shivering in the ambulance.

"Was there another rape?"

He quickly turned his head to look at the ambulance behind him. The back doors were wide open as the paramedics tended to Anna Swayze. He turned back to Tina.

"We don't know yet, Tina. She needs to go to the hospital and get a rape test kit."

Tina and her cameraman tried to barge past Darren to interview the woman in the ambulance. More police officers blocked their way, so Tina shouted a question while the cameraman took a close-up video of the bruised and battered woman.

"What happened to you? Did the dead police officer rape you?"

Anna Swayze just looked over at Tina and didn't answer. She was too weak and too hurt to acknowledge Tina's questions.

Tina then turned her attention to the cameraman to sign-off on the breaking news story. She knew there would be more follow-up later.

"This is Tina Evanston Reporting for NBC6 Investigators."

Casey Collins had rented a car and was driving back to Tallahassee when she heard the NBC6 Investigators News live simulcast report on the radio. She was shocked and pulled over to the side of the road. She heard Tina ask Darren, *"Is it a dead Slayton brother?"*

At that exact moment, Casey immediately knew one of her brothers was dead, and she immediately knew who had killed him. *Which one was it? And where was my other brother?*

She reached for her cell phone and called Darren.

CHAPTER FORTY-EIGHT

Who Dunnit?

Backroad

Outside of Miami

An hour later, Casey Collins arrived at the crime scene. They had cordoned off the entire area with yellow police tape, and there were numerous red numbered markers scattered around denoting evidence for forensic analysis. Her dead brother was still lying on the gravel shoulder, being examined by the Miami Medical Examiner.

Anna Swayze had given a brief statement to Darren about what had happened and then was taken to the hospital in the ambulance. They would conduct a more detailed interrogation following her recovery and release from the hospital.

The NBC6 Investigators News crew had been joined by several other television stations, news vans, media, and print reporters, and all had been moved to an area further away from the crime scene but close enough to keep track of what was going on.

Darren needed Casey to positively confirm the identity of the dead body. She was completely dispassionate as she looked at his lifeless face, "Yes, that's Police Officer Angelo Slayton," she confirmed to the Miami Medical Examiner, as he jotted on a notepad. Angelo had a birthmark on his neck that Gus didn't have. That was the only way she could tell which identical twin brother it was.

She turned to Darren, "What happened?"

"When we arrived here this morning, a woman was handcuffed spread-eagle in the cage of that Miami police cruiser." Darren pointed to the cruiser's cage, "She told us she had been abducted and badly beaten and raped by two men who looked identical. The only difference was, one was in a police uniform and smelled of scotch and cigarettes, and the other was in plain clothes and smelled of beer." He pointed to the dead Slayton brother, "She identified this one, Angelo, as one of the rapists and said she saw him at McCabe's Irish Pub downtown playing pool last night. She thinks the other rapist, probably Gus, was shot but got away."

Casey looked perplexed, "Shot? By who?"

Darren shook his head, "Based on what the victim told us; they took turns beating and raping her until someone came along in a black and white car that looked like another cop, in a cop uniform. She said a gunfight ensued, and Gus, Angelo here, and the shooter were all shot." He looked over at the dead man, "Apparently, Angelo was killed first, and then I assume Gus was shot, but ducked down and started shooting back. The shooter scrambled back to the black and white car and escaped while Gus continued shooting."

"That means Gus is still out there," Casey said, "armed and wounded."

"And, dangerous! She thinks the shooter was also wounded." He pointed to the blood on the ground, "We'll know after we get the DNA from all of this blood."

"Could she identify the shooter?"

Darren shook his head, "No. It was dark, and the Blood Moon last night obscured her vision, so she couldn't make an identification. She said he looked white, tall, and average body weight in a police uniform with a handgun."

She nodded her head, "I'd like to thank that 'hero.'"

"Hero? I don't know if that's the right categorization. She was scared the shooter was going to shoot her too, but instead, I assume Gus Slayton fired back and the shooter sped away. She said that strange music was playing. She thinks it was Gershwin again, *Rhapsody in Blue*. Then, she said Gus Slayton crawled over to the second police cruiser that Angelo had apparently driven here, and drove away."

Casey walked over to the police cruiser and examined the cage. The bloody handcuffs were still dangling inside the cage, "Oh my God, like a chained animal." Anna Swayze's clothing was scattered on the floor of the cruiser.

They were talking in private, so she confided in Darren, "It's what they used to do to me... For years."

Darren's eyes widened, "Wow, Casey."

She looked away from Darren and sobbed, "I know. It was awful. My father would come into my bedroom first after my mother fell asleep and play 'Rhapsody in Blue' on the CD player."

Darren was surprised, "Your father?"

"Yes, my father. 'Rhapsody in Blue.' *Blue* is a cop thing. You know, *Blue* uniform, *Blue* cap, *Blue* blood, *Blue* lens, *Blue* curtain."

He looked at her compassionately, "I know."

She continued, "He didn't want my mother to hear him screwing her daughter. The music, *Rhapsody in Blue*, veiled any noise coming from my bedroom."

"So that explains the music."

"Then, my brothers would take their turns." She looked back over at the dead body, "I'm glad he's dead. I only wish I had killed him... and Gus."

Darren was sympathetic, "I can't say I blame you... Did *you* kill him?"

Casey looked up at him, "No, I didn't. I wanted him dead, but there are so many others who also wanted them both dead."

Darren was subdued, "Well, as you know, the usual suspects are the victims or the victim's family members or relatives or... well, *you*."

Casey denied it, "As I said, I'm glad he's dead, but I didn't kill him."

Darren wanted to eliminate her as a suspect, but she had motive and opportunity, "You've been missing for the past twelve hours. Where have you been?"

Casey understood his suspicions; after all, she was the first to know they were proven guilty by the DNA, "As I expected, Brendan was furious that I didn't tell him the Slayton brothers were my brothers. When I told him the DNA proved my brothers had raped and murdered his daughter, he accused me of lying to him. When I told him, I would recuse myself... he fired me."

Darren was listening intently, "That doesn't explain where you were all night."

Casey had to quickly come up with an alibi to protect Brendan. Being the good detective that she was, she had already figured out that Brendan killed her brother. Especially since she had the conversation with him last night, and he explicitly ordered her not to tell the District Attorney... until the next morning. That gave him the opportunity to carry out his plan, and he certainly already had the motive.

She knew he had to avenge the rape and murder of his daughter and the death of his wife. She knew he was a former Marine and had experienced guns and killing in the war. She also knew he would need an alibi, and she decided *she* would become his alibi.

She looked away, "About 45-minutes after Brendan hung up the phone on me, he called me back in my hotel room. He said he was sorry, but he was distraught now that he knew who the killers were. And especially distraught that they were my brothers. He said he was in Palm Beach and wanted to see me."

Darren was listening intently, "Did you see him?"

She looked back at him with tears in her eyes, "Yes, I told him to meet me at the Marriott Hotel lounge. I told him I would be there waiting for him. I told him I needed a drink, badly. He said he did too."

Darren realized the Governor and Casey were his two prime suspects in the Slayton brother's killing, and if they were together all night, that would eliminate them because each of them would be the alibi for the other, "What time did this take place?"

Casey instinctively looked at her watch while devising her story, "About an hour later, I guess it was around ten o'clock, Brendan walked into the Marriott Hotel lounge, and we sat down at a table and talked... and drank. We drank a lot."

Darren was piecing together the timelines in his mind as he was interrogating Casey. Based on Anna Swayze's recollections, he estimated the Slayton brother was killed a little before three o'clock in the morning, "I presume the bartender can confirm that you both were there?"

Casey really was at the bar at that time, although not with the Governor. She had to take the chance, "Yes, and so will the bar tab. I billed it to my hotel room."

Darren acknowledged her story. He would double-check all of her alibi's anyway. After all, he was a detective. But he was hoping it was all true, "Okay, so go on."

"We had several Martinis together." Her bar tab could prove that because she did have several Bombay Gin Martinis, but, just not *with* the Governor, "Brendan was understandably upset. We drank together, talked together and cried together until the bar closed after 1:00 a.m."

Darren knew that still gave either or both of them time to commit the murder. Besides himself, they were the only other people in the world who knew the Slayton brothers were the confirmed killers. They each had a motive, "So, where did you go after the bar closed?"

Casey looked down at the ground for a moment to compose herself, and then looked back up into Darren's eyes, "We went to my room. Brendan spent the night with me."

Darren was a little surprised by that, "So, you're telling me you slept with the Governor... All night?"

"Yes, Darren." She started sobbing, "We were both going through hell - me with my psychopathic brothers, and he with the death of his daughter and wife. We were drinking, and with all our years of friendship and working together, we turned to each other and mutually bonded. We fell in love."

She was crying, tears were rolling down her cheeks, but Darren still needed more answers, "What time did he leave?"

"He left in the morning. I was asleep."

Darren was still working the timelines in his mind, "So, you don't know what time he left?"

Casey realized what Darren was doing, and she knew that she had to make it after the time of Angelo's murder, which she presumed was early in the morning, "I was drained. It was all very emotional."

"Casey, I need to know what time he left."

She understood that, "I think it was around 5:00 a.m. when he returned to Palm Beach."

"Where was he staying?"

She knew he would double-check that too, "The Breakers Hotel."

"So, you spent the night together in bed, and then he returned to Palm Beach at 5:00 a.m. Is that right?"

"Yes, that's right. I didn't kill my brother."

"I believe you. The question is, *who* did?"

"They were horrible men. Lots of people had a motive."

"Why didn't you answer your phone? I've been calling you all morning, and Betsy has been calling you as well."

"I turned my phone off. I need some downtime. I needed some time to think about my relationship with Brendan and my life. As you now know, I've had a pretty awful childhood, and adulthood hasn't been a panacea either."

"We both left messages everywhere."

"I know. It wasn't until I heard your girlfriend, Tina, on the radio ask: *Is it a dead Slayton brother?* That I knew something had happened."

CHAPTER FORTY-NINE

Wound Care [26]

Cleveland Clinic Hospital
Miami, Florida

It started raining hard as Gus Slayton parked his police cruiser in the employee parking lot of the Cleveland Clinic Hospital in downtown Miami. It was a dark, overcast night, and the blinding rain obscured the parking lot lights. He lit up a fresh joint with his Zippo lighter embossed with a rippling American flag and a police badge silhouetted among the folds, "To Protect and Serve" in bold blocks at the base and inhaled the weed through his nicotine discolored teeth. The drug helped ease the pain from the gunshot wound in his shoulder.

He dragged the smoke deep into his lungs, as he scrutinized the midnight shift scurrying to their cars after work, dodging the rain in a pulsating canopy of bouncing umbrellas. He had bandaged his left shoulder, using his police EMT kit, but he was still bleeding from the bullet lodged in his wound. His plan was to kidnap a nurse who could help him with his injury.

As the flow of medical personnel subsided, Gus spotted a middle-aged woman in a white nurses' uniform walking down the aisle near his police cruiser. She was juggling her umbrella and digging into her pocketbook for keys as she searched for her car.

He flicked what was left of the joint out the window, grabbed his police-issued Glock 9mm handgun and handcuffs, and staggered toward her as she unlocked her car's driver side door. She had just started to lower her umbrella to get in when he accosted her.

He jammed the gun into her head, "Don't scream, or I'll kill you."

The gun assault hurt her head and triggered a primal fear in her that verged on panic, "What do you want from me?"

He knew his police cruiser was hunted, and he needed to abandon it, "Unlock the car doors. I just need a ride." He pushed the gun harder into her head, "Now!"

Her head started to bleed. She had a feeling of imminent danger as she pushed the button on the driver's side door to unlock all four doors on her car. She pleaded, "Please don't shoot me. I have children."

He opened the rear passenger door behind the driver's seat, "Do as I tell you, and you'll live. Get in and drive." He got behind her in the car and pressed the gun to her head. He directed her to drive to a rundown ghetto area near Grove Street in Miami.

She started the car and drove as he ordered.

He had found a fleabag motel frequented by prostitutes and drug addicts, where the clerk didn't ask any questions, especially after he saw the police badge. He didn't want any problems with the law. The dried blood from his gunshot wound had blended with his dark blue police shirt, and the clerk didn't notice the blood and didn't really care anyway, especially since Gus had rented the room for a week and paid with cash.

Like a flickering, grainy slow motion, old-time black and white movie, the nurse pulled her car into the wet, misty parking lot at the Grove Street Motel and searched through her rain-drenched windshield for a place to park.

Gus directed her to park her car in front of the door to his rented motel room and back into the space so the license plate number would not be visible. He knew the State of Florida only required the license plate on the rear of the car, which now faced the motel instead of the parking lot. He put the "Do Not Disturb" sign on the doorknob as they entered the rundown motel room.

Cheap drapery covered the windows, and the walls were painted a dingy pea-green. A queen-sized bed was against the center of the wall, facing the door. The bedspread was old, wrinkled, and stained as if most people never bothered to get under the sheets. An acrid odor of dirty underwear combined with stale body odor and cigarette-smoke permeated the room. The fluorescent lights harshly revealed moldy carpet and discolored walls. A green neon vacancy sign outside the motel window flashed continuously, giving an eerie film noir feeling to the putrid room.

On either side of the bed, cheap wooden night tables supported cracked ceramic lamps with mildew stained, tarnished yellow lampshades. A bottle of Johnny Walker Red scotch and a pack of cigarettes were on one of them. His portable police radio scanner was on the bureau opposite the bed to monitor law enforcement activity, especially as it pertained to him, alongside an outdated cathode-ray tube television.

He immediately turned on the television to NBC6 news and gawked for a moment at beautiful Tina Evanston, as she reported the tail end of her latest news update:

BREAKING NEWS!
The Rhapsody Killers

". . . police are looking for Gus Slayton in Miami. He is armed and dangerous. Authorities believe he is wounded and seeking medical care."

"This is Tina Evanston Reporting for NBC6 Investigators."

He pushed the nurse over toward the bed with the Glock 9mm handgun, "Are you right-handed or left-handed, Nursey?"

Her eyes moved from the television to the Glock 9mm gun in his hand, but she didn't want to ask questions at this point. She stuttered as she answered him, "I'm... I'm right-handed."

The bedframe had a metal headboard, so he handcuffed her left hand to the frame. Then, he placed the Glock on the bureau, so the nurse couldn't reach it, and started to remove his police uniform. He was aching as he slipped out of his shoes and trousers, and he needed help to remove his shirt.

She thought he was going to rape her and started to cry, "Please... I drove you here, as you wanted. Please let me go."

"I'll let you go, after you help me with this gunshot wound in my shoulder, Nursey." Gus instructed her to carefully help him to remove his police shirt so she could examine his wound. He grabbed the bottle of scotch from the night table and took a long, hard swallow as he laid down on the bed. He was in excruciating pain.

She took off his bloody shirt and saw the wound. Her nursing instincts immediately kicked into gear, and she reached over for the police issued EMT kit, fully stocked with medical instruments and medications. She was a caregiver because that's what nurses do, so she opened the EMT kit and started to take care of his wound.

CHAPTER FIFTY

Collision Course [26]

Grove Street Motel

Miami, Florida

After a couple of days, the nurse was able to mend Gus as best she could under the circumstances. She had cleaned and bandaged his wound with the police EMT kit, and, as a thank you, he beat her and raped her. She was hurt and scared, and after she had finished nursing his wound, he handcuffed both of her hands to the metal headboard on the bed frame above her head. She was lying on her back, naked from the waist down, unable to move her arms or hands. He used his gun to threaten her as she lay on her back in the bed next to him.

They were lacking food, but Gus was not strong enough yet to make a food run, and he certainly would not allow the nurse to leave the motel room unescorted. He thought about ordering pizza delivery, but he didn't want to draw attention to the room or his condition to a deliveryman. He figured they would go to a fast-food drive-thru window to get hamburgers and fries at some point.

The maid was curious about the "Do Not Disturb" sign constantly on the door, but for her, it was one less room to clean, so she disregarded it.

Gus drank from what was left of the bottle of scotch and smoked a cigarette as he watched the NBC6 Investigators news on the outdated

262

television in the motel room. Tina Evanston announced an All-Points-Bulletin for his arrest, with his "Wanted" photograph broadcast nationwide. She also said they hadn't found Angelo Slayton's killer yet, and they had very few leads in the case.

Gus thought to himself; *it didn't take a rocket scientist to figure out who the shooter was.* He knew who had killed his brother. He eventually recognized the voice, the size and shape of the shooter, and, of course, the motive. The Governor wanted revenge for the rape and murder of his daughter. And now, Gus wanted revenge for the killing of his brother. They were both on a collision course with each other.

The nurse heard Tina Evanston, too, and saw the Wanted photograph of her abductor. She realized who Gus was, and it frightened her even more. A serial rapist and killer had kidnapped her. She had already been beaten and raped, would she be killed next? She knew her family would be frantically looking for her.

Gus was drunk and sexually aroused watching Tina Evanston on television. He stroked himself as he leaned over to taunt the nurse, "So, now you know who I am, Nursey. I'm famous," he said with a callous laugh, "What do you think of that, Nursey?"

She was frightened and sobbed, saying, "Please let me go. I won't tell anyone. I promise."

He slipped off his underwear and fondled himself. He was hallucinating, "Oh, I'm not done with you yet, Nursey. You're not as gorgeous as Tina Evanston, but you'll have to do for now."

Gus fantasized that she was Tina, "I've got a nice present for you, Tina." He loved the power of being in control, "The law must be obeyed, Tina."

She cried, "No, no, I'm not Tina. Please let me go."

He climbed on top of her while her hands were still handcuffed over her head, "You be nice to me, Tina, and I promise I won't hurt you...

too much," Gus said, laughing. He smelled of scotch, cigarettes, and stale body odor. He slapped her face and forced himself inside of her.

She was crying and struggling to free her hands, but her wrists started bleeding. She was powerless. All she could do was just lie there while he raped her.

---

[26]. *Police Officers Mark Vara and Lindsay Craig*
Police Brutality in Buffalo, NY:

Police Officers Mark Vara and Lindsay Craig were charged with police misconduct and brutality to Nurse Anna Townsend arising from events that began at Townsend's residence. The charges of abuse by police included: unlawful arrest, unlawful imprisonment, trespass, excessive force, battery, slander, malicious prosecution, negligence, and intentional infliction of emotional distress. Police Officer Mark Vara grabbed Anna from inside her home, pushed her down her porch stairs, and threw her onto the concrete sidewalk outside after handcuffing her. She fractured her ankle.

CHAPTER FIFTY-ONE

Motive

Governor's Mansion
Tallahassee, Florida

The Governor returned to Tallahassee with a wounded leg that L.B. had hastily bandaged so he wouldn't have to go to the hospital and report the shooting. He felt both gratified and justified in having killed one of the men that raped and murdered his daughter and caused the death of his wife, but he wanted the other brother dead as well.

He realized he hadn't planned it very well, given the spontaneity of his vengeance, and he probably made a lot of mistakes. Notwithstanding the fact that there were no eyewitnesses, except the rape victim, who he felt certain could not have recognized him in the dark Blood Moon lit night, the forensics might implicate him. He had experience with law enforcement when he was District Attorney, and he knew the bullets could definitely be connected to the gun he used. But, he also knew, they would have to locate the gun first - to make a match - which was now permanently lost after he had tossed it into the Atlantic Ocean. He thought about his response to interrogation about the gun's whereabouts and played it out in his mind:

"Where is the gun, Governor?"

"Oh, it fell out of the car as I was opening the door. Sorry."

"Where did it fall out of the car?"

"In the Atlantic Ocean."

It just didn't sound plausible; he would just have to say he didn't have a gun. He figured they would never doubt the word of the Governor. *Would they?*

The other problem was his blood was all over the crime scene, and his DNA could incriminate him. He wasn't sure if any of the DNA databases had his DNA or not. It might be in some Marine Corps DNA database from over 40-years ago if they checked there. If they still had it?

His biggest problem was motive. He definitely had it, and the entire world knew it. Law enforcement always suspected family members first in any murder investigation, and he had "motive" stamped all over his forehead.

He also had opportunity. He was in Palm Beach, a short distance from Miami and The Breakers valet could attest to the fact that he drove off alone, in the direction of Miami, if he was paying any attention at all, which, given the curiosity written all over his face when the Governor retrieved the unmarked patrol car, he probably was. Although, he had no regrets, and he would do it all over again if he had to, he was fearful that he might get caught. The idea of spending the rest of his life in prison was petrifying.

Upon returning to The Breakers Hotel, the Governor parked the bloody and bullet-riddled patrol car in the self-parking lot so it wouldn't draw attention to the car or himself with the valet or bell service. Thankfully, the patrol car had an EMT first-aid kit, which he used to stop his leg bleeding, before heading back to The Breakers. He rolled up the bloody police uniform military-style, put it back into the laundry bag, and changed back into his civilian clothes before returning to the hotel.

The Governor had a slight limp from the gunshot wound and tried to be as obscure as possible returning to his hotel room at five o'clock in the morning, but the ever-attentive clerk at the front desk had recognized him, "Good morning, Mr. Governor."

He quickly faked a feeble excuse, trying to be as anonymous as possible, "Oh... good morning. Couldn't sleep. Just went out for a walk."

The clerk practically screamed across the foyer, "If there is anything I can do to help Governor, please let me know."

The Governor just waved back. *You can shut-up,* he thought.

Once in his hotel room, he crossed over to his security guard's adjoining room and woke L.B. out of a sound, snoring sleep, "L.B., L.B., wake-up, I've been shot!"

L.B. awoke to the surprise of the Governor of Florida, waking him in his bed, "Brendan, what happened? Are you, all right?"

He shook his head, "No, I'm not. It's a long story, L.B., but I've been shot in the leg. I need your help."

L.B. would do anything the Governor asked of him, "Of course, Brendan. Anything you need." He jumped out of bed, "Let me see your wound."

L.B. spent the next two hours mending Brendan's bullet wounded leg with his own professional EMT first-aid kit he always kept with him in his suitcase. Fortunately, as part of his job, he had extensive medical training, and, when he examined the Governor's wound, he could see the bullet had passed completely through the thigh muscle based on the bullet exit hole. He thoroughly cleaned and disinfected the wound, then injected antibiotics with a hypodermic needle and bandaged the leg again with sterile gauze pads and rolls wrapped around the wound.

The Governor gave him a detailed explanation of the Slayton brothers shooting in Miami, while L.B. played doctor and administered pain pills and a sleeping pill. After which, the Governor passed out, with the "Do Not Disturb" sign on his hotel room door. He would eventually heal physically, but would he heal emotionally and mentally?

The sun was rising over the Atlantic Ocean as L.B. examined the patrol car in the self-parking lot. He could see in the morning light that the driver's side seat and carpet were blood-soaked. The driver's side door had bullet holes in it, as did the front bumper and rear trunk. He knew he could clean it and repair the bullet holes himself so no one would ever know what had happened.

CHAPTER FIFTY-TWO

Gone but Not Forgotten

FDLE Regional Operations Center
Miami, Florida

The Governor's Rape Task Force meeting was originally planned to announce the DNA match and arrest warrants for the Slayton brothers with Casey Collins in charge; but now, instead, they were assembled to brainstorm the identity of the killer of Angelo Slayton with Darren Turner in charge. Casey Collins was gone, but not forgotten.

The District Attorney issued an arrest warrant for the surviving Slayton brother for rape and murder. Gus Slayton was a wanted man and assumed to be wounded, based upon the victim, Anna Swayze's eyewitness account of the shooting. An All-Points-Bulletin had been issued to be on the lookout for Gustavo Slayton, assumed to be armed and dangerous.

The investigative team sat on both sides of the long rectangular table in the glass conference room with the large whiteboard behind Agent Turner at the front of the room. Directly across the room on the opposite wall was Lieutenant Weller and Sergeant Benjamin, attending the meeting from Tallahassee via the video monitor.

Darren stood up with a black magic marker and wrote "Angelo Slayton's killer" at the top and underlined it. Then, he wrote potential suspects underneath and drew a line over to the left with the number one, "Let's start listing the suspects with a motive to kill the Slayton brothers. I'll start with the murder victim's family members. At the top of my list is the Cara Jones family." He wrote Cara Jones next to the number one and under that "father," "mother," and "sister."

Sheriff Robertson was closest to that investigation and spoke up first, "Cara's father, Sam Jones, found his daughter's body at the bottom of the 70-foot high bridge the Slayton brothers threw her from. As you would expect, Mr. Jones was livid and vowed revenge for his daughter's murder."

Darren interrupted, "Unfortunately, losing Cara devastated Sam Jones so badly that he died of a heart attack shortly after Cara's murder. So, naturally, he's off our list of killers."

Robertson continued, "True. But by that time, her sister, Cynthia, and her mother, Joyce, had lost two loved ones, Cara *and* Sam, because of the Slayton brothers, and they wanted retribution." He reached over and switched the video monitor to display the computer feed. He typed on the keyboard and video from Cara Jones sister's and mother's television remarks displayed on the screen:

> *"I'm so outraged," said Cynthia Jones, Cara's sister. "It's egregious to think this could happen in this day and age. It makes me relive my sister, Cara's murder, all over again."*
>
> *Cynthia said she and her mother were sickened and disgusted by the recent news events and cannot believe this is happening.*

"Tina Evanston interviewed Joyce Jones on NBC6 News, here's the text of what she said:"

> *"I just don't want our family to appear that we are against the police. We have the utmost respect for the department and the majority of the police officers. It just seems that after all these years, there should be a better*

*way to identify the bad ones. Thank goodness times have
changed, and at least some of the women who are harassed
or taken advantage of do come forward and report these
incidents. When there is a pattern of behavior of controlling
women through sexual advances, there is the chance that
the actions may escalate, and another person's life might
be in danger. I want to encourage any woman who finds
herself in such a situation to speak up and report it. By
doing so, she may save the life of another innocent young
woman. It could have saved Cara's."*

*"This is Tina Evanston Reporting for NBC6
Investigators."*

Darren added, "Besides Gus Slayton, who has vanished into thin
air, our only eyewitness, Anna Swayze, said Angelo Slayton's killer was
male, so either the Jones women disguised themselves really well to look
like a male, or they hired somebody else to do it."

Sheriff Robertson probed deeper, "Or, our eyewitness was mistaken
about gender."

"True. It could be a case of mistaken identity or an impersonator."
Darren assigned responsibility to Sheriff Robertson, "Sheriff, check
their alibis for last night, for both of them. Also, see if there might be
an accomplice."

He acknowledged the directive, "Got it."

Darren turned back to the whiteboard and wrote number two next,
"OK, Kimberly Merrick, next." He looked at the faces of Weller and
Benjamin on the video screen, "You two have been tirelessly dedicated
to working the topless bar interrogations. What do we know?"

They all laughed for a moment to break the tension in the room.

Weller began, "Bridger Merrick, Kimberly's widower, has been a
basket case ever since Kimberly's murder. He's the one that retraced
her route when she didn't arrive home on time and initially discovered

her red Jeep Wrangler on the side of the road, with her driver's license missing from her wallet."

Benjamin continued, "Bridger told us he can't sleep at night, and when he does, he has nightmares about his wife. He was seething with anger when we interviewed him. His eyes were red-rimmed and ringed with dark circles."

Weller completed the dialogue, "He said when he closes his eyes, he sees his wife lying on a hospital examining table in a bag unzipped from head to chest. One side of her face is beaten beyond recognition."

Darren interjected, "Do you think he was angry enough to become a vigilante?"

Weller answered, "Not sure, but we'll check on his alibi for last night."

Darren turned back to the whiteboard and wrote number three next, "OK. The highest-profile murder, of course, is the Governor's daughter." He looked around the conference table, "Casey and I have been focused on this one, and it has gotten very complicated." He put down the magic marker, "The prime suspect would normally be Susan Scott's father. He would be the most likely to want revenge. However, Susan's father is our Governor and the head of law enforcement, FDLE, in the State of Florida."

Dennis Hollis voiced his misgivings, "He's also the father of a murdered daughter who wants vengeance. I don't think we can discount that just because he's the Governor and our boss."

Darren agreed, "Yes, that's true. I agree."

Hollis questioned, "What about the buried pirate treasure investigation? Is that still active?"

"From what we know, Susan discovered a legend about an Indian boy spotting pirates on Seminole Indian tribal land about 200 years ago, but we haven't uncovered any connection to buried treasure as a motive to kill her." Darren shook his head, "That appears to have been a blind alley."

Hollis continued, "Any idea where the Governor was last night?"

Darren had his suspicions about Casey's story. Still, he realized he needed to share just enough information with the detective team to make them think he was unbiased in his investigation... although he wasn't, "According to Casey, the Governor has an alibi."

The detectives in the room all looked at each other questioningly. Hollis asked, "What happened to Casey, and how come she knows the Governor's alibi?"

"That's where it really gets complicated. It turns out that the Slayton brothers were *her* brothers. That's why she recused herself." Darren paused to let that sink in with the team.

The entire room let out a collective, "What?"

"Angelo was her brother, and he abused her as a child, which also makes her a suspect in his murder."

Sheriff Robertson was surprised, "What? Casey was the Slayton brother's sister?"

Darren let out a sigh, "I know it's hard to believe. But yes, she was their sister, and they both abused her when she was young. That means she had motive."

Hollis voiced skepticism, "I can't believe that."

"I know. I know. I can't believe it either. But she had a plausible motive and opportunity. She was in Miami, and he was killed in Miami. We can't ignore that." Darren realized he would have to disclose some basic facts to clear them of suspicion, "And then, to complicate things even more... She was having a love affair with the Governor after his wife passed away."

The entire room started buzzing.

Darren continued, "So, Casey said they were together last night at the Marriott Hotel in Miami. She was the Governor's alibi, and he was her alibi?"

Hollis interjected, "Oh my God. Is there any way to verify their alibis?"

"Basically, it's just their word. I checked with the hotel, and Casey was checked in, and she had a bar tab until after one o'clock in the morning that I verified. She told me that after cocktails, they went to her room for the night and the Governor left at about 5:00 a.m."

Hollis was eager to clear Casey, "The murder was estimated at 3:00 a.m., so if that's verifiable, neither he nor Casey could have done it. Right?"

Darren was leading his team to the presumption that Casey and the Governor were innocent, "Yes, according to the Medical Examiner and the victim, Anna Swayze, the Slayton brother was killed between 2:30 a.m. and 3:00 a.m."

Darren wondered if Casey really was innocent and if he could actually arrest her if she wasn't. He wasn't sure he could. He loved her and felt she had suffered enough throughout her life.

CHAPTER FIFTY-THREE

Alibi

Governor's Mansion
Tallahassee, Florida

Casey was sure Brendan had killed her brother and needed to make him aware of the alibi she had created for him – and for them both really - because she knew Darren would eventually interrogate them separately and compare their timelines. She drove to the Governor's Mansion in Tallahassee and rang the doorbell. She knew she would not be welcomed with open arms.

L.B. answered the front door, "Casey, what are you doing here? You know Brendan doesn't want to see you."

She pleaded with L.B., "Please L.B., I need to talk to him. It's important."

L.B. reluctantly opened the door to let her in, "This better be good, Casey. He's in the library."

"It is L.B. Thank you."

Casey walked to the Governor's library and knocked on the massive mahogany door.

Brendan opened the door and immediately started to close it on Casey. He screamed, "GET THE HELL OUT OF HERE AND LEAVE ME ALONE!"

Casey pleaded with him, "Brendan, please don't close the door. I *need* to talk to you."

He continued to try to close the door on Casey, but she jammed her foot inside the threshold to keep it ajar, "Why should I? You have a lot of nerve showing up here like this. You lied to me, and your brothers killed my daughter *and* my wife."

"I didn't lie to you! I just had to be sure my brothers were really guilty before I needed to tell you. Otherwise, it wouldn't have mattered. And I had nothing to do with your daughter's murder or your wife's death. I'm sorry my brothers are psychopaths, but it's not my fault. It's just an unfortunate travesty of birth that they were my brothers at all. I wish I could change that."

He listened to her while he continued pushing on the door to keep her out, "What do you want, Casey?"

She was still outside the doorway, "Can I please come in and talk to you?"

"Just go away, Casey. Let me grieve in peace. I don't want you here."

Casey stubbornly pushed on the door, "Brendan, I really need to talk to you. Please, just let me in. It's very important."

He backed off the door, and Casey walked into the library, "Since you won't go away, I guess I have no choice."

It was a warm and cozy room surrounded by mahogany bookshelves filled with legal and governmental books and magazines. They sat down on his couch, and she turned to face him.

She decided not to accuse him first and cause him to go on the defensive, "I created an alibi for you that I need you to know about. I recounted it to Darren this morning. We have to collaborate together for it to work."

He was in denial, "An alibi for what? I don't need an alibi."

"Brendan, I know you killed my brother Angelo, and I'm glad you did. I only wish you had gotten Gus as well."

He was silent.

"You and I are prime suspects, so I created an alibi for us. I told Darren you came to the Marriott Hotel Lounge in Miami at about 10:00 p.m., we had drinks until after 1:00 a.m. when they closed the bar, and then you spent the night with me in my hotel room. I told him you returned to Palm Beach at around 5:00 a.m. By the way, I actually was in the bar until after one o'clock, and I have receipts to prove it. But I was there alone."

Brendan thought about it for a moment, and it worked. *He left The Breakers in Palm Beach at around 9:00 p.m., which the valet could confirm. He could have arrived at the Marriott Hotel in Miami at 10:00 p.m. Casey says she has proof of cocktails in the bar until after 1:00 a.m. That's good. Then, coincidentally, the front desk clerk at The Breakers Hotel saw him arrive at 5:00 a.m. It all fits together,* "Well, if I needed an alibi, that's a good one. No way to prove I wasn't in your room with you."

"Believe me; you need an alibi. And so, do I."

"Just out of curiosity, where were you really last night?"

Casey looked down at the floor, trying to compose herself, "It devastated me when it was proven my brothers had raped and killed Susan and more devastated when you called me a liar and fired me." She looked back at him with tears in her eyes, "I shut off my phone, went down to the bar at the Marriott Hotel, and drank several Martini's. When that didn't help, I went outside to the dock overlooking the Intercostal Waterway. I wanted to jump in. I was just so sick and tired of the abuse and pain, the struggles and failures I've endured, that, after I finished drinking the Martinis, I decided I just didn't want to live anymore."

"I have had a horrible life. My father and brothers raped me for years; my husband was murdered soon after we were married, and then you... you said you never wanted to see me again and fired me. I just wanted to end it all."

She was crying uncontrollably, and Brendan approached her and held her in his arms, his anger subsided. He didn't want to lose another person in his life, "Casey, Casey, don't you ever do that. You're a wonderful woman. And... I love you."

"This elderly fisherman saw me trying to commit suicide. He looked like Captain Ahab from 'Moby Dick.' He talked me down and saved me."

He hugged her tighter, "Thank God."

She looked up at him while still in his arms, "You can talk to him. You can talk to the bartender. That's where I was."

"I believe you."

She was still crying, "I'm glad you killed my brother. He was a horrible man, and they both deserve to die. I just don't want to see you get punished for doing the right and just thing for Susan and your wife... and me!"

CHAPTER FIFTY-FOUR

Verification

Governor's Office
Tallahassee, Florida

Darren needed to verify both the Governor's alibi and Casey's alibi for the night of the murder. Since Casey had already given him her alibi, he needed to question the Governor to see if his version of events matched up with Casey's version of events. Then, he would interrogate Casey further to piece together the timelines of each of their versions of the story, because he suspected that it really was, a "story," which was why he went alone.

He had been cooling his heels in the Governor's vestibule, wondering what was taking so long. The meeting was almost an hour behind schedule. As Darren waited, the security guard, dressed in a police uniform, was standing at attention on the sidelines. And then, the Attorney General for the State of Florida, quickly whizzed past him, into the Governor's office. Darren assumed the Attorney General would be at the meeting to legally defend the Governor during his interrogation, but he wondered about the security guard. *Why was he there?*

Darren had spent the previous evening preparing a list of questions to substantiate the Governor's alibi and had it beside him in his briefcase as he sat waiting. He felt confident the story could work for Casey and the Governor, but he needed eyewitness testimony or forensics to vindicate them. He had checked out Casey's story with the Marriott and The Breakers hotels and double-checked with their staff, computer and security systems, to verify the events that Casey had propositioned were consistent. Except for Gus and Angelo's blood, none of the DNA at the crime scene was identifiable.

Finally, the Governor's secretary directed Darren into his office. The security guard followed close behind him.

Darren smiled and extended his hand to greet the Governor, "Hello, Governor. Thank you for meeting with me."

The Governor returned the handshake and introduced his Attorney General and then his security guard standing behind Darren. His expression stern, he directed Darren to a chair in front of his massive desk, "Please, sit down, Darren."

The Attorney General sat in a side chair next to the Governor, and the security guard stood behind him. Where Darren sat, an extraordinarily oversized window behind the Governor's desk angled the sunshine right into his eyes, making it difficult to see. The Governor's massive ornate Renaissance executive desk and maroon leather executive chair sat well above Darren, while the chairs in front of the desk had been purposely lowered so the Governor always looked down on his visitors. Psychologically, the size and positioning of the furniture was intended to be a power play to make people feel intimidated, and at this point, Darren definitely felt intimidated.

Darren squinted up into the bright sunlight shining through the window behind the Governor's chair and squirmed in his seat, feeling overwhelmingly apprehensive about how to conduct his interrogation of the Governor of the State of Florida. He locked his hands together, not trusting what they might do if allowed a little freedom.

The Attorney General ran his fingers through his closely cropped salt-and-pepper hair and placed his notepad on the side of the Governor's desk. When Darren sat down, the Attorney General handed him an official letter typed on the Governor's official letterhead.

Darren glanced at the letter in his hand and looked back at the Governor, "What is this all about, Governor?"

The Attorney General answered, "The Governor is maintaining all of his fifth amendment rights not to incriminate himself. As the Attorney General, I need to legally protect the Governor and the State of Florida."

Darren could feel perspiration accumulating around the starched collar of his white cotton shirt, and his stomach ached. He knew the Governor needed to protect himself, and he couldn't let them know he was really on their side. His morals and principles, his sympathy for the Governor's losses, and his affection for Casey, all overpowered his sense of duty to his badge to defend scum like the Slayton brothers. Since he was the principal investigator, he could control the narrative.

"I understand, Mr. Attorney General, but this is just an informal interview to corroborate some of the facts surrounding the Governor's whereabouts on the night of Angelo Slayton's murder. All the victim's family members are considered suspects until we can validate their alibis. We are interviewing everyone, including the Governor."

The Governor swiveled his chair, listening.

The Attorney General answered, "Very well. Ask your questions."

Darren took his clipboard with the questions he had prepared the previous evening out of his briefcase, "Where were you on the night, or actually the early morning, of Angelo Slayton's murder?"

The Governor looked at his security guard behind Darren before he answered the question, "I was at The Breakers Hotel in Palm Beach, promoting the Veterans America Fashion Show Charity event. The hotel and hundreds of guests can verify that."

Darren: "Yes, I know. I've checked that out. But, what about after the event?"

Governor: "Well, I had dinner with the senior management of the Veterans America Organization and then retired to my room for the night at about 8:00 p.m., L.B., my security guard, can verify that. He was with me the entire trip."

Darren turned around in his chair to look up at the security guard standing behind him.

L.B. looked down at Darren sitting in the chair and confirmed the Governor's statement, "Yes. I was in the dining room of the hotel during dinner, and then after dinner, the Governor went to his room for the evening. I am his eyewitness."

Darren: "But, at some point, Governor, you left the hotel that night."

Governor: "That is correct. It upset me when Senior Agent Casey Collins confirmed to me that the Slayton brothers had raped and killed my daughter and that they were actually *her* brothers. She informed me she wanted to recuse herself from the investigation."

Darren: "She was just following the compulsory protocol of FDLE."

Governor: "I understand, but I felt she had lied to me. I wanted to talk to her in person, so I drove to the Marriott Hotel in Miami to meet with her. I'm sure you've already gotten a statement from the valet confirming that. I left at about 9:00 p.m. and was at the Marriott by about 10:00 p.m."

Darren: "I did. However, there is no record of you calling Casey from your hotel room at The Breakers, except that she called you to inform you of the DNA match and her recusal. And the Marriott Hotel has no record of you being there."

Governor: "I assumed she would need a drink following our conversation and go to the bar. I parked the car in the self-parking lot and walked into the Marriott Lounge alone. We had several cocktails and talked until after 1:00 a.m. The bar tab can verify that."

Darren: "Yes, I have verified Casey was at the bar having cocktails, but I don't have proof you were there with her."

The Attorney General intervened, "Do you have any proof he wasn't there?"

Darren: "No. Unfortunately, the bartender doesn't remember. Which in and of itself is unusual since he is the Governor of Florida. You would think the bartender would recognize him."

Attorney General: "Well. I don't know about that. If he doesn't remember, he doesn't remember. It was late at night. Maybe he was just tired."

Darren continued. "What about after cocktails, Governor? Where did you go?"

The Governor looked over at his Attorney General, who already knew about his relationship with Casey, but didn't know he *was* guilty of killing Angelo Slayton, "Well, Casey and I have a relationship that evolved after my wife passed away. We love each other. We went back to her hotel room, and I spent the night with her."

Darren: "When did you leave the Marriott Hotel, Governor."

Governor: "I left the next morning at about 5:00 a.m., give or take, to return to The Breakers because I knew I needed to travel to Tallahassee that day."

Darren: "The hotel clerk at The Breakers in Palm Beach said he saw you enter the hotel at about 5:00 a.m. How could you leave Miami at 5:00 a.m. and arrive in Palm Beach at the same time?"

Governor: "Well, maybe I left the Marriott earlier, or maybe the clerk was mistaken. I don't remember. It was all very emotional for me. I really wasn't concerned about the time."

Darren: "Governor, do you own or have access to a gun?"

Governor: "No. As you probably know, I was in the Marine Corps, and I was in the Vietnam War, but nowadays, as Governor, I have a security guard with a gun to protect me, and I don't need my own gun anymore." He looked back at L.B.

Darren: "According to the Marine Corps, you carried a Black Sig Sauer M17 Strike-Fired 9mm pistol while in the military. Where is that gun, Governor?"

Governor: "I turned it in when I was honorably discharged."

Darren: "The Marine Corps claims it went missing after you left the service?"

Governor: "I don't know anything about that."

The Attorney General interrupted, "Agent Turner, I think you've gotten all the questions answered you need at this point. I am ending this interrogation."

Darren blinked in the bright sunlight and shifted in his seat. Whatever fire was in his belly, felt like he had swallowed a feral cat and it was clawing its way out through his stomach wall.

The Governor sat stone-faced, his arms crossed over his chest.

The Attorney General broke the silence and handed Darren a business card, "Agent Turner, if you have any more questions, please contact me. Thank you." He stood up and ended the session.

A sick feeling festered in the pit of Darren's stomach. He stood up and prepared to leave, "Thank you. I'll be in touch." They both shook hands. He looked over at the Governor, "Thank you, Governor." He wanted to wink and nod, but he thought that would be a little too obvious.

Darren turned to leave the Governor's office, and L.B. followed him out the door. L.B. watched him go to the elevator and leave the building.

It was true the Governor stayed at The Breakers Hotel in Palm Beach, and when Darren checked the computer for his room, it showed he left his room at 8:42 p.m. and returned at 5:06 a.m. the next day. Given that time frame, he would have had time to kill Angelo Slayton in Miami at 3:00 a.m., get rid of the gun, and return to The Breakers Hotel in Palm Beach by 5:00 a.m.

The Marine Corps said that a Black Sig Sauer M17 Strike-Fired 9mm pistol went missing right around the same time that the Governor was discharged. Like many soldiers, he might have kept his weapon as a memento. Based on the bullets, Darren knew the murder weapon was a Sig Sauer 9mm pistol.

He also verified Casey was at the Marriott Hotel lounge until after 1:00 a.m., based on her bar tab, but he couldn't verify if the Governor was there with her or not? The bartender said it was a busy night, and he doesn't remember if anyone was with Casey or not? Also, Casey said the Governor left her hotel room at 5:00 a.m. and the computer for her room showed her door opened at 5:16 a.m., but it appeared that she was returning to her room, not leaving it, because it showed she left at 10:02 a.m. Also, the desk clerk at The Breakers Hotel said he saw the Governor at 5:00 a.m. That didn't fit either, because it would take an hour to drive from Miami to Palm Beach, meaning that, if Casey was being truthful, the Governor couldn't have arrived at The Breakers Hotel until at least 6:00 a.m.

It just didn't add up. The timing of events was inconsistent with facts and physics. Darren was an agent of law enforcement, he had a sworn duty to uphold the law, and he knew their stories and their timelines had some big holes in it. However, he also knew they were both good, upstanding, law-abiding people who had contributed immensely to society. Plus, they were his friends whereas the Slayton brothers were rapists and murderers. He had to choose between Casey and the Governor, or the Slayton brothers.

CHAPTER FIFTY-FIVE

Reinstated

FDLE Headquarters
Tallahassee, Florida

Brendan figured that, under the circumstances, it would be prudent to have Casey back at FDLE, to control the investigation, for his benefit, and hers. Casey would continue to report directly to him and run the same organization she had prior to her dismissal. That way, the investigation of their alibis would have to go up the chain of command to Casey, and eventually to him before any action could take place. Brendan knew how the system worked, and he worked it.

Plus, he was concerned about Agent Darren Turner's line of questioning. He was getting too close for comfort. Now, Agent Turner would have to report to Senior Agent Collins, and she could monitor his investigation.

The Governor reconstituted the Rape Task Force to be the Slayton Task Force, intended to both arrest Gus Slayton for rape and murder, and find Angelo Slayton's killer. Although, he was obviously more concerned about finding Gus since he already knew who had killed Angelo.

One of the first things Casey did was put Rachel Slayton under twenty-four-hour surveillance and protection from Gus Slayton. Casey was using her as bait, assuming Gus might contact her for money and, or a hideout, while he was on the run. Rachel would eventually be relocated to Naples, Florida as she requested, as part of the Witness Protection and Relocation Program, but not until the arrest and conviction of Gus Slayton.

Casey was also worried Gus could identify his brother's killer since he was close to the shooter and could conceivably recall the details of what happened that night - that the Governor, Casey, and L.B., had worked so hard to conceal. They were the only ones that knew everything about the Governor being wounded, the bloody police uniform, the missing waterlogged gun, and the blood and bullet holes in the patrol car that L.B. had since thoroughly cleaned and repaired. They also didn't know whether Gus had recognized the Governor either visually or audibly since Brendan had spoken to the Slayton brothers prior to the shootout.

The more she thought about it, the more she realized that it would be better if Gus were *killed* instead of captured.

The other problem was if Gus recognized the Governor had been the killer of his brother, he would want revenge. Casey realized that if she could figure out Brendan had killed Angelo, then so could her brother. A father would want to avenge his daughter's rape and murder, and Gus would want revenge for his brother's killing. She couldn't let Gus hurt her again by killing Brendan.

It would be better if Gus were *killed* instead of captured.

Darren walked into her office, "I just dug up another interesting little factoid. I talked to the Seminole Indian Police Captain, and he told me that the Slayton brothers met with him to discuss the pirate buried treasure. They said they were following up on my interview with the Seminole Indian Chief and needed a few additional facts."

Casey looked surprised, "Following up on your interview? What kind of additional facts did they need?"

He sat down, "Seems they were very interested in the exact location where the Indian boy encountered Pirate Gasparilla and his crew digging 200-years ago. The Police Captain showed Gus the approximate location in Big Cypress on a map. The brothers were quite attentive."

Casey wondered whether Gus might hide out there and search for the buried treasure, "Interesting. What else did he tell you?"

"He said he told them there probably wasn't any buried treasure map and probably wasn't any buried treasure, but that the Governor's daughter had gone to the Seminole Indian museum, AH-TAH-THI-KI in Big Cypress to research Seminole Indian artifacts, the afternoon prior to meeting with the Seminole Indian Chief."

Casey started putting the pieces of the puzzle together, "That's probably how they stumbled onto Cara Jones. They were on the Tamiami Trail after the meeting or after going to the Seminole Indian museum. As we know, they saw her when she stopped at the Chevron Station for gas."

Darren agreed, "Right. And get this... they were at the Seminole Indian Reservation on the same day they killed Cara. She was just at the wrong place at the wrong time. They saw her, followed her, and then pulled her over in the deserted area by the Tombs."

"Oh, my God. It sounds about right based on the videotape. Did they ever go to the museum? They were probably trying to find the treasure by following Susan's tracks."

"I don't know. I asked Sheriff Robertson to find any video surveillance at the museum to confirm it. The Seminole Indians have video surveillance everywhere. My hunch is that they went there to search for clues."

"Mine too."

"You probably know Gus better than anybody. Where do you think he would go?"

"He probably knows we have Rachel staked out, so he wouldn't go there. If he's wounded, he would need first-aid or medical attention depending on how badly he's hit."

"We've checked every hospital and clinic in the area and haven't found any sign of him."

"What about his police cruiser? Any chance of finding that?"

"Normally, we can track the location of any police cruiser by its computer, but apparently, Gus disabled it, so we can't track it."

CHAPTER FIFTY-SIX

Perfect Storm

Fisher Island
Miami, Florida

Fisher Island had at one time been connected to Miami Beach, as one continuous stretch of coastline, until the City of Miami developed as a commercial port and dredged the shipping channel named, "Government Cut," dividing the north-end from the south end of the Miami Beach peninsula, creating Fisher Island.

The rain suddenly turned into a torrential downpour, as streaking bolts of lightning burst throughout the blackened sky into the vast Atlantic Ocean. Thunder rumbled raucously, and fierce winds pounded the powerful surf on the beach below Tina Evanston's exquisite penthouse condo on Fisher Island in Miami. Tina had chosen Fisher Island as her home for privacy. It was only accessible by boat, ferry or helicopter, and far enough away from the hustle and bustle of the city to escape when she wanted to, but still close enough to Miami to get there when she needed to.

Agent Darren Turner sipped a glass of red wine on the screened veranda, as he watched the thunder and lightning tempest in the distance, over the turbulent horizon, "Wow, Tina. This is spectacular. I love watching storms roll-in across the ocean like this."

The ferocity of the storm and flashes of lightning added an eerie dimension of power and strength to a city already revered as the epicenter of Florida's hurricane coast. It looked as though the storm was not above the Atlantic Ocean but emerging from within and aiming directly at Miami.

Tina sat down next to him, also with a glass of red wine, and put her arm around him, "I'm glad you like it. I love listening to the waves pounding on the beach during a storm. It helps me sleep better at night."

Darren smiled and leaned over to kiss her on the lips, "Honey, I think we'll both sleep *very well* tonight."

She kissed him back and picked up her glass for a toast, "Yes. I'll drink to that." They clinked their glasses, and both took another drink of wine. She wanted him relaxed and off-guard tonight.

She invited Darren to her condo Saturday night because she had a strong suspicious instinct about the entanglements of the Governor, Casey Collins, and the Slayton brothers. She doggedly pursued the actual story angle one way or another... like a dog with a bone. She knew Darren had some of the answers, but his loyalty to Casey would not allow him to divulge what he knew. Tina was determined to get to the bottom of it, and she knew she had the one persuasive weapon Darren would respond to - SEX.

It was forecast to be a stormy weekend, perfect stay-in-bed weather in the rain. She would question him, using her feminine charms, to find the holes in the official FDLE story, and find the truth about what he really knew and what was actually reality. After all, that's what investigative reporters do. She had the benefit of being a sexy, beautiful woman, and she was going to use it to her advantage. She knew he was vulnerable, plus; she was actually very fond of Darren, anyway. So, it would be a win-win-win.

She took another sip of wine and waited for Darren to do the same, "So how is the investigation going now that we're down to one Rhapsody Killer?"

He lowered his glass and looked out at the Atlantic Ocean light show, "Right, we have one down and one to go. Gus Slayton is out there somewhere, and probably wounded, so we'll get him, eventually."

Tina massaged the back of his neck with her fingers and took another sip of wine. She waited for him to follow her lead. And he did, "Any suspects for Angelo Slayton's killer?"

He could feel the wine beginning to relax him as Tina continued to caress his neck, "Umm, we are checking the alibis of all the victim's family members and friends. So far, everyone has checked out."

"Including the Governor?"

"Yes, the Governor has an airtight alibi."

She thought about his answer for a moment, and then leaned over and kissed him sensually on his lips, "Baby, you taste good."

He kissed her back and started moving in for more, "You taste good too. How about watching the storm from your bedroom where we can relax?"

"I was just thinking the same thing." Tina took her glass of wine and turned toward her adjacent bedroom, which had the same view of the storm, but from a different angle.

Darren grabbed the bottle of wine and his glass and followed her. He was anticipating an amorous evening.

Lightning flashed, and thunder followed loudly as Tina folded back the bedspread and bedsheets. She fluffed up the pillows and turned to Darren, "Pour us some more wine, baby. I'll be right back." She headed toward her bathroom.

The bedroom was exquisitely decorated with a king-sized bed positioned in the middle of the room to take advantage of the ocean views and twin matching nightstands with Alabaster table lamps on either side of the bed. The ceiling had recessed lighting, designed to set the mood for romance, and exotic murals and paintings on the walls depicted partially nude Victorian couples in erotic positions. The room had over-sized sliding glass doors, overlooking another veranda and the Atlantic Ocean, which were opened wide to allow the sound of the pounding surf to be heard in bed.

Darren poured the wine and set a glass down on each nightstand. He removed his jacket and shoes and casually laid down on *his* side of the bed.

Tina returned in a sexy negligée and laid down on the bed next to him. She reached for her wineglass and toasted them again, "Here's to us, baby."

Darren's eyes widened with anticipation, as he leered at Tina's sheer black lace, intimate nighty as she climbed onto the bed. He grabbed his wine glass and clinked her glass, "To us, honey."

She waited until he finished drinking and cuddled closer to him, as another flash of lightning lit up the room. Thunder followed, "So, tell me more about the progress you're making with the Slayton Task Force. What's the Governor's alibi?"

Loose lips sink ships, and Darren's lips were loosening, "He was with Casey Collins all night."

This revelation surprised Tina. She had no idea they were romantically involved, "Wow. He certainly recovered quickly from his wife's death."

Darren poured more wine from the bottle into their glasses, "I guess they have a long history of working together, and after his wife Mary died, they naturally grew closer."

Tina took a long drink of wine after learning this new eye-opener, "How romantic."

The wine was having the predictable effect on Darren, and Tina was getting an earful, "Yes. He was initially angry when he found out she was related to the Slayton brothers, but that has long since subsided."

Tina almost spit her wine out but acted completely composed toward Darren, so he would not realize how astonished she was. She coughed slightly to clear her throat, "What was her relationship to the Slayton brothers?"

Darren leaned his neck back as she ran her fingers up his mullet hairstyle in the back of his head, "Oh, that feels good."

She brought her wineglass to her lips, and Darren followed suit and took another sip, "What was her relationship to the Slayton brothers?" Tina repeated and started to unbutton his shirt.

Darren reached down to unbuckle his pants, and he blurted out, *"Sister."*

Tina leaned forward to look Darren in the eyes as she stopped unbuttoning, "Oh, my God. *Sister?* She's their sister?"

He was so mellow at this point he didn't fully comprehend her surprised reaction, "Yes, she's their sister."

Tina started composing the breaking-news headline story in her head, as she said, "So, the Governor was in bed with the sister of the men who raped and murdered his daughter, and probably also caused the death of his wife?"

Darren finished unbuttoning his shirt and tossed it onto the floor next to the bed, "I guess you could say that. But, technically, he didn't know she was their sister, and she didn't know they were the killers, until later when the DNA evidence proved it." He moved closer to Tina, trying to arouse her.

Tina was still mentally composing her news story as Darren removed his pants and attempted foreplay with her.

Tina was no longer in the mood, "Hold on, Darren, is this information public?" She got out of the bed, walked over to the open sliders, and looked out at the storm. As she was thinking, a giant bolt of lightning flashed down toward the ocean, and the sound of thunder rumbled throughout her bedroom.

CHAPTER FIFTY-SEVEN

Missing Person

FDLE Headquarters
Tallahassee, Florida

Gus Slayton's police cruiser was discovered at the Cleveland Clinic Hospital parking lot about the same time they reported a nurse missing from the hospital. Casey studied the police report of the missing nurse, paying particular attention to the description of her car. She knew there had to be a connection. Gus was wounded, and needed medical attention, and a nurse had been kidnapped in the same vicinity as his police cruiser at the hospital. He needed her medical expertise and her car.

If they could find the car, they would find him.

Casey issued an All-Points-Bulletin for the nurse's car. A description of her car along with the license plate number was broadcast on every television, radio station, and newspaper in Miami. Darren was already in Miami, wining and dining Tina Evanston, and Casey wanted to remain in Tallahassee with Brendan, so she directed Darren to work with Officer Dennis Hollis and the Miami FDLE team to find the nurse's car. The remainder of the Slayton Task Force were already on their way down to Miami. They surmised the car, the nurse, and Gus Slayton would all be together, wherever the car was located.

Darren and Hollis discussed it on the phone with Casey, "The obvious hideout for Gus would have been the nurse's residence, but she had three kids and a husband living there. The husband had reported her missing."

Casey was brainstorming, "The police EMT kit, radio scanner, and all the weapons were missing from the cruiser, so they could still be hold up in her car somewhere, doing wound care. He had enough ammunition to hold off a small army."

Hollis agreed, "He's very dangerous at this point. Like a wounded animal."

"I know. Maybe he's back at the site of the pirate buried treasure he was searching for, while the nurse mends his wound?"

Darren shot that theory down, "The Seminole Indian police have already been scouring the Everglades, and there's no sign of them or her car. We also checked Angelo's apartment building, and they're not there either. He might have commandeered a house, or an abandoned building somewhere."

Hollis added, "We are checking with every hotel and motel in the area. We've called the desk clerks and gave them descriptions of Gus, the nurse, and the car. But so far, nothing."

Casey looked at the missing person's police report again, "You've got to go door-to-door looking for that car. Unless it's hidden in a garage somewhere, it has to be found. I'll put a $10,000 reward out for information leading to the location of that car."

Both Darren and Hollis agreed it was a good idea, "That should get the attention of somebody near to the car."

Casey was thinking, *it would be better if Gus were killed instead of captured.*

Tina Evanston and the NBC6 Investigators broke the story first after Darren called her immediately after hanging up the phone from Casey:

BREAKING NEWS!

The Rhapsody Killers

$10,000 REWARD for information to locate this car:

A photograph and description of the nurse's car's make, model, year, color, and license plate number followed the breaking news headline.

Call: (850) 555-1212.

"Police are searching for this vehicle last seen at the Cleveland Clinic Hospital in Miami. There is a $10,000 reward for information leading to the location of this car. They have established a special phone line to collect any relevant information: (850) 555-1212."

"This is Tina Evanston Reporting for NBC6 Investigators."

The Grove Street Motel's maid had the television on as she cleaned the motel room adjacent to Gus Slayton's motel room. When she heard Tina Evanston announce the breaking news headline, she sat down on the edge of the bed to see the details of the reward. Her eyes moved from Tina's face to the caption at the bottom of the screen: "$10,000 REWARD" in capital letters. *They have established a special phone line to collect any relevant information: (850) 555-1212.*

The maid copied down the license plate number, and the phone number displayed on the television screen and then walked over to the window of the motel room. She pulled back the curtain and looked at the rear-end of the car, backed into the space for the room next door with the "Do Not Disturb" sign. The license plate number matched the number that she had copied down from the breaking news story. She picked up the phone and dialed FDLE.

Gus Slayton's eyes were glued to Tina Evanston on the television, watching the breaking news story. He knew the reward would be a problem. He would listen closely to the police radio scanner from now on, to monitor where the police were looking.

CHAPTER FIFTY-EIGHT

SWAT Team

Grove Street Motel

Miami, Florida

Agent Turner worked with Officer Dennis Hollis and FDLE in Miami to organize a SWAT Team to capture or kill Gus Slayton at the Grove Street Motel. Lieutenant Mike Weller and Sergeant Jon Benjamin had arrived from Tallahassee, as well as Sheriff Alan Robertson and Detective Piper from Southwest Florida. The SWAT team was on high-alert. They knew Gus Slayton was armed and dangerous. His police issued Glock 9mm and other more lethal weapons were missing from his police cruiser, including an AR-15 semiautomatic rifle they had to assume he had with him in the motel room, and that he was probably aware of the reward broadcast.

Time was running out, and he could be prepared for their assault.

The SWAT team consisted of a dozen black-and-white police cruisers, plus a black SWAT van loaded with a combination of police, sheriff deputies, and an additional contingent of FDLE agents headed by Agent Darren Turner, and an arsenal of powerful weaponry. They gathered a block away from the Grove Street Motel to get organized.

They were concerned about his hostage, and whether the nurse was still alive. They thought he might have killed her after she outlived her usefulness, but they had to assume she was alive and needed to be rescued.

Turner carefully studied the blueprint of the motel building supplied by the Miami Building Department. The maid had provided the room number, confirmed by the motel front desk clerk, and he reviewed the configuration of the motel room and the internal walls and doors with the SWAT team members. Other than Gus Slayton's motel room, the entire motel had been covertly evacuated.

He also examined the floor plan of each room, contiguous with Slayton's room from the top to bottom, each side, and all potential escape routes. It was a two-story structure with a stairway in the middle of the building that went from the first-floor motel rooms to the second-floor motel rooms. He directed police to sneak into the room above Slayton's just in case he tried to break through the ceiling.

He ordered police snipers onto the rooftops of adjacent buildings and coverage of the alleyways in the back of the motel building as well.

"Judging by the location of Slayton's motel room," Turner said to the team, "we'll need to blast through his front door and surprise him before he can get to his weapons." He pointed to various places on the blueprint as he spoke, "There's a bathroom window over here that needs to be guarded in case he tries to bolt out the back of the building when we go in the front."

"Piper," Sheriff Robertson snapped, "get some men on that window and, while you're at it, make sure they monitor the back window over here." He gestured to the rear of the motel on the blueprint.

"You got it, Sheriff." Piper barked his orders into the police walkie-talkie, on a special frequency, to teams assembled in strategic locations around the building. It was almost like a gangland hit from the old days, but legal.

Agent Turner took a large piece of paper and placed it on top of the blueprint. He had drawn a crude diagram with the layout of the motel room, and the potential escape routes to the alleyways, "According to the motel clerk, this window here leads to an alleyway which winds around to a street on the other side." He indicated several locations on the diagram, "Slayton could use that escape route to get away from us."

"We'll barricade it," Weller replied, "I'll send half a dozen men back there to head him off, just in case he gets any ideas." He turned and conveyed the order to Benjamin next to him.

Sheriff Robertson looked at Turner, "Okay, we're ready."

Turner responded, "FDLE goes in first."

"Fair enough. We'll back you up with a dozen deputy sheriffs and police officers on either side while you're going through his front door."

Turner gave his troops a final look, "I want him dead or alive. Either way, I want this to end today, right here and right now."

The FDLE team wore black bulletproof vests with FDLE emblazoned on the front and back, and black helmets with miner's lights. They carried M16 military assault rifles over their shoulders as they slowly, quietly moved down the street. Only minutes before, pedestrians and civilian cars had been blocked off from entering the street at either end. Unmarked police vehicles had been placed within the cordoned-off area, so they already had the motel surrounded.

Hollis's team climbed onto the front curb to paste a few ounces of "C4" explosives onto each of the three hinges on Slayton's motel room door. They hoped that the explosion and element of surprise would give them an advantage. Turner gave Hollis the signal.

Immediately, *BOOM! BOOM! BOOM!* Hollis triggered the explosives that splintered the door off its hinges with a loud blast, and within seconds the team raced into Gus Slayton's motel room. They charged into the room, rolling onto the floor to avoid potential gunfire from Slayton.

There was no gunfire, and there was no Gus Slayton! As Hollis rose to his feet, he quickly surveyed the darkened motel room with the bright light glaring from his helmet. He moved with his team, searching the closet and the bathroom as they went. There were no rifles or guns,

301

and the closet was empty. Gus had moved out, leaving behind the unmistakable stench of urine and cigarette smoke, and an empty bottle of Johnny Walker Red scotch.

Hollis switched on the lights and saw a woman lying on the urine-stained bed, handcuffed to the metal bedframe, gagged and beaten, "Oh, my God."

Turner burst into the room and glanced at Hollis, "It looks like he figured it out before we got here." He walked over to the woman to un-gag her, as the other team members gathered in the same area, "Are you, all right?" He pulled the cover up over her waist and searched his pockets to find a key to the handcuffs.

The woman was shaking and crying, "No! I'm not all right. I've been kidnapped, raped, and beaten, and I haven't eaten in days."

Hollis called for an ambulance, "We have help on the way, ma'am. Are you the nurse from Cleveland Clinic Hospital?"

"Yes," she said, crying.

Turner tried to console her, "I'm sorry. Do you know where he went?" He found a key in his jacket and unlocked the handcuffs.

She rubbed her wrists and stuttered, "He... He left soon after he saw the reward posted on the television and listened to the police radio scanner... After he beat and raped me again. He took the radio scanner, weapons, and the medical kit with him."

Turner looked at Hollis, then asked her, "How bad is the wound? Is he still bleeding?"

She looked up at Turner, "It was really bad, a couple of days ago. I got the bullet out and bandaged the wound. It stopped bleeding."

Sheriff Robertson entered the room after he crawled through the bathroom window and walked through the mess on the floor. He sized up the situation, "No Slayton and no guns!"

302

"Where is *he* now? And where are *they* now?" Turner asked absentmindedly, feeling a sense of desperation, "He has the weapons and had time to prepare. He's not running. Just changing headquarters."

While the police searched his ransacked motel room, Gus Slayton was driving up I-95 North out of Miami, wedged tightly between an eighteen-wheel semi-truck hauling Walmart merchandise and a recreational vehicle trailing a boat. He tried to conceal the car and its license plate from the police and highway patrol looking for the stolen vehicle.

He knew the minute Tina Evanston posted the reward on television, and it was just a matter of time before he would get ratted out. He listened to the police radio scanner constantly to track the progress the police were making.

In the middle of the night, before the police could beat the trail to his location, he shoved the radio scanner, guns, and the medical kit out the motel room's back bathroom window and crawled out. To his surprise, there was a car in the back lot with its keys still in the ignition. He took it.

Now he was on his way to Tallahassee.

CHAPTER FIFTY-NINE

Retribution

Governor's Mansion

Tallahassee, Florida

The Governor woke up early the next morning and stood by the window of his bedroom, looking out over the finely manicured grounds of the Governor's Mansion. It was a sunny, crystal clear morning with a crisp breeze blowing. An assortment of bright green trees decorated the grounds, and dazzling rays of sunshine filtered through the trees. He could see squirrels foraging for breakfast and hear the sounds of birds chirping in the branches.

He thought about the failed invasion of the Grove Street Motel yesterday by the SWAT team and wondered where Gus Slayton had gone. Based on the report Casey received, the kidnapped nurse had mended his shoulder wound, and he still had a cache of weapons with him. *Where could he be heading?*

Brendan needed some time to think, to figure out his next move, and to figure out his life. He was upset with himself for not seeing the obvious implications of their contrived alibi, dreamed up by Casey and supported by his devoted, long-term friendship with L.B. He was furious that Slayton had outsmarted the SWAT team at the motel. But mostly, he was angry with himself for not killing Gus in Miami when he had the chance. He should have been faster and shot both of them before Gus could get his gun out and duck down to shoot back at him.

He struggled with his emotions. The regret he felt over his failure to kill Gus Slayton had transformed into rage and resentment over what Gus Slayton had done to his life. It worried him that Agent Darren Turner could uncover the truth - that he had killed Angelo Slayton - before he could avenge his daughter and wife's death by killing Gus Slayton.

As hard as Casey and L.B. tried, they filled their alibi with holes and dubious timelines, and he knew Tina Evanston smelled a cover-up and she was hot on his trail with lots of television resources. The investigative reporter had dreams of "star power," and a ruthless front-page revelation about the Governor's assassination of Angelo Slayton could be just the ticket.

He needed to devise a strategy to deal with everything that had happened to him. He needed a change of venue and decided to take a drive, by himself in his BMW, to help clear his head.

Casey was still in bed, and he stared at her, sleeping peacefully and wondered, *how could this beautiful woman be related to those monsters?* He left a quick note on her nightstand that read, *"I went for a drive to think. Be back soon. I love you, B."*

He imagined strolling on the beach with the wind at his back, the smell, and feel of sparkling clear saltwater spraying on his face and bright sun warming him overhead. Maybe the change of scenery would be good for him. He got dressed, collected some gear, and went downstairs. L.B. was also still asleep.

He backed his Beemer out of the garage and drove out to the roadway towards Apalachicola Beach. When he stopped at the traffic light on Monroe Street, the driver's side window suddenly shattered, and he felt something whiz by his ear. *BLAP!* Then, incredibly, the rearview mirror exploded into a thousand pieces. *BLAP!* He instinctively ducked down into the driver's seat just as the steering wheel splintered from something hitting it. *BLAP!* It took him a moment to register that someone was shooting at him. *Not again,* he thought to himself.

He stepped on the gas and turned right toward the police station, just as he heard the metal shattering as bullets struck the trunk of his car. *BLAP! BLAP!* He quickly looked behind him as he accelerated and saw a car following him at full-speed. *BLAP! BLAP!* More bullets splintered through the car's interior, barely missing his head. Then, a bullet ripped through his left arm. *BLAP! BLAP! BLAP!* Blood gushed from the wound.

He saw the police station up ahead and several police officers out front, as he frantically steered away from the shooter. He barely avoided hitting one of the police officers and rammed into a police cruiser parked in front of the station, slamming on the brakes and screeching the tires. A loud explosion followed the crash. Broken glass and shattered debris from the collision burst into the air and splattered onto the ground.

The sudden accident shocked the police officers, and they encircled the Governor's car, with guns drawn. Bitter smoke from the smashed car fumed around all of them.

CHAPTER SIXTY

Emergency Room

Tallahassee Memorial Hospital

Tallahassee, Florida

Just after 9:00 a.m., L.B. received a phone call from the police department, notifying him the Governor was in the hospital with a gunshot wound to his left arm. He ran upstairs to tell Casey what had happened, but she already knew and was ready to go.

FDLE had informed her of the attempted assassination of the Governor while driving his car near Monroe Street. She ordered the Forensics Team to examine the Governor's smashed Beemer at the police station for whatever evidence they could recover from the ambush. It was riddled with bullet holes.

Casey and L.B. raced to Tallahassee Memorial Hospital to check on the condition of Brendan.

When they arrived, Casey and L.B. flashed their badges as they hurried into the building, "Where is the Governor?" Police and FDLE agents packed the emergency room.

An emergency room doctor working behind the reception desk saw the badge and realized who Casey was, "He's in the operating room. We have him sedated. They're removing a bullet from his left arm."

She was frantic, "How is he doing?"

The doctor looked at the clipboard in his hand, "He's going to be ok. The bullet fractured the humerus bone in his left arm, so he'll be in a cast for a while, and he has a slight concussion when he hit his head in the car crash. We also found what appears to be a prior bullet wound in his leg that was infected, but we have no record of any other gunshot wound? Does FDLE know anything about that?"

L.B. spoke up, "It was a recent hunting accident. I'm his security guard. I was with him when it happened."

The doctor looked surprised, "Did he go to a hospital to be treated?"

L.B. was fabricating the story as he answered the doctor, "No. I'm also an Emergency Medical Technician, and I knew the bullet had exited his leg, so I just bandaged it."

The doctor admonished him, "Well, you might want to go back for a refresher course. When we removed your bandage, the wound was badly infected. You should know better than to treat a bullet wound at home. He needed to be taken to a hospital."

Casey interrupted, "How bad is the infection?"

The doctor turned to answer her, "We are treating it with antibiotics. It should be ok, eventually, but it complicates the treatment of his arm gunshot wound. Why is the Governor getting shot so much?"

Casey looked over at L.B. before she answered, "That's why I'm here." She wanted to make it look official, to calm the doctor's suspicions so he wouldn't report it to the authorities. "FDLE is investigating both shootings."

The doctor looked relieved, "I'm glad to hear that. Unless you have other questions, I suggest that you wait for the surgeon to finish the procedure, then we'll know more about the Governor's condition."

"Thank you, doctor."

He turned and looked at another clipboard.

An hour passed, and now the emergency room was being invaded by news reporters asking questions about the Governor's attempted assassination, *"Who shot him? Why? What was his condition?"* She could hear the flurry of questions from the waiting room. She knew the reporters would eventually discover the leg wound also, and that would probably be a headline as well: *Governor shot twice. Who wants him dead? Why?*

The surgeon finally entered the waiting room, "Are you Senior Agent Casey Collins from FDLE?"

She jumped up out of her chair, "Yes, I am. How is the Governor?"

He looked over at L.B., "And you are?"

"His security guard, doctor."

The doctor looked at him warily, "Well, I guess you aren't doing a very good job."

L.B. felt guilty enough, without being reprimanded by another doctor, "He went out early in the morning. He said he wanted to be alone. How is he?"

The doctor turned back to Casey, "He's in recovery. We have him in a private room with a security guard." He looked back at L.B. "A *hospital* security guard. He has a broken humerus bone in his left arm, a concussion from hitting his head in the accident, and an infection in his right leg from a prior recent bullet wound. Do you know anything about that? We will need to report it to the authorities."

"I am the authorities!" Casey looked at L.B., "The Governor and L.B. were hunting together, and they had a shooting accident. FDLE is investigating both shootings."

The doctor looked over at L.B. again, deviously, "Maybe the Governor should think about replacing his security guard?"

Casey was anxious to end the inquisition, "Can you take me to see the Governor?"

The Governor was lying in bed, holding his left arm in a sling. His head was bandaged, and he looked visibly shaken.

Casey ran over to him and gently hugged him, "Brendan, how are you feeling? What happened?"

Still sedated from medication, he was groggy, "I've had better days."

The three of them were in the room alone, so L.B. asked, "Do you have any idea who might be trying to kill you?"

"A... as a matter of fact," Brendan stuttered, struggling to talk, "My guess is Gus Slayton. He probably identified me from Miami with his brother, and he's still on the loose." He looked over at Casey, "Nice family you have."

Casey didn't think it was funny, "Well, I'm glad to see your sarcasm is still intact."

"He probably followed you this morning. Figuring you would be at home," said L.B. thinking out loud.

Brendan mocked him, "Good thinking, Sherlock Holmes."

Collins straightened up and looked over at L.B, "He'll probably try again. We need to get more security for this room."

L.B. was on the defensive, "I'll be here around the clock, Casey."

Casey realized L.B. was sensitive because now the Governor had been shot twice, and it was his responsibility to protect him, "Good L.B., but we need police protection, not a hospital security guard outside the door."

Brendan slurred his words because of the sedative, "I hope you can find Gus Slayton soon."

Casey again thought, *it would be better if Gus were killed instead of captured.* "I hope so, too, I want to keep you alive."

Brendan agreed, "Me, too."

L.B. had previously reviewed Gus Slayton's file, "From what we know, you're lucky he only winged you. His file shows him as a sharpshooter; he doesn't miss his target."

Brendan paled further, "Oh, my God. If he doesn't see news he killed me, he's likely to try again."

Casey concurred, "Yes, we don't want to give him a second chance. I think you were lucky this time around."

He looked down at his wounded arm, "Funny, I don't feel so lucky."

"Just be thankful you're still alive. He rarely misses."

"It was very scary out there when those bullets were flying."

"I can imagine it was. I'll have a team of agents assigned to you around the clock." She looked over at L.B., "In addition to L.B."

CHAPTER SIXTY-ONE

Investigative Reporters

Miami International Airport

Miami, Florida

Tina Evanston sat in first-class on the early morning American Airlines flight to Tallahassee, along with several other senior investigative reporters from Southeast Florida covering the Governor's assassination attempt.

The plane was still on the tarmac at Miami International Airport, delayed for an hour because of maintenance issues. She didn't like the sound of that. *What does that mean anyway? The engine or a lightbulb?*

She could hear kids screaming and parents yelling in the coach section. She felt sorry for her camera crew and production team, also in coach, as she sipped a Bloody Mary and tasted a warm toasted bagel for breakfast, waiting for the plane to depart. She was, after all, a television star, and she deserved first-class treatment.

She had gotten an earful from Darren over the weekend, and her suspicious instincts hammered doubts in her mind about the official FDLE storyline. Now, the grapevine rumored another gunshot wound to the Governor's leg from a previous incident. *What was going on?*

His daughter was raped and murdered. Her killer Angelo Slayton was ambushed and killed, with his brother, Gus, wounded and still on the run. His wife was dead from a heart attack, and now, suddenly, he's romantically involved with a Senior Agent at FDLE, who reports to him

312

and is the sister of the killers. And now he had a wound in his arm from an assassination attempt, in addition to the previous mysterious gunshot wound in his leg? It was getting juicier and juicier.

She thought about writing a book. It could be a bestseller. What would she entitle it? *Sunshine State Governor? The Secret Life of Florida's Governor? Gunfight at the Governor's Corral? Governor Bang, Bang? The Governor's Mistress?* Any of those titles could work.

The first-class flight attendant cringed as Agent Darren Turner pulled back the curtain that alienated the coach section and encroached on the first-class cabin. She started to reprimand him for entering her hallowed territory, but then observed his familiarity with Tina Evanston and backed off. Unfortunately, FDLE policy does not fly agents in the first-class cabin, so it relegated him to the coach section on his way back to Tallahassee.

His weekend liaison with Tina turned out to be disappointing. She spent most of the time interrogating him or traveling to the television station, leaving him alone at her condo to watch the seagulls, beach, and surf, following the storm.

"Hello, Tina, can I buy you a cocktail?" Darren was joking, knowing drinks were free in the first-class cabin.

"Ha, thank you, Darren, that's very generous of you, but probably I should offer you a cocktail instead." She signaled the flight attendant, who was listening attentively anyway.

The flight attendant feigned a smile, "What would you like to drink, sir?"

Darren looked over at Tina's cocktail and remarked, "I'll have what she's having." Mimicking the scene from the movie *When Harry met Sally.*

The flight attendant didn't get the humor in that, "OK, I'll get you a Bloody Mary."

Tina smiled, "You want an orgasm?"

"Now that you mention it, let's join the 'Mile High Club.'"

Tina laughed, "I doubt that 'Nurse Krachett,' would let us get away with that." Referring to the "rule enforcement," flight attendant.

He was standing in the aisle and turned around to scout the flight attendant, "Ha, you're probably right. She doesn't look like much fun."

The flight attendant returned with Darren's Bloody Mary and handed it to him, "Here you are, sir."

Darren took the cocktail, "Thank you."

Tina raised her glass for a toast, "Here's to our esteemed Governor. Cheers."

Darren clinked his glass to hers, "Hopefully, he'll survive. Cheers."

They both took a drink and then Tina turned very serious. She had a plan, "What is going on with him, anyway? I can't believe he's dating the sister of the men who raped and killed his daughter, and probably his wife. And now the gunshots and assassination attempt. What is that all about?"

Darren peered over his glass as he looked down at Tina, "I really don't know. I guess Casey had admired him since they began working together when he was the District Attorney, and she was a detective."

Tina looked back at him quizzically, "And then his wife was killed by her brother. How convenient. Makes you kind of wonder."

Just then, the Captain came on the speaker, "Ladies and Gentlemen, they have cleared us for take-off. Please be seated with your seatbelts fastened firmly around your waist. Flight Attendants, prepare for take-off."

Darren looked back at Tina, as the flight attendant collected their glasses, "To be continued. See you in Tallahassee."

Tina smiled as Darren returned to his seat in coach.

CHAPTER SIXTY-TWO

Mass Pandemonium

Tallahassee Memorial Hospital
Tallahassee, Florida

Cameras, microphones, miles of wires, throngs of reporters and newscasters from everywhere descended on Tallahassee Memorial Hospital to cover the assassination attempt on the Governor of Florida. Police and National Guard Troops were stationed tactically throughout the hospital to control the mass pandemonium and protect the Governor.

Outside was a massive traffic jam caused by dozens of news vans with satellite dishes transmitting breaking news updates back to their respective newsrooms and television stations; and law enforcement cruisers and police cars with rolling red and blue lights. Strobe lights lit up the night, and it looked more like daytime. Occasionally, an ambulance would try to squeeze through the commotion to get to the Emergency Room with lights flashing and siren squealing, and the police would clear a path to let it get through.

Gus Slayton knew exactly where the Governor was, but getting close enough to kill him would be difficult. He figured all the confusion might provide him with an opportunity to reach his target if he looked official. He watched the special treatment the ambulances were getting from afar and figured that could be a good cover for him, along with his police uniform, so he could carry his weapon into the hospital. If he could commandeer an ambulance, he could get into the hospital posing as a police officer, and get to the Governor's room. But could he get back out? He lit up a cigarette and contemplated his strategy.

The radio in his stolen car broadcast a newsflash from Tina Evanston simulcast on NBC6. Gus turned the volume up higher:

BREAKING NEWS!

Governor Brendan Scott Shot

"… shot this morning on Monroe Street, driving from the Governor's Mansion. He is being treated at Tallahassee Memorial Hospital for a bullet wound in his left arm. They gave no motive for the shooting, and the perpetrator is still at large. Unexpectedly, the doctors also discovered another recent bullet wound in his right leg. His security guard claimed it was from a hunting accident a few weeks ago, but the surgeon I interviewed at the hospital further speculated the wound did not appear to be from a hunting rifle and had become infected because the gunshot had not been treated at a hospital. FDLE is investigating both incidents. They brought in the National Guard and the FBI to protect the Governor and help with the investigation. Anyone with any information is asked to call the FBI hotline at (800) 555-1212."

"This is Tina Evanston reporting from Tallahassee Memorial Hospital."

Gus was fuming smoke out of his mouth as he hollered at the radio, "Hunting accident? Bullshit. I got him. I knew it. That's my gunshot wound in his right leg. Yes!" This was just further confirmation that the Governor had killed his brother, and Gus had wounded him as he fled, "Damn, I should call you, Tina. You're right nearby. I can give you some real breaking news, Darlin'. Maybe we could have some fun in the back of my stolen car too." He laughed viciously.

Later that night, Gus rented a room at the Red Roof Inn down the street from the hospital. Given all the police activity because of the assassination attempt on the Governor, the front desk clerk was not surprised to have a police officer check into the motel. He paid cash so he couldn't be traced.

Once inside the room, Gus took the Tallahassee telephone directory and started calling the local hotels, searching for Tina Evanston. He figured she would check into one of the more upscale hotels in Tallahassee. He phished for her room with each of the front desk clerks, "Hello, can I speak to Tina Evanston, please?"

The front desk clerks searched through their guest directories, "Hmm. I'm sorry, but we don't have Tina Evanston registered here."

He abruptly hung up and tried the next hotel until he eventually got a confirmation at the Hilton Doubletree Hotel across from the State Capitol Building. The hotel clerk connected the call to Tina Evanston's room.

Tina anxiously picked up the telephone receiver, hoping it might be a news update from the hospital, "Hello?" she said brightly.

"Hello, Tina. It's Gus Slayton."

Tina was totally stunned but also suspicious, "*Gus Slayton*. Really? Where are you?"

"Well, let's just say I'm in the neighborhood, Darlin', and I miss seeing you since we met at McCabe's in Miami."

She had a sarcastic response, "Well, I miss you too. You're very popular. Everyone is looking for you."

"Well, Darlin', my brother is dead, as you know, and I want to give you an exclusive interview about that and everything else that's happened. Maybe we can have a little *quid pro quo*? You know what I mean?"

Tina was excited to have an exclusive interview with Gus Slayton. It could be the big break she was hoping for. But she was also frightened and hesitant, "First of all, how do I know it's really you?"

He laughed into the receiver, "Well, Darlin', I shot the Governor this morning in his BMW on Monroe Street and his right leg after he killed my brother and wounded me in Miami. I used my Glock 9mm, not some hunting rifle that's being reported. How's *that* for exclusive breaking news?"

Tina was practically shaking with anticipation. She knew some of these were facts only the killer would know, "The Governor killed your brother?"

"Yes, he did, Darlin', and I will kill *him* for that! He was disguised as a police officer, and we thought he was just another cop looking for some action with our girl, Anna, but he suddenly started shooting at us. He hit Angelo in the chest and killed him. I dove to the ground with my gun firing back at him. He got me in the shoulder, and I got him in the leg."

The thought of making a pact with the devil made Tina feel as if she might be taking one more step down toward a horrible abyss. She challenged the devil in this hellish trade, "Okay, Gus Slayton. You have my attention."

Gus was getting aroused, just talking to her on the telephone, "I knew I would, Darlin'. I want to meet, but you need to agree to a few basic terms first. You can interview me, but no cameras and no cops. Just you and me, Darlin'."

Tina would have agreed to anything at this point to get an exclusive interview with Gus Slayton, "Okay, where and when?"

"Go down to the hotel lobby. I'll pick you up outside in ten minutes."

She was surprised, "What? Now? You want to meet now? It's almost midnight."

"Yes, Darlin'. I don't want to give you any time to call your police buddies. If you're not there in ten minutes, the deal is off." He hung up.

Tina heard the click, then the hum of the dial tone. She looked at the phone receiver in her hand and panicked at the prospect of meeting him. He was a rapist and murderer, but she was an investigative reporter, and she could have an exclusive interview with Gus Slayton, the most wanted man in America. It could get her on national television. It could make her a worldwide star. She thought again about the book deal she imagined earlier, but with a new title, *The Governor Assassin*. It would be a bestseller and could also ultimately be a movie.

She picked up her cell phone to call Darren and grabbed her voice recorder and notepad. She slipped her snub-nose .38 caliber handgun into her handbag, first checking that it was loaded. She had a permit for it and had checked it with her luggage.

She closed the door behind her and hurried down toward the lobby, talking on the way to the elevator. The clock was ticking, "Darren, it's Tina. I'm doing an exclusive interview with Gus Slayton tonight."

Darren was groggy from sleep, but her revelation quickly woke him up, "What? When? Where? How?"

She pressed the down button in the hallway for the elevator, "Right now. He's meeting me at the Doubletree Hotel."

He practically stood up in bed and screamed, "TINA, DON'T DO IT. THIS MAN IS A KILLER."

"Darren calm down. I have my gun, and I'm turning on the 'location finder' on my cell phone so you can track me." She held out the phone as she walked into the elevator and turned on the location finder app.

Darren was frantic, "Tina, seriously, don't do it. He'll rape or kill you or both."

The elevator bell rang, signaling the ground floor, and the doors opened, "Got to go, Darren. I'm turning my ringer off." She clicked the end button and muted her cellphone. She walked past the bar, which had a few late holdovers watching the Governor's hospital scene broadcast live on the several flat-screen televisions on the walls, and out to the cement steps outside.

An older, tan, nondescript Buick pulled up to the steps driven by a man in a police uniform.

Gus Slayton grinned broadly when he spotted Tina standing alone in front of the Hilton Doubletree Hotel, looking more beautiful than ever. He got aroused watching her chest jiggling ever so slightly as she stepped down the stairs toward his car. He opened his window, "Well, hello Darlin'. You look beautiful tonight."

She walked around the front of the car and opened the passenger side door to get in. Once inside, she was all business, "Hello, Gus Slayton. I have a lot of questions for you. Pull into the parking lot so we can talk."

"Now hold on, Darlin'. Not so fast." He quickly slapped handcuffs on her wrists and grabbed her handbag, "I was born at night, but not last night," he said, laughing. He opened her handbag and peered inside while Tina tried to wrest it away from him.

"Give that back to me. That was not part of the deal."

"Well, looky here, Darlin'... You got yourself a little peashooter and a cell phone. No doubt with a location finder." He tossed the handbag out the window and stepped on the accelerator, "Nice try."

Now, Tina was terrified and realized she might have made a huge mistake, "What are you doing? Where are you taking me?"

CHAPTER SIXTY-THREE

Kidnapped

Tallahassee Hilton Doubletree Hotel

Tallahassee, Florida

Darren called Casey on her cellphone to tell her about Tina's meeting with Gus Slayton, "Casey, Tina just called me. She is meeting Gus Slayton. Tonight."

Casey was alarmed, "What? Where? Why?"

He held the phone to his ear with his shoulder and dressed as quickly as he could, "At the Doubletree Hotel. He promised her an exclusive interview with him. I told her not to go, but she wouldn't listen to reason."

"Oh, my God."

"I'm really worried about her." Darren followed the location finder for Tina on his cellphone. It showed the Hilton Doubletree Hotel on Monroe Street. She was still there, "Meet me at the Doubletree Hotel."

"I'm on my way."

Darren arrived before Casey and found Tina's handbag on the cement steps outside the hotel. He looked inside and saw the handgun and her cellphone. Casey pulled up a minute later. She got out of the

321

car and walked over to Darren, "He must have tossed her handbag out when she got into his car."

They heard police sirens in the distance, coming toward the hotel.

Casey looked at the handbag he was holding and agreed, "We have to find that car. We have the description and license plate number of a Buick stolen from the Grove Street Motel in Miami. That must be what he's driving. The police saw it when Gus shot at Brendan. We are already searching for it in Tallahassee."

Darren looked at Casey. He was distraught, "He's going to kill her, Casey."

Several police cruisers arrived with rolling lights and sirens. The officers got out of their cruisers and surrounded Casey and Darren.

She got on her cellphone to FDLE headquarters. Lieutenant Weller was working the late shift and answered on the second ring, "We need to put out an emergency alert on that Buick stolen by Gus Slayton in Miami. Slayton has kidnapped Tina Evanston from NBC6 News. She's in that car with him, and he's armed and dangerous. Put out an All-Points-Bulletin to Police, National Guard, the FBI, and the news media with a full description of the car and license plate number. Also, post a $25,000 reward for information leading to the location of that car."

They launched a frenzied search for the car, Gus Slayton, and Tina Evanston. Police, National Guard, and News helicopters filled the air with bright lights glaring throughout the darkened night on the streets and highways below, hunting for the stolen car. They had no idea where Gus would be heading, but frantically scoured Tallahassee and its outskirts looking for him. It was like searching for a needle in a haystack.

Darren was frantic too, "Where would he take her, Casey? You know him better than anyone."

Casey racked her brain, probing for places that may be familiar to Gus in Tallahassee. She started brainstorming out loud, "Well, I doubt he would take her to a motel or someplace public where she could be seen and scream for help."

"I agree. So maybe someplace secluded, like a garage, a field, the woods, a vacant building, a boat?"

Casey felt a lightbulb flash in her head, "A boat, or maybe a beach." She turned and looked at him. "I was married on a beach. My brothers were furious when I got married. They're control freaks and felt weird ownership of me, because of our perverted relationship. I didn't invite them to the wedding, but I had the feeling they were there, anyway."

"You mean like wedding crashers?"

"No, they never came out in the open, but I could feel their presence. I felt some kind of psychic connection from years of living together and being abused by them."

"Where did you get married?"

"Saint George Island, off the coast of the panhandle. It's a hunch, but it's a secluded beach, especially off-season. He's not that familiar with Tallahassee, but he knows that island. He might go there."

"It's all we have right now, Casey. Let's go."

They headed toward Saint George Island in Turner's police car. Casey got on her cellphone to update Weller and Benjamin and directed them and the search parties to head to the island. She didn't want to use the police scanner because she knew Gus would monitor it, "Lieutenant Weller, I have a hunch Gus Slayton may be heading to Saint George Island. We are traveling down Route 319 toward Route 98 to Apalachicola Beach. Alert all parties not to reveal this on the police scanner because Gus has one."

Gus Slayton had the police scanner on loud and clear as he drove toward Saint George Island. He heard all the squawking from search parties and other police activities, but nothing about his destination, "OK, my beauty. Ask your questions."

Tina was struggling with the handcuffs, trying to release them, "Can you take these off?"

He looked over at her hands, "Well, no, I don't think so, Darlin'. At least, not right now. How about a little *quid pro quo*?"

Tina hesitated, "Like what?"

Gus glanced over at Tina and laughed, "Well, like I'll be nice to you, and then you be nice to me later."

Tina decided to put her anger on hold. Gus was reeling her in, and she wanted to hear what he had to say, especially if it could help her career, "What are you suggesting?"

"Well, look now, you want an exclusive interview with me, and I want you to be nice to me. A little *quid pro quo*. You know what I mean?"

Tina didn't trust him, "No! That's not part of the deal."

"My little sister, Casey, is probably frantically searching for you right now." He didn't mention his main objective out loud. He had been obsessed with Tina's beauty and allure ever since he had first laid eyes on her. He wanted her. He wanted her badly.

She wore her blonde hair up in a clip and was dressed casually, probably because she hadn't planned to go out. She wore very little makeup, but in Gus's opinion, she didn't need any makeup. Her natural beauty shone through.

Gus grinned. He leaned over and strained to smell the fragrance Tina was wearing. It excited him to be close enough to her to experience her live, instead of seeing her on television. He looked at her breasts, covered tonight with a white button-down blouse he was looking forward to unbutton, *quid pro quo*.

CHAPTER SIXTY-FOUR

The Hunt

Route 98

Apalachicola, Florida

Casey called L.B. at Tallahassee Memorial Hospital from her cellphone as they drove to Saint George Island, to check on the Governor's condition and give him a status update, "How is Brendan?"

L.B. was groggy; he was sleeping in the chair next to the Governor's bed, "Good morning, Casey, or should I say good night?" He looked over at the beeping monitors hooked up to the Governor, "Brendan is resting and recovering. Doing all right."

"Good. Unfortunately, we're not! Gus kidnapped Tina Evanston tonight. We're searching for them right now."

"Oh my God, Tina Evanston." Brendan sat up, and L.B. conveyed the phone to him.

"What happened, Casey?" The Governor winced in pain as he talked on the phone.

"Gus promised Tina Evanston an exclusive interview to lure her into a trap and then kidnapped her. I think he is going to Saint George, where I got married. It's probably the only destination Gus is familiar with in Tallahassee."

It surprised Brendan. "Your brothers were at your wedding?"

"They weren't invited, but I knew they were there covertly. I sometimes think I have a sixth-sense with my brothers because of our perverted relationship. Too much to get into right now."

"Perverted is an understatement."

"Tell me about it."

"Casey, it's supposed to rain. The bridge might be treacherous." The Governor knew that the four-and-a-half-mile-long Bryant Patton Bridge to Saint George Island was one of the longest bridges in Florida, "It's a narrow, two-lane bridge, not well-lighted and slippery when it rains."

"I know, but there's no other way to get there except by boat or air, and we don't have much time. I've also got Lieutenant Weller and Sergeant Benjamin and a team of FDLE agents and police on their way."

"What do you need from me, Casey?"

"I think we have everything we need, Brendan. Darren and I are driving there now, and we'll rendezvous with the contingent of law enforcement officers at the Buccaneer Inn."

"Be careful, Casey, and keep us informed of your progress."

L.B. took the phone and clicked off.

The Governor was worried. It was very personal to him, and he didn't like sitting in a hospital while Casey hunted for the man that killed his family and wounded him. He wanted to do something, "L.B., help me get dressed."

He painfully uncovered himself and got out of the hospital bed.

CHAPTER SIXTY-FIVE

Quid Pro Quo

Bryant Patton Bridge
Saint George Island, Florida

The windshield wipers slapped rhythmically back and forth as rain started falling, first as an intermittent drizzle, then as a steady downpour. It was chilly and foggy, and the roads were slippery. Gus turned onto Route 300 toward the four-and-a-half-mile-long Bryant Patton Bridge across Apalachicola Bay. He was headed to the Buccaneer Inn, a lost little motel directly on the Gulf of Mexico near the Saint George's Island Lighthouse.

He had only been there once before, as an uninvited guest, to Casey's wedding to Jeremy Collins, along with his brother, Angelo.

Gus remembered from Casey's wedding that, in-season, it was a bustling tourist destination on Saint George Island Beach. But now, it would be quiet and deserted until next season. He recalled it was surrounded by multi-family homes and a recreational vehicle park that would be vacant this time of year. He would be undetected in the laid-back motel on this far-off island. He looked forward to reciprocity with Tina after she interviewed him. *Quid pro quo.*

Tina was thinking about the questions she wanted to ask Gus as they drove. Although the details of the entire scheme were beginning to emerge, she knew Gus was still holding back some of the missing pieces. He was the lynchpin, "Gus, where are you taking me?"

"A quiet little place on the Gulf, where we can talk and *quid pro quo*, Darlin'." He glanced briefly at Tina and then turned his attention back to the slick road crossing the bridge.

Tina shifted sideways in her seat to look directly at Gus with her handcuffs on her lap, "Gus, why don't you turn yourself in? Maybe you can save yourself?"

Gus admired her gorgeous tanned legs as her skirt rode up when she repositioned herself, "With all due respect, Darlin', I'm afraid that's just not going to happen." Gus shrugged to signify the frustration of his dilemma, "I want revenge for my brother. He would do the same for me."

Tina figured that would probably be his answer, but she had to try anyway, "What does that mean?"

The rain fell harder on the windshield, as Gus fidgeted, "That means killing the Governor. Revenge. Pure, sweet revenge, Darlin'. Plus, now he's screwing my little sister."

Tina knew Gus was a couple of sandwiches short of a picnic. He seemed purely mercenary, "So that's it, pure revenge and hatred? What's the payback?"

Gus turned the windshield wipers up to a higher speed as the rain came down harder, "I'm afraid so, Darlin'. Revenge *is* the payback."

Tina could see his mental wheels turning as he weighed his options. She put her thumb on his scale, "Both of you are vindictive men. Gus, you know you'll end up in jail or dead. I have the feeling you don't want that. And what about your wife and son?"

Gus knew he was backed into a corner. He mopped a drip of sweat from his brow, knowing she was probably right. He looked sideways at her again, "I'll figure it out. I always do. Start asking your questions, *quid pro quo*, Darlin'."

Tina turned to briefly glance out the rear window, hoping they were being followed, but it was dark, "To begin with... Why? Why did you rape and, in some cases, murder these women? You had a family, a career. *Why?*"

Gus glanced in the rearview mirror, "The killings were an accident. We didn't intend to kill them. It just happened."

Tina looked surprised, "You just happened to kill three women?"

Gus grimaced, "Those deaths were accidental."

"Did you know Susan Scott was the Governor's daughter?"

"No, we didn't. That was another mistake. As far as I can tell, it was just an unfortunate twist of fate. We didn't know she was the Governor's daughter."

"What about the other murders?"

"Well, Kimberly was running away in the dark, and I didn't see her trip and fall as I chased after her. I accidentally stepped on her."

"That was more than just a step, Gus."

He looked over at her, "I know." Then, looked back at the road, "And with the girl from Everglades City, we were searching for that buried pirate treasure or treasure map on the Seminole Indian Reservation, you kept talking about on the news. We just happened to see this beautiful young woman at a gas station on the Tamiami Trail at night and followed her. We pulled her over for a traffic ticket."

"You mean Cara Jones? That was unfortunate."

"Yes, Cara. She refused to cooperate with us and scratched Angelo's face. I guess he lost his temper and hit her."

"She was strangled, Gus."

"I know. Sometimes Angelo got a little out of control. He strangled the Governor's daughter too, while he was having rough sex with her."

"Rough? Wow, I guess so. What about the buried treasure?"

Gus laughed cynically, "Ha. That was a wild goose chase. What a waste of time."

"Did you find it?"

"No, we didn't find it. After we heard about it from you on the television news, we searched for it, but it was a dead end. I don't know if it ever really existed?"

"And the music, *Rhapsody in Blue*. What was that all about?"

Gus looked back at her, remembering the song, "It's a turn on. 'Blue' is a cop thing. Power and authority, you know? It has a strong beat that added to our sexual fantasy. Maybe I'll play it for you later."

"No, thanks, Gus."

He laughed again, "Ha. I'm not asking for your permission. Anyway, our father played it to disguise any noise from Casey while he was screwing her. Then me and Angelo would take our turns."

Tina was sickened by that, "That's disgusting, Gus."

"She's more than a sister to us. Family traditions. You know what I mean?"

Tina looked ahead at the bridge crossing, "Speaking of your sister. Casey Collins was charged with finding you and arresting you. How did you feel about that?"

"Well, she was charged with heading the Rape Task Force. At the time, she didn't know she would be hunting down her brothers. We have a special connection with our little sister. We are more than just family."

"What do you mean, *more than just family?*"

"It's complicated. I told you. She's more than a sister to us. She's more like a soulmate to me. It's complicated; I'd rather not go into it right now."

"Again, I ask you *why?* Why did you and your brother think you could rape all these women and get away with it?"

"We were on a power trip. It was within our power to deprive those women of their physical safety, security, privacy, freedom, and life, if and when we choose to unless they complied with our demands. It happens all the time."

"And your demands were for sex?"

"Yes. It was easy. I'm sure you've heard the term 'Rape Cops,' we get sex in return for leniency. We learned from our father and his father before that. I guess we came to see ourselves not merely as enforcers of the law, but as the law itself."

Tina could smell the salt air from the Gulf of Mexico and see Saint George Island through the rain in the distance, "Weren't you afraid of getting caught and going to jail?"

Gus laughed, "We had the entire criminal justice system behind us to carry out our threats. 'The Blue Curtain.' We could tell them, 'Call the police. Who are they going to believe?'"

"That is, unfortunately, true." Tina already knew this from her own investigation. There is great systemic resistance against prosecuting a police officer. If a victim decides to file a criminal complaint, she would have to present an extremely compelling story to the police and state's attorney to counter their reluctance to pursue the complaint. She would have to be able to convey that, in addition to common forms of abuse, the abuser exploited his professional status and power to control and terrorize her.

Gus drove onto the Saint George Island and turned right onto Gulf Shore Drive West, toward the Buccaneer Inn.

Route 319 from Tallahassee to Apalachicola was interspersed with FDLE, and police cruisers headed in the same direction with lights and sirens on. Weller and Benjamin tried to catch up to Darren and Casey, but Darren had a head start. They were almost to Route 98 at Alligator Point.

CHAPTER SIXTY-SIX

Deja Vu

The Buccaneer Inn
Saint George Island, Florida

When Darren pulled into the wet, misty parking lot at the Buccaneer Inn, Casey spotted a tan Buick similar to the car stolen in Miami. It was parked in a space in front of a motel room adjacent to the Inn's restaurant, where she had held her wedding reception.

A line of FDLE and police cars followed them in succession. They surrounded the Buccaneer Inn. Helicopter airspace was prohibited within 25 miles of the island to ensure Gus would not be alerted, and civilians and the news media were blocked from crossing the bridge until law enforcement had the situation under control.

They had ordered the news media not to broadcast the developing story for Tina Evanston's safety, and because she was one of their own, they complied. They worried Gus would hear or see a report on the radio or television and change plans to elude the police.

Searching through the rain-drenched windshield, Casey suddenly became aware of a familiar memory that subconsciously triggered an alarm inside of her head. At first, it was a distant, nagging feeling, until her cognitive perception triggered a primal fear that verged on panic. As she tried to confirm her feelings, she realized she was staring at her brother's stolen car, parked directly where her husband Jeremy had parked their car outside of the motel room they stayed in on their wedding night. Could Gus have gotten the same motel room? *That definitely was perverted.*

In a flickering, grainy slow motion, like an old-time black and white movie, she reminisced about Jeremy on her wedding day standing in that same doorway. His black tuxedo was glaringly contrasting against the bright white door of the motel room. He picked her up and carried her over the threshold, as his new bride.

Then, she thought about his murder and started connecting the sinister dots. *Could Gus and Angelo have assassinated her husband out of perverted jealousy and possessiveness of her? Is that why he's here with Tina?*

Darren used his cell phone to avoid using the police scanner and told one of the fellow officers to confirm that the license plate was that of the car stolen in Miami. Gus had once again backed the car into the parking space to hide the view of the license plate number from the parking lot.

A couple of police officers huddled together and crawled under the small overhang from the roof above the motel building, trying to stay dry. Casey watched as they reached the front of the motel room door behind the rear-end of the Buick and shined a small flashlight at the license plate on the car. They then retraced their steps backward, far enough away to call Darren back and confirm that it was the stolen Buick.

Darren clicked his cellphone off, "Well, that's definitely the stolen car, so your hunch was correct. Gus and Tina are here."

Casey was deep in thought, "Darren, I think I just had another clairvoyant-like revelation."

Darren looked at her quizzically, "Casey, what are you talking about? Tina is probably in trouble in there with Gus Slayton. We have dozens of police surrounding his room. We have to do something. Now!"

She was resolute, "It might be connected to Tina's kidnapping."

Darren was impatient, "What is it, Casey?"

She reached for their weapons case in the backseat and strapped a hidden gun holster onto her ankle under her slacks, "I think Gus and Angelo assassinated my husband, Jeremy. They were here secretly during my wedding, and Jeremy and I stayed in that same motel room on our wedding night. Gus obviously wanted the same room we stayed in. I think I'm the key to Tina's abduction." She placed her gun in the ankle holster and slid another smaller gun from the weapons case into her bra. She was hoping one of them would not be detected.

Darren was confused, "What are you doing?"

She stared back at him, "Darren, I'm the one he's really after. Why else would he come here? I need him to exchange Tina for me." She opened the passenger door.

Darren reached over to grab Casey, "Casey, no. Stop. He'll kill both of you."

She leaned down to talk to Darren through the car's door, "It's hostage negotiations. I'm going in. Have everybody stand-down until directed otherwise." She closed the door and started walking toward the motel room.

Darren immediately got on his cellphone and directed law enforcement to stand down as he watched Casey walk away.

Lieutenant Weller and Sergeant Benjamin finally arrived and pulled up next to Agent Turner and watched Casey walk toward the motel. Weller rolled down his window, and Darren did the same, "Where is Casey going?"

Gus wore his Glock 9mm in a shoulder holster and had his AR-15 semiautomatic rifle leaning against the wall in the motel room. He had the shades closed tightly, the television on a news channel, and the police scanner on the bureau.

Tina was handcuffed to the bedframe. She struggled with the handcuffs on her wrists and her arms over her head as she laid on her back on the bed, just like the nurse, "Gus, would you please uncuff me?"

Gus turned and sauntered over to Tina. He looked forward to his *quid pro quo* with her. He ran his hand over her face and then down to her breast, "You are so beautiful, Darlin', and what a great body."

Tina grappled with the handcuffs, trying to free herself, "Don't you touch me. Get your hands off me."

His expression changed to a mock disappointed pout, "Now, Darlin', we had a deal. Remember? I gave you a very insightful interview. Now, it's time for a little *quid pro quo*." Gus started unbuttoning Tina's blouse and unsnapped her bra.

Tina screamed at him, "GUS. STOP IT. I NEVER AGREED TO THIS."

Gus turned and walked into the bathroom. He quickly returned with a washcloth, which he shoved into Tina's mouth to shut her up.

Tina struggled to avoid being gagged, but all she could do was mumble through the washcloth stuffed into her mouth.

Gus grinned and slid her skirt off, "That's better, Darlin'. Now, remember, *quid pro quo*. I held up my end of the bargain. Now it's your turn." As Gus started to strip off her panties, there was a loud bang on the motel door.

Casey banged hard on the motel door with her fist, "GUS. IT'S CASEY. OPEN THE DOOR. NOW!"

CHAPTER SIXTY-SEVEN

Family Reunion

The Buccaneer Inn

Saint George Island, Florida

Gus turned to face the loud banging on the motel door, then looked back at Tina, "I guess we have company."

Tina let out a muffled scream and struggled with her handcuffs.

Casey banged hard on the door again and repeated herself, "GUS! OPEN THE DOOR! IT'S CASEY! OPEN THE DOOR! NOW!"

He screamed back at the door, "ARE YOU ALONE?"

She answered, "YES! AND I'M UNARMED!"

Gus pulled his Glock out of its holster and pointed the gun toward the ceiling as he walked over to the motel door. He unlocked the door and put his hand on the doorknob, "HANDS UP IN THE AIR, LITTLE SISTER!"

She responded, "MY HANDS ARE UP IN THE AIR!"

Gus opened the door, "Well, isn't this nice. You passed Detective Course 101. You figured out where I was going. Come on in, Sis." He surveyed the parking lot outside his motel room. Law enforcement had him surrounded. Police cruiser headlights were glaring at him as he let Casey inside the room. He closed the door behind her, "A little family reunion. Hands against the wall, Sis." He frisked her body up and down from behind.

"I told you, I'm unarmed." She expected him to find the ankle holster and gun. In fact, she wanted him to find it, because she knew that, as a cop, he expected her to be armed. Finding it would satisfy him he had disarmed her.

He grabbed her ankles and felt the gun, "Unarmed, Sis? What's this little peashooter?" He pulled the gun out of the holster and tucked it into his belt.

"Oh, I forgot about that. I am a cop after all," she joked, trying to lighten up the situation.

"Alright, turn around. Sit down over here." He waved his Glock toward a chair he placed in the middle of the room.

"Nice to see you again, Gus." She said sarcastically. Casey looked around the room, with fond memories of the last time she was in it... With Jeremy on her Honeymoon. She looked over at Tina, handcuffed to the bed she had once shared with her husband long ago. Tina was gagged and nude except for panties, "Is Tina hurt?"

"She's fine, Sis. You just interrupted a little foreplay, that's all." He pointed his gun toward Tina as she tried to scream through the washcloth.

Casey was tempted to attack him right then with the element of surprise while his gun was pointed away from her, but she knew he could overpower her, "Give it up, Gus, you're surrounded by two dozen troopers."

"Maybe, but I have a hostage. A very famous and beautiful hostage. Miami's NBC6 news goddess." He waved his gun toward Tina again and then back to Casey, "In fact, now I have *two* hostages. The famous and beautiful girlfriend of the Governor of the State of Florida. Wow. My little sister."

Casey appealed to him from the chair, "Let Tina go, Gus. I'll be your hostage."

He just grinned, "I guess I'll be making the decisions around here, Sis. How is your boyfriend doing, anyway? He was lucky I didn't get a clean shot at him."

"He's recovering from *both* times you shot him."

"What a shame. Hard to believe I missed him twice. How does it feel knowing your boyfriend killed your brother?"

Casey wanted to get an answer to her most important question, "Did you kill Jeremy, Gus?"

He started laughing, "For a detective, it certainly took you a long time to figure that one out."

"Did you?"

"Of course, I did. You belong to Angelo and me. We are family. He had no right to marry you. You belong to me for life! Or death!"

Casey was hoping his life would be a short one, "You bastard. I loved him." At that moment, she wanted to take the gun, hidden in her bra, and kill him right then, but he was pointing his Glock at her.

Gus shouted his resentful reaction, "YOU BELONG TO ME! Not Jeremy and not the Governor." Then he added, "I'll take care of him next."

Darren had the police plant a microphone in the room next door to Gus's motel room, and he listened to Gus screaming at Casey. He wanted to do something, and he wanted to do it immediately. Both of the women he loved were being held hostage by this madman, and he had all the firepower he needed, armed and ready, and sitting right outside his door. He wanted to storm the room when Gus would least expect it and exploit the element of surprise. He put on his bulletproof vest and dialed his cellphone to inform the Governor of his plan. He knew it would continue to get more and more difficult if he let it drag out. He wanted to act now, and the Governor agreed.

Darren, Weller, and Benjamin assembled the police and FDLE agents with stormtrooper shields, ready to attack the motel room. He listened to the microphone again to gauge the timing of his attack.

Casey tried to defuse the situation by psychologically capitalizing on his perverted affection for her, "You're right, Gus. We have loved each other all of our lives. Release Tina, so we can be alone together."

"I don't know about that, Sis. You chose a room with a king-size bed. Maybe we can have ménage au trois together?"

When Darren heard Gus suggest *"ménage au trois,"* he made his decision. He was going in.

Suddenly, *BOOM! BOOM! BOOM!* The motel door shattered as police used C4 to blow off the hinges. Darren barged into the room with Weller, Benjamin, and a dozen police officers behind them with their guns ready to shoot.

Gus grabbed Casey and used her as a human shield in front of him. He started shooting, *BAM! BAM! BAM! BAM! BAM!* He fired his Glock and backed up to reach his AR-15 semiautomatic rifle for more firepower. He shot Benjamin and two police officers in the head and wounded two others. Darren, Weller, and the other officers aimed their guns at Gus, but he continued to hold Casey in front of him for protection. It was a standoff.

Darren had his M16 semiautomatic rifle pointed at Gus, and Gus had his Glock pointed at Darren. Five officers were down, and Gus was holding Casey in front of him. They couldn't shoot, "Give it up, Gus. You're surrounded."

The two wounded officers were moaning in pain on the floor. Weller leaned down and felt Benjamin's neck for a pulse. Nothing. He then checked the other two police officers shot in the head. They were all dead! He stood up and shook his head to Darren.

Darren looked from Weller to Gus, "So, now you've killed three police officers Gus, in addition to all your other murders. Give it up."

Gus looked at the dead police officers on the floor and then back at Darren, "It was self-defense. Look, Agent Turner, I have two hostages. I want a helicopter, and I want all of you out of here, or I will kill both Tina and Casey. One at a time. Tina will be first."

Darren looked over at Tina, gagged and lying mostly nude on her back on the bed with her arms over her head, handcuffed to the bedpost. She was struggling with her handcuffs and trying to scream.

Gus pointed his gun at Tina, ready to shoot her, "Your decision, Agent Turner. I'm going to count to three. I need to hear your decision before I get to 'Three.' One... Two..."

As Gus pointed his Glock toward Tina before he could get to "Three," Casey suddenly reached for the gun in her bra and twirled her body around to release herself from Gus's grip. *BAM! BAM! BAM!* She fired three bullets into his chest in rapid succession, as she screamed, "YOUR TURN TO DIE, GUS!"

The jolt from her shots caused Gus's Glock to discharge towards the bed, wounding Tina in her left arm. Gus staggered backward toward the wall, bleeding. Then he aimed his Glock at Casey and shot back at her, instinctively. She was hit in the chest and fell to the floor, wounded and bleeding. Gus was shocked, holding his hand to his bloody chest and staring down at Casey. He knew he was dying, so he aimed his Glock at her head and started to pull the trigger to kill her, "WE DIE TOGETHER, LITTLE SISTER!"

Before Gus could pull the trigger, Darren fired his M16 at Gus to save Casey. Weller and the police fired relentlessly now that Casey was out of the line of fire. An eruption of bullets barraged Gus and riddled the motel room, knocking out the television and the police scanner. Broken glass and shattered debris from the gunfire burst around the air and splattered to the floor. Gus Slayton was dead.

Just as suddenly as the shooting started, they raised their rifles high in the air and stopped the bombardment. It was suddenly eerily quiet, except for the constant tapping of the rain outside and the sound of the air conditioner blowing cold air into the room. Bitter smoke encircled all of them.

Darren surveyed the surreal spectacle of wreckage in front of them. Twisted metal shards and glass were scattered everywhere. He frantically raced over to Casey, laying on the floor in a pool of blood. She was unconscious and bleeding badly. Gus was next to her, slumped over the AR-15 he had been attempting to reach. His bloody dead torso was riddled with bullets and wreckage.

Darren leaned over to feel Casey's neck for a pulse. He yelled to Weller, "Get an ambulance, fast. She needs CPR." He fervently started pumping Casey's chest and began CPR. He looked up and screamed at Weller, "WHERE IS THE GODDAMN AMBULANCE?"

Sirens in the rain announced the ambulances were approaching.

CHAPTER SIXTY-EIGHT

Lifeless

The Buccaneer Inn
Saint George Island, Florida

A steady stream of headlights started crossing over the lengthy Bryant Patton Bridge after they lifted the blockade, following the death of Gus Slayton.

News media, reporters, cars, television production trucks, and mobile broadcast vans were racing toward the Buccaneer Inn. A lone helicopter hovered overhead with powerful, bright lights illuminating Saint George Island below, headed in the same direction.

It was frantic chaos in the crowded motel room with police and FDLE agents treating the wounded laying on the floor in pools of blood. An ambulance finally arrived, and two paramedics sprinted from the vehicle carrying big yellow boxes. A third grabbed the gurney out of the back cabin and wheeled it into the demolished motel room. Another ambulance appeared, and a third was on the way.

Darren signaled the paramedics over to Casey to give her immediate medical attention, and then he raced over to Tina to check on her condition. Other paramedics took care of the wounded police officers.

342

The paramedics split their focus, one leaning over Casey, checking pulse, eye response and breathing, the other turned attention to Tina, who was on the bed screaming in pain after Darren removed the gag from her mouth. He removed her handcuffs and covered her as the paramedic tended to her wounded arm.

The head tech signaled another paramedic when he was finished with his triage, and they gingerly slid Casey's body onto the gurney. She was in critical condition with a gunshot in the center of her chest. They inserted an IV bag needle into her arm, and they placed a plastic mask over her nose and mouth to squeeze oxygen into her lungs. The paramedic spoke into his radio microphone, and they raced the gurney out of the motel room.

The ambulances were lined-up next to each other, ready to transport the injured to the hospital. The paramedics with Casey reached the back doors of the first ambulance. They pushed the gurney into the ambulance cabin, forcing the legs up as they shoved it into the back and climbed in behind it. They hooked her up to medical technology, which monitored, poked, and pierced Casey to check her vitals.

The helicopter landed in the parking lot several yards away from the ambulances and police cars swarming around the motel room.

L.B. and the Governor waited anxiously as the helicopter rotor slowly wound down so they could disembark. L.B. reached over for the Governor's cane and helped him down the steps to the ground, then held the Governor's arm as he limped with his cane over toward the ambulances.

The Governor and L.B. reached the ambulance after the paramedic glided Casey's gurney into the ambulance cabin. The paramedic looked bleak when they came to the back of the ambulance. L.B. wiped his wet hands on his jacket and glanced down at Casey's bloody injury. She looked lifeless. The paramedic recognized the Governor as rainwater dripped down his face, and L.B. helped him climb into the ambulance cabin and onto the seat next to Casey. The Governor tenderly wiped the raindrops from her forehead.

The Governor suggested using his helicopter to take Casey to the hospital quicker, but the paramedic said the ambulance was better medically equipped to take care of her.

CHAPTER SIXTY-NINE

Hope Was Everything

Ambulance

Saint George Island, Florida

The siren shrieked loudly as the ambulance raced back over the Bryant Patton Bridge toward the emergency room at George E. Weems Memorial Hospital in Apalachicola. The paramedic worked desperately to revive Casey as they crossed over the four-and-a-half-mile-long bridge.

Brendan gazed down at her unconscious face and reflected on all they had been through together. His daughter Susan raped and murdered by the Slayton brothers, his wife dead from a heart attack caused by the Slayton brothers, the revelation Casey Collins was their sister, then he killed Angelo Slayton and wounded Gus Slayton in Miami, Gus shot him back - wounding him in Miami and attempting an assassination in Tallahassee. He had fallen in love with Casey, and now she was lying here dying after her own brother shot her. *What could possibly be next?*

As the ambulance splashed through puddles on the rain-drenched roadway, he watched the paramedic struggle to resuscitate Casey, and considered what the future held in store for them. L.B. interrupted his thoughts, "Brendan, you know she killed Gus Slayton to save your life. He would have never given up."

"Yes, I know. I owe her, big time. For both of our lives. But first, I'm going to take her on a romantic trip to Paris and marry her after she recovers."

L.B. watched the paramedic working feverishly to save Casey and then surveyed the blinking lights and sounds of the medical equipment connected to her body. He knew from experience that the chances of her survival were doubtful at this point. He wanted to say, *Brendan, she's already gone, she's not going to make it.* But he didn't. Something in the devotion to life, the reverence of the moment, maybe a glimpse into what they had suffered so long together, kept him silent.

Brendan looked at L.B. with tears in his eyes, then looked down at Casey and squeezed her hand, "She's got to make it."

At this point, all he had was hope.

Hope was everything!

EPILOGUE

Star Power

Cleveland Clinic Hospital
Miami, Florida

Casey Collins was in critical condition when she barely made it to the emergency room at George E. Weems Memorial Hospital in Apalachicola. The bullet from Gus Slayton's 9mm Glock had pierced her heart, and she was intubated and wheeled into the Operating Room immediately upon arrival. Her prognosis was guarded!

Tina Evanston's bullet wound had fractured the humerus bone in her left arm when Gus was jolted backward by the deadly gunshots from his sister. Tina would be in a cast for a while but would eventually reach a full recovery. Ironically, her wound was almost exactly analogous to the gunshot to the Governor's arm from Gus's same Glock in Tallahassee.

They transported her back to Cleveland Clinic Hospital in Miami from Apalachicola by helicopter, paid by NBC6 News. The management of the television station thought it would be a *Neilson Ratings* bonanza to have their star investigative reporter broadcast the story of what she had been through with Gus Slayton, the Governor, and the Rape Task Force, live from her hospital bed in Miami.

Since she was a television star, they admitted her to the VIP section of the hospital, complete with mahogany cabinetry, an oversized flat-screen television constantly tuned to NBC6, and a picture window view of the Atlantic Ocean. They filled the room with flowers and get-well baskets from her family, friends, and fans. The bed was surrounded by beeping monitors and intravenous medical devices attached to her body.

Darren Turner visited her daily, and he was going to be featured in the forthcoming prime time exclusive broadcast from NBC6 News: "Slayton Brothers: The Rhapsody Killer Cops." It was sure to be an explosive exposé of law enforcement's Blue Curtain and a ratings goldmine for the television station. The theme song would be, *Rhapsody in Blue.*

In the meantime, Tina started writing the book she had dreamed of, with Gus Slayton as the main character. She used everything she had learned from her interview with him, and while listening to everything said by both Gus and Casey while she was gagged and handcuffed to the bed at the Buccaneer Inn.

She was thankful there was no *quid pro quo* necessary, thanks to Casey Collins' surprise intervention. Casey would also be an important character in her book, although she wasn't sure if she would live or die at this point. Only time would tell.

She intended the book would chronicle the Slayton law enforcement family lineage from the grandfather to the father as Chiefs of Police, on to the sons, Gus and Angelo Slayton, as police officers and their abuses. She would explain how sexual abuse is a learned behavior handed down from father to son, like a family tradition. She would also feature Rachel Slayton and her son since they were no longer in the Witness Protection and Relocation Program following the death of Gus Slayton. She hoped her son would be spared the "family tradition," since the Blue Curtain had now been virtually discredited.

She thought the most interesting part of her book, would be about Casey Collins, and what she had been through growing up with an abusive father and identical twin brothers, and how she had been charged with tracking down her own brothers for the rapes and murders. Of course, her relationship with the Governor, and how that evolved following the death of his wife, would also play a crucial part in her book. Plus, her courage and determination to overcome all of her abuses and obstacles to rise to the position of Senior Agent in FDLE. Tina hoped Casey would live to receive the honors she deserved, bestowed upon her.

Instead of the title *The Governor Assassin* she decided to entitle the book *Rapist in Blue* because it would be based on the *Blue Curtain* that protected the Slayton brothers, and other police officers when they abuse their authority as law enforcement to rape and murder women and hide behind *The Badge of Betrayal*. She wanted the book to focus on the ultimate betrayal when law enforcement subverts its motto, "To Protect and Serve," and becomes the attacker instead of the defender.

It would be non-fiction based only on the facts about Casey (Slayton) Collins life.

She envisioned it would be a bestseller, resulting in a movie deal where she would play herself as the Investigative Reporter, exposing The Rhapsody Rapists and Killers as cops. Tina would "Star" in the movie and perhaps win an academy award!

THE END

POSTSCRIPT

Quote from Diane Wetendorf from the Battered Women's Justice Project: [27]

Society grants members of Law Enforcement enormous power over citizens to enable the police to keep the peace and preserve social order. They are granted a great deal of freedom to use their judgment regarding which laws to enforce, when, and against whom. This wide range of options and power can sometimes lead to the abuse of their authority. Unfortunately, some police officers come to see themselves not only as enforcers of the law, but as the law itself. Every police abuser reminds his victim that it is within his power to deprive her of her physical safety, security, privacy, freedom and life, if and when he chooses, unless she complies with his demands.

Most "abusers" are not able to enlist the help of the Criminal Justice System to carry out their threats, but abusers within Law Enforcement are. officers tell their victim, "Call the police. Who are they going to believe?" There is great systemic resistance against prosecuting a police officer. If a victim decides to file a criminal complaint, she will have to present an extremely compelling story to the police and state's attorney to counter their reluctance to pursue the complaint. She will have to be able to convey that, in addition to common forms of abuse, the abuser exploited his professional status and power to control and terrorize her.

BIBLIOGRAPHY

[1] **USA Today - Records of Police Officer misconduct published after nationwide search:**

At least 85,000 Law Enforcement Officers across the United States have been investigated or disciplined for misconduct over the past decade, an investigation by USA TODAY Network found.

Officers have beaten members of the public, planted evidence, and used their badges to harass women. They have lied, stolen, dealt drugs, driven drunk, and abused women.

Despite their role as public servants, the men and women who swear an oath to keep communities safe generally can avoid public scrutiny for their misdeeds.

The records of their misconduct are filed away, rarely seen by anyone outside their departments. Police unions and their political allies have worked to put special protections in place, ensuring some records are shielded from public view or even destroyed.

\#

Reporters from USA TODAY, its 100plus affiliated newsrooms and the nonprofit Invisible Institute in Chicago have spent more than a year creating the biggest collection of police misconduct records.

Obtained from thousands of state agencies, prosecutors, police departments and sheriffs, the records detail at least 200,000 incidents of alleged misconduct, much of it previously unreported.

The records obtained include more than 110,000 internal affairs investigations by hundreds of individual departments and more than 30,000 officers who were decertified by 44 state oversight agencies.

Among the findings:

▌ Most misconduct involves routine infractions, but the records reveal tens of thousands of cases of serious misconduct and abuse. They include 22,924 investigations of officers using excessive force, 3,145 allegations of rape, child molestation and other sexual misconduct and 2,307 cases of domestic violence by officers.

▌ Dishonesty is a frequent problem. The records document at least 2,227 instances of perjury, tampering with evidence or witnesses or falsifying reports. There were 418 reports of officers obstructing investigations, most often when they or someone they knew were targets.

▌ Less than 10% of officers in most police forces get investigated for misconduct. Yet some officers are consistently under investigation. Nearly 2,500 have been investigated on 10 or more charges. Twenty faced 100 or more allegations yet kept their badge for years.

The level of oversight varies widely from state to state. Georgia and Florida decertified thousands of Police Officers on grounds ranging from crimes to questions about their fitness to serve; other states banned almost none.

That includes Maryland, home to the Baltimore Police Department, which regularly has been in the news for criminal behavior by police. Over nearly a decade, Maryland revoked the certifications of just four officers.

We're making those records public

The records that USA TODAY and its partners gathered include tens of thousands of internal investigations, lawsuit settlements and secret separation deals.

They include names of at least 5,000 Police Officers whose credibility as witnesses has been called into question. These officers have been placed on Brady lists, created to track officers whose actions must be disclosed to defendants if their testimony is relied upon to prosecute someone.

USA TODAY plans to publish many of those records to give the public an opportunity to examine their police department and the broader issue of police misconduct, as well as to help identify decertified officers who continue to work in law enforcement.

Seth Stoughton, who worked as a Police Officer for 14 years and teaches law at the University of South Carolina, said expanding public access to those kinds of records is critical to keep good Cops employed and bad Cops unemployed.

"No one is in a position to assess whether an officer candidate can do the job well and the way that we expect the job to be done better than the officer's former employer," Stoughton said.

"Officers are public servants. They police in our name," he said. There is a "strong public interest in identifying how officers are using their public authority."

Dan Hils, president of the Cincinnati Police Department's branch of the Fraternal Order of Policemen union, said people should consider there are more than 750,000 law enforcement officers in the country when looking at individual misconduct data.

"The scrutiny is way tighter on Police Officers than most folks, and that's why sometimes you see high numbers of misconduct cases," Hils said. "But I believe that policemen tend to be more honest and more trustworthy than the average citizen."

Hils said he has no issue with USA TODAY publishing public records of conduct, saying it is the news media's "right and responsibility to investigate police and the authority of government. You're supposed to be a watchdog."

The first set of records USA TODAY is releasing is an exclusive nationwide database of about 30,000 people whom state governments banned from the profession by revoking their certification to be law enforcement officers.

For years, a private police organization has assembled such a list from more than 40 states and encourages police agencies to screen new hires. The list is kept secret from anyone outside law enforcement.

USA TODAY obtained the names of banned officers from 44 states by filing requests under state sunshine laws.

The information includes the officers' names, the department they worked for when the state revoked their certification and – in most cases – the reasons why.

The list is incomplete because of the absence of records from states such as California, which has the largest number of law enforcement officers in the USA.

Bringing important facts to policing debate

USA TODAY's collection of police misconduct records comes amid a nationwide debate over law enforcement tactics, including concern that some officers or agencies unfairly target minorities.

A series of killings of black people by police over the past five years in Baltimore, Chicago, Sacramento, California; and Ferguson, Missouri; and elsewhere have sparked unrest and a reckoning that put pressure on cities and mayors to crack down on misconduct and abuses.

The Trump administration has backed away from more than a decade of Justice Department investigations and court actions against police departments it determined were deeply biased or corrupt.

In 2018, then-Attorney General Jeff Sessions said the Justice Department would leave policing the police to local authorities, saying federal investigations hurt crime fighting.

Laurie Robinson, co-chair of the 2014 White House Task Force on 21st Century Policing, said transparency about police conduct is critical to trust between police and residents.

"It's about the people who you have hired to protect you," she said. "Traditionally, we would say for sure that policing has not been a transparent entity in the U.S. Transparency is just a very key step along the way to repairing our relationships."

Contributing: James Pilcher and Eric Litke.

---

[2] Police Officer Joseph James DeAngelo – The "Golden State Killer"

CNN NEWSFLASH - April 24, 2018: The "Golden State Killer" was a Police Officer.

Police Officer Joseph James DeAngelo, sworn to protect the public from crime as a Police Officer, was living a double life, terrorizing suburban neighborhoods at night. The time frame of the crimes prove that he was a Police Officer when he committed the crimes. He became California's most feared sadistic serial killer and serial rapist in the 1970s and 1980s and was dubbed the "Golden State Killer." He murdered at least 13 people, committed more than 50 rapes and burglarized over 120 homes, during his 12-year reign of terror.

His perseverance, reconnaissance and ability to escape manhunts, as well as the intricate knots he used to bind his victims, led detectives to believe that he had served in the military or in law enforcement. He did both. As a Police Officer, he had the knowledge and the training, that helped him commit and cover-up his crimes. Plus, he could monitor the status of police investigations as an official member of the police department.

The Golden State Killer usually struck at night after carefully planning his attack ahead of time, even down to the smallest details. He studied his victims' schedules, broke into their homes and unlocked windows or removed screens in preparation for his return. He turned off porch lights and hid shoelaces and ropes to use later to bind his victims. In one assault, he hid in a couple's closet, waited for them to fall asleep and then attacked them. When the husband reached for a gun next to him in bed, the attacker shined his flashlight on the bullets he was holding. He had already emptied the gun.

To commit his crimes, DeAngelo would slip in through the backdoors and windows of victim's homes in the dark. He had peculiar and cruel rituals that he inflicted on his victims. His victims included women home alone and women at home with their husbands and children. He would rape the women with their husbands present and then murder them both.

Police Officer DeAngelo killed at least 13 people in California: February 2, 1978, he shot Brian and Kate Maggiore, killing them both. December 30, 1979, he killed Doctor Robert Offerman and his wife, Alexandria Manning, he raped her and shot them both. March 13, 1980, he tied up Lyman and Charlene Smith with a drapery cord and raped the wife before fatally bludgeoning them both with a fireplace log. August 19, 1980, he bludgeoned Keith and Patrice Harrington with a blunt object, after raping the wife. February 1, 1981, he raped and murdered Manuela Witthuhn, while her husband was in the hospital. July 27, 1981, Cheri Domingo and Gregory Sanchez were bludgeoned to death with a garden tool. May 4, 1986, he brutally raped and murdered 18-year-old Janelle Cruz with a pipe wrench, in her family's home.

#

Wikipedia:

1978

- On the night of February 2, 1978, a young Sacramento couple, Brian Maggiore (a military policeman at Mather Air Force Base) and Katie Maggiore, were walking their dog in the Rancho Cordova area, close to a cluster of five East Area Rapist attacks. A confrontation in the street caused the couple to flee, but they were chased down and shot dead. Some investigators suspected the couple had been murdered by the East Area Rapist because the killings occurred in the vicinity of the attacks and one shoelace was found near the crime scene.

358

- On October 1, an intruder broke in and tied up a Goleta couple. The attacker alarmed them by chanting "I'll kill 'em'" to himself. When he left the room, the man and woman made attempts to escape, during which the woman screamed. Realizing the alarm had been raised, the intruder fled on a bicycle. A neighbor, who was an FBI agent, responded to the noise and pursued the perpetrator, who abandoned the bicycle and a knife and fled on foot through local backyards. The attack was later linked physically to the Offerman–Manning murders by shoe prints and the same roll of twine being used to bind the victims.

- On December 30, Dr. Robert Offerman, 44, and Dr. Debra Alexandra Manning, 35, were found shot dead at Offerman's condominium on Avenida Pequena in Goleta. The bindings on Offerman were untied, indicating he had apparently lunged at the attacker. Neighbors heard the gunshots, but failed to respond to them, attributing them to innocuous causes. Paw prints from a large dog were found at the scene, leading to speculation that the killer may have brought it with him. There is evidence that he fed the dog some leftover Christmas turkey from the refrigerator. The killer also broke into the adjoining residence, which was vacant at the time, and stole a bicycle from a third residence in the same complex. The bicycle was later found abandoned on a street to the north of the crime scene.

1980

- On March 13, Charlene Smith, 33, and Lyman Smith, 43, who was about to be appointed as a Judge, were found murdered in their home in Ventura. Charlene Smith had also been raped. A log from the fireplace was used to bludgeon both the victims to death. Their wrists and ankles had been bound with a drapery cord. An unusual Chinese knot, known as the diamond knot, was used on their wrists. The same knot had been noted in the East Area Rapist attacks in Sacramento, with at least one confirmed case publicly known.

- On August 19, Keith Eli Harrington, 24, and Patrice Briscoe Harrington, 27, were found bludgeoned to death in their home on Cockleshell Drive in the Niguel Shores gated community in Dana Point. Patrice Harrington had also been raped. Although there was evidence that the Harringtons were bound at the wrist and ankles, no ligatures or murder weapon were found at the scene. The Harringtons had been married for three months at the time of their deaths. Patrice Harrington was a nurse in Irvine, while Keith Harrington was a medical student at the University of California, Irvine. Keith Harrington's brother Bruce later spent nearly $2 million supporting California Proposition 69 (2004), which allows for DNA collection from all felons and certain other criminals in California.

1981

- On February 6, Manuela Witthuhn, 28, was raped and murdered in her home in Irvine. Again, while the body showed signs of being tied before being bludgeoned, no ligatures or murder weapon were found. The victim was married, but her husband was recuperating from an illness in the hospital; thus, she was alone at the time of the attack. A lamp and crystal curio were removed from her house, presumably by the killer. Detectives also remarked that Witthuhn's television was found in the backyard, which was possibly the killer's attempt to make it appear as a botched robbery.

- On July 27, Cheri Domingo, 35, and Gregory Sanchez, 27, became the 10th and 11th murder victims of the Original Night Stalker. Both were attacked in Domingo's house on Toltec Way in Goleta, several blocks south of the Offerman–Manning crime scene. Their murder was linked to the Original Night Stalker by DNA left at the scene. He is believed to have broken into the home in Goleta, which was up for sale at the time of the attack. Law enforcement believe the attacker may have worked as a painter or related role in the Calle Real Shopping Centre.

It is unknown how the Golden State Killer selected Domingo and Sanchez as victims. Domingo's daughter was staying with friends on the night of the attack and her son was with family members out of state. The home in Goleta belonged to Domingo's family and she was staying there temporarily. The offender had entered the property via a small window in the bathroom. Sanchez had not been tied and was shot in the cheek, although not fatally. He was then bludgeoned to death with a garden tool taken from the property. Some believe Sanchez may have realized he was dealing with the man responsible for the Offerman–Manning murders and made a desperate attempt to tackle the killer rather than be tied up. As in the Offerman–Manning case, no neighbors responded to the sound of the gunshot. Sanchez's head was covered with clothes pulled from the closet. Bruises on Domingo's wrists and ankles indicated she had been tied, although the restraints were missing. She had been raped and bludgeoned. A single piece of shipping twine was found near the bed, and fibers of an unknown source were scattered over her body.

1986

- On May 4, Janelle Lisa Cruz, 18, was found raped and bludgeoned to death in her Irvine home. Her family was on vacation in Mexico at the time of the attack. A pipe wrench was reported missing by Cruz's stepfather and was thought to be the murder weapon.

These murders in Southern California were not initially thought to be connected by investigators in their respective jurisdictions. One Sacramento detective strongly believed the East Area Rapist was responsible for the Goleta attacks, but the Santa Barbara County

361

Sheriff's Department attributed them to a local career criminal who had subsequently been murdered. Investigating the crimes that did not occur in Goleta caused local police to follow false leads related to men who had been close to the female victims. One suspect, later acknowledged to be innocent, was charged with two murders. Linking all of the cases together was achieved almost entirely via DNA testing, which was not done until many years later.

---

[3] <u>NYPD Martins and Hall Police Rapes in New York. November, 2017</u>

Two New York Police Department officers took turns raping handcuffed, Anna, in the backseat of their police van in Coney Island, NY.

Police Officers Eddie Martins and Richard Hall stopped a car driven by a young, beautiful woman and made her remove her bra and expose herself to prove that she wasn't hiding anything. They handcuffed the woman and arrested her on drug charges.

Martins then raped the handcuffed woman in the back seat as Hall drove and watched in the rear-view mirror. They stopped and switched places in the van. Hall forced the woman to perform a sex act on him.

Later they drove back to the 60th precinct and dropped Anna off, telling her to keep her mouth shut. Anna went to Maimonides Medical Center and underwent a sexual assault exam. DNA found on Anna matched both detectives and video surveillance showed her leaving the police van at 8:42 p.m. that evening.

Officers Martins and Hall were charged with first-degree rape, first-degree criminal sexual act, second-degree kidnapping, totaling 50 charges. Both officers face up to 25 years in prison.

#

(CNN) Two NYPD officers who have been accused of taking turns raping a handcuffed 18-year-old woman in the back seat of their police van in Coney Island in September have voluntarily resigned.

Eddie Martins, 37 and Richard Hall, 33, appeared on their own at New York Police Department headquarters on Monday "and quit their employment with the NYPD," according to a statement from the NYPD.

Martins and Hall were arraigned last week on a total of 50 charges, including first-degree rape, first-degree criminal sexual act and second-degree kidnapping, the Kings County District Attorney's Office said.

NYPD Commissioner James O'Neill said the charges "tarnished all of the admirable things accomplished by other, good officers every day in neighborhoods across New York City."

"Had these charges been upheld in an upcoming departmental trial, I would have fired them immediately," O'Neill said in a statement on Monday.

Both officers pleaded not guilty to all counts, according to the district attorney's office. Martins was released on $250,000 bail and Hall was released on $150,000 bail. Each could face up to 25 years in prison if convicted.

An attorney for Eddie Martins, Mark Bederow, said his client's resignation "has no impact on how we will prepare to defend the case."

"It's true that [Martins] resigned today, but we're going to be focusing all of our efforts on confronting the indictment in Brooklyn and spending all of our time demonstrating that the charges against him are absolutely false," Bederow said.

An attorney for Richard Hall did not return CNN's request for comment.

The rape allegedly occurred on the evening of September 15 when Martins and Hall, plainclothes detectives, left their post without authorization and drove to Calvert Vaux Park in Brooklyn, the district attorney's office said.

There, the officers stopped a car driven by an 18-year-old woman with two male passengers. The detectives made her remove her bra and expose herself to prove she wasn't hiding anything, said Michael David, an attorney representing the 18-year-old.

They handcuffed the woman and arrested her on drug charges and told the male passengers to leave and pick up the young woman later, the district attorney's office said.

Martins allegedly told her that he and Hall are "freaks" and asked her what she wanted to do to get out of the arrest, the district attorney's office said. Martins allegedly then raped the handcuffed woman in the back seat as Hall drove and watched in the rear-view mirror.

The detectives then allegedly stopped the van in Bay Ridge, about 4 miles from the park. After they switched places in the van, Hall forced the woman to perform a sex act on him, according to prosecutors. Later the officers drove back to the 60th precinct and dropped off the woman, telling her to keep her mouth shut, the district attorney's office said.

The young woman went to Maimonides Medical Center and underwent a sexual assault exam, prosecutors said. DNA found on the woman matched both detectives, while video surveillance showed her leaving the police van about 8:42 p.m. that evening, according to prosecutors.

David said his client feels the officers should have been fired immediately after the alleged incident, "instead of this dragging on for seven or eight weeks now."

"She wants their conviction. She wants them then in jail. She's not going to feel safe until they're behind bars," David said.

A pretrial conference is scheduled for January 18.

<u>1981 Governor Brendan Byrne Daughter Rape in New York City,</u>
<u>New York</u>

New Jersey Governor Brendan Byrne's 25-year-old daughter, Susan, was dragged into an alley and gang raped by two men on the Upper East Side of Manhattan. Susan was attacked while she was returning to her car on East 78th Street between Second and Third Avenues at 12:40 a.m. She was alone at the time and had been socializing at Jim McMullen's, a bar at 1341 Third Avenue, frequented by sports celebrities.

Susan was taken to Lenox Hill Hospital in New York City, where she was treated for her bruises and rapes.

Her attackers were never located. The crime remains unsolved in the New York City cold case files.

#

<u>United Press International:</u>

NEW YORK -- New Jersey Governor Brendan Byrne's 25-year-old daughter was dragged into an alley by two males on the Upper East Side early today, authorities reported.

There were reports the young woman had been sexually assaulted but police and the governor's office in Trenton could not confirm this.

Governor Byrne was reported in route to Manhattan. John Farmer, Byrne's press secretary, said he could not confirm or deny the reports the governor's daughter had been raped.

"What I can confirm is that she (Susan) was accosted apparently sometime around midnight," he said.

Farmer said Miss Byrne, who attends school in New York, but lives in Morven the governor's official residence in Princeton, was in the city visiting friends when the incident occurred.

"Naturally, it scared the hell out of her," Farmer said. "She called home and didn't have to be hospitalized and came home to Morven last night."

Farmer said the incident occurred on the Upper East Side of Manhattan.

New York City police would say only that a 25-year-old woman was dragged into an alleyway in the same area and assaulted by two male Hispanics. The woman was attacked while she was returning to her car on East 78th street between Second and Third Avenues at 12:40 a.m.

Asked whether the victim was Byrne's daughter, one officer said: "We are required by law to withhold the identity of a victim of a sex crime ... We can't confirm or deny it."

Police said the woman, who apparently was alone at the time, had been socializing at Jim McMullen's, a bar at 1341 Third Ave. frequented by sports celebrities and was returning to her car when she was accosted.

Police said the woman was taken to Lenox Hill Hospital, where she was treated and released.

---

[5] Associated Press – November 1, 2015:

When an Oklahoma City Police Officer was charged last year with sexually assaulting or exploiting 12 women and a teenage girl, The Associated Press wanted to know how often officers nationwide are accused of sexual misdeeds. The question has no easy answer because no federal accounting of police misconduct exists. However, most states have standards and training commissions that can strip officers of their law enforcement licenses for misconduct. That administrative process is commonly known as decertification.

Over a yearlong period, the AP collected and analyzed decertification records nationwide from 2009 through 2014. Of the nearly 9,000 cases in which officers were decertified, about 1,000 officers lost their licenses for conduct that the AP found included sexual assault, sex crimes such as possessing child pornography and misconduct that ranged from propositioning citizens to consensual but prohibited on-duty intercourse.

The AP compared the cases to a federal government standard to determine whether the officers' actions amounted to sexual assault or involved other forms of sexual misconduct. The U.S. Justice Department defines sexual assault as "any type of sexual contact or behavior that occurs without the explicit consent of the recipient," including forced sexual intercourse or sodomy, child molestation, incest, fondling and attempted rape.

While the AP's review is the most comprehensive available — 41 states provided decertification information — the number is an undercount. Some states did not provide information and even among states that did, some reported no officers removed for sexual misdeeds even though cases were identified via official records and news stories.

Six states, including some with the nation's largest law enforcement agencies, said they did not decertify officers for misconduct and kept no official tally of officer wrongdoing. They are California, Hawaii, Massachusetts, New Jersey, New York and Rhode Island. Three states — Louisiana, Maryland and North Carolina — did not provide information to the AP. The District of Columbia said it had no process for certification.

Standards for revoking an officer's license varied: Almost every state in the U.S. can decertify an officer convicted of a felony. More than 30 have the ability to also decertify for misconduct that may not be criminal. But some states have no reporting requirements, leaving it to local law enforcement to seek the removal of an officer's license or instead let him or her quietly leave the force.

The quality of information in the decertification records also varied widely.

Florida provided the most detailed review, sharing copies of its statewide database of officers" employment histories and discipline reports. Georgia supplied spreadsheets with the names and offenses of

367

officers disciplined for misconduct and access to an online database of information. About 20 states provided a list of all decertified officers" names, agencies and dates and reasons for decertification.

Minnesota refused to name the officers it decertified, though it provided their agencies and reason for decertification. Oklahoma refused to let the AP review all of its files and released records only for officers it said were decertified for sexual misconduct.

In determining whether an officer had committed sexual misconduct, the AP mostly relied on what a state gave as its reason for decertification. But a cause for decertification was not always clearly stated in the records. Some states gave vague reasons, such as "conduct unbecoming an officer" or "voluntary surrender," for officers who the AP later found — through additional state information, court or other official records, or media accounts — had actions that met the federal definition of sexual assault or constituted another sex crime or sexual misconduct.

Not all decertified officers face charges or a trial, where the standard of proof is "beyond a reasonable doubt." State commissions generally apply a "preponderance of the evidence" standard in deciding whether to revoke a law enforcement license.

The AP found fewer than a dozen cases among the sex-related decertification's it studied in which an officer was acquitted in court or later on appeal. Those officers' licenses were not reinstated and the cases were included in AP's count. It is also possible for officers to appeal their decertification's and later regain their licenses.

A yearlong Associated Press investigation uncovered about 1,000 officers in six years who lost their licenses to work in law enforcement for rape, other sex crimes or sexual misconduct. The number is unquestionably an undercount because it represents only those officers who faced an administrative process known as decertification and not all states take such action or provided records. California and New York, for example, did not provide records because they have no statewide process for decertification. Even among states that provided records, some reported no officers removed for sexual misdeeds even though the AP discovered cases via news stories and court records.

Below are 10 cases from across the U.S. that reflect how such crimes can occur and the devastation they leave behind. Most of the officers have been convicted and are serving time. Some await trial.

SERGIO ALVAREZ

Sergio Alvarez, 40, of the West Sacramento Police in California, is serving 205 years to life after being convicted of kidnapping five women and then raping them or forcing them to perform oral sex. The victims testified at Alvarez's criminal trial last year, recounting how he picked them up while they walked alone in the darkness along a strip known for prostitution, drugs and homelessness. Investigators found a personal "spycam" that Alvarez used to record some of the sex acts. One of the women referred to Alvarez as a "Creepy Cop" she tried to avoid but couldn't. California doesn't decertify officers for misconduct, though Alvarez relinquished his badge when he was arrested.

WILLIAM NULICK

William Nulick, 44, of the Tulare County Sheriff's Office in California, is awaiting trial after being charged with sexually assaulting four women in 2013. Two who speak only Spanish claim Nulick pulled them over and led them into remote areas, asking for sexual favors in lieu of writing them tickets. Two others claim to have been groped in inappropriate pat-downs. All told, Nulick faces 18 criminal counts, including oral copulation under the color of authority, accepting bribes in the form of sexual favors and false imprisonment. At a preliminary hearing, Detective Paul Gezzer said one victim told him she "was afraid she was going to die." Nulick's attorney, Galatea DeLapp, said her client admits accepting a sexual favor as a bribe but denies a charge of false imprisonment. Nulick resigned from the sheriff's office. California doesn't decertify officers for misconduct.

JONATHAN BLEIWEISS

Jonathan Bleiweiss, 35, of the Broward Sheriff's Office in Florida, began serving a five-year sentence in February after he was accused of bullying about 20 immigrant men living in the country illegally into sex acts. The victims shied away from testifying, so prosecutors reached a plea deal revolving around false imprisonment charges, allowing Bleiweiss to escape conviction on any sexual offenses and thus avoid being labeled a sex offender. Prosecutors said he used implied threats of deportation to intimidate the men. His guilty plea means the state will decertify him.

MICHAEL GARCIA

Michael Garcia, 39, of the Las Cruces Police in New Mexico, was sentenced last year to nine years in prison for sexually assaulting a 17-year-old girl interning at the department. Garcia, at the time assigned to a unit investigating child abuse and sex crimes, was one of the girl's mentors. The victim said the assault made her give up her dream of being an officer and left her crippled by depression, anxiety and nightmares. In court, she said Garcia "took my spirit away from me" and that "it had never occurred to me that a person who had earned a badge would do this to me or anybody else." Under questioning by an investigator, Garcia said a brief lapse had cost him his career: "Three minutes for the rest of my life." Garcia was ordered to forfeit his law enforcement certification.

DANIEL HOLTZCLAW

Daniel Holtzclaw, 28, of the Oklahoma City Police, is scheduled for trial Monday, accused of sexual offenses against 13 women, including rape, forced oral sodomy and sexual battery. He has pleaded not guilty. The former college football star is accused of targeting mostly poor women from the same rundown neighborhood. Prosecutors say he often used the same ploy of accusing the women of concealing drugs beneath their clothes, then directing them to expose themselves. Central to their case is GPS data they say place him at the scenes of the alleged crimes. Oklahoma City Police Chief Bill Citty says Holtzclaw took advantage of those made vulnerable by their pasts; some of the accusers have criminal records. "It's somebody that he as a Police Officer felt like he had power over. And he abused that power," he said. Holtzclaw has been fired. He declined comment and his attorney did not respond to messages.

WILLIAM RUSCOE

William Ruscoe, 46, of the Trumbull Police in Connecticut, began a 30-month prison term in January after pleading guilty to second-degree sexual assault of a 17-year-old girl he met through a program for young people interested in law enforcement. The girl said she began receiving text messages from Ruscoe that grew sexual and that he eventually professed his affection for her and gave her a silver bracelet with a heart-shaped charm that said "Made with Love." In an incident at the officer's home, he removed her cadet uniform and sexually assaulted her. At one point, she said, he handcuffed her. Ruscoe has been decertified.

DARRELL BEST

Darrell Best, 46, of the Metropolitan Police Department in Washington, D.C., pleaded guilty in October to sexually abusing two teenagers who were members of the church where the officer was head pastor. The girls said the abuse occurred on several occasions and included incidents at Best's church and police headquarters. The officer also pleaded guilty to producing child pornography after detectives found sexually explicit pictures of the victims on his phone. "It takes a particular type of depravity, boldness and recklessness for a sexual predator to take photographs of his victim," the government argued in a court filing. Best is due for sentencing in February; his plea agreement calls for an 18-year prison term. His attorney, Nikki Lotze, called his guilty plea "an important step in accepting responsibility." The police department said Best resigned in August. The District of Columbia says it does not decertify officers.

REX NEWPORT

Rex Newport, 47, of the Colville Police Department in Washington state, was sentenced last year to 2½ years in prison for unlawful imprisonment with sexual motivation and other charges. Newport had entered an Alford plea, which allows a defendant to plead guilty while maintaining innocence. According to a detective's report, a woman said Newport followed her home from a bar and entered her apartment in the remote town near the U.S.-Canadian border. According to a probable cause affidavit, she went to a neighbor's apartment when he left to take a call on his radio, fearing he would come back to attack her. She saw him come and go and thought it was safe to return, but he was waiting inside. Newport handcuffed her, then removed the cuffs before having sex with her. After she reported the assault, police identified four other women who accused Newport of propositioning them while on duty. The state decertified Newport.

WALTER NOLDEN

Walter Nolden, 34, of the San Antonio Independent School District Police, was released from jail last year after being given a yearlong sentence related to improper searches of young girls. Nolden was a campus officer at Page Middle School, where six girls in seventh and eighth grade made similar accusations – that the officer had them expose their breasts or peered down their shirts when he conducted searches for drugs. Some of the girls claimed he groped them. Nolden ultimately pleaded no contest to a charge of official oppression. One of the girls said Nolden told her the search was necessary "to make sure she didn't have anything." Nolden was decertified.

CHRISTOPHER STEIN EPPERSON

Christopher Epperson, 37, of the Wasatch County Sheriff's Department in Utah, is serving three years" probation in the sexual assaults of two inmates. Epperson pleaded guilty to two federal counts of deprivation of rights under color of law for the offenses in 2009 and 2010 while he was a deputy sheriff working in the county jail. He had groped two female inmates. A separate civil lawsuit against Epperson, the county and the sheriff's department was filed by one of the women nearly five years ago but remains ongoing; the second woman later joined the litigation. The lawsuit alleges a pattern of behavior by Epperson that began with flirtation, smiles and winks and grew more serious to include forcing one woman to be photographed shirtless and to fondle the officer and attempted sodomy. Epperson has voluntarily relinquished his state law enforcement license.

---

[6] Philip Stinson, J.D., Ph.D

An associate professor of criminal justice at Bowling Green State University. Dr. Stinson's primary area of research is police behaviors, including police crime, police corruption and police misconduct. He is the principal investigator on a research project funded by a grant from the National Institute of Justice (NIJ) at the U.S. Department of Justice to study police crime across the United States. His current research project, Police Integrity Lost: A Longitudinal Study of Police Crime, is supported by the Wallace Action Fund of Tides Foundation. Dr. Stinson's research has been published in numerous peer-reviewed journals, including Criminal Justice Policy Review, The Prison Journal, Victims & Offenders and Journal of Crime & Justice. His research has also been featured in many news publications, including The Washington Post, The Wall Street Journal, The New York Times and FiveThirtyEight.com. Phil Stinson has appeared on CNN, PBS, NPR, CBC, BBC, Sky News, CCTV, Radio Sputnik, Democracy Now. HuffPost Live and numerous other media outlets worldwide. He teaches a variety or undergraduate and graduate courses at Bowling Green, including Criminal Law, Procedural Rights, Criminal Courts, Criminal Justice Ethics, Criminal Justice Policy Analysis and Law, Evidence & Procedure in Forensic Science.

---

[7] 2017 Deputy Evan Cramer Police Rape in St. Lucie, Florida

A young Florida woman named Kelly, was pulled over by Sheriff's Deputy Evan Cramer for a minor traffic violation. However, instead of simply writing a ticket and moving on, he proceeded to use his police authority to kidnap her, throw her in the back of his cruiser, drive her to a vacant car lot and rape her.

Afterwards, Kelly went to Lawnwood Regional Medical Center in Fort Pierce, Florida, and underwent a rape test. DNA evidence from the semen on Kelly's clothing and body, obtained though the rape test kit was later confirmed to match the DNA of Deputy Cramer.

Prosecutors later identified a second and third victim as well.

Deputy Cramer was previously employed by the Sanford Police Department in Florida and had been recommended for termination due to improper conduct and abuse of authority.

#

The Free Thought Project:

Fort Pierce, FL — For the majority of people who see those red and blue lights turn on behind them as they drive down the highway, your adrenaline spikes, your heart races and the last thing going through your mind is, "I am being protected right now." While most of these stops end with a promissory note of extortion for a victimless crime, sometimes, especially for women, things can get quite dangerous.

As the Free Thought Project has reported countless times, all too often, Police Officers will abuse their authority to force unwilling victims into performing sexual favors in exchange for leniency. Also, many times, there is no quid pro quo and Police Officers will simply rape people they pull over — case in point, Daniel Holtzclaw.

A young Florida woman has learned the hard way about police rape last week when she was stopped by St. Lucie County Sheriff's Deputy, Evan Cramer, 28.

According to Sheriff Ken Mascara, Cramer pulled over his latest victim last Tuesday night for a minor traffic violation. However, instead of simply writing a ticket and moving on, Cramer proceeded to use his authority to rape this woman.

Cramer is accused of telling the victim she had multiple warrants out for her arrest and said she could avoid jail time if she granted sexual favors, Mascara said.

According to police, Cramer then kidnapped his victim, threw her in the back of his cruiser, drove her to a vacant car lot and raped her.

Immediately after it happened, his frightened victim then went to the local hospital to report she'd been raped.

"She was terrified," said Sheriff Ken Mascara. "You could hear it in her voice. You could see it. It was palpable."

Cramer was arrested the next morning after a brief investigation. He was charged with sexual assault/battery and unlawful compensation, the sheriff's department said. He is currently being held on a $850,000 bond.

Mascara told the media last week that it is, indeed, likely, that Cramer had done this before and urged any potential victims to come forward.

"He made comments to this victim that support that he's done this in the past," the sheriff said. "He actually compared her to other victims. It's apparent there are some other victims out there, based on his own statements."

"During a time in our nation when respect for law enforcement is at an all-time high, incidents such as this quickly erode that trust and respect," Mascara said. "I want to apologize to our community and other members of the law enforcement family for the dishonorable actions of this one person."

While this apology sounds okay, perhaps Mascara should apologize for hiring this officer with such a troubled past in the first place. After the arrest, WPBF looked into Cramer's past — what they found was trouble.

<u>Oklahoma City Police Officer Holtzclaw Police Rapes in Oklahoma</u>

<u>Cable News Network and Wikipedia:</u>

January 22, 2016 – Oklahoma City Police Officer Daniel Holtzclaw, convicted of rape and other charges after he preyed on African-American women for over six months, was sentenced to 263 years in prison. Holtzclaw was convicted on 18 of 36 counts, including four counts of first-degree rape and four counts of forced oral sodomy.

The police investigation brought together 13 women who were willing to testify; published reports did not include information on any possible further women who were not willing to testify. The earliest woman discovered was from December 20, 2013, a woman who said she had been arrested for drug possession, was hospitalized and forced to give oral sex while she was handcuffed to her hospital bed. She said that he again made sexual advances to her on several occasions after she was released from jail. The woman said that she was led to believe that she would be released if she performed oral sex on Holtzclaw. "I didn't think that no one would believe me", she testified at a pretrial hearing. "I feel like all police will work together."

On February 27, 2014, Holtzclaw allegedly pulled up to a woman who was sitting in a parked car outside her house, fondled the woman's breasts and told her "I'm not going to take you to jail. Just play by my rules." He returned to her home repeatedly and broke into it once. At his trial she said she did not notify the police because she did not believe anyone would believe her because "I'm a black female."

In early 2014 Holtzclaw allegedly forced a woman who was admittedly a drug user to expose her breasts and genitals in order to avoid arrest.

- March 14, 2014: Holtzclaw stopped a woman who was walking to a friend's house, asked her if she was in possession of any drugs and forced her to expose her breasts.

- April 24, 2014: Holtzclaw stopped a woman who was prostituting herself for drugs. He drove her home and when they arrived he forced her to perform oral sex and then raped her.

- April 25, 2014: Holtzclaw pulled a woman over saying he was taking her to detox in jail; he instead drove her to a field and raped her, leaving her there after he was done.

- May 7, 2014: Holtzclaw stopped a woman while she walked to her cousin's house. After finding out she had some warrants, he forced her to perform oral sex and then raped her behind an abandoned school.

- May 8, 2014: According to a later investigation, "A woman, known in court documents as T.M., reported that an unidentified officer forced her to perform oral sex after he found a crack pipe in her purse. Although she filed a police report later that month, no connection was made to Holtzclaw at the time."

- May 21, 2014: Holtzclaw drove a woman to a secluded area and gave her an ultimatum: sex or jail. She performed oral sex on him and then he raped her. In an interview the woman said that she first thought it was a "cruel joke of some hidden-camera show" until she realized that he was serious. She said she "had been jailed many times before and knew the math: a 15-minute ride downtown, two hours to be booked, up to a day of waiting to move to a cell, hearings drawn out over weeks or months," and then decided to give into his demands, which she figured would only take about six minutes.

- May 26, 2014: Holtzclaw stopped a woman and touched her breasts and put his hand in her pants. The woman said she did not tell the police because she didn't think she'd be believed.

- June 17, 2014: According to an investigation, "A 17-year-old female is first stopped by Holtzclaw when he arrives to investigate a verbal dispute between two of her friends. Later, he tracks her down while she is walking home, threatens to arrest her for an outstanding warrant and then takes her to her mother's house, where he forces her to perform oral sex and have intercourse with him on the enclosed porch."

- June 18, 2014: Around 2:00 a.m., Holtzclaw had an encounter with a 57-year-old grandmother, Jannie Ligons, who would ultimately be the one to spark the investigation

- June 18, 2014: The final sexual incident occurred on the same day as the encounter reported by Ligons. According to testimony, Holtzclaw stopped a woman as she left a hotel where she had been staying with her boyfriend. After running a check on her he took her to a desolate area and raped her. She told her boyfriend about the attack and he told her that she should report the rape to the police. "He is the police", she responded.

- November 2014: In November three more victims came forward, bringing the total to 13. Previously unidentified DNA which had been found on Holtzclaw's pants was found to match that of a 17-year-old girl who had come forward regarding the June 17 event. Another woman said she was walking on May 22 when Holtzclaw stopped her to check for warrants. When he found that there were no warrants out for her he said he would jail her if she didn't have sex with him; he then forced her to perform oral sex and raped her. A third woman said that he told her he was bringing her to detox but instead brought her to an isolated area and raped her. Ten more counts, including "first-degree rape, second-degree rape by instrumentation, forcible oral sodomy and sexual battery" were filed against Holtzclaw, who was still on paid leave.

Prosecutors said Holtzclaw selected victims in one of Oklahoma City's poorest neighborhoods based on their criminal histories, assuming their drug or prostitution records would undermine any claims they might make against him. Then, he would subject them to assaults that escalated from groping to oral sodomy and rape, according to the testimony of 13 victims. Holtzclaw, whose father is a police lieutenant on another force, waived his right to testify.

Two of those women shared their stories with CNN on Wednesday, recounting horrific memories of being forced to perform sexual acts by a serial rapist with a badge who was supposed to protect and serve.

Because the victims are black, race has been regularly invoked in the case. His trial began in November and was criticized by activists after an all-white jury was chosen. Protesters repeatedly gathered outside.

Attorney Benjamin Crump, who represented the families of Trayvon Martin and Michael Brown, has criticized the media, asking, "Where is the national outcry for their justice?"

Crump praised the sentence Thursday saying it was "a landmark victory."

"All the women were victims, from the 17-year old teenager to the 57-year old grandmother. This is a statement for 400 years of racism, oppression and sexual assault of black women; a statement of victory not only for the "OKC 13," but for so many unknown women," Crump said in a statement.

One of Holtzclaw's victims, Jannie Ligons, grandmother of 12, was among those who spoke at the sentencing on Thursday.

In an interview with CNN this week, she recalled driving down Lincoln Street when Holtzclaw pulled her over and told her she was swerving, "which was untrue," she said. He told her to get out of the car. "He put a flashlight on my chest. He told me to pull my pants down to my knees. I did that but real quick and pulled them back up again. He pulled out his flashlight and shined it on my privates. I said. "Sir, you not supposed to do this. He said, 'Get back into my vehicle.' I did what he said. I began to get very, very scared," Ligons said.

She remembers him telling her, "Damn, you got a big ass."

"I thought he was going to kill me because I had seen his face and could tell on him and he was an officer and had to know he wasn't supposed to do this," she said.

That's when Holtzclaw ordered her to perform oral sex, she said. Her mind racing and tears gushing from her then-57-year-old eyes, she was both disgusted and terrified.

"I tried to perform oral sex," she said. "And trying to talk, I kept saying, 'Sir, please don't make me do this.' I said, "Are you gonna shoot me?" He said, "I promise I am not. I didn't believe him. I kept seeing his gun while he was making me do this right there on the street. I was sitting in the passenger side of the car and he was standing there. It was so horrifying. It was unreal. I cried and cried," Ligons said.

Finally, he let her go and "I decided right then If he didn't kill me I was going to tell on him," she said.

Rape in a hospital bed

She picked up her daughter and went to the police station. Investigators interviewed her and sent her to the hospital. She soon learned she was the last in a string of sexual assaults and rapes committed by Holtzclaw.

"The detective I talked to in the hospital came in and she believed me. While she was writing the report she said, "I got a good idea who it was," " Ligons said. "I was relieved at first, but then I wondered why he was still on the street if they knew who it was."

Ligons told reporters after the verdict was announced last month that she had to enter therapy and later "had a stroke behind this."

Another victim, 24-year-old Shandegreon "Sade" Hill, told CNN she was intoxicated the night Holtzclaw arrested her.

He promised to get her prior charges dropped, but while she was handcuffed to the hospital bed trying to detox, he raped her, she said.

"He started to touch me. He touched my breast. From there, I just didn't know what to think. I am in his custody because whatever he tells me in my mind I just did it. As far as I know I could wind up dead in the hospital saying I was overdosed," Hill said.

380

"He violated me. And made me give him oral. He stuck his hands into my privates. He done everything against my will, " she told CNN, her voice shaking and angry.

Holtzclaw continued to pursue her, even following her to her home and stalking her on social media, she said.

These are just two of the stories from the 13 victims, one of whom was 17 at the time and testified she was raped on her mother's front porch.

Grandmother brought him down

Ligons" report would be the one that finally yielded Holtzclaw's arrest. After she went to police and media outlets, investigators found another dozen victims. She now has a civil lawsuit pending against the former officer and the city, filed on behalf of several victims. Hill has filed a state civil lawsuit against Holtzclaw and Oklahoma City.

Crump has called Ligons "a true hero -- not just for black women but all women."

"The statistics on rape victims reporting the crimes against them are low to being with. This grandmother had the strength to come forward not just against her assailant but against a Police Officer. That is a frightening thing to do," he said.

Holtzclaw was a former linebacker on the Eastern Michigan University football team and graduated with a degree in criminal justice.

Prosecutors say his ruthless scheme began during a June 2014 traffic stop. He was fired from the force in January 2015 after an internal investigation.

"Your offenses committed against women in our community constitute the greatest abuse of police authority I have witnessed in my 37 years as a member of this agency," Oklahoma City Police Chief Bill Citty wrote in the termination letter, according to CNN affiliate KFOR.

LAPD Valenzuela and Nichols Police Rapes in California

Two Los Angeles Police Department officers repeatedly raped and sexually assaulted four women while on duty. They took turns like a tag team, one partner served as the lookout, as the other carried out an attack in the backseat of the police car that they drove together.

They targeted specific women and threatened them with arrest if they did not comply with their demands. Officer Valenzuela also assaulted women with a gun.

They were charged with more than a dozen felony counts, sentenced to 25 years in prison and ordered to register as sex offenders.

#

February 17, 2016 - Los Angeles Times:

Two officers from the Los Angeles Police Department have been charged with repeatedly raping and sexually assaulting several women while on duty.

The men threatened their victims with arrest if they did not comply with their demands and abused at least some of the women in the backseat of the unmarked police car they drove together, according to court records.

Luis Valenzuela, 43 and James C. Nichols, 44, face more than a dozen felony charges, each stemming from allegations that they raped four women from late 2008 to 2011, according to a complaint filed Tuesday by the county district attorney's office. They are accused by prosecutors of forcing some women to have sexual intercourse and others to perform oral sex. Valenzuela also is accused of assaulting one woman with a gun.

The charges carry a possible punishment of life in prison.

Both men were arrested by detectives from their own department and held on more than $3.5 million bail. They are scheduled to appear in court. The men and their attorneys could not be reached for comment.

"It is a wonderful development, although it is years overdue," said Dennis Chang, an attorney representing two of the women. "It's a ray of light that these women will finally see some justice."

The LAPD placed the officers on unpaid leave more than two years ago after a stop-and-start internal investigation that was launched when a woman came forward to report the men.

Detectives from an elite investigative unit eventually took over the case in 2014 and reworked it in an effort to gather sufficient evidence for prosecutors to bring a criminal case against the men.

"These two officers have disgraced themselves, they've disgraced this badge, they've disgraced their oath of office," a somber Chief Charlie Beck told reporters. "I am extremely troubled by what they've done."

Beck declined to say much about the investigation, but said the case included dozens of interviews, forensic analysis, long-term surveillance and search warrants. Detectives also retraced the officers' movements, he said, checking prior contacts they had made and going to Hollywood in search of other potential victims.

Beck said investigators worked a difficult case, complicated by the fact that the officers "preyed on folks that are sometimes reluctant witnesses, reluctant victims."

"When we got the district attorney's assurance that she would file, we went out and physically tracked down these — and I use the term loosely — officers and put them in handcuffs," Beck said.

The Times first wrote about the allegations against Nichols and Valenzuela in 2013 when LAPD detectives sought a search warrant to confiscate the men's computers and phones.

An affidavit that accompanied the warrant described a dark pattern of behavior. The pair, who worked together as narcotics officers in the LAPD's Hollywood Division, were accused of targeting women they had arrested for drug possession and, in some cases, had used in their narcotics work as confidential informants.

They repeatedly used the threat of jail to get women into an unmarked Volkswagen Jetta they drove on duty and took them to secluded areas where one of the officers demanded sex while the other kept watch, the warrant alleged.

One woman, who settled a lawsuit against the police department for $575,000, was arrested in 2010 by the officers, Chang, her attorney, said in an earlier interview with The Times. The officers then offered to help free her from custody and win her a lenient sentence if she agreed in exchange to work for them as an informant on other investigations.

Over the next year, Nichols and Valenzuela confronted the woman repeatedly, telling her they would no longer help her unless she had sex with them, Chang and the affidavit said. She agreed, she told investigators, out of fear the officers would send her back to jail if she refused.

Valenzuela later showed up at the woman's apartment while he was off duty and, several months later, had sex with her in the backseat of an unmarked undercover car while he was working, according to the affidavit. Nichols, the woman told investigators, brought her to a hotel and, on a later encounter, had sex with her in her apartment, the affidavit alleges.

The first woman to accuse the men came forward in early 2010. She told a supervisor in the Hollywood narcotics unit of being stopped by the officers more than a year earlier, according to the affidavit. The woman, who worked as an informant, said Valenzuela had threatened to take her to jail if she refused to get in the car, then got into the backseat with her and exposed himself, telling the woman to touch him, the affidavit said.

An attempt to look into the woman's claim went nowhere when the detective assigned to the case was unable to locate her, according to the affidavit.

A year later, however, another woman gave a similar account to a station supervisor after being arrested. She recounted how two officers driving a Jetta had pulled up alongside her as she was walking her dog in

Hollywood in 2009. The officers, whom she recognized as the same Cops who had arrested her previously, ordered her into the car.

Valenzuela then got into the backseat with the woman and handed her dog to Nichols, who drove the car a short distance to a more secluded area where Valenzuela forced her to perform oral sex on him, according to police records contained in the warrant.

The department's internal affairs office reopened the case, but for reasons not explained in the warrant, the investigation stalled again for the next year and a half. During this time, police records show, the officers were transferred to different divisions.

Then, in July 2012, a man left a phone message for the vice unit at the LAPD's Northeast station, where Nichols was assigned. The man relayed a conversation he had had with a prostitute, who said patrol officers in the area were picking up prostitutes and letting them go in exchange for oral sex, the warrant said.

It is not clear how, but from this lead an investigator identified two more women who reported encounters in which Nichols and Valenzuela coerced them into performing sex acts in exchange for leniency.

Beck had harsh words for the officers, saying they had abused their authority as Police Officers.

"It's a violation of public trust," the chief said. "That's what makes it so horrific."

---

[10] Charlotte Police Officer Griffin Police Rape and Murder in North Carolina

Police Officer Josh Griffin, serving a life sentence for the murder of Kimberly Medlin, a cocktail waitress he'd pulled over in his police cruiser, finally confessed to killing her, after years of vehement denials.

Kim disappeared while driving home at 3 a.m. on March 29, 1997, from her job at a Charlotte Strip Club. Her red Jeep was found at 4 a.m. on the side of a road with the engine idling and the lights still burning. Her purse and cash were on the seat, but she and her driver's license were missing.

Police Officer Griffin, used the blue lights on his cruiser to stop Kim. He then handcuffed her and drove her to a deserted road to rape her. When she tried to flee, he hit her, stomped on her back and strangled her. Investigators found his shoeprints on the back of her sweatshirt.

Her dead body was found the next morning in a field, partially hidden under brush, leaves and tree limbs. She had been strangled and her neck was broken.

July 21, 2005 - AP North Carolina News:

CHARLOTTE, N.C. -- A former Monroe Police Officer, serving a life sentence for murder in the 1997 death of a cocktail waitress he'd pulled over in his police cruiser, confessed four years ago to killing the woman after years of vehement denials.

Josh Griffin told an agent with the State Bureau of Investigation in 2001 that he killed Kim Medlin, former Union County District Attorney Ken Honeycutt and former Monroe Police Chief Bobby Haulk told The Charlotte Observer.

"The statement was essentially a confession to the murder. He just minimized his actions," said Honeycutt, who has a transcript of what Griffin told the agent.

Medlin, 26, disappeared while driving to her Union County home about 3 a.m. on March 29, 1997, from her job at a Charlotte strip club. Her red Jeep was found about 4 a.m. at the side of a road with the engine idling and the lights burning. Her purse and cash were on the seat, but she and her driver's license were missing.

Medlin's body was found the next day in a field at the end of a deserted cul-de-sac. She had been strangled and her neck was broken. Prosecutors said Griffin was a stalker who had seen Medlin months earlier and commented on her good looks. Griffin, then 23, was off-duty but was wearing a uniform and used the blue lights on his cruiser to stop Medlin, prosecutors said.

Griffin drove Medlin to the deserted industrial road, prosecutors said. When she tried to flee, they said, he hit, stomped and strangled her. Investigators found shoeprints on the back of her sweat shirt.

In the confession, Griffin admitted the shoeprints were his, Honeycutt said. He said he threw his boots in a retail store's trash bin and cut up Medlin's license and flushed it down a toilet.

Griffin claimed he owed drug dealers money for steroids and was told he could pay the debt by stopping Medlin and turning her over to them, Honeycutt said. Griffin said he killed Medlin while the drug dealers were holding them at gunpoint.

Griffin was unable to describe the drug dealers to investigators. "He basically said one was kind of average looking and the other sort of ordinary looking," Honeycutt said. "Not too tall, not too short, kind of average. That's not the way Police Officers are trained to describe people."

Haulk and Honeycutt said the Police Officer Griffin claimed took part in Medlin's killing had an alibi. The SBI again interviewed him, they said and he passed a polygraph test.

Retired Sgt. Sonny Rogers told the newspaper on Wednesday he was the one Griffin fingered. The SBI on Wednesday would only say its agents conducted interviews based on statements made by Griffin after he was convicted. Bridger Medlin, Kim Medlin's widower, said he has known about Griffin's confession for several years.

"I'm glad for his conscience that he can finally admit to it. But we - the family of Kim Medlin - knew it," he said. "The only ones this may help are those who lack rational thought and question whether he is guilty. There will be no doubt now."

Haulk, who retired last fall, said Honeycutt told him and others about the SBI investigation and confession but swore them to secrecy. Officials were afraid going public would hurt their case if it had to be retried. Griffin's defense attorney Kevin Barnett said in 2000 that appeals of the murder conviction had been exhausted.

Griffin, 32, is serving his sentence at the Hoke Correctional Institution, a medium-security prison near Raeford. He declined to talk to the newspaper.

---

[11] **Tamiami Trail of Tears** – From forthcoming book by Edward Caputo

[12] **Pirate Gasparilla - Wikipedia**

José Gaspar, also known by his nickname Gasparilla (lived 1756 – 1821), is an apocryphal Spanish pirate, the "Last of the Buccaneers," who is claimed to have roamed and plundered across the Gulf of Mexico and the Spanish Main from his base in southwest Florida. Details about his early life, motivations, and piratical exploits differ. However, the various versions agree that he was a remarkably active pirate during Florida's second Spanish period (which spanned from 1783 until 1821), that he amassed a huge fortune by taking many prizes and ransoming many hostages, and that he died by leaping from his ship rather than face capture by the U.S. Navy, leaving behind an enormous and as-yet undiscovered treasure.

---

[13] 2014 Boynton Beach Police Officer Maiorino Rape in Florida

Police Officer Stephen Maiorino, was charged with armed sexual battery and armed kidnapping. On October 15, 2014, Maiorino attacked and raped a 20-year-old woman at gunpoint on the hood of his police cruiser.

The woman wrote in her court filing that she was threatened with a DUI arrest, unless she performed oral sex on him in the police station parking lot. "I cooperated because I was scared."

Maiorino then drove her a short distance away to another location, described as an abandoned field and when the car stopped, Maiorino pointed his gun at her and told her to get out of the car, she said. "I got out, scared for my life and in shock," she wrote.

During the assault, the officer held her face down on the hood of his police cruiser with his right hand, and pointed a gun at her with his left. After that, when they both got back in the police cruiser, Maiorino took the clip out of his gun and showed her the bullets. Maiorino, said, "If you tell anyone what just happened, I will find you and I will kill you."

She took investigators to the site of the assault, where they found a condom, a condom wrapper and other materials with her DNA on it. Her DNA was also found on Maiorino's underwear, police said.

#

SUN SENTINEL:

OCT 31, 2014 | 4:30 P.M.

A woman who accused a Boynton Beach Police Officer of rape said she was in his patrol car when he started flirting and telling her that he "liked what he saw," according to newly released documents detailing her allegations.

Stephen Maiorino, 35, who has served on Boynton's force for eight years, pleaded not guilty Friday to charges including armed sexual battery and armed kidnapping in the alleged Oct. 15 attack.

Maiorino raped the 20-year-old woman at gunpoint on the hood of his police cruiser, according to a police affidavit.

Two days after the incident, the woman filed a request for a restraining order against Maiorino and detailed the horror she felt as his flirtation turned into an assault, records show. After being threatened with a DUI

389

arrest, she performed oral sex on him in the police station parking lot, she wrote. And it was just the beginning of her hour-long ordeal, police said.

"I cooperated because I was scared," the woman wrote in her court filing.

Maiorino then drove her a short distance away and when the car stopped, Maiorino pointed his gun at her and told her to get out of the car, she said.

"I got out, scared for my life and in shock," she wrote.

On Friday, Circuit Judge Caroline Shepherd ordered the officer held without bond.

Michael Salnick, a West Palm Beach attorney who represented the officer, entered the not guilty plea on his client's behalf. Salnick also asked that Maiorino be evaluated to determine whether he should continue to take his current medications.

"There are two sides to every story," Salnick told the Sun Sentinel after Friday's hearing. "This case will definitely be headed to trial."

Maiorino and the woman accusing him of the rape met, because a man she had been riding with on Oct. 15 was stopped by police after a pursuit, according to a police affidavit.

The friend was subsequently arrested and charged with fleeing and eluding, resisting officers without violence and DUI, police records show.

His car was towed, leaving the woman stranded with a dead cellphone. Maiorino came to the scene to bring her back to the police station, where relatives would pick her up, according to the affidavit.

She and officer made it to the station, but then he took her to another location, described as an abandoned field, to continue the assault, police said.

During the assault, the officer held her face down on the hood of his cruiser with his right hand and pointed a gun at her with his left, according to the affidavit. After that, when they both got back in the police cruiser, Maiorino took the clip out of his gun and showed her the bullets, the woman wrote in her court filing.

Maiorino, according to what the woman wrote, said, "If you tell anyone what just happened, I will find you and I will kill you."

A complaint against Maiorino was made just a few hours after the woman was returned to her relatives.

She took investigators to the site of the alleged assault, where they found a condom, a condom wrapper and other materials with her DNA on it. Her DNA was also found on Maiorino's underwear, police said.

Maiorino turned himself in to the jail Thursday.

Seven days after the alleged attack, the woman's request for a restraining order against Maiorino was granted, according to documents filed in the Palm Beach County Circuit Court. The order also required that Maiorino turn in his guns to the Palm Beach County Sheriff's Office and not use guns or ammunition.

Maiorino is on unpaid administrative leave from the police force and "will be fired," Boynton Police Chief Jeffrey Katz said Thursday.

---

[14] 1990 Indian River Police Officer Tim Harris Police Rape and Murder in Florida

Florida Highway Patrol Police Officer Tim Harris pleaded guilty to the first-degree rape and murder of Jacksonville resident, Lorraine Hendricks, in a heavily wooded area in the median of I-95 in northern Indian River County.

March 4, 1990, FHP Police Officer Harris, stopped Hendricks, for wearing headphones while driving south to a dental appointment in Broward County. Hendricks' car was later found abandoned along the highway, with all her possessions inside, except for her driver's license and car registration. Officer Harris was assigned to patrol that section of I-95, but Harris's patrol records didn't show that he had stopped Hendricks or checked her car. It wasn't until days later, that searchers found her decomposed body under a pile of brush.

Four weeks after her body was found, Police Officer Harris confessed that he took Lorraine Hendricks into the wooded median, raped her, and strangled her with her own underwear.

In September 1990, Harris was sentenced to twenty-five-years to life in prison.

#

The Palm Beach Post:

INDIAN RIVER COUNTY- A former Florida Highway Patrol trooper judged guilty of murdering a female motorist along Interstate 95 in 1990 says he should be eligible for consideration for parole from state prison in the next few years, according to court documents.

"The Department of Corrections records are incorrect (in saying the life sentence is for the duration of [my] natural life)," former trooper Timothy Harris, 54, wrote in his motion filed in Indian River Circuit Court.

In September 1990, Harris was sentenced in Vero Beach to life in prison after he pleaded guilty to first-degree murder of Jacksonville resident Lorraine Hendricks in a heavily wooded area in the median of I-95 in northern Indian River County.

Harris' handwritten motion asks the Indian River Circuit Court to decide whether he should be eligible for a parole review after he serves 25 years in prison. He's been in prison for about 21 years.

Circuit Judge Robert Pegg plans to rule on Harris' motion after getting the State Attorney's response to Harris' claim. Assistant State Attorney Nikki Robinson said she isn't ready to comment. She plans to file her response within the next few weeks.

Pegg has set a deadline for mid-May for getting written opinions.

Around midday March 4, 1990, Harris, who was then 32, stopped Hendricks, 43, for wearing headphones while driving south to a dental appointment in Broward County.

Earlier in her life she had been a model for the FHP's Arrive Alive publicity campaign.

It wasn't until days later searchers found her decomposed body under a brush pile, meanwhile Harris continued patrolling that area of I-95. The eight-year FHP veteran even stopped along the highway and talked to searchers.

The search started after her car with all her possessions inside, except for her driver's license and car registration were found abandoned along the roadway.

Initially, investigators did not investigate law officers patrolling the area, as they had tips that there were various vehicles, but not a patrol car seen near the crime scene. As other leads didn't produce any suspects, investigators began questioning Harris at length.

Hendricks' car was left along the highway the day he was patrolling that section of I-95. But Harris's patrol records didn't show his stopping Hendricks or checking her car.

After lengthy interviews, Harris admitted he took Hendricks into the wooded median and had sex with her. Four weeks after her body was found, Harris confessed that he strangled her with her own underwear.

He partially blamed the murder on his having a mental breakdown because of being estranged from his wife, who lived with their two children about seven miles from the murder scene in northern Indian River County.

Now the former Sebastian Police officer contends the state Department of Corrections is misinterpreting his court sentence. Court records show the sentence is for life. There is a notation his minimum mandatory sentence is 25 years.

One of Harris' former public defenders, Phil Yacucci, who now is a St. Lucie County Judge, said he doesn't recall the sentence including a possible parole.

The State Department of Corrections is looking into Harris' contentions. "As I understand the law, parole was abolished in 1983 so anyone sentenced after that can't be eligible," said DOC spokeswoman Ann Howard.

Yet Harris said when he was sentenced, Circuit Judge L.B. Vocelle, now deceased, "clearly states ... (Harris) would be sentenced to life (with a) 25-year minimum-mandatory term) and would be eligible for parole" after that, according to his court motion.

At the time of his sentencing in 1990, Harris said, "I'm not going to be able to forget what happened. And I know there's nothing I can say to make things change."

At the time Hendricks' parents, of Jacksonville, said they would have preferred the death penalty for Harris. However, they said they also just wanted the matter to be resolved.

"If the appeal process was used, it could go on for the next 10 to 12 years," her father Frank Dombroski said at the time of Harris' sentencing. "I don't feel that, emotionally, we could survive."

---

[15] 2014 Police Officer Sergio Alvarez Rapes in West Sacramento, California#

Police Officer Sergio Alvarez prowled the streets in his police cruiser during his graveyard shift and used his police authority to abduct and rape women. He used phony DUI stops and computer warrant searches to single out his victims, who he attacked in his patrol car or in dark alleys from 2011 to 2012.

Alvarez preyed upon prostitutes, drug addicts and other "down-and-out" women, that he believed would not report his assaults. He occasional videotaped some of his sex acts with his victims on a personal "spycam."

His wife, Rachel Alvarez, was also raped and abused by her husband, and testified against him at trial. She was relocated to Naples, Florida as part of the "Witness Protection and Relocation Program." Sergio Alvarez was found guilty of 18 counts of kidnapping, rape and forced oral copulation.

He was sentenced to 205 years in prison.

#

The Sacramento Bee:

Police Officer Sergio Alvarez rapes in West Sacramento, California. Sergio Alvarez's estranged wife likened him to a firestorm that destroyed everything in his path. His family. His home. His marriage. His law enforcement career. The lives of the women he kidnapped and raped.

"Sergio did not choose to stop raping women; he was stopped," Rachel Alvarez wrote in a statement that was read in the courtroom on the day of his sentencing. "Sergio's fire destroyed my community. My children's sense of security was destroyed, too. The women Sergio hurt will never forget and will never trust law enforcement again."

Rachel Alvarez described a violent man out of control, who "lost the moral compass and direction in his life." His moods became darker, his increasingly suspicious behavior "alarming."

Alvarez in the letter said she finally packed up their three children, pets and clothes and fled out of state to escape a man who, "became my abuser, not my husband or friend."

A year after West Sacramento Police Officer Sergio Alvarez was convicted of prowling the streets during his graveyard shift and using his position to abduct and rape at least half a dozen women, the city agreed to pay $2.8 million to four of his victims.

The settlement covers a lawsuit filed in Yolo Superior Court. Combined with two other settlements in federal court, one still awaiting approval by a judge, the city has agreed to pay a total of $4.11 million to Alvarez's victims.

"With the conclusion of the criminal and civil cases, the police department of West Sacramento is relieved that the legal aspects of this horrible event have been resolved," Bruce Kilday, an attorney representing the city, said in a prepared statement. "The victims of Alvarez's criminal acts can continue with the healing process and the police department can continue regaining the trust of the people of the city they serve."

The Alvarez case was one of the department's darkest scandals. The officer was accused of preying upon prostitutes, drug addicts and other women, described in court as "down-and-outers," that he believed would not report his assaults.

Alvarez used phony DUI stops and computer warrant searches to single out his victims, some of whom he attacked in his patrol car or in dark alleys from 2011 to 2012. As sexual assault victims, the women have not been publicly identified.

One of the victims reported her assault to police in September 2012 and Alvarez was indicted and arrested in 2013 after an investigation.

He was found guilty of 18 counts of kidnapping, rape and forced oral copulation in 2014 and sentenced to 205 years in prison.

Alvarez's crimes also destroyed his own marriage to Rachel Alvarez, with whom he had three children and who fled their home with the kids and drove across the country to escape him.

Sacramento attorney Robert Buccola, who represented the four victims in Thursday's settlement, said, "Alvarez was not the sharpest knife in the drawer and he did sloppy work."

"But there was no indication prior to the time this matter came to the attention of the department that he was a sexual predator," Buccola said.

Kilday said the investigation into Alvarez included reviewing all vehicle stops and record checks the officer made over a one-year period and contacting women to determine if they had been subjected to improper conduct.

---

[16] 2007 Austin Police Officer Fennell Rape and Murder in Texas

Police Officer Fennel, is suspected of killing his fiancée, Stacey Stites because he was angry that she had sex with a black man, Rodney Reed. Fennel allegedly strangled Stites to death with a belt. The pickup truck that she was driving was found in a parking lot adjacent to Rodney Reed's home, but the driver's seatbelt was buckled, leading investigators to suspect that the car was last driven by a Police Officer not Stacey.

DNA from semen found in Stites' body matched Rodney Reed, and the evidence presumed that he had abducted, raped and strangled her. Rodney Reed was convicted of the murder and sentenced to death but he claimed that he was innocent. Reed admitted that he was having sex with Stites and accused Fennell of the murder when Fennell found out about the affair. Fennell staged the evidence to make it appear that Reed was guilty. Furthermore, Fennell's face was scratched and Stacey's fingernails were clipped, to eliminate Fennell's possible DNA evidence. Because Reed had sex with Stites earlier, on the day that she was murdered, the DNA evidence indicted Reed as the guilty party.

However, in October 2007, Fennell pled guilty to kidnapping and sexual misconduct, for raping a woman involved in a domestic disturbance call that he handled as a Police Officer. Fennell confessed to committing this crime of sexual violence and his conviction for this crime was consistent with his long history of violence and also made him a suspect in the murder of Stacey Stites. Officer Fennell's confessions were relevant in demonstrating Reed's probable innocence.

Fennell was sentenced to up to 10 years in prison for the kidnapping charge and an additional two years for the charge of improper sexual conduct. In addition, Rodney Reed's lawyers presented testimony from noted forensic pathologist, Dr. Michael Baden, who concluded that Stites had not been raped and had been killed before midnight, a time that pointed to Fennell as the killer, not Reed.

#

The Austin Chronicle:

Jimmy Fennell, 45, went to prison for raping a woman in his custody in 2007, when he was a Georgetown Police Officer. However, he was an original person of interest in the 1996 murder of his fiancé Stacey Stites. Fennell's ties to Stites, and the high-profile capital murder case involving Rodney Reed, have kept him in the spotlight for years.

Reed has always maintained his innocence. For years, his legal team has pointed to Fennell as Stites' true killer.

Fennell's legal problems bolster Reed's argument of innocence, says Reed's attorney Bryce Benjet. "Jimmy Fennell has now twice confessed to committing this crime of sexual violence," said Benjet. "Mr. Fennell's conviction for this crime is consistent with his long history of violence and the ample evidence that made him a suspect in the murder of Stacey Stites over a decade ago. ... Mr. Fennell's recent confessions are certainly relevant in demonstrating Mr. Reed's innocence."

Stites was found dumped on the side of a rural Bastrop County road in April of 1996. She was 21. Reed was convicted of raping and strangling Stites as she made her early morning commute from Giddings to a Bastrop grocery store, according to court records. At the time of her death, Stites was days away from marrying Fennell, a rookie Giddings Police Officer at the time.

Reed's defense team has worked for years to expose new evidence that, they say, undermines Fennell's alibi and alters the time-of-death estimate prosecutors used to convict Reed.

Reed's team says forensic evidence shows Stites died earlier than portrayed at trial, and Fennell could have killed her in their apartment.

"Of course [Jimmy] continues to profess his innocence. He loved Stacey Stites. He was engaged to be married to her and the individual who raped and murdered her is properly on death row," said Fennell's attorney, Robert M. Phillips. "Rodney Reed was convicted by a jury of twelve. He's failed in any number of appeals to convince various judges of both technical and substantive problems with his case and that's because he richly deserved the sentence that he got."

Reed was granted a week-long hearing in Bastrop District Court last October. The visiting judge overseeing the hearing recommended the State Court of Criminal Appeals not grant Reed a new trial. The visiting judge's decision is not final.

Fennell was called to testify at the hearings, but he said in a written statement that he would invoke the Fifth Amendment and was ultimately not called into the courtroom.

---

[17] Medley Police Firing Range:

Sgt. Valerie Deant peered into a stack of garbage at a Medley shooting range last month and saw a photo of her brother. His face had bullet holes.

Turns out that North Miami Beach police used a photo lineup of men arrested 15 years ago to help its sniper team practice its marksmanship. All of the photos were of black males, one of whom happened to be Woody Deant.

When the story was published, it ricocheted around cyberspace, causing considerable consternation at a time when relations between police and the black community have been strained around the country.

Woody Deant posted on his Facebook page: "ATTENTION..... To all my friends, Facebook friends and family. I have fallen victim to criminal profiling by the North Miami Beach Police Dept."

He also posted: "We are targets...."

The fact that North Miami Beach police honed their aim by shooting a gallery of black men is no reflection on police-community relations in the city, said Maj. Kathy Katerman.

"We have other targets, too," she said. "We don't just shoot at black males."

She said the photo gallery should have been disposed of before North Miami Beach Cops left the range and Sgt. Deant's group — she's with the Florida Army National Guard — came in.

Katerman said North Miami Beach sharpshooters also take aim at mugshot lineups of Anglos and Hispanics. She said the department finds it useful to use lineups with faces that share similar characteristics. It was just an unfortunate coincidence that Woody Deant's photo was a target the same day that his sister was using the range for her annual weapons training qualification.

The television station reported that Woody Deant was arrested 15 years ago while a teenager in connection with a drag race in which two people were killed.

His sister called him right after finding the photos.

"The picture actually has like bullet holes," Woody Deant told NBC 6. "One in my forehead and one in my eye. ... I was speechless."

Deant said he spent four years in prison, but that's all behind him now. "I'm a father. I'm a husband. I'm a career man. I work nine-to-five," he told the TV station.

Using photo lineups for target practice doesn't seem to be a common practice among local police departments. Miami-Dade, the county's largest force, doesn't do it; nor does Miami or Miami Beach.

H.T. Smith, a prominent local attorney and civil rights icon who served in the Army during Vietnam, said his unit never considered taking target practice shooting at images of real people — not even the president of North Vietnam.

"Of course, it's offensive. You shouldn't be shooting at faces anyway," Smith said. "It's inconsiderate. And it starts at the top. In a multi-ethnic community, you should not have a system set up with one set of people."

On Thursday, North Miami Beach Police Chief J. Scott Dennis denied that his department has a racial issue but said that his officers should have used better judgment. He said that the sniper team included minorities, that no one would be disciplined and that no department policies were violated.

Late Friday, the city responded to the public outcry over the sniper target shooting story. A mass email was sent to media outlets with photos of other targets used by the city's two snipers. Among them: A photo of Osama Bin Laden and another of a man holding a gun to woman's head.

In a five-paragraph statement Dennis said the department realizes how, taken out of context, the photo of the six black males in the photo lineup may appear to be offensive.

"For that reason," Dennis said, "I immediately suspend the sniper training program as we conduct a thorough review of our training process and materials, ordered commercially produced training images and opened an investigation into the matter."

---

[18] <u>1997 Las Vegas Police Officer Arthur Lee Sewall Jr. Police Rape and Murder in Nevada</u>

Construction workers found 20-year-old Nadia Iverson's body, in an apartment they were renovating at 1226 Reed Place in Las Vegas, with a gunshot wound to the head.

The Metropolitan Police Department sent Iverson's rape kit for testing in March 2016, and police said that Las Vegas Police Officer Arthur Lee Sewall's DNA matched the DNA tested in her rape test kit. Sewall was charged with raping and killing her.

Sewall faces one count of murder with a deadly weapon and two counts of sexual assault with a deadly weapon.

#

US News:

May 8, 1997. Construction workers found 20-year-old Nadia Iverson's body in an apartment they were renovating at 1226 Reed Place, near Washington Avenue and Martin Luther King Boulevard in Las Vegas, with a gunshot wound to the head.

Las Vegas Police Officer Arthur Lee Sewall Jr. was charged with raping and killing her. The Metropolitan Police Department sent Iverson's rape kit for testing in March 2016 and police said that Sewall's DNA matched the DNA tested in her rape kit.

Sewall faces one count of murder with a deadly weapon and two counts of sexual assault with a deadly weapon.

Metro said detectives interviewed Sewall, who had been living in Reno, on Jan. 11 and the next day issued a warrant for his arrest in the murder case. Metro said he was being moved to Clark County Detention Center.

Past crime

Metro first arrested Sewall in a February 1997 video surveillance sting operation at the now closed Del Mar Motel, 1411 Las Vegas Blvd. South. Police accused him of forcing a woman to perform sex acts on him while he was on duty, the Las Vegas Review-Journal reported then. Sewall resigned from Metro in March 1997.

He joined Metro as a corrections officer in 1990 before joining the police force in 1992, police said.

He was sentenced in 1999 to five years of probation after pleading guilty to two counts of oppression under color of law. While awaiting sentencing, Sewall was arrested in San Diego in the solicitation of a prostitute but was allowed to stay on probation.

Christopher Orem, Sewall's defense attorney at the time, declined to comment on Sewall's recent arrest. Then-district attorney Stewart Bell declined to comment through a representative.

In August 2004, the month his probation was expected to expire, authorities learned of a month's long string of probation violations.

Probation officers found a gun and knife in Sewall's San Diego home. Sewall failed to regularly submit reports to probation officers and he was removed from a sex offender counseling program for noncompliance, then-prosecutor Doug Herndon told the Review-Journal in 2004.

Starting in October 2004, Nevada Department of Corrections spokeswoman Brooke Keast said, Sewall served about a year and a half in prison for oppression under color of law. Keast said he was released on parole nine years to the day after Iverson's death.

Untested kits

Iverson's rape kit was among the nearly 6,500 untested kits that had accumulated in Southern Nevada from 1985 through 2014. Metro said a 2015 grant from the New York County district attorney's office funded the testing of her kit.

Las Vegas police were recently awarded $2.7 million to help test the long backlog of untested kits. About 5,600 of the 6,473 kits in Southern Nevada were within Metro's jurisdiction, said Kim Murga, Metro's crime laboratory director.

Murga said the work her office does can help the families of victims find closure. She said Sewall's DNA was collected in 1999 as a result of a parole and probation directive. For Iverson, Murga said, closure will come with the court proceedings.

"Certainly, Mr. Sewall has some things to answer to in terms of how his DNA was found in the tested kit," Murga said.

CHP Officer Peyer Police Rape and Murder in San Diego California

Patrol Officer Craig Peyer murdered Cara Knott, 20, a student at San Diego State University, the night of December 27th after he pulled her car to a darkened Mercy Road exit-ramp north of downtown San Diego, called The Tombs. He tried to have sex with her, but when she refused, he strangled her with a piece of rope and beat her with a blunt object which killed her.

He then placed her body on the hood of his police car, to eliminate any possible evidence inside of his car and drove her body up to the top of the bridge. He threw her body off the 70-foot high bridge into a dry creek bed, where it was discovered the next morning, along with her white Volkswagen Beetle.

He was sentenced to twenty-five years to life in prison.

#

Los Angeles Times:

On December 27th, 1986 20-year-old, SDSU college student Cara Knott was travelling southbound on Interstate 15. Cara was on her way home from an evening at her boyfriend's home in Escondido to her parent's home in El Cajon. Craig Peyer, on duty CHP patrol officer, flashed lights at Knott to pull off the freeway to an isolated off ramp. It is thought the situation with Knott became physical when, she threatened to report Peyer's behavior. Peyer beat her with his flash-light and strangled her with rope from his patrol car. He then disposed of her body by throwing her off an abandoned bridge into the brush below.

Two days after the murder Peyer was featured on a KCST- interview ride along for a segment related to self-protection for female drivers. Peyer's face had scratches on it during the interview. Following the broadcast several calls by other female drivers were received by the authorities. A new picture of Patrolman Peyer began to emerge. Peyer had a reputation of following female drivers and pulling them over in the same secluded location as Cara. Though most of the callers insisted Peyer was nice and non-threatening, they felt an uneasy creepiness about him. All of the woman were of approximate age and physical characteristics to Cara. Several other patrolman (and woman), became suspicious of Peyer as many of them knew Peyer had a tendency to make tickets at the secluded off ramp. On one early morning briefing a colleague joked with Peyer asking if he had killed Cara Knott. The room became quiet, and Peyer began acting odd. It was then that suspicion became outright and open.

Officer Peyer was arrested 21 days later in connection with Cara Knott's death. The 1st trial ended in a hung jury. Upon retrial, the first-ever conviction of murder by an on-duty CHP officer. In 1988 Peyer was sentenced to 25 years to life.

Judge Link bound Peyer after listening to 57 witnesses produced by the prosecution over a five-day period. Nineteen young women testified that Peyer pulled them over while they were driving at night on Interstate 15 and ordered them to drive down the darkened Mercy Road off-ramp, where he engaged some women in conversations that lasted as long as one hour and 40 minutes. All of the women testified that Peyer stopped them for minor infractions, usually for having a faulty headlight or taillight.

Several witnesses, including CHP officers, testified that they saw scratches on Peyer's face the night Knott was murdered.

Gary Harmor, a serologist with the Serological Research Institute in the Bay Area, testified that a blood spot found on Knott's sweat shirt matched Peyer's blood type. Harmor said that he used a complex and sophisticated scientific test to match the so-called genetic markers derived from the blood spot on the sweat shirt to genetic qualities found in a sample of Peyer's blood.

Although Harmor did not say that the blood spot on the sweat shirt definitely came from Peyer, he said that only 1.33% of the world's population has similar genetic markers in their blood. This percentage amounts to one in every 75 Caucasians and not at all in non-Caucasians, Harmor said.

Gold Fiber Studied

The list of scientific evidences also included a microscopic piece of gold fiber found on Knott's sweat shirt. A San Diego police hair-fiber expert testified last week the fiber matched thread samples found on the California Highway Patrol patches taken from Peyer's uniform jacket.

Peyer is the second CHP officer ever charged with committing murder while on duty. In 1984 CHP Officer Michael Gwaltney was convicted in a civil rights homicide case stemming from the rape and killing of a young woman he stopped in the desert near Barstow.

As tragic as this these events were the story of Cara Knott was far from over.

The location near where Knott was found is home to a memorial garden of oak trees to honor her and other victims of violent crime the result of efforts spearheaded by her father. Sam Knott became a nonstop advocate for crime victims following his daughters murder. He campaigned tirelessly for local and state law enforcement agencies to install technology that would allow them to monitor the whereabouts of their officers at all times. He also pressed law enforcement to ease the standard 48-hour waiting period before issuing a missing-persons bulletin to officers in the field. The loss of Cara plagued Sam and many persons attribute Peyer to Sam's early death as well. Sam died within feet of where Cara's body was recovered. His heart simply gave way, and he died of a heart attack.

With the arrest of San Diego Police Officer Christopher Hays after sexual assault accusations and the conviction of SDPD officer Anthony Arevalos two years ago, the family is upset that these types of cases can and still are happening within the San Diego Law Enforcement ranks.

"I'm so outraged," said Cynthia Knott, Cara's sister. "It's egregious to think this could happen in this day and age. It makes me relive my sister Cara's murder all over again."

Cynthia said she and her mother were sickened and disgusted by the recent news events and cannot believe this is happening.

Joyce Knott wrote to 10News:

"I just don't want our family to appear that we are against the police. We have the utmost respect for the department and the majority of the officers. It just seems that after all these years there should be a better way to identify the bad ones. Thank goodness times have changed and at least some of the women who are harassed or taken advantage of do come forward and report these incidents. When there is a pattern of behavior of controlling women through sexual advances, there is the chance that the actions may escalate and another person's life might be in danger. I want to encourage any woman who finds herself in such a situation to speak up and report it. By doing so, she may save the life of another innocent young woman. It would have saved Cara's."

---

[20] <u>2010 LA Sheriff Deputy Jose Sanchez Police Rapes in California.</u>

Sheriff Deputy Jose Rigoberto Sanchez, a seven-year veteran of the LA Sheriff's Department, spotted a 24-year-old woman at a gas station in Palmdale California on Sept. 22, 2010. He ran her license plate and discovered that she had an outstanding arrest warrant. Sanchez followed her car for a while and then pulled her over.

She acknowledged to Sanchez that she had been drinking and he conducted a Breathalyzer test which confirmed that she was over the legal limit. Deputy Sanchez drove the woman out to a secluded spot and raped her in the back of his patrol car.

He was sentenced to nine years in state prison after pleading no contest to one count of rape while under the color of authority and one count of soliciting a bribe.

#

She was driven to a dark road in the desert in the back of patrol car. The sheriff's deputy parked in a secluded spot in Palmdale and told her to walk to the front of the car.

It was there, the woman said Friday in court, that the L.A. County deputy raped her and changed her life forever.

"You essentially murdered a part of me and I'll never be able to get it back," the victim tearfully said as she stared at her attacker, Jose Rigoberto Sanchez. "A Police Officer is supposed to protect and serve. I had nowhere to run because the one who I should have been able to run to for help was the one harming me."

Following the woman's statement, Sanchez, who pleaded no contest to one count of rape while under the color of authority and one count of soliciting a bribe, was sentenced to nine years in state prison. Los Angeles County Superior Court Judge Terry A. Bork also ordered Sanchez to register with the state as a sex offender.

The woman said she believed Sanchez, 29, deserved "far more" time behind bars. The Times generally does not name victims of sexual assaults.

According to a probation report released Friday, Sanchez spotted the then-24-year-old woman at a gas station in Palmdale on Sept. 22, 2010. He ran her license plate and discovered she had an outstanding arrest warrant, the report states.

Sanchez followed her car for a while and then pulled her over. She acknowledged to Sanchez that she had been drinking, according to the document, which was based on police reports and interviews.

After conducting a Breathalyzer test, Sanchez said she was over the legal limit, the report states. He told her she was "hot" and asked what she would do to avoid arrest before telling her to lock her car with her cell phone and purse inside the vehicle. He then placed her in the back of his patrol car without handcuffing her, the report says.

Sanchez drove the woman out to the desert, raped her against the hood of the patrol car, then drove her back to her car, the probation report says. He followed her home and asked for her phone number to "mess around" again, the report states. Out of fear, the woman told authorities she gave him her number.

Prosecutors say that two nights later Sanchez, a seven-year veteran of the sheriff's department, pulled over a 36-year-old woman for investigation of driving under the influence and solicited a bribe in the form of sexual activity. With the help of a friend the woman refused, the report states.

On Friday, Sanchez, who was shackled and wearing an orange jumpsuit, was stoic. He mostly looked down at the defense table as his first victim berated him.

"I know that at some point you will get out of your prison, but me? I am stuck in mine for the rest of my life," she said, adding that she had been diagnosed with post-traumatic stress disorder after the assault.

She said she lived in fear during the three years the crime was under investigation and he was not in custody.

The woman filed a civil lawsuit against Sanchez, the county and the Sheriff's Department in November 2011.

---

[21] <u>1982 Los Angeles Police Officer George Gwaltney Police Rape and Murder in California</u>

LOS ANGELES - Jan. 11, 1982 - California Highway Patrol Officer George Gwaltney, was convicted of committing a murder while on duty. He handcuffed aspiring actress Robin Bishop after a routine traffic stop, off a deserted stretch of Interstate 15 in the Mojave Desert, raped her in his patrol car, then shot her to death in the head.

Medical evidence during the nearly six-week trial linked Gwaltney's semen, which contained a rare antibody, with stains found in the backseat of his patrol car and in Miss Bishop's jeans. The strongest evidence was Gwaltney's dismantled gun found in his locked pickup truck. The barrel, grips and chamber were missing.

Gwaltney was sentenced to life in prison.

LA Times:

LOS ANGELES -- A former California Highway Patrol officer was sentenced to life in prison for being convicted of violating the civil rights of an aspiring actress found shot to death in the Mojave Desert.

George Gwaltney, 42, was convicted of handcuffing Robin Bishop after a routine traffic stop, having sex with her in his patrol car, then shooting her in the head. The jury said Gwaltney violated the civil rights of the 23-year-old Cedar City, Utah native.

The verdict in the six-week trial came in the second day of jury deliberations.

Gwaltney was indicted by a federal grand jury after two state court juries deadlocked in favor of acquittal on first-degree murder charges.

The indictment charged the former officer violated the civil rights of Miss Bishop, who lived in Las Vegas, Nev., by raping and killing her after stopping her car in January 1982.

Gwaltney, the first CHP officer charged with committing a murder on duty, reported finding Miss Bishop's body off a deserted stretch of Interstate 15 on Jan. 11, 1982.

He listened quietly as the unanimous verdict was read, but his wife sobbed. Defense attorney Brian Robbins said he would appeal.

'The U.S. Attorney's Office wanted this conviction bad and they spent unlimited amounts of money to win it,' Robbins said. 'This was a key prosecution for the government and money was no object.'

Robbins said an appeal would be based in part on the prosecution's introduction of medical evidence during the nearly six-week trial linking

Gwaltney's semen, which contained a rare antibody, with stains found in the back seat of his patrol car and in Miss Bishop's jeans.

'That kind of test, at this point in time, is not appropriate in a criminal case,' Robbins said.

Jury foreman Ray Loehr said the five-woman, seven-man panel took only one vote. The strongest evidence, he said, was Gwaltney's dismantled gun found in his locked pickup truck. The barrel, grips and chamber were missing.

'There was no accounting at any time by the defense as to how that gun frame could be explained in the condition it was in,' Loehr said.

---

[22] Milwaukee Police Officer Cates Police Rape in Wisconsin. January 29, 2012

When a brick crashed through her bathroom window and somebody began kicking in her front door, the 19-year-old single mother of two in Milwaukee dialed what are supposed to be the most trustworthy three numbers: "911."

Within minutes, two Police Officers responded. Police Officer Cates asked to see the broken window and she led him down a narrow hallway to a bathroom in the back. The Cop she had summoned to protect her, instead chose that moment to grab the back of her head by her hair and sodomize her. Then he raped her.

Her revulsion in the aftermath of the rape was so visceral that she vomited as she ran outside, screaming incoherently about being raped. She was handcuffed and arrested by Officer Cates and told at the stationhouse that she was being charged with assaulting a Police Officer.

Eventually, Internal Affairs confronted Cates with DNA evidence linking his semen to the rape test kit of the victim. On January 11, 2012, the jury convicted Cates of raping her and sentenced him to the maximum of life in prison.

When the brick crashed through her bathroom window and somebody began kicking in her front door, the 19-year-old single mother of two in Milwaukee dialed what are supposed to be the most trustworthy three numbers.

"I called 911 for help," she later said in court. "I didn't call 911 to be the victim."

Within minutes, two Police Officers responded. One took her 15-year-old brother outside to speak to him. The other Cop, Police Officer Ladmarald Cates, gave her boyfriend $10 and told him to go the store and get some water. She told him that he was welcome to chilled water from her refrigerator.

"I only drink bottled water," Cates said.

Her boyfriend has a pronounced limp and set off with no promise of returning soon. Cates asked to see the broken window and she led him down a narrow hallway to a bathroom in the back. She felt sure that jealous neighbors had attacked her happy home because she dared to defy what seemed surely to be her fate as an inner-city teenage single mom.

"I wanted to be a good example to my kids," she would later say. "I wanted to learn something, be somebody."

She had returned to high school as a mother of two and after graduation she had continued on to the University of Wisconsin, where she was studying criminal justice with the thought of becoming a Police Officer or a lawyer.

"I thought I was going pretty good," she would recall.

She now stood on a floor littered with broken glass and pointed to the brick. The Cop she had summoned to protect her instead chose this moment to grab the back of her head by her hair and sodomize her. Then he raped her.

Her revulsion in the aftermath was so visceral that she vomited as she ran outside. The Cop's partner had become concerned when he did not immediately see Cates and called for back-up. Other Cops began arriving and saw a woman screaming incoherently about being raped.

Cates appeared and grabbed her by the waist, spinning her around. Her swinging feet may or may not have struck the partner. She was handcuffed and taken in, told at the stationhouse that she was being charged with assaulting a Police Officer.

She became more coherent but no less outraged and vocal as she continued cry out from a holding cell that she had been raped. She also continued to vomit. The other Cops dismissed her as a liar.

After 12 hours, she was interviewed by internal affairs and taken to a hospital, where a rape kit was used to collect evidence. She was then taken to the county jail and held for four days before being released without actually being charged.

She took her story to the Milwaukee District Attorney's office. A prosecutor subsequently wrote, "While I did find the victim's version of events credible, I did not believe that her testimony would be strong enough to successfully prosecute Officer Cates."

In other words, Cates was still a Cop and she was still an inner-city teenage single mom. She stopped going to school as she fell into a deep depression, making two serious suicide attempts.

"It was killing my soul," she says.

She who had so desperately wanted to be a good example for her 3-year-old boy and 2-year-old girl began to wonder if they should even be with her.

"Sad and crying all the time," she says. "I didn't know if I wanted my kids around, me being upset like that about something that happened to me."

Meanwhile, internal affairs confronted Cates with DNA evidence linking him and the victim. He told three different stories, finally saying there had been a voluntary sexual encounter. His victim read in the newspaper that he had been fired for lying and for "idling and loafing" on duty, words that mocked what had been done to her.

"That really pissed me off," she says.

She took some comfort in knowing Cates was not going to be answering any more 911 calls. But he still had not been held accountable for what he did to her.

"It wasn't really justice," she says. "It didn't say he hurt me."

She was sinking only deeper into despair when she went on the Internet and chanced up a photo of an eminent Milwaukee defense lawyer named Robin Shellow.

"She had a beautiful smile," the victim recalls. "It was just her smile and the look in her eyes…She's not mean and she's a woman … She looked like she could understand me…She looked like she would help."

She went to Shellow's office.

"I just was giving it a shot. I didn't think nothing was going to come of it." Shellow proved to be everything her photo suggested. Shellow also happened to have just finished a case in federal court and she had the number handy for the prosecutor who had been her opponent. Assistant U.S. Attorney Mel Johnson came to her office with an FBI agent to interview her new client. He not only found her credible, he was willing to prosecute.

"He was a very nice guy," the victim says. "He kind of made me not afraid."

As the case headed for trial, Gina Barton of the Milwaukee Journal Sentinel reported that Cates had been investigated for illegal behavior on five previous occasions, three of them involving sexual misconduct. Two of those were with prisoners. The third was with a 16-year-old and that case had been referred to the Milwaukee district attorney's office, which declined to prosecute. The priors came as no surprise to the

19-year-old who was now accusing him of raping her while he somehow remained employed as a Cop.

"I knew it," she says. "The way he treated me, I knew he had to have hurt somebody else before."

But, the law prohibited the prosecution from using Cates's history to sway the jury. The case was still a she-said-he-said as the victim took the stand. She had been counseled and steadied by Shellow right up to this moment. She was now on her own.

"I am here today because Officer Cates is a very bad man," she said. Shellow says that her client was a terrific witness. The victim herself feels otherwise, faulting herself for not being able to convey the enormity of what happened. She does say, "It felt good to look at him and tell him what he did. He was looking at his shoes." She also felt that whatever her shortcomings he was sure to be convicted.

"I thought it would be guilty," she said. "I felt it in my stomach. Anybody with two eyes could see this dude was an animal."

On January 11, the jury convicted Cates of violating the victim's civil rights by raping her.

"I just heard the "guilty" and then I left because I was so emotional," she says.

She returned to court on Jan. 18, to see Cates remanded, pending sentencing in April, when he faces a maximum of life in prison.

"I didn't feel happy," she says. "I felt like, "Finally, it's over.""

She could not help but feel sympathy for Cates's children.

"They didn't do anything," she says.

She has chosen to accept the anonymity accorded a sex crime victim as she resumes being the hero of her own particular life. She is back to being the mom she wanted to be for her own kids. And she plans on continuing her studies next semester, though she has seen enough of the legal system to have a new career goal.

"A nurse or a doctor," she says.

1999 Lafayette Sheriff Deputy Randy Comeaux Police Rapes in Louisiana

Sheriff Deputy Randy Comeaux was branded the serial "South Side Rapist," because he preyed on the women of Lafayette, Louisiana, from the early 1980s through 1995. Comeaux, like many rapists, was a repeat offender.

The FBI studied the case for a psychological profile that suggested that the serial rapist worked in law enforcement as a security guard, Police Officer or deputy. He was a deputy, in a position of power and he took advantage of that. DNA evidence taken from his covertly obtained cigarette butt matched evidence from six rape cases.

He is serving six life sentences for the six rapes.

#

Daily Press:

The search for a serial rapist who preyed on the women of Lafayette, La., from the early 1980s through 1995 is detailed. Despite using the most advanced methods available to them, the investigators came up empty until an anonymous phone call tipped them to a suspect: sheriff's deputy Randy Comeaux. DNA evidence taken from a cigarette butt confirmed that he was their man.

Lafayette, LA., police had used all the conventional approaches in probing a serial rapist, including a task force comprised of investigators from five different agencies.

The attacks started in the early 1980s and continued through 1995, remembers Lafayette Police Lt. Jim Craft.

"We could positively link six of the cases and suspected the same person in seven to nine others," Craft said.

416

Like the East End cases, the attacks were sporadic.

"Sometimes, we would go two to three years without one," Craft said. "Then they'd come all at once."

The FBI studied the cases for a psychological profile that suggested the serial rapist worked in law enforcement as a security guard, Police Officer or deputy.

After the task force disbanded in 1998 with no arrests, Craft said his police chief showed him a copy of an article about geographic profiling in Police Chief magazine.

The department invited Kim Rossmo to Lafayette, in hopes a geographic profile might narrow the field of possible suspects.

"We had no preconceived ideas about profiling," said Craft. "We thought if it could help us, fine. If not, at least we gave it a shot. We didn't want to leave any stone unturned."

Rossmo used the background of the attacks to establish a perimeter, or boundaries within an area the rapist might live or work, that - when placed over a map pinpointing the crime sites - formed a triangle.

As the investigation progressed, an anonymous caller named a sheriff's deputy as the rapist.

Investigators took saliva from the deputy's cigarette butt and submitted the specimen to a lab for DNA analysis. Craft said the DNA matched evidence from six rape cases.

When police arrested the deputy, Randy Comeaux, on Jan. 18, 1999, he was living just a block outside of the triangle.

But during the serial rapes, he resided precisely in the middle of the triangle, Craft said.

Detective Randy Comeaux was considered a "top notch" member of the Lafayette, Louisiana, Parish Sheriff's office for nearly 20 years. He was known by his colleagues as an outstanding investigator and a "really nice guy." Lafayette, Louisiana is the heart of Cajun country with typical southern friendliness and a very close community.

When Comeaux was arrested in 1999 for the rape of more than seven women over a 13-year span, Lafayette was stunned. Comeaux randomly chose his victims, broke into their homes and sexually assaulted them by gunpoint. In 1999, someone called in an anonymous tip about the serial "South Side Rapist" being on the sheriff's department. Comeaux was soon after identified through a composite sketch and finally caught through a DNA match.

Comeaux is serving six life sentences for the six rapes.

---

[24] <u>1987 Sheriff Deputy David Keith Rogers Rapes and Murders in Bakersfield, California</u>

A navy veteran and father of two, born in 1947, Rogers moved to Bakersfield, California, at age 30, finding employment with the Kern County Sheriff's Department a year later.

He spent five years on beats where prostitutes were numerous, and he was fired March 22, 1983, for taking nude photographs of a hooker in a local cemetery.

On appeal, the state Civil Service Commission reduced his punishment to a 15-day suspension, and Rogers returned to duty in June 1983. (The prostitute in question failed to appear at this hearing, and she has not been seen since.) Assigned to the county jail, Rogers was accused of beating up an inmate in April 1984, but the charges were ultimately dismissed. He returned to active patrol in June 1986.

On February 21 of that year, the bullet-riddled body of Kay Bradley, a 21-year-old Los Angeles prostitute was fished out of a canal near Lamont, in Kern County. The fatal bullets were fired from Sheriff Deputy David Keith Rogers gun, and the same weapon was identified a year later, on February 8, 1987, when Tracy Clark, a pregnant 15-year-old hooker, was found dead in the same canal.

Arrested five days later, after background investigation revealed his "unusual interest" in prostitutes, Rogers admitted owning the murder weapon, reported stolen from a local tavern in 1982.

Large quantities of pornography were discovered in Rogers's home, and detectives learned that he had once taken his teenage son on a tour of hooker-infested streets, to teach the boy that prostitutes were "scumbags." Prosecutors declared that the missing 1983 witness was "very much on the list" of potential victims, but Rogers was finally charged with two counts of homicide.

Convicted on one count each of second-degree murder (Kay Bradley) and first-degree murder (Clark), Rogers was sentenced to die on the latter charge.

---

[25] Maryland Police Officer Macklin Charged with Raping Woman at Traffic Stop

Authorities say it may not be Officer Ryan Macklin's first crime, and they are looking for other victims to come forward. Macklin has been suspended, and stripped of his gun and badge. The woman told police that the officer allegedly attempted to touch her breast before ordering her to move her car behind a store, according to charging documents. Behind the store, the officer allegedly forced the woman to perform oral sex on him and told her he wanted to have sex with her.

The alleged assault was interrupted by a witness whom the woman had called earlier. The officer returned to his cruiser and left the scene. The witness later corroborated some of the woman's account of the assault, which was also backed up by video evidence.

Police said Macklin was on duty and in uniform, and driving a marked police cruiser at the time.

Prince George's County Police Chief Hank Stawinski said at a news conference that the woman came forward "several hours" after the incident with the encouragement of friends. Police said they do not know why Macklin allegedly targeted the driver. "The charges against this officer are highly troubling," Stawinski said. "Officers take an oath to protect others, not to abuse their authority in order to victimize someone. Those who live and work in Prince George's County deserve the very best from the men and women of this department."

---

[26] <u>Buffalo Police Officers Vara and Craig Police Brutality in New York. May 9, 2014</u>

Police Officers Mark Vara and Lindsay Craig were charged with police misconduct and brutality to Nurse Anna Townsend arising from events that began at Townsend's residence on May 9th, 2014. The charges of abuse by police included: unlawful arrest, unlawful imprisonment, trespass, excessive force, battery, slander, malicious prosecution, negligence and intentional infliction of emotional distress.

Police Officer Mark Vara grabbed Anna from inside her home, pushed her down her porch stairs and threw her onto the concrete sidewalk outside after handcuffing her. She fractured her ankle.

#

ARTVOICE:

In the US District Court, Western District of New York, a Buffalo woman, Anna Townsend, is suing the City of Buffalo, the Buffalo Police Department, Police Commissioner Daniel Derenda and two Police Officers, Mark Vara and Lindsay Craig, for violating her civil rights under 42 U.S.C § 1983, known as "Section 1983".

Townsend, who is represented by Buffalo attorney Matthew Albert, is alleging unlawful seizure, unlawful arrest, unlawful imprisonment, trespass, excessive force, battery, slander, malicious prosecution, negligence and intentional infliction of emotional distress arising from events that began at Townsend's residence on May 9th, 2014 which she alleges violated her constitutional rights as established in the Fourth and Fourteenth Amendments.

This is a serious case of alleged police misconduct and brutality and, with Albert representing the plaintiff, the stakes are not small. The Buffalo attorney has become the leading lawyer in this city for people who have alleged abuse by police.

---

[27] Diane Wetendorf

A life-long advocate who pioneered the field of Police Officer-involved domestic violence. Her work has resulted in thousands of advocates learning how to safely help survivors and untold numbers of battered women knowing "they are not alone, they are not exaggerating and they are certainly not crazy."

Diane is the author of Police Domestic Violence: A Handbook for Victims, the first book written specifically for survivors of police-perpetrated domestic violence; When the Batterer Is a Law Enforcement Officer: A Guide for Advocates; as well as Crossing the Threshold: Female Officers and Police-Perpetrated Domestic Violence, a groundbreaking book for women in law enforcement. Her latest book, "Hijacked by the Right: Battered Women in America's Culture War," closely examines how domestic violence has become the new front of the war on women. Her careful analysis of the Family Justice Center movement shows how political and religious conservatives are impacting social services and opportunities for all women and their families.

In 1996, while director of counseling for a community domestic violence agency, Diane created a unique program which provided specialized counseling, legal and advocacy services for victims of officer-involved domestic violence. She worked collaboratively with police departments to develop policies, provided systemic advocacy to professionals nationwide, trained community advocates and provided thousands of hours of individual and group counseling. In 2002, Diane established an independent corporation dedicated to providing advocacy, training and consulting services specific to police-perpetrated domestic violence. Diane has extensive experience conducting workshops and seminars for local, state and national audiences. Topics included victim safety and intervention, the unique dynamics due to the abuser's profession, working with survivors who are also in law enforcement and collaboration between advocates and law enforcement agencies. She served as an expert witness in the U.S. and Canada and was a consultant to the Battered Women's Justice Project.

ABOUT THE AUTHOR

Edward Caputo is an entrepreneur, author, investor, developer and former Chief Executive Officer of a number of highly successful technology companies, which he founded and built during his career in business. He pioneered outsourcing to India, rode the first Internet wave, engineered an Initial Public Offering at the peak of the Dot-com bubble in 1998 and sold out in a cash-only deal right before the Dot-com bubble burst and the technology stock market crash of 2001. He was awarded Ernst & Young, Master Entrepreneur.

Other books and screenplays published or in development:

Death Cross – published fact-based, dramatized Wall Street business murder mystery thriller

Tamiami Trail of Tears - non-fiction about Florida history and Seminole Indian genocide

The Caregiver - non-fiction about hospital elderly healthcare problems

Yahoo, Yahoo - non-fiction Internet history and the founding of Yahoo

How to Build a Business - non-fiction self-help for entrepreneurs

Cruisin' Cuisine: Eat, Drink, Cruise – Global Travelogue and Recipe Cook Book

Endowed – comedy movie screenplay about a fictional, well-endowed playboy

Contact: Edward Caputo

www.edwardcaputo.com

ed@edwardcaputo.com